*[signature]* 12/01/19

There are numerous ethical issues which arise every day in the world of medical science, religion, and healthcare. Many of them are related to new technologies invented to solve life's problems. When such inventions and their use go against the religious dictates of a people and what they hold dear in their faith life, there may arise a moral impasse which can affect such people for better or for worse.

The Magisterium of the Roman Catholic Church condemns in vitro fertilization (IVF) as a morally unacceptable method of human reproduction. But when Father Cletus Nicholas McCarthy is outed in court as the first IVF-conceived Catholic priest, Pope Benedict XVI must do either of two things: annul his ordination without any canon to back his action and risk a backlash from the people, the press, and the general public, or let him be and continue to exercise his priesthood, thereby indirectly endorsing IVF as morally acceptable. Either way, he cannot win. In the throes and turmoil of it all, coupled with the demands of other huge problems in the Church, the pope, already advanced in age, resigns his papacy. Was Fr. McCarthy the last straw that precipitated the Supreme Pontiff's resignation? Your guess is as good as you believe it...or not.

# THE
# MIRROR
# APOCALYPSE

JOHN AYANG

LifeRich Publishing is a registered trademark of The Reader's Digest Association, Inc.

LifeRich Publishing books may be ordered through booksellers or by contacting:

LifeRich Publishing
1663 Liberty Drive
Bloomington, IN 47403
www.liferichpublishing.com
1 (888) 238-8637

ISBN: 978-1-4897-1185-4 (sc)
ISBN: 978-1-4897-1186-1 (hc)
ISBN: 978-1-4897-1187-8 (e)

Library of Congress Control Number: 2017905913

Print information available on the last page.

LifeRich Publishing rev. date: 5/23/2017

To my parents, Martin and Dymphna, who taught me the value of honesty and hard work and who, themselves, were great storytellers. To my uncle, Augustine, who nurtured my vocation, and all my teachers and mentors for being such wonderful people.

Jennifer's thoughts were inundated with Barbara's words of admonition. She was not to grieve so much that she distressed the child in her womb. She understood her perfectly well, both of them being nurses and knowing full well the implications of fetal distress and possible miscarriage. That, of course, was not an option on Jennifer's list of things she would welcome.

"That's him living inside you," Barbara kept reminding her in the days leading up to the funeral. "That child is the only handle you've got on him. Lose that, and you lose everything of the person you loved so dearly."

Jennifer thought that was the most profound way to perpetuate the memory of Father Cletus McCarthy. And it was a very real one. She was carrying his child and, metaphorically speaking, she was carrying Cletus McCarthy...The first Cletus McCarthy came from the test tube—produced, not begotten—according to Catholic doctrine. The second Cletus McCarthy will come from her womb—begotten, not produced—according to Catholic doctrine. He will be the new beginning for the McCarthy family. He will start the lineage of the begotten, not the produced or adopted. She will name him Cletus McCarthy.

# PART I

*In blowing your nose,*
*you must expose your teeth.*

— YORUBA PROVERB

# HOUSTON, TEXAS

## OCTOBER 9, 2012

IT WAS JUST like another Tuesday morning as Father Cletus "Nick" McCarthy eased his Lexus SE 350 into the parking lot at the back of the Downtown Chancery. The car hissed to silence as he turned off the engine and pulled out the ignition key. It was not a particularly sunny day, but it wasn't gloomy either. The early morning fog, the tell-tale sign of the rains of the previous two days, had just lifted. All around were the typical signs of mid fall as Mother Nature seemingly conferred her rainbow attire of brilliantly colored foliage on the trees and shrubs that lay thick at the outskirts of the city's concrete jungle, and even the ones that sparsely dotted it. Traffic seemed to be snaking its way insipidly along the streets that crossed each other at right angles between the high rises. Pedestrian traffic was sparse and Fr. McCarthy thought this was somewhat untypical of the usually boisterous Downtown Houston. A few of the beautifully colored leaves lay on the ground around the bases of the trees that lined the block on which the Chancery building stood. For a brief, ridiculous moment, he felt greatly piqued at nature for such irony: 'The shame of it all!' he thought. 'Why should death sever the leaves from their trees at just the highest moment of their glory when they finally break free of their greyish verdant monotony to provide such visual delight to men?' He couldn't understand. Looking away angrily he glanced at the dashboard of his car, and the time on the car LED read 10:12 a.m.

Always conscious of the bad traffic situation that Houston was famous for, Fr. McCarthy had started out quite early to beat it to his ten-thirty appointment with the Cardinal. He was a big stickler for punctuality. So, arriving eighteen minutes early wasn't bad at all. It gave him ample time to recollect himself, marshal his thoughts, and rehearse the right opening words before going in to meet with the Cardinal.

But what were the right opening words with which to start a discussion on a case that was no case at all? He wondered. He knew that a couple had called the Chancery to report him to the Cardinal for stopping them from receiving Holy Communion. And he knew who they were. Fr. Brady Callahan had left that much for him on his voice mail. What baffled him was why the Cardinal should summon him over such a trivial matter. It had been a long time since he was 'summoned to the Principal's office,' as his staff members at the parish usually joked when he would call any of them into his office for a discussion. His last summon was during his second-year theology, eight years previously, when he posted a controversial article on the Seminary *Popular theology* board. After that he knew to avoid such summons if he was to be selected for ordination in his final year.

He unclicked his seatbelt, reclined slightly back, creased his forehead and pondered hard over nothing. Thoughts refused to form logically in his mind or, at least, assume some coherence. His mind dangled between a void and a fleeting cacophony of words: *Confusion. Injustice. Ignorance. Change. Who is right? Who is wrong? What is right? What's the morality of it? Cafeteria Catholics. Are Church teachings out of date? Is the famous Catholic mentality changing? Who is really a true Catholic these days? Are Bishops losing control, no longer able to get their flock in lock step?*

Another quick glance at the dash board showed he had seven minutes left. Suddenly peeved at feeling like a trapped game he opened the car door and pushed it too fast and so hard that it bounced back on its hinges and slammed into his knee cap with a painful thud as he put out his leg to alight from the car. He hissed with pain and gave voice to some unpriestly choice word. Quickly taking a hold of himself he glanced around self-consciously, and was glad nobody was within earshot. Not that it mattered, but a passer-by hearing the dirty "F" word coming from a black-coated, Roman-collared, white man, would have added to the confusion that was eating up the world. 'Yes, the world is giddy with confusion,' he thought. He grabbed his desk diary on the passenger side of the front seat, banged the car door to – gently this time – and walked round from the parking lot in the back to the front doors of the Chancery building, effortful in concealing the pain in his knee by consciously refusing to limp.

"Come in, Father Cletus. Come in," the Cardinal said, as Fr. McCarthy stood by the open office door, about to announce his presence. "Just in time before I get spirited off to the next meeting. You know I have so many meetings during the day with so many groups that I sometimes think it is only the good Lord keeping me from collapsing with an attack of *meetingitis*."

"God morning, Eminence," Fr. McCarthy said, taking the Cardinal's proffered hand and permitting a spurt of mirthful laughter to escape him at the latter's humor. "That must be a strange illness I guess," he added.

"Very strange indeed," the Cardinal concurred, waving Fr. McCarthy to a chair. "One that hasn't yet come under the purview of the medical community, but which will add to their list of odd diagnoses when it does." He took his seat in the high-backed leather swivel chair behind the ornate, glossily polished mahogany desk. A slender-looking man of sixty-two, Umberto Cardinal Pacino Felice, at five feet, eight inches, oozed a strong presence that always gave his visitors the impression of a powerful church lord. He had an equally strong baritone voice that seemed to be ringing from a throat thoroughly washed by countless gulps of good Italian Chianti. His eyes were piercing like an eagle's, separated by a ridge of beaklike nose. 'Typical Italian trademark,' Fr. McCarthy thought. With a thin-lipped mouth and a cheek slightly dimpled, he looked like he was forever wearing a very faint toothless smile as a tribute to his Italian name, Felice, which means joy. A wavy mane of hair, slightly thin at the forehead, neatly brushed back and well cropped around the neck region gave the Cardinal the persona of primness. Equally swathed in black coat and a Roman collar, the only thing that distinguished him in rank from Fr. McCarthy was the silver chain diagonally crossing his chest from the right shoulder to a pocket under his left breast, hiding his pectoral from view. He settled in his chair, looked at Fr. McCarthy straight and inquired, "How is Our Lady Queen of Peace these days? I hope the good parishioners are behaving, and everything is peaceful." He smiled impishly, at his acrid humor.

"We are trying our best, Eminence," Fr. McCarthy replied, searching for the right words to match the Cardinal's effort at conversation openers. "Our Lady of Peace is okay, though at times not very peaceful. But the parishioners are generally very supportive, and they tell me they always pray for me."

"Good to hear that, Fr. Cletus," the Cardinal affirmed. "Good to hear that, especially now. You really have a lot on your mind. We all do. And we all need lots of prayers, Fr. Cletus. I pray for you: not just you but all my priests. Hopefully, you are doing the same for me."

"Thank you, Eminence. I do pray for you too. In fact, I pray for all Bishops, I know it can be a little bit hectic at the top."

"Thank you, Fr. Cletus. But we are here to talk about you. I know it's quite hectic for you too, right now."

"Yes, Eminence," Fr. McCarthy bit his lips, realizing he was beginning to sound patronizing. He didn't miss the gentle chiding in the Cardinal's voice. He thought he got a little too excited.

"Fr. Cletus, I'm sure the Vicar for Priests, Fr. Brady, informed you of the reason why I wanted to have a discussion with you. Please, look at this session as a friendly chat, a conversation within which you and I will try to explore together how best to handle the crisis. You understand?"

"Your Eminence, I do," Fr. McCarthy replied. "But I don't know that I can call the situation a crisis. I mean, the Eshiets did something quite contrary to the teachings of the Church. *Donum Vitae* clearly states that In Vitro Fertilization is not an acceptable solution for infertility for Catholics. Moreover, the entire process separates the unitive and procreative ends of marriage and makes the child so conceived, a manufactured product instead of a begotten person. I believe this has deep moral implications, Eminence." He concluded, somewhat professorially.

"And a scandal for the rest of the faithful too, Fr. Cletus, I agree with you," the Cardinal concurred. "You were right in suspending…um, what's their name?" He briefly consulted a paper on his desk. "Oh, yes, Edidiong and Ima Eshiet. You were right to suspend them from the Sacraments for using IVF to conceive a baby contrary to Church teaching. Also, as their letter of complaint indicates, they weren't, and are not ignorant of Church teaching on the subject. What I want to ask you, though, is whether they talked to you before they made the decision."

"Your Eminence, they did," Fr. McCarthy replied, beginning to feel at ease, seeing, at least, that the Cardinal seemed to be leaning toward supporting him. "We had a couple of lengthy sessions during when I expounded to them the moral teachings of the Catholic Church concerning the new reproductive technologies springing up every day and everywhere around us. The Eshiets are well educated and they understood everything. What just escapes me is why, understanding perfectly well, the moral, and even the spiritual implications of their action, they went ahead with the decision to use IVF."

"I see in this letter they wrote, they signed it, Doctor and Doctor Mrs. Eshiet?"

"That's right, Eminence," Fr. McCarthy replied. "Edidiong is an Obstetrician/ Gynecologist. And the wife is a PhD, Pediatric Nurse. They both work at Mercy and Children's Hospital here at the Medical Center."

"I didn't know that. I thought they were academic doctors. Well, either way, I think there is a bit of academic arrogance at work here. It really seems these are not your average 'good' Catholics, always ready to agree with *Father* because '*Father* has said it.' That's why I wanted to talk to you to make sure you are confident and comfortable in your own skin, and strong in your stand, which I support one hundred per cent. But you don't need to worry too much. Stacy Donovan, our Attorney, will handle everything. All you need to do is to articulate the position of the Church on reproductive technology if you are called to the stand."

"Stacy will handle everything! Wait ..., Your Eminence," Fr. McCarthy stuttered, looking confused. "I think you have lost me. I'm not quite sure I follow... or, that I understand what you mean by 'if you are called to the stand.'"

"Oh, I thought you were served your own papers?" The Cardinal said, looking confused, too. "This legal notice of a suit citing discrimination and emotional battery came in yesterday. Haven't you got your copy?"

"I am sorry, Eminence. I'm usually off on Mondays. So, yesterday I visited the bay area for the day and came back late. I had no time to check my mails. I also, forgot my Secretary is on vacation this week. I came this morning because I got the message left on my voice mail by Fr. Brady Callahan. So, immediately after morning Mass I decided to come here first thing."

"Well, a letter from the law firm of Turner and Stendhal is probably waiting in your mail box for your attention," the Cardinal said. "The Eshiets allege that your act of denying them Holy Communion amounts to discrimination, emotional battery and unjust stereotyping. They also allege that you have not treated others who are in the same situation as they are, as you have treated them. They are asking for damages in unspecified amount for the emotional pain and social degradation that your action has caused them. Their suit names you and the parish, then myself and the Archdiocese of Galveston-Houston, as defendants."

"Fr. Callahan didn't apprise me of this in the message he left on my voice mail," Fr. McCarthy complained feebly and pointlessly. His heart beating irregularly in his chest.

"Perhaps, he thought that you had already got your notice, or he just decided to spare you from worrying too much before meeting with me or some other possibility," the Cardinal said, trying to calm him, as it looked. "But, as I said, there is nothing to worry too much about here. The Church is not a stranger to lawsuits. Compared with what we have gone through in the past, this one seems a bit frivolous. The hearing is not until November ending, more than a month. And that, I would say, leaves Stacy enough time to prepare a defense. She probably would want to talk to you. Or, again, she may not see that as necessary. Only make sure there is no other parishioner who has blatantly repudiated Church teaching on the issue and has not been appropriately sanctioned as the Eshiets allege in their suit."

"I can't recall any, Your Eminence," Fr. McCarthy said, creasing his forehead in obvious but needless effort.

"That, I believe you, Father," the Cardinal replied. "But if you, by any chance, discover a case like that which had not come to your notice don't hesitate to call Stacy. She is an expert in these matters; and a very smart lady."

Fr. McCarthy thought that was very comforting to know. Feeling he had gotten more support from the Cardinal than he had hoped for, he sighed with relief. But he was still confused, wondering what the world was coming to when folks would sue at the drop of a hat over what they have no right nor moral standing to sue. 'Where has the respect of Catholics for a priest of God gone to?' He wondered, feeling insulted by the suit and raging impotently at such an affront.

———

"Can you believe that?" Fr. McCarthy raged, a glass of screwdriver—orange juice spiked with vodka—in hand. "I can't believe a couple of African block heads would have the guts to sue me for stopping them from Holy Communion when they know full well they did something immoral."

"Whoa-o! Whoa-o! Take a grip on yourself, Nick," Fr. Charles Polanski chided his friend. "Please, don't let such a frivolous situation rob you of your priestly demeanor. Maybe you shouldn't be knocking back that screwdriver so fast."

"I'm sorry, Charlie," Fr. McCarthy mellowed. "I got carried away. You know, I drove to the Chancery quite peeved at the poor Cardinal, thinking he gives ear too much to disgruntled parishioners over irrelevant complaints. I never knew he had a lawsuit on his hands, thanks to me. No.

Thanks to my libertine, highly educated parishioners! Tell me something Charlie. Why are Catholics no longer respectful of priests and Church teachings? Where has the famous Catholic loyalty of yesteryears gone to?"

Fr. Polanski stood pensive for a few seconds. Then he said, "I have a theory, Nick," and poured himself a generous measure of the screwdriver, dropped his bulk into the settee and warmed to his theory. "The Nordic tribes have a masquerade dance during the harvest season. When they wear their masks women and children run from them in fear and awe, shrieking. When they put aside their masks after the dance to sit down and eat and drink with the rest of the folk and everybody sees who were behind the masks, women and children can then sit beside them laughing and making fun of their awkward dance steps." He took a gulp of the screwdriver and paused for effect.

"So, what's the point of your theory?" Fr. McCarthy asked, barely keeping from laughing it off as ridiculous. "What connection has your theory, as you call it, to my being sued for discrimination?"

"Did I hear you ask why priests are no longer respected and Church teachings no longer followed religiously?" Fr. Polanski asked, dubiously.

"Sure, I did," Fr. McCarthy replied.

"Then my theory has a lot to do with your case, Nick," Fr. Polanski replied, shifting his bulk and crossing one leg over the other. He took a sip and continued. "You see, before Vatican II Council and the great aggiornamento of John XXIII, when priests used to wear black cassocks and berets, say Mass in Latin facing the wall away from the people, and generally veiling everything, there was much respect for priests. That was because there was a great mystique surrounding the person of the priest and everything he did. After Vatican II, the altar rails were knocked down, the priest ditched the black beret and black cassock and faced the people. Great emphasis was given to lay participation in the liturgy, lay Communion Ministers were created to serve at what was the exclusive turf of the clergy, and the mystery language of Latin was retired to make room for the vernacular: everything was basically demystified. Now, the masqueraders without their masks – the priests without the mystique aura – are no longer intimidating to 'women and children:' the laity."

Fr. McCarthy stopped pacing and sat down opposite his host. He was always impressed at his older friend's sagacity. As he was listening to his explanation, nay 'theory,' on why priests have lost respect among their flock, he felt he wasn't let down.

"I think you're beginning to make a lot of sense, Charlie," he said, ponderously. "But, why? One would have thought making the liturgy more participatory and demystifying things to make them understandable would be much more welcome than esotericism!"

Fr. Polanski chuckled and said, paternally, "You should become a student of human nature, Nick. Once you demystify sacred objects and persons you divest them of the sacredness too. You make them banal and insipid." He took another sip and continued in mock disappointment, "I thought you were going to corroborate my theory by mentioning the pedophilia scandal."

"And I thought that was going to be the thesis of your theory," Fr. McCarthy countered. "Because I have a rebuttal ready for that."

"And what would be your rebuttal, my dear Nick?"

"You cannot condemn a whole barrel of apples because of a few rotten ones," Fr. McCarthy stated, almost with the impudence of a cocksure teenager. Fr. Polanski heaved his bulk from the settee and moved toward the kitchen, saying dismissively, "Go back to school, Nick, and register in Human Psychology 101. Are you hungry?" He asked, proceeding to open the pans and pots he had on the stove.

"Oh, c'mon, Charlie. You know what am talking about?" Fr. McCarthy pursued his righteous rebuttal. "Moreover, the media was feeding the frenzy of the people, blowing everything out of all proportion to sell paper." He took his place at the table as Fr. Polanski put a plate and cutlery in front of him and settled opposite him for a lunch of spaghetti and meatballs. "I know part of the anger had to do with the fact that Catholic moral teaching especially in sexual matters is viewed by some people as too rigid. It was as though they were saying to the Church, 'We've caught you now in your own trap you SOB.' And I know some people still have a gripe with the Church over *Humanae Vitae*. But, what the heck! Truth sometimes hurts."

"Tut, tut!" Fr. Polanski exclaimed in mock surprise. "You are suddenly becoming very intelligent."

"Yeah, I guess you can mock me now," Fr. McCarthy said, ruefully. "But I hate the whole business of stereotyping and profiling people. I have not sexually abused any child. Nobody should judge me by the mistakes of a few misguided priests."

Fr. Polanski forked a load of spaghetti into his mouth and spoke through the mash, "Stereotyping and profiling is what we do every day, Nick."

"It's not what I do," Fr. McCarthy protested feebly.

"Yes, it is," Fr. Polanski countered.

"It isn't."

"It is."

"Isn't."

"'Is. You just did it barely half an hour ago. You referred to your complainants as 'African block heads,' remember?"

"Charlie, c'mon, that's not stereotyping, you know it," Fr. McCarthy said, exasperated. "And besides, I said that in a feat of anger, you know."

"Nick, if you accept that people do stereotype people every day in different forms and in different ways, you will understand that I am not indicting you," Fr. Polanski mellowed. "You talk about anger. Don't forget that the lawsuit against you might be a grandchild, so to speak, of the anger over *Humanae Vitae* which you just mentioned."

"But that's a longstanding teaching of the Church, and what it predicted are all coming true in our day," Fr. McCarthy said, matter-of-factly.

"I wish it were about the truth of predictions, Nick," Fr. Polanski said. "The fact is: whether longstanding, long-sitting, or long-squatting, there is something that is not fitting in well with popular opinion of Church moral teaching on sexuality. Don't ask me, because I don't know what it is."

"What do you mean?" Fr. McCarthy asked, confused.

"How many families do you have in your parish, and what is the median age?"

"Eight hundred families, give or take," Fr. McCarthy replied, not seeing where his host was leading. "I would say the median age is about fifty-two, or thereabouts."

"What percentage of that number, those married in Church in the eighties up to the nineties, have more than two children?" Fr. Polanski drilled on.

"I see where you are going," Fr. McCarthy conceded. "But I will answer truthfully. I would say, not up to ten percent."

"Boom! That must be good news for the Church," Fr. Polanski said, sarcastically.

"What do you mean, Charlie?"

"You see, after their first child or second child, our wonderful Catholic people took to practicing abstinence all the days of their lives." He pushed out his chin and addressed an imaginary figure on the couch, "Move over celibate priests and monks, there's a new group of sex abstainers in town! They have never heard about the pill, tubal ligation or vasectomy. These ninety percent, typical of every parish, were, and are very loyal to Church sexual moral teachings. Curran and McCormick were just naysayer wafflers. Thank God they got rapped on their knuckles for impudence…"

"Okay, Charlie. Okay. Okay, you've made your point," Fr. McCarthy said, vexing visibly. "Quit your sarcastic rant."

"Who said am ranting?" Fr. Polanski said, faking a hurt. "I'm just crying that there was an elephant in the house, and it is still there." He added after a pause, "It doesn't matter. I'm probably the only one who sees it, and that makes me the wacky one."

"You aren't wacky, Charlie," Fr. McCarthy said, somberly. "You're just saying it like it is. And I think I like it that way. But I think I prefer the truth straight without the sarcasm."

"Gosh! I think am on cloud nine. There is nothing like a good lunch," Fr. Polanski said, changing the subject and getting up to clear the table. "Coffee, or dissert?" He asked.

"No sweets for me," Fr. McCarthy replied. Glad that his host had changed the topic. "But coffee is okay. I still have a long day ahead." He began to feel a bit at ease. The conversation was getting too tense for comfort. Yet, there was no denying that his host had given him a lot of food for thought. "Thanks," he said, curtly, as Fr. Polanski placed his coffee in front of him. Then he remembered to be a gracious guest, "The spaghetti meal was good."

"Don't blame me. Blame the makers of the Ragu sauce," Fr. Polanski said, good-naturedly, settling down for his own coffee with a generous slice of brownie.

The two friends sat for several seconds, silently bemoaning the loss of clergy respect among their flock. Then Fr. McCarthy rose and thanked his host again before making his exit to return to Our Lady Queen of Peace Church.

## OCTOBER 9, 2012

"*IN NOMINE PATRIS, et Filii, et Spiritus Sancti,*" Father McCarthy intoned, loud and clear.

"*Amen,*" the congregation behind him responded in an equally resounding chorus.

"*Gratia Domini nostri Jesu Christi, et caritas Dei, et communicatio Sancti Spiritus sit cum omnibus vobis,*" he continued.

"*Et cum spiritu tuo,*" the congregation responded, fluently. Father McCarthy was pleased. 'The Latin Mass should be very easy,' he thought to himself. 'It would be as if the Church had not left off its official language for quite some time.' He wondered why some priests were riled when they got the "Motu Proprio" from the Holy See. 'The thing is as easy as ABC! Even the people of God have not forgotten their beloved Latin language.' He felt quite delighted and proceeded to the penitential rite.

"*Fratres, agnoscamus peccata nostra...*" He found himself at this point holding the Host. Self-conscious, he thought, 'I think I should do the Liturgy of the Word, first. I shouldn't consecrate the Host yet.' He dropped the Host into the paten and looked around to see whether the congregation had noticed his little snafu. To his despondent surprise, he saw an empty Church behind him. The pews looked rickety and tattered. He stood speechless for a few seconds, wondering where the earlier chorus response came from. Just then the Church Laity Council Chairman walked in swathed in a golf cap, a Nike polo shirt, and khaki pants with tennis shoes.

"Father, the people are all in the parish center," He announced, a shade too excitedly to Father McCarthy's irritation.

"In the Parish center?" Father McCarthy asked, confused. "Doing what?"

"Celebrating the new language," he continued with the same excitement.

"But ... We are using the new language here!" Father McCarthy said, plaintively, visibly confused. "Well. Latin is not new... I mean, we are renewing its use again."

"Well, the people like the new language better," the Chairman continued, stubbornly, talking beside the point. "Come, let's go celebrate," he called out, still excited.

"I can't leave saying Mass half way." Father McCarthy said resolutely. "I have to finish the consecration, at least." He turned again to face the altar and the wall.

"Okay, Father," the Chairman said. "I will ring the bells and hold the back of your chasuble."

As Father McCarthy picked up the host again he thought, 'The wall! Why am I facing the wall? That was discarded years ago, as obsolete. Maybe that is the reason the people left.' He meant to drop the host in the paten again, but decided against it. He determined to follow through with the consecration and get done with it, and join the celebration in the Parish hall, perhaps. He held the Host and bent slightly over it.

"*Hoc est enim, corpus meum. Lava me, Domine, ab iniquitate mea.*" He stopped, feeling a tinge of shame and guilt at the same time, at having mixed up the words of consecration. 'What's wrong with me?' He thought. He looked hard at the page of the Sacramentary and tried to correct himself, but the words kept dancing and blurring up. He gave up, thinking, 'the poor Chairman doesn't know Latin after all.' He lifted the Host and held it up, but there was no sound of the bell. He turned slightly to look and see why the Chairman wasn't ringing the bells. There was nobody behind him. To his horror, he discovered that he was stark naked, except for a white V underwear that barely covered his buttocks. Terribly embarrassed, he unthinkingly dropped the Host and grabbed the altar cloth to wrap it around himself to hide his nakedness. The altar cloth stuck to the altar and refused to give, causing him to pull with force. In his panicky scramble, he accidentally dislodged the candle stick and it fell on the bells which started ringing, interminably, with a loud shrill.

———

Father McCarthy bolted upright to a sitting position on the bed, still clutching at the altar cloth which was now, of course, his bed sheet. The foot end of the sheet was tucked underneath the heavy mattress, and he realized he had been pulling vigorously but futilely at it. He let go of the sheet, breathing heavily and feeling beads of perspiration forming on his forehead. The phone shrilled two more times and went dead. A woman's voice crackled to life to leave a message.

"Hi, Father McCarthy. This is Stacy Donovan at the Chancery. Please, give me a call when you get this message. My number is..."

He threw off the bed sheets and slid out of bed. He was vexed and did not want to wait out the rest of the message. He knew Stacy's number at the Chancery, anyway.

"What a weird dream!" He said, aloud. He looked down at himself and was thankful to see that he wasn't naked, though that wouldn't have mattered in the sanctuary of his bedroom. In fact, he was still fully clothed in his clerical attire. The screwdriver and the big lunch of spaghetti at Father Polanski's was enough to send him into a good afternoon nap, despite the coffee he quaffed to wash it down. He remembered coming into the bedroom and sitting on his bed, but didn't remember tucking himself in for the unplanned siesta. The clock on the reading lamp stand beside the head of the bed read 3:35 p.m. He crossed the room and pulled open the curtain over the South window. The room became flooded by a bright afternoon light. Part of the sun's rays flashed through to fall on the chest of drawers to the East side of the bed. Fr. McCarthy was partially blinded for a moment and squinted to adjust his vision. From the window of his room, the sky outside was sparsely clouded in grey and white. The white clouds looked like huge balls of cotton, irregularly shaped, and broken at intervals to show a smoky blue that let through huge shafts of sunlight. Down below, to the right, was an expansive golden red, orange, and yellow foliage, themed with deep green, stubbornly holding out and seemingly resolute on defying the climate, though it was middle of autumn. The scene looked like one giant carpet of wild beautiful colors, severally dotted by scattered roof tops of equally assorted colors. To the left was Main Street, from which several other streets forked off. A few of the roads crossed to the right and disappeared, peeping out at intervals, as it were, under the thinning autumn foliage. The tributary roads had scanty traffic while Main Street had a lot of vehicles of assorted sizes, make and color; all weaving in and out among themselves, vying for right of way. Father McCarthy knew it would soon be rush hour.

"God's creation," he muttered under his breath. "All rushing to wrap up the business of the day." He was glad that the thick glass window was designed to shut out much of the outside noise. All that he could hear from the hustle and bustle below was a muffled din. He turned and stared at the bed and the rumpled sheets, and wondered what the embarrassingly weird dream he had just had could portend. He was not born when Catholic Mass used to be in Latin. But they had Mass in Latin every Wednesday at the Seminary, though it was Mass of the 1973 *Novus Ordo*, not of the Tridentine brand. And, facing the wall! Why was he facing the wall instead of facing the people in the pews? The greatest puzzle of all was his utter nakedness at the altar. What was the meaning of it all? He knew that the Church taught that dreams fall among the categories of things that a good Catholic should not believe in. Though Joseph's dream in the Old Testament is taught as having come true when his brothers bowed down to him in Egypt. And, another Joseph in the New Testament had a dream not to divorce the Mother of the Lord, which he believed and obeyed. "And it was credited to him as righteousness," he muttered wryly, chuckled guiltily under his breath and shook himself out of his revelry to avoid being conflicted. This was not the time to get conflicted about Church doctrines. Maybe it's only the Josephs who should deal with dreams. So, he decided to leave dreams to the Josephs of this world while occupying himself with matters of the moment. He wished, though, he could find his Joseph right then. Turning away from the window he sat down on the settee and picked up the phone to dial Stacy's number at the Chancery.

The phone was picked up from the other end on the second ring.

"Chancery Legal Office. Donovan speaking," came a woman's voice.

"Miss Donovan. Father Cletus," he announced.

"Oh, thank you, Father, for returning my call," Stacy said, as though she was the one needing his favor. "I need to touch base with you to discuss a few things. The Cardinal told me he met with you this morning. Is that correct?"

"Yes. That's correct," Father McCarthy confirmed.

"Okay, you already know what it's all about," she continued. "First, I want to assure you that it is nothing to worry about. We will soon get it fixed and everything will be alright. It's a shame that some people would make a big deal out of such a minor thing. But that's how it is and we must face it. It will be okay. I just need to ask you a few questions and get some papers prepared for the preliminary hearing.

"I'm ready, Ms. Donovan," Fr. McCarthy said, adjusting his weight on the settee to a more comfortable position.

Just as Stacy Donovan had said, the questioning session was very brief. They had gone a little over ten minutes, and mostly about the background to the case, a little description of the Eshiets and their mindset, the relevance of the action of denying them Holy Communion to the specific canons in the Code of Canon Law, and the discussion process leading up to their action of choosing to use IVF. Fr. McCarthy was glad he could demonstrate his intellectual acumen in canon law, his pastoral knowledge of sacramental administration, and the deep theological reasoning behind his action. To his surprise, he discovered during the conversation that Stacy was not totally wet behind the ears as far as canon law was concerned. For instance, she asked to know whether the act of using IVF is an occult offense that could be treated in the internal forum or an offense that drew diriment impediment to the reception of the sacraments. She asked to know whether the penalty was *ferende sententiae* or *latae sententiae*, and whether he, Fr. McCarthy, had the proper authority to impose it within the community of worshippers that constituted his congregation. Did he warn the Eshiets of the consequences of their act if they chose to ignore his advice? Did he check to see that there was no other defaulter that was not similarly sanctioned? Fr. McCarthy was impressed by the thoroughness of Stacy's inquiry. Stacy herself was all apologies for subjecting him to that kind of grilling.

"These things are necessary for me to know to prepare my briefs for the preliminary hearing," She had said. "I intend to make sure that this doesn't go to trial. It is a minor thing that should be settled outside the court."

"I appreciate your invaluable help, Ms. Donovan," Fr. McCarthy said.

"You're welcome, Father," Stacy replied. "Don't put too much on it. I'm only doing my job. I only wish this would be over in a short time so that you can relax and face your parish work in peace."

"Certainly, Ms. Donovan," Fr. McCarthy said, amused at the unintended pun on the word 'peace.' "I'll be glad once I can put this behind me."

"Good," she replied. "Don't hesitate to call me if you have any questions. Thank you for your time, Father."

"No, Ms. Donovan," he replied. "I should be thanking you. Please, have a good afternoon."

"You, too."

The phone went dead on the other end.

Fr. McCarthy continued holding the receiver for a few more seconds before setting it back in its cradle. For some reason, he felt thankfully relieved. The deep questions that Stacy asked and the professional way she did it while she kept assuring him at the same time gave him a lot of confidence and trust that she was going to handle everything. She was a doctor of jurisprudence in civil law, after all, and had a licentiate in Canon Law as well. He leaned back and looked at his watch. It was 4:51 p.m. He wondered whether he had any other engagement that evening. Heaving himself up, he crossed the room into his study for his desk diary. The only entry in pencil was a Hispanic couple that was scheduled for Confession at 4:30 p.m. His heart sank. They had probably come and waited for him till they got tired and decided to leave. He knew the couple very well. Sometimes they were so respectful to a fault. That might account for their not coming over to the rectory to ring the doorbell and inquire for him when they didn't see him in the confessional, and he failed to show up. Feeling angry at himself, he buttoned up his shirt collar, pulled the white plastic strip into place and rushed out to the Church. To his great relief, he found them in the pews – man, wife, and three children – saying their prayers. He went over and apologized softly to them, beckoning them to come into the confessional. Once inside, he draped the purple stole over his neck, flipped on the green light switch to indicate that he was ready for the first penitent.

The door to the penitent cubicle creaked open and shut with an annoying whine, and Fr. McCarthy made a mental note to ask the maintenance man to put some grease on the hinges.

"Bless me, Padre, um…porque… um…soy un pecador…" a man's voice said timidly from behind the screen, then went silent. After a couple of seconds, the voice came back, "hablas Espanol, Padre?"

Fr. McCarthy had not prepared himself for a Spanish language penitent. He thought they spoke English as most of his Hispanic parishioners did. Feeling world-wearied he responded insipidly, "un poquito," and regretted his response immediately.

The man launched into rapid Spanish monologue, sometimes sobbing uncontrollably, at other times proceeding courageously, punctuating at intervals with, "lo siento, padre; lo siento mucho." Fr. McCarthy's Spanish wasn't pitifully bad. He could understand a lot of it, but he was unable yet to keep pace with the owners of the language, especially when they rattled it off like nobody's business. As he sat listening he tried but failed to figure out how he was going to advice his penitent. So, he picked up his usual prop card and resolved to just read the formula of absolution once the man would get done off-loading. 'The good Lord is a polyglot. After all he created the many languages. So, he understands his penitent and will forgive him,' Fr. McCarthy thought as he sat back waiting for the first sign from the man that he was done.

# HOUSTON, TEXAS

## OCTOBER 23, 2012

STACY WAS IN COURT for the preliminary hearing. So, also, was Patrick Turner of the *Turner and Stendhal Law Firm*. They stood up as the judge came in and took her place on the bench.

"Mr. Turner, your client is suing the Reverend gentleman, his pastor, for discrimination, stereotypical persecution, unwarranted public shaming, and emotional battery. Is that correct?" Judge Anieno Montgomery asked, primly, as judges tend to do when they are about to begin hearing a case.

"Yes, Your Honor," Patrick Turner responded. He was bald and stocky in physique, and stood not more than five feet five. His baldness swept from one temple, over the top and crown of his head to the other temple, leaving a clump of severely thin hair atop his broad forehead, like a miniature island. The rest of the hair continued from behind one ear, across the back of his head, and terminated behind the other ear. It was primly cropped, well-oiled, and brushed into waves, as though to appease and dissuade it from completely disappearing and leaving a totally shorn pate in place. He wore a pin-striped designer suit and wreaked of a Giorgio Amani cologne, bearing with him all the aura of a successful and prosperous legal personage. Of course, Turner & Stendhal was a high-profile law firm, usually handling equally high-profile cases. And they made a fortune, too, on torts. Big pharmaceutical companies feared Turner & Stendhal. Healthcare systems reviewed their ethical policies frequently to avoid any lawsuit that might bring them face to face with Turner & Stendhal. Their prosecutorial tactics were ruthless. Stacy knew this, and she wondered why the firm should condescend to take such a minor case of a griping parishioner who was prevented from receiving Holy Communion. She found that odd, and became a little wary. From what Fr. McCarthy told her, she knew the Eshiets were highly successful as an obstetrician/gynecologist and a pediatrician. They probably made enough money to pay Turner &

Stendhal in cash. She thought another reason might be because the suit named the Cardinal and the Archdiocese as co-defendants, the general, but unstated, opinion being that the Catholic Church had a lot of money. And, so, every lawyer would want to pounce on a suit that named a Catholic diocese. She watched with a tinge of disgust as Patrick Turner presented his case.

"Would you please state your case fully, Mr. Turner?" Judge Montgomery prompted.

"Yes, Your Honor," Patrick Turner replied. He cleared his throat and began. "Your Honor, on Sunday, May 17, 2012, my client, Dr. Edidiong Eshiet, a devout and well-meaning Catholic, a financial member in good standing with the Church, walked up to receive Holy Communion at a service in his Church. To the utter surprise and undeserved embarrassment of my client, he was publicly shamed and belittled...."

"Objection!" Stacy called out, standing.

"Hold, Mr. Turner," Judge Montgomery ordered as she raised her hand to stop him. "What are you objecting to, Ms. Donovan?"

"Your Honor, Counsel is trying to whip up your sentiments with his choice of words," Stacy said, plaintively.

"Let me be the judge of that, Ms. Donovan," Judge Montgomery said, looking at Stacy with a very faint smile. "Also, there is no need to object to any of Mr. Turner's statements since the case is not on trial yet. You will have the opportunity to present your own side, as well." She continued, addressing Patrick Turner, "and may I state here that you do not impress me with how maudlin you sound, Mr. Turner. All that I need from you now are the bare facts of the case."

"Yes, Your Honor," Patrick Turner demurred and continued. "My client, as I said, was denied Holy Communion in full view of the congregation, thereby subjecting him to humiliation and disgrace. As if that wasn't enough, my client's wife was subjected to the same public shaming by the Reverend Cletus McCarthy, in the same service. This act was mean, and constituted emotional battery of my client and his wife. Moreover, it was a glaringly arrogant act of discrimination against my client, as no other person in the same circumstances has ever been subjected to such treatment." Stacy was almost half way up to protest before she remembered Judge Montgomery's instruction and sat down again. Patrick Turner continued, "Accordingly, my client is asking for damages in the sum of five million dollars.

"Five million dollars?!" Stacy shot up from her seat.

"Sit down, Ms. Donovan," Judge Montgomery ordered, mildly. "And may I remind you again that no interruption is necessary at this stage. You will have your turn to state your case. Is that clear, Ms. Donovan?"

"Yes, Your Honor," Stacy responded, grudgingly, and sat down again.

"Mr. Turner, you may proceed," Judge Montgomery said. "But, first, let me ask you a question: Are you serious about your client's demand, or are you just kidding?"

"Your Honor, at Turner & Stendhal, we don't kid around," Patrick Turner said, looking directly at Judge Montgomery, as if to let her know it was insulting to even think, let alone suggest, that he was kidding.

"I didn't think you do," Judge Montgomery said, with a tinge of sternness. "And, hopefully, you're not, because, considering the nature of the case, I do not see the reason behind your client's bogus claim."

"Your Honor, this is a high-profile case, considering the personages involved. And the Catholic Archdiocese of Galveston-Houston is a highly powerful entity which…."

"Counsel," Judge Montgomery interrupted. "Save your lecture for the jury. I'm fully aware of the nature of the case and, though I am not Catholic, I know a lot about the Catholic Church. That is irrelevant to my concern, which is that your client is asking for a bogus amount which may not even be demanded in a homicide case."

"My client is a highly respectable…"

"Mr. Turner, do you have any more facts to state?" Judge Montgomery sternly interrupted again.

"Um…" Patrick Turner vacillated, then added, "No, Your Honor."

"Then you may assume your seat," Judge Montgomery directed.

Patrick Turner bowed sanctimoniously and took his seat, seemingly unruffled by the judge's cutting remarks, but not looking too pleased, either. Judge Anieno Montgomery turned and nodded to Stacy, with that air of authority that said, 'You may now proceed with my permission.' Stacy stood up, buttoned and pulled down her jacket, and tugged at her skirt to straighten it. She jerked her head to one side and daintily pushed a lock of hair into place.

"Your Honor," she began in a matter-of-factly tone of voice. "I propose that you dismiss the suit brought against my client by Turner & Stendhal because it is a non-issue and, ipso facto, my client has no case to answer." For a brief moment, Judge Montgomery looked somewhat perplexed at

Stacy. Patrick Turner looked incredulous, too, shifting his gaze from Stacy to the judge and back to Stacy, and then back to the judge.

"And what makes it a non-issue, Ms. Donovan?" Judge Montgomery asked, seemingly with a faint smile.

"The Catholic Church, Your Honor, is an autonomous entity with its own rules and regulations to which members voluntarily commit themselves, agreeing to keep those rules, thereby implicitly accepting to be sanctioned accordingly, in case of a dereliction," Stacy stated in one breath.

"Objection!" Patrick Turner bolted upright in his seat.

"Mr. Turner!' Judge Montgomery called sternly, banging her gavel at the same time. "Only speak when you are permitted to do so. You had your turn, remember? If you have rebuttals or more facts to add, you will be given the chance to do so."

"But, Your Honor, the Catholic Church is not...," he began, and was stopped abruptly by the loud cracking sound of the judge's hammer smacking into the gavel. He took one look at Judge Montgomery's visage and lowered himself slowly into his seat.

"Miss Donovan, does that give the Catholic Church the privilege to discriminate?" Judge Montgomery asked.

"No, Your Honor, it doesn't," Stacy responded, confidently.

"Then why is the case a non-issue?" Judge Montgomery asked, more out of curiosity than for the need to get the facts.

"Because membership in the Catholic Church is purely voluntary," Stacy continued doggedly. "Once you consent to belong to the Church, you also consent to be sanctioned if you break the rules."

"You are moving in circles, Ms. Donovan," Judge Montgomery said, with faint impatience. "I fail to see where you are going with this argument."

"Your Honor, an analogy might help," Stacy insisted.

"Okay, let's hear your analogy," Judge Montgomery said, putting one elbow on the desk and resting her chin on her fist, slightly leaning to one side in the manner of a wise professor patiently waiting out an impertinent student who is trying to dispute a proven theory.

"Take, for instance, the NFL," Stacy warmed to the challenge. "The NFL is governed by rules and regulations that coaches, players, and referees are supposed to follow. If a player, coach, or referee breaks any of those rules, that person incurs appropriate penalties and sanctions. No one has ever sued the NFL for discrimination because he was sanctioned for breaking the rules because said rules and regulations are known to the defaulter beforehand. To litigate such penalties or sanctions would constitute a non-issue because the NFL would have no case to answer."

"Very impressive, Ms. Donovan," Judge Montgomery said, nodding faintly in agreement. "I think I can grant you that."

"Thank you, Your Honor," Stacy said with a slight bow. "Based on the argument so advanced, I pray the court to dismiss the case as frivolous and lacking in merit."

"Your Honor!" Patrick Turner's hand shot up in the air, like a town council voter.

"You may speak, Mr. Turner," Judge Montgomery obliged, graciously.

He stood up, looking pleased for the first time, and even wearing a faint smile. "I agree perfectly with my learned opponent's analogy. The unfortunate thing, however, is that she is laboring the obvious and, hence, her argument is beside the point."

"This is getting interesting," Judge Montgomery said and sat back, again, like a wise professor gauging the wit and wisdom of two impertinent students sparring to prove their intellectual superiority over each other. "Mr. Turner, let's hear you demonstrate the irrelevance of this analogy."

"That every entity or corporation has the right to establish and implement its set of rules and regulations and to sanction its members in case of dereliction is not on trial here, Your Honor." Patrick Turner rose to the challenge, too. "But that such a corporation, through its agent, has shown gross partiality and discrimination in applying such rules and penalties or sanctions…THAT is what is on trial. My client was singled out and subjected to public humiliation bearing on a case for which another defaulter has not been appropriately and equally sanctioned. It is a case of discrimination and, perhaps, racial oppression. That is what I am prosecuting, Your Honor, I pray the court that this case be brought to trial."

Stacy's hand was up in the air. Judge Montgomery also raised her hand, motioning Stacy to hold her peace. She jotted down some notes on her pad, looked up at Patrick Turner, and inquired, "Again, Mr. Turner, for the record, you seriously insist that you intend to prove a case of discrimination?"

"Yes, Your Honor," Patrick Turner replied.

"You also bring in the 'race card', alleging racial oppression."

Stacy squirmed in her seat, but held her peace as Judge Montgomery held out her hand again to stop her from interrupting.

"Mr. Turner, I realize that your client is Black," Judge Montgomery continued. "And as is quite obvious, I am also Black."

"Yes, Your Honor," he replied, bobbing his head back and forth in emphasis.

"And so, you realize that brining in the race factor takes the case a notch higher and more serious?"

"I am perfectly aware of that, Your Honor," he assured her. "And I intend to prove my case accordingly."

"Ms. Donovan, do you have anything more to say?" Judge Montgomery asked, looking prim again.

"Your Honor, I do not see why this case has to go to trial based purely on speculation about a discrimination that has not been substantiated."

"That will be substantiated, Ms. Donovan," Patrick Turner addressed her directly.

"If you have evidence of the alleged discrimination why not produce it?" Stacy sparred angrily. "You know you are required to make such evidence available to me for examination and proper preparation of the defense of my client."

"I know all that, Ms. Donovan," he said. "The evidence in this case is a person, whom I will produce. You will have all the freedom to examine that person and make your defense at that time."

"I think both of you are done," Judge Montgomery said. "In the absence of any further facts to present, I will move the case to trial."

"But, Your Honor..." Stacy began, but was interrupted by the judge.

"Both of you will receive notification of the date of trial by mail. By the way, Miss Donovan, Prosecution is usually not bound to share evidence when a trial is not yet fixed. Once you get your trial date, you can negotiate the sharing of evidence. For now, this preliminary hearing is adjourned," the judge stated as she banged the gavel, got up, and walked into her chambers.

Stacy was really piqued at the outcome of the preliminary hearing. She felt she did not get a fair adjudication from the judge. She stood there for a couple of minutes, perplexed at the turn of events. Then she gathered her papers into her briefcase, zipped it, and stalked out petulantly. At the door, Patrick Turner gave her a mock compliment.

"That was quite an impressive analogy, Ms. Donovan."

"Thank you, Mr. Turner," Stacy responded, primly. "Forgive me if I can't say the same for your performance, though."

"Ah, I'm not much for the show, that's understandable," he countered, acridly.

"You certainly thirst for blood when you smell money, don't you?" Stacy asked, almost hissing, her face a mere six inches from his face. Then she stalked out with an air of arrogance before he could think of a rebuttal.

"Women!" Patrick Turner muttered under his breath, smiling wryly. "They can never lose with grace." Tucking his briefcase under his arm, he walked out to his car.

———

Later that morning, Stacy drove straight from the court to Our Lady of Peace Catholic Church. She was just four blocks away from the Church when a police car parked by the curb flashed its red, blue, and orange lights. Startled, she instinctively switched her foot from the gas to the brake pedal. She looked at her speedometer and realized she was doing almost fifty miles on a thirty-five-mile-an-hour suburb road. Her heart missed a beat and pounded furiously against her chest. There was only one stoplight before she turned left onto the side street where the rectory of Our Lady of Peace Church stood. As she approached, the light turned yellow. Under normal circumstances, she could have made it across before it turned red, but she decided against the impulse and slowed her BMW convertible to a stop. A glance in her side mirror showed that the police car was still at the spot where it was. Whoever was behind the wheel did not appear to be interested in following her. She thought the flash was a warning, yet she was unsure if it was for her or another driver. Whoever it was for, she was greatly relieved that she didn't get a ticket, which would have exacerbated the bad taste she had from her encounter with Patrick Turner in Judge Montgomery's courtroom earlier that morning. After what she considered a major defeat—failing to persuade the judge to throw out the case and not move it to trial—she wasn't ready to encounter any superior airs from a cop. It would have been much worse if the cop recognized her as an attorney breaking traffic regulations. She resolved to just go and break the bad news to Father McCarthy and then head back to her office at the Chancery to attend to regular office matters. Maybe that would soothe her mood. She wondered why she decided to drive to the rectory instead of breaking the news to him on the phone and leaving it at that.

The light turned green and Stacy had no time to answer her own question, nor was she interested in manufacturing an answer. She was still too piqued at the morning-gone-wrong to dwell on a Q-and-A game. Turning left onto Lamar Street, she drove for ten minutes and turned left again into the driveway of Our Lady of Peace rectory. The driveway was curved for easy entrance and exit, a clever use of the twenty by thirty feet of space between the rectory and the street. Being a perfect bow, it could take up to six cars parked along the curb, something that would be impossible to pull off with a straight driveway perpendicular to the rectory and the street. The rectory seemed to have been designed by someone with foresight and good planning. The main entrance was on the opposite side, facing the rectory, separated by a large parking lot. The side facing Lamar Street could also serve as a main entrance, though it was rarely used except by private visitors. Stacy pulled up and parked directly in front of the rectory, parallel to the three concrete steps leading up to a lightly ornate door. The rectory and the church building, by their architectural design, both appeared to have been erected in the early 1950s. She made a mental note to ask Father McCarthy when it was built.

"Good morning, Miss Donovan," a voice called out from the doorway, startling Stacy, who was busy pressing and holding the button that was bringing out the roof and glass windows of her convertible into place. She did not want to take chances with Houston weather. It could rain at the drop of a hat.

"Good morning, Father," Stacy called in response. She had not heard the door open, but Father McCarthy was standing there holding it. Dressed in his clericals—a Spanish-style black jumper over black dress pants and black shoes—with a crew-cut hairstyle neatly trimmed at the sides and around the back, and combed into a nice clump over his forehead, Father McCarthy looked quite handsome. She felt a slight flutter in her stomach, but quickly composed herself and asked, half teasing and half surprised at his quick appearance, "Do you always stay by your door, or were you expecting me?"

"No. Why?" Father McCarthy asked, then added, "I stay inside the house. In fact, I was upstairs."

"Well, then, you must be quicksilver, Achilles, or some sort of lightning, to move that fast from upstairs. I wasn't even out of the car yet when you opened the door."

"Oh, I just happened to look through the window and spotted your car wheeling into my driveway," Father McCarthy said. "I like your ride," he concluded, giving Stacy's convertible an appraiser's eyeing-over.

"Oh, thank you," Stacy demurred, hanging her handbag over the crook of her left arm and stretching her suit skirt, which was slightly tight, accentuating her hip and back curves.

"Graduation gift from my dad. It's almost ten years old. It gets me where I need to go, though," she added, chuckling.

"A priority function well fulfilled," Father McCarthy concurred. "Come inside, please, and tell me that everything is going well so far."

"The news is not good, Father," Stacy said somberly. "Judge Montgomery insisted on moving the case to trial."

"Move the case to trial?!" Father McCarthy said, almost yelling. "Goodness, gracious! It's not worth the trouble! Since when did the court sink to that level of wallowing in frivolities?" he asked rhetorically, throwing his hands in the air in exasperation. He started pacing, visibly agitated.

"I'm terribly sorry." Stacy was all apologies. "Once Patrick Turner insisted that he could prove a case of discrimination, I couldn't persuade her to throw out the case or even to let it be settled out of court."

"Discrimination, my foot," Father McCarthy said, visibly livid. "Is it because the Eshiets are Black? I could equally stop any White folk from Communion if they committed the same moral scandal of using IVF as a method of conception, which the Church expressly prohibits. I guess no one would cry 'discrimination'! Since the anti-discrimination laws, everyone has to walk on eggshells where minorities are concerned."

"Well, Father," Stacy said. "I know it's hard, but I don't think you really had to walk on eggshells. Besides, I don't think their argument alleging discrimination will be premised on race, although there is no telling how far Patrick would go to prove his case."

"What if they drop it like a bomb at the trial?" Father McCarthy asked.

"That would be to your advantage, Father," Stacy replied confidently.

"What do you mean?" Father McCarthy asked. He stopped pacing to look at Stacy.

"That would give us the grounds to ask Judge Montgomery to recuse herself from the case," Stacy said, slipping into a conspiratorial mood. "And the only other judge whom I know the case would go to is Judge Mendes. Victoria Mendes."

"Why would she recuse herself?" Father McCarthy asked, confused.

"She's Black," Stacy said.

"Oh, I see," Father McCarthy said, looking every bit like a person who had, in fact, seen where this case was heading. "So, I am accused of discrimination by a Black couple, and I am to be prosecuted before a Black judge."

"Wait a minute, Father," Stacy said, raising a hand to calm Father McCarthy. "I think you are taking me out of context. I am not saying that Judge Montgomery would not be fair, or that she is incapable of giving a fair judgment in a case of racial discrimination, even where the plaintiff is Black."

"So, what are you saying?" Father McCarthy inquired.

"All I am saying is that I would capitalize on the scenario to pressure her to recuse herself from the case. That would give me another chance to try to persuade the next judge to either throw out the case or, worse, order an out-of-court settlement."

"Okay, I see where you are going," Father McCarthy conceded, then countered, "What if she refuses to recuse herself?"

"Then we will have no option but to slug it out in the legal ring," Stacy said, again using that confidential tone which Father McCarthy was beginning to like. He thought Stacy exuded confidence and was smart enough to handle Turner & Stendhal.

"Well, that still doesn't make me feel any better," Father McCarthy said, doggedly. "Knowing that both my opponent and my judge are Black doesn't make me very confident in the justice system."

"Father, do me a favor, please," Stacy said, softly. "Can you drop the 'Black' thing for once and relax? It's not going to be what you think, I can assure you. And, by the way," she added. "I'm kind of Black, too."

"What do you mean?" Father McCarthy asked, creasing his forehead with incredulity.

"I'm half Black," Stacy said.

"What do you mean, 'half Black'?" Father McCarthy pursued, still incredulous.

"Well, one-quarter Black, if you like," Stacy corrected herself.

"Yeah, keep going," Father McCarthy urged, almost mockingly.

"That's where it ends." Stacy chuckled and said, "Father, don't look at me as if I'm nuts. Seriously, I consider myself one-quarter Black. My father is mulatto. He's the one who's half Black. His mother was Black and his father was Irish. I'm a carbon copy of my mom, who's Swede. You haven't met my mom. When you do, you'll see what I mean."

"Would you like a cup of coffee or a glass of wine?" Fr. McCarthy asked suddenly. "And, please, sit down." He pointed her to a chair by the breakfast table."

"Whoa!" Stacy exclaimed. "Nice to see you getting back to normal and becoming civil and hospitable."

"I apologize. I got carried away," Father McCarthy said.

"First time coming into your house, you offer me no seat, and we've been talking for almost fifteen minutes, trying to calm you down," Stacy said, sounding relieved. "Good to see you're recovering yourself."

"I apologize," Father McCarthy said again. "I guess getting the bad news that the case is set for trial, and knowing my accuser, the judge, and my lawyer are all Black, is enough to make me forget my manners. So, if you don't mind, let me be honest: I am offering you a seat and coffee or wine because I am desperately trying to keep, at least, one Black person on my side." Fr. McCarthy had found his sense of humor.

"I thought bribery was a mortal sin...?" Stacy began to say.

"... which kills the life of God in the soul. Yeah, I know," Fr. McCarthy finished her sentence for her, chuckling wryly.

Stacy broke into uncontrollable laughter. She laughed so hard, her whole body was rocking. She rolled from side to side. Her laughter was so full of mirth and gaiety, it became contagious. Soon Father McCarthy was rocking in laughter, too.

"You need to go to confession, Father," she said in mock chiding, barely able to contain her guffaw. "But first, let me have my coffee. A lot of desk work is waiting for me at the office, so, I need something to keep me awake."

"Alright, coffee coming," Fr. McCarthy said, almost announcing it. He crossed the room and poured two cups of coffee—one for Stacy and one for himself, then called, "sugar?"

"Yes, please," Stacy responded.

"Cream?" he called again.

"Just a little drop," Stacy said.

"Oh, I thought women liked a lot of cream in their coffee," Fr. McCarthy teased.

"No, I only like a little cream in my coffee, not the other way around," Stacy said as Fr. McCarthy set her cup in front of her. "That's one of the bad habits I inherited from my dad. My mom drinks coffee, too, and my siblings. Matter of fact, it's a family thing. We are a clan of coffee guzzlers."

"As far as I know, I'm the only one in my family who drinks coffee," Fr. McCarthy said. "The rest of the family follows the tea-drinking tradition of the English. Don't ask me where and when they picked up the habit because I don't know, and we're not even English."

Fr. McCarthy and Stacy settled down to their coffee with occasional small talk in between gulps. Eventually, Stacy glanced at her watch and decided it was time to get back to the Chancery office. She thanked Fr. McCarthy for the good brew, hung her handbag on the crook of her left hand, and stretched out the right for a handshake. Fr. McCarthy took it and pumped it briefly, praying her again to do her best for him and for the Church. Stacy assured him again and turned to leave, but noticed a pouch-covered Wilson racket leaning against the corner of the wall, with a can of tennis balls beside it.

"Do you play tennis?" She asked, looking excited.

"Yes, Ma'am, I do," Fr. McCarthy responded and asked, "Do you?"

"I'm a big fan of tennis, and I play when I have time," she responded, still excited.

"Well, then," Fr. McCarthy said. "Maybe you could join us tomorrow at St. Mary's Seminary. Fr. Polanski and I are playing on the Seminary court. Greg, my parish council chairman, is coming, too. We could play doubles, since you will make a fourth person." He was becoming excited.

"Yeah, I would love to," Stacy said. "What time?"

"Four," he responded.

"Mm! Four is a bit early for me," Stacy said. "That's the time I usually leave the office, but I will see what I can do."

"We can start late," Fr. McCarthy offered, graciously.

"Well, the doubles won't be until I arrive," Stacy pointed out. "But you can start playing without me."

"That's right," he concurred. "But we'll be expecting you."

"I'll be there," Stacy confirmed. "A bit tardy, though." She stretched out her hand again for a shake.

———

The following day, at three forty-five in the afternoon, Fr. McCarthy nosed his car onto Memorial Drive, heading for St. Mary's Seminary. Fr. Polanski sat beside him, chewing a wad of gum. They drove in silence for most of the way. Both were in their tennis gear: white polo shirts, white shorts, and white Nike tennis shoes. Fr. McCarthy wore a blue band around his head and another on his left wrist, like a pro. Fr. Polanski wore a white cap that bore his alma mater insignia of Notre Dame University, in South Bend, Indiana. He had grown tired and stopped explaining to his critics that the reason why he wasn't a football nut, but preferred tennis, even when he was still at Notre Dame, was precisely because he wasn't a Mick, but a Polack. Nobody could tell whether he always said that in jest or was serious about it. But Fr. Polanski was one person who didn't care about making jokes or using derogatory terms at his own expense. Some say it was subterfuge, a kind of defense mechanism against his critics. Since he himself was a veritable social critic, he would first criticize himself or apply to himself any racially motivated insults current in popular talk. That way his critics were robbed of anything to say to hurt his feelings, if they got upset with him. Always referring to himself as a Polack was probably, also, a play on his name.

Fr. McCarthy was almost the opposite. A prim and loyal firebrand of the Church, defender of orthodoxy, guarded in speech, a veritable fan of Pope Benedict XVI, although he had schizophrenic outbursts of anger when frustrated. He knew this, and would often be ashamed of it later whenever it got the better of him in an unguarded moment. He enjoyed the company of his friend, Fr. Polanski, his wisecracks, and his sagacity, despite his scathing criticisms of the Church. Some priests who knew them well thought they were like a pair of shoes, always complementing each other, though never quite agreeing with each other on many things. On such occasions, they followed the unwritten rule of agreeing to disagree, moving on and not in the least ruffled by each other's outspokenness. In any case, Fr. McCarthy cherished and cultivated the sounding board he discovered in Fr. Polanski. He often mused to himself that Fr. Polanski, though sixteen years his senior, had become a father figure in his life, making up for what he missed from his real father who, though not really estranged from his priest son, was, nevertheless, reserved in character. Father McCarthy never really enjoyed a conversation with his father on an intimate level, but there was a kind of mutual respect between them, the kind that he would gladly lose for a warmer relationship. Since he met Fr. Polanski, he never really missed the warm presence of his adopted father in his life.

He slowed his car to thirty-five mph, since there was ample time, and cleared his throat. "I had a moment of weakness yesterday when I was with Stacy Donovan," he began.

"Oh, my dear, Nick. My dear Nick," Fr. Polanski said, patronizingly. "Always remember what your spiritual director taught you in the seminary: when talking to a beautiful lady, look straight at her face or forehead, but never at her booby bosom, her curvy waistline, or her shapely legs. Say the *Ave Maria, Ora pro Nobis* ejaculation silently in your mind."

"Okay, Charlie. Hold it! Hold it!" Fr. McCarthy interrupted, chuckling tolerantly at his friend's raunchy spiritualizing. "I'm not talking about *that* weakness."

"You're not?"

"No. I'm talking about my usual nemesis. I had an outburst of anger when Stacy gave me the discouraging news that the judge was moving my case to trial."

"Oh, I see," Fr. Polanski said, getting serious. "And why was that, if I may ask? Surely you knew that the case might be moved to trial?"

"I thought the judge would see the frivolity of it and just dismiss it," Fr. McCarthy said plaintively. "The case lacks merit, Charlie. You know that. The Church has the authority to make laws governing her subjects and to enforce such laws…"

"Here we go again," Fr. Polanski said, exasperatingly.

"You know what I am talking about, but that's not what worries me, in any case," Fr. McCarthy quickly assured. "It's the racial angle they are trying to create in the case."

"Again, with Blacks constituting only nine percent of your parish population, don't tell me you didn't see that coming, Nick," Fr. Polanski said.

"Maybe I did, but just thought they wouldn't dare play that card," he responded. "But now that situation is aggravated by the fact that the trial judge is Black."

"Okay, I didn't know that," Fr. Polanski said, somberly. "I now understand your fears."

"Good, I now put my fears into question form," Fr. McCarthy said, relieved that his friend was beginning to agree with him. "Do you think that I will have a fair trial considering the situation of things?"

"Mmm, let's see," Fr. Polanski heaved his bulk to one side and continued in measured tones. "I would say it's fifty-fifty. Let's just say the judge knows she was sworn onto the bench as a custodian of justice. And don't forget, too, that Cardinal Felice is a popular and powerful figure, not just in the Church, but in the city, also. I doubt whether the judge would risk offending him by being unfair."

"Well, Charlie," Fr. McCarthy responded. "As you said, it's fifty-fifty. You never know who has an axe to grind with the Church and may find in this case the opportunity to embarrass the Cardinal. But I will take the fifty-fifty wager, though fifty out of a hundred ain't too consoling."

"It ain't too discouraging, either," Fr. Polanski countered. "Now can we quit the glum side of things and talk about tennis?"

"Of course, of course," Fr. McCarthy livened up. "Let's see. Where shall we begin? Shall we begin by agreeing that I'm going to beat you in the first two sets?"

"I would pawn my racquet first thing tomorrow morning, and send my tennis gear to the Salvation Army, Nick! True to God!" He responded, pretending to feel insulted at such an outrageous claim.

"Okay, Charlie, take it easy," Fr. McCarthy cautioned. "Go easy on the pre-fight boast, and don't swear a big Herodian oath that you might regret having to make good on when I beat you."

"Nick," Fr. Polanski called, looking at Fr. McCarthy with a faint indulgent smile. "Just admit you are an amateur tennis player coming to learn from a professional. Tell you what?

"What?"

"I'll fete you sumptuously at *Fogo de Chao*, complete with any wine of your choice to wash it down, if you return my first service. It's a Brazilian restaurant in the southwest part of the city."

"Oh, get off it, Charlie," Fr. McCarthy dismissed. "Doesn't it occur to you that you might be presuming too much here? Remember, meals at *Fogo de Chao* don't come cheap. So, I caution you again, don't be a Herod." He pressed hard on the brake pedal to bring the car to a stop, as he nearly jumped the red light. "By the way, I invited Stacy. Hopefully she can make it. She said she might be running late."

They were at the last stoplight before the gates of the Seminary. From there, they could see the large compound with its tall buildings of dull red bricks. The life-size statue of the Blessed Virgin Mary could be seen from the lights. The well-mowed lawns dotted with tall pine trees and lined with equally well-trimmed bushes and flowers bestowed an atmosphere of tranquility on the campus that made it feel almost like a seventeenth-century monastery. The lights changed to green and Fr. McCarthy drove a block and turned left onto the main avenue of the Seminary campus.

The seminarians were still engaged in their afternoon studies when Fr. McCarthy and Fr. Polanski pulled up in the parking lot adjacent to the tennis courts, twin courts of concrete done to Wimbledon standard, painted deep green with white lines and grey nets, the funding of which was donated in memory of Bishop Nold by some rich couple who wished to remain anonymous. Greg was already there sitting in the open door of the driver's side of his Toyota RAV 4, his legs out on the tarmac. He was talking to someone on the phone. He quickly ended his phone conversation as the two clerics alighted from their car still debating who was going to trounce the other and who was going to have to eat the humble pie. Greg put his cap on and moved toward Fr. McCarthy and Fr. Polanski.

"Good afternoon, Greg," Fr. McCarthy called out. "I see you were quite early."

"Yeah, I am," Greg responded. "I guessed coming to play with two priests meant I needed to arrive on time so I won't have to go to confession for tardiness."

"Well, what can I say," Fr. McCarthy replied. "Sounds like it was a good plan."

"Good afternoon, Greg," Fr. Polanski greeted and added, "Your mama raised you well. Being on time is evident of good upbringing."

"There you go," Greg demurred, taking Fr. Polanski's proffered hand. "Good afternoon, Father. Mama always said, 'Don't you be late for your appointment with a priest'. I tell ya, I've always tried my very best since then."

"Evidence of good upbringing," Fr. Polanski concurred again.

"Don't worry, Greg," Fr. McCarthy interjected. "The only person who should go to confession after the game is Charlie here, for bogus pre-game boasting."

Fr. Polanski stopped in his tracks, feigning a tripping misstep. He turned to Greg and said, "This guy would debate St. Peter at the Pearly Gates, that he is the Redeemer and not Jesus." He turned to Fr. McCarthy and all but commanded, "Get onto court and let me give you a whooping for impudence."

"I will let you priests play first," Greg conceded. "I'll watch your hands so when I come in, I won't spoil the tempo."

"Why not get in with Nick and let's warm up first for a couple of minutes," Fr. Polanski said.

"Yeah, Greg, let's do a warm-up first," Fr. McCarthy agreed. "I have invited Ms. Donovan, the Archdiocesan attorney, to join us. We can play doubles today."

"Okay, looks like it's gonna be a great evening," Greg said as he lightly returned Fr. Polanski's warm-up service.

Fr. Polanski, Fr. McCarthy, and his parish council chairman played the warm-up game for about ten minutes. Eventually Fr. Polanski called for a formal game. Greg took the sideline to await his turn while playing the umpire.

"Ball!" Fr. Polanski called, threw the bright yellow ball from a freshly opened can, high up in the air, and swung his racket.

*Whack!*

"Five love," Greg called out. Then he noticed that Fr. McCarthy was still motionless in the crouching position he took, racket ready in hand, seemingly waiting for the ball. Fr. Polanski noticed it, too, and both looked quizzically at Fr. McCarthy.

"What?" The latter asked plaintively, pretending to be ignorant of why they were looking at him sideways. "You called service and I'm waiting for the ball." Fr. Polanski and Greg broke out laughing.

"Father, the ball was served," Greg said, amid heaves of laughter.

"Was it?" Fr. McCarthy asked, feigning surprise and sending the other two into another merry guffaw.

"Okay, Nick," Fr. Polanski said, barely able to rein himself in. "I repent for that brutality. That was my special 215-mph service. I thought you would live up to your pre-game boast. Otherwise I should have treated you to a gentler service. Get to the other side. I'll try and be merciful."

"Alright, Charlie. No need to laugh till you tear up. I concede that that went by so fast, I couldn't even react to it," Fr. McCarthy said. "Don't be merciful. Just serve."

The two clerics battled each other for twenty minutes and three games before Fr. McCarthy agreed to let Greg take his turn, having lost all three games without scoring any advantage. After two games, which Greg also lost, Fr. Polanski allowed Fr. McCarthy and Greg to play each other, while he rested, sitting on the hood of their car, sipping cold lemonade from the ice chest they had brought.

Stacy was an hour and fifteen minutes late and was all apologies. She was impeccably dressed in a white polo shirt, white cap, white short skirt with white knickers underneath, and a pair of white tennis shoes that looked very new. Her gear was all Nike. Her well-chiseled, slender legs and her very slim abdomen revealed someone who took her gym time seriously. Fr. McCarthy again caught himself wondering why she wasn't married. Such an intelligent woman with such a killer body! He quickly shook off the irreverent revelry and welcomed her to the game. Stacy was introduced to the others. They played six games in doubles and two rotating games each in singles. Fr. McCarthy was surprised that Stacy could play so well. She got one game with Fr. Polanski and dislodged him twice at game point before he could beat her at the third. Fr. Polanski was equally surprised at her prowess. During small talk between games, Stacy managed to squeeze in an invitation to dinner at her mom's place in two days' time. Greg politely declined with some 'good' excuse. Fr. McCarthy had a lot at stake to say "no" to a dinner invitation from Stacy, and Fr. Polanski, a self-proclaimed lover of gourmet dinners, was bereft of even a bad excuse for declining, and decided to tag along. As the evening was beginning to get dark and they were preparing to go, Stacy decided to take Greg aside for a ten-minute conversation. Those were ten very fruitful minutes, as she later confessed to Fr. McCarthy.

# HOUSTON, TEXAS

## OCTOBER 26, 2012

FR. MCCARTHY WAS IMPRESSED and awed at the same time with the opulence of the Donovan residence. Ensconced in a calm non-descript part of South Post Oak Boulevard, not quite two miles from former US President George H.W. Bush's home, which sat on a four-acre lot, facing a miniature, man-made, rectangular lake that was not more than 1,200 square feet. The lake spewed four fountains at its four corners which glowed beautifully at night in crimson and yellow, opal blue and turquois, indigo and pink, green and crystal white. Four black-gilded stands, topped with white, opaque light globes—five on each stand—lined the short fifty-foot driveway on either side leading up to the ornate arc that stood like a sentry in front of the house. On the arc was inscribed the words, "Welcome to the Donovans'." It appeared black against the dull red color of the arc during the day, and at night it glowed neon white. Ten feet beyond the arc was the main entrance of what, to Fr. McCarthy, looked like a palace. Immediately behind the entrance was a six-foot-wide arcade that split to the left and right, skirting a twenty-by-twelve-feet swimming pool. It was railed off at the end facing the main entrance.

At the opposite end, overlooking the pool, were three large doors. The middle door opened into a large dining area, the left door opened into a large sitting room set theater-style with an eight-by-six-feet movie screen over a low fire place that was alive with artificial electric flames that looked red hot, but were, in fact, cooler than Lake Placid in winter. The third large door on the right opened into another sitting room, furnished in the regular way with a central glass-topped coffee table and settees of costly synthetic fabrics. Another door from that sitting room to the far right opened into a game room with a pool table and other games. A corridor ran between the dining area and the second sitting room, leading to two guest rooms at the far end. A staircase from the same corridor led upstairs to the Donovans' private rooms. All the bedrooms were upstairs. The dining room and the second sitting room had high, gilded ceilings ornamented with gold linings. At the center of each room was a large crystal candelabra that glowed during the day and sparkled beautifully during the night. The sheer architectural complexity of the entire edifice was awe-inspiring. And Fr. McCarthy and Fr. Polanski drank all of it in as Mrs. Donovan bobbled around giving them a short tour of the building. The furnishings, too, were all of very costly brocade and satin material, carefully chosen by Mrs. Donovan herself. Fr. McCarthy could tell that she was an expert decorator, as she explained how she came to decide which material should go where and which furniture should stay where.

Family photographs and single ones, intermingled with scenic paintings and pictures, were stationed at strategic positions all over the house: on the mantel piece, over the window ledges, on small high tables that seemed to be made just for that purpose, and so on. Each photograph, painting, or scenic picture had a history which Mrs. Donovan was only too glad to throw out in short summaries. Fr. McCarthy couldn't help wondering whether she had worked as a tour guide or as an appraiser of art works before. And there were not a few art works in wooden sculpture and porcelain, too. Mrs. Donovan took it all in stride in her wonderful, short historical summaries. When she eventually led them around to the large dining room, they had spent almost twenty minutes touring the house.

"I hope everybody is hungry after the tour," Mrs. Donovan called out, obviously announcing her wish rather than asking a question, as she started pulling out the seats.

"You bet, Mrs. Donovan," Fr. Polanski replied, good-naturedly.

"Good," she said and continued pulling out the chairs. "I did that on purpose."

"What? Pulling out the seats?" Fr. Polanski asked, breaking Mrs. Donovan's monologue and faking wariness, as if she had implied something ominous was about to happen.

"Nope. The tour," she replied. "A short walk or brief exercise before dinner usually whets the appetite. Fathers, would you please do us the honor of sitting at the heads of the table?" she asked as she assigned the two clerics to opposite ends of the table.

"Is Mom lecturing y'all, expounding on her 'healthy-eating-habits theory'?" Stacy quipped as she came in from the kitchen, bearing a service pan full of fried rice. She placed it on a pad on the table and added for the benefit of their guests, "She believes in lots of eating rituals, like which course should go first and which should be eaten last, what type of dressing matches what type of salad, and so on."

"Well, I think good eating order is health-inducing," Fr. McCarthy said, glad to be able to chip in a word edge-wise to match Mrs. Donovan, who, throughout the brief tour, chattered excitedly. "For instance, you wouldn't eat your dessert before the main course."

"Brilliant, Father!" Mrs. Donovan concurred excitedly. "Brilliant! My daughter doesn't believe eating is an art. She and her dad…they just throw food in their mouths, masticate, and ingest it. That's all. By the way," she added as an aside, "Geoffrey is away on a business seminar. He will be back in a day or two."

"We do derive the same nutritious value," Stacy contested as she got a pan of roasted beef from their cousin to put on the table while the latter went back to bring other food items from the kitchen to the dining area. "So, why waste time on needless protocols? What's the difference?"

"It's that between a lawyer and a real estate agent slash interior decorating expert," Mrs. Donovan said, facetiously. "The one doesn't care about taste, the other does. Sit beside Father, dear." She pointed to the seat on the right of Fr. McCarthy and Stacy moved over dutifully. Mrs. Donovan proceeded to assign seats to her son and their cousin, a pretty young lady, probably not older than fifteen or sixteen. The young man appeared to be in his mid-twenties, with a quiet, almost lugubrious, demeanor. They nodded acceptance of their positions and went back to bring more food items to the table. It was obvious from the inception that Mrs. Donovan enjoyed her role as the matriarch of the small Donovan clan.

"I thought lawyers were supposed to be a class with a taste for protocol," Fr. Polanski said, picking up the conversation. "I mean, I have always admired court decorum and procedures which probably beat the Catholic Mass, stratifying the room into bar and bench, addressing the presiding judge, 'Your Honor,'…"

"'Your Worship,' in parts of Europe…" Fr. McCarthy interjected.

"Yes, of course," Fr. Polanski said, welcoming the addition. "And referring to a lengthy appeal to judge or jury as 'praying the court,' and admission of guilt as 'confession.'"

"Whoa! Father," Stacy said, pleasantly surprised. "You know quite a lot about court intricacies and decorum."

"Brilliant, Father!" Mrs. Donovan approved, excitedly. "Positively brilliant!" It soon became clear that every statement with which she agreed was brilliant. And she herself exuded brilliance, too, as Fr. McCarthy came to conclude. A middle-aged woman on the high side of fifty, she looked younger than her years. Except for a few lines on the outward sides of her eyes and two faintly visible lines crossing her neck, she could pass for forty. Like Stacy, she was a paragon of beauty, Unlike Stacy, she carried herself stately about in an air of superiority that seemed second nature to her, but devoid of arrogance, and Fr. McCarthy couldn't help but notice the uncanny resemblance in bodily features, even if mother and daughter were given to indulgent sparring, each trying to promote hers as the better profession. In fact, their personalities were somewhat different. Fr. McCarthy thought mother and daughter were highly learned and intelligent as he recalled his conversations with Stacy in previous days. Listening to her mother was a delight. Though she was chatty, she was not unbearably so. And she made a lot of sense when she spoke.

"You see, Fathers. That's where the difference between lawyers and the rest of us lies. They use art in their profession, but to make money. We appreciate art for the beauty of it," Mrs. Donovan said, teasing her daughter.

"Oh, C'mon, Mom. Are you kidding me?" Stacy sparred with mock vexation. "Since when did real estate agents prospect for land, built or refurbished houses, and give them away for charity? And since when did you finish decorating a house without sending a bill?"

"The money is secondary for us," Mrs. Donovan replied cleverly. "We're like the priests…"

"In what way?" Stacy challenged.

"Priests don't charge money for their services. They get stipends. Isn't that so, Father?" Mrs. Donovan asked, not really waiting for an answer. "We interior decorators don't charge our clients. There is no adequate payment for beauty. We get honoraria."

"Okay, Mom. That's where we're even," Stacy said. "We're like priests, too. We don't charge money. We receive compensations. Shall we pray and eat before the food gets cold?"

"Actually, both of you are right," Fr. McCarthy said, adding ruefully, "We don't charge parishioners for our services. We only take up collections." His remark cracked everybody up in raucous guffaw. Mrs. Donovan paid her usual compliments of 'brilliant' in between heaves of laughter. When she could hold it, she invited Fr. McCarthy to pray the grace before the meal. He did. Mrs. Donovan insisted on serving the priests, an idiosyncrasy which, according to her, she contracted from her mother who believed guests should always be served the first round of the meal, after which, they can serve themselves seconds and thirds. Everyone enjoyed the meal and conversation. Fr. McCarthy and Fr. Polanski took turns spinning yarns about their seminary days, while the Donovans listened with rapt attention, fascinated to learn that life inside the seminary was, in many ways, markedly different from life in secular universities, but also, in some ways, similar. Their stories were so entertaining that even the young Donovan, Stacy's brother, lost his lugubrious demeanor and chuckled at intervals. Their cousin kept smiling coyly, and Mrs. Donovan and Stacy forgot, for a moment, to fight over whose profession was the better one. Mrs. Donovan didn't permit herself to be outdone, as she regaled them with stories of her college sorority exploits with Stacy playing the part of the critic, always ready to point out where her mom had embellished the facts. Eventually, she steered the conversation to Fr. McCarthy, broaching the subject of his pending lawsuit.

"I hear that one of your parishioners is suing you for discrimination. Is that true?" she asked, addressing Fr. McCarthy.

"Yes, Mrs. Donovan," Fr. McCarthy replied with a tinge of embarrassment. "The suing couple did something they shouldn't have done as Catholics. When they were sanctioned, they took offense and decided to sue me, alleging discrimination."

"But, why discrimination?" Mrs. Donovan asked, genuinely confused. "Where's the discrimination in being sanctioned for what you have done wrong?"

"Mom, it's a complex issue," Stacy interjected. She was afraid Fr. McCarthy would bring in the race factor and complicate the conversation, seeing as her family was of mixed blood. "They are alleging that Fr. McCarthy has not sanctioned other offenders in the same situation, that he singled them out," she added, attempting to steer the conversation away from a discussion about race.

"But is that true? What was the actual offense?" Mrs. Donovan asked, still genuinely puzzled.

"Mom, you don't need to know that," Stacy said, beginning to feel cagy. "We are taking care of the issue at the Chancery legal office."

"That's okay, Stacy," Fr. McCarthy said, raising his hand slightly to calm her. "She needs to know because it is a common issue concerning Church teaching. This couple used the new reproductive technology of pre-implantation genetic screening and in vitro fertilization to conceive a child."

"But isn't that against Church teaching? I have read the document from the Congregation for the Doctrine of the Faith that came out on that issue, and I think Pope Benedict says the Church does not endorse IVF for Catholic couples," Mrs. Donovan said.

"That's precisely the point, Mrs. Donovan," Fr. McCarthy replied, glad for an ally in her.

"I think the couple is probably angry about other things, too," Fr. Polanski interjected. "Maybe they feel the Church is too restrictive or too absolutist in its moral dictates. We encounter a lot of people, especially in the liberal camp, who tend to think that way."

"This couple sounds, to me, like they are from that camp," Mrs. Donovan surmised. "Are they Caucasian or Hispanic?

"Mom!" Stacy was getting alarmed. "That is irrelevant…"

"They are Africans," Fr. McCarthy interjected. "From Nigeria, and highly educated. The husband is an obstetrician/gynecologist and the wife is a pediatrician. So, it's a kind of academic arrogance, too."

"Fr. McCarthy, you don't need to field Mother's every question," Stacy said with a tinge of authority, perhaps to remind Fr. McCarthy that she was the one to call the shots as his attorney.

"But, dear, it's not like this is classified information," Mrs. Donovan protested feebly. "It's a lawsuit, and you can bet that since it involves the Catholic Church, it will be all over the papers and the television."

"Like I don't know that," Stacy parried. "Again, we're handling that at the Chancery office, Mom. And I'm on top of it. So, if you don't mind, can we please change the subject?" With that, Stacy got up while asking, "Anybody for dessert, coffee, or something?"

Her brother and their cousin, sensing an opening, grabbed the cue and quickly got up to start clearing the table for dessert. They were glad to leave the table, as the conversation was getting intense. Fr. Polanski, too, was relieved that Stacy requested a change in subject. He was all the time trying to catch Fr. McCarthy's attention to give him a signal to change the subject, but it seemed the latter was ready to indulge Mrs. Donovan further, perhaps to feed the need to prove his righteous innocence.

"Coffee for me," he called out.

"Fr. McCarthy?" Stacy inquired.

"A sliver of dessert, no coffee," Fr. McCarthy responded curtly, feeling slightly, but indirectly, rebuked by Stacy's reaction to her mom. He accepted in his mind that he was beginning to go too far. And Stacy was right.

He needed to be guarded in talking about the lawsuit, even with well-meaning people such as his lawyer's mother. He made a mental note to defer everything to Stacy in the future. After all, she was his attorney.

Mrs. Donovan herself did not seem ruffled at all by her daughter's souring humor. As Stacy moved to the kitchen to prepare desserts and coffee, she leaned forward and said in hushed tones for Fr. McCarthy's and Fr. Polanski's benefit, "I have never seen a young lady so fiendishly protective of her profession and her clients."

"I heard that," Stacy called from the kitchen and Mrs. Donovan grimaced funnily, barely stifling a smile while drawing her finger across her closed mouth, from left to right, indicating that her mouth was zipped. She got up to join the rest of the kitchen crew in preparing and getting the desserts and coffee to the table. Fr. Polanski spotted a football jersey in a glass case, hanging at the far end of the room, close to the corridor. He decided to use that to begin a new line of conversation for dessert time.

"Who plays football?" he inquired loudly, directing the question to Mrs. Donovan in the kitchen. "Your husband or your son?"

"Geoffrey," Mrs. Donovan began.

"Junior," her son interjected before she could add another word.

"Junior, of course. How forgetful of me," Mrs. Donovan pretended to correct herself. "Geoffrey, Jr. is the football player, not Geoffrey, Sr. Thank you, Son, for not letting your demented mom mix things up." She came back to the dining table with cups of coffee and small spoons on saucers. "He always thinks I'm so old that I would have a senior moment forgetting to add the suffix when I'm referring to him."

"I'm not saying you're old, Mom," Geoffrey, Jr. protested. "I was just trying to say that I'm the one who plays football, not my dad."

"What school do you play for?" Fr. McCarthy asked, more by way of trying to diffuse the tension between mom and son before it escalated into an all-out argument.

"Strake," Geoffrey, Jr, replied. "I used to play for Strake Preparatory."

"Geoffrey is in transition now," Stacy chipped in, arriving at the table with a tray of assorted sweets, her cousin hot in tow with a pot of freshly brewed coffee, which she set on a pad on the table. "Geoffrey, Jr., I mean to say." She quickly corrected herself while their mother rolled her eyes and stifled a chuckle as Stacy kicked her gently under the table. "He is going to college next fall. Aren't you, Junior?"

"Yeah," he replied, looking at his sister warily, and, having determined that she wasn't making fun of him, he continued, "I'm going to the University of St. Thomas in the fall to study Business Administration."

"That's a good Catholic college," Fr. Polanski said, supportively. "It's well run, too."

"I'm excited for him," Mrs. Donovan said. "Though I had thought he would want to attend the seminary."

"Mom, don't put him on the spot," Stacy chided gently, again kicking her mother under the table.

"I'm not putting him on the spot. I'm just saying what I thought he would like," Mrs. Donovan countered. "But he decided otherwise, so there is no putting him on the spot." Stacy placed a saucer with a generous slice of pecan pie in front of Fr. McCarthy and was about to do the same for Fr. Polanski, but the latter declined and asked for only coffee instead. Fr. McCarthy half-heartedly protested the huge size of his pie then went ahead and ate all of it, anyway. He declined to drink coffee because, as he put it, he didn't want to keep vigil while the rest of the world slept. Fr. Polanski gulped down his coffee and praised it as the best brew he had ever tasted. Stacy thanked him for the compliment and looked pleased because he liked her coffee. She asked her mom whether she wanted a cup of her exquisite brew. The latter declined and announced a different type of dessert altogether.

"I'll have a glass of wine, instead," Mrs. Donovan announced and started to get up.

"I'll bring it, Mom," Geoffrey, Jr. offered, and rushed from the table in the direction of the cellar. "What should I bring, Mom?"

"Ooo! Here comes the wine party," Stacy said, teasing. "He loves wine. That's why he's quick in offering to fetch it."

"Bring *Che Gaucho*," Mrs. Donovan called after her son. "Malbec Merlot," she added, to specify. Fr. Polanski glanced furtively at Fr. McCarthy and the latter recalled his friend's remark about ladies who drank wine by their brand names. Fr. Polanski's psychology was that such women were wont to exude power, and they ran the house while their husbands were the laid-back type, happily available for just honey-dos. Fr. McCarthy concluded in his mind that his friend was probably right after all. Though Mr. Donovan was not home that evening so he could observe him, he concluded that Mrs. Donovan pretty much ran things in their miniature palace. She was the undisputed queen and matriarch of the Donovan clan, though it seemed that Stacy would not always grant her that 100% sway. She wasn't draconian or unbearable, but she exhibited the character of a woman who loved order and some measure of control. Stacy had earlier informed him that she suspected that her mother's constant harassment of her to get married and settle down was not so much because of her concern for Stacy's future as for the need to get rid of a challenging voice in the family. But having watched Mrs. Donovan that evening, Fr. McCarthy mentally disagreed with Stacy. His opinion of Mrs. Donovan was that of a woman, a pleasant lady, who loved things to go orderly and well. He particularly loved her support of Church teaching. If he could describe her, ideologically, he would call her a moderate conservative. And that was the group that Fr. McCarthy felt comfortable with.

After their dessert, the dinner group unconsciously divided itself into pairs. Geoffrey, Jr. and his cousin cleared the table and went to put the kitchen in order before retiring to their rooms to play video games. Mrs. Donovan and Fr. Polanski reclined where they were and continued small talk about this, that, and those; nothing particularly important. And Stacy invited her client, Fr. McCarthy, to the pool room for a game of billiards. Fr. McCarthy was not a billiards player, but he was an admirer of the game. So, he gladly welcomed the opportunity to learn to play. Stacy was not a bad teacher, as it soon became apparent that something else was beginning to brew between him and his attorney. He was conscious of the fact that he was tipsy because of the wine he drank, but he wasn't so sure whether Stacy herself was not more than tipsy. She was a bit too chatty, and brushed against him several times. Once, in pretense of trying to teach him how to hold the billiard stick perfectly, so he could get a perfect knock of the ball into the hole, she stood behind him and literally pressed her soft, ample bosom against his back. And this added, in no small measure, to the warm, fuzzy effect that he was already having from being tipsy. Although he was a bit leery at the beginning, after a few brushes, he decided to relax and enjoy the teasing, if that was what it was. That turned out to be a bad idea. He suffered a stiff erection for his errant judgment. By the time he came out of his lesson knocking balls into holes in a table, he had to learn to manage the bulge in his crotch so it wouldn't show. He walked slightly stooped and with legs slightly apart, making it appear as though he had had too much to eat. He was thankful to see that Fr. Polanski was already outside by the pool. Mrs. Donovan, still pinching the stem of her wine glass, was gesturing to emphasize what she was expounding upon.

"There you are," Fr. Polanski said, looking relieved to see Fr. McCarthy.

"Mrs. Donovan, I must say it was a wonderful evening. I wish we could stay longer, but I have an early appointment tomorrow."

"Yes, Mrs. Donovan, it was a very pleasant evening and I enjoyed myself immensely," Fr. McCarthy concurred. "I'm afraid we must run now. I have an early schedule, also. Thank you for the wonderful dinner. It was the best I have had in years."

"Don't blame us if we brag about it. It was delicious," Fr. Polanski added to the compliments.

"Oh, don't make a fuss about it. I'm sure it wasn't anything near what your moms cook for you, or your housekeepers in the rectory," Mrs. Donovan demurred. "Thanks for the compliments, though."

Mrs. Donovan then gathered Fr. Polanski with one hand into a tight hug, still deftly pinching her wine glass, now almost empty, between her thumb and two forefingers, her third and fourth pinkies sticking out as ladies of class are wont to hold their wine glass or cigarette pipe. She gave Fr. McCarthy a hug, too. Stacy came out on cue, gave Fr. Polanski a brief hug, then Fr. McCarthy, holding on to him a little bit tightly and longer. Then she released him and, looking straight into his eyes, said, "Don't worry. Everything will be alright." Then she pecked him on the cheek and moved briskly away into the house, turning at the door to call out, "Good night, Fathers."

"Good night, Stacy," they chorused. "Good night, Mrs. Donovan."

"Good night, Fathers," she responded. "Please drive safely."

As they went out to their car. Fr. McCarthy was thankful that the pressure in his crotch had eased. He put the key in the ignition and asked incredulously, "Charlie, did you see that?"

"Okay, Nick. That's what they mean by 'attorney-client privilege'," Fr. Polanski said wearily. "So, shut up and drive, if you don't mind. It's past my bed time already."

Fr. McCarthy looked at Fr. Polanski, trying to decide whether to counter his statement or let go. Eventually, he decided to let go and turn the key in the ignition. The engine came alive and he shifted the gear lever to D, easing the car out onto the road. A rustling sound behind the passenger side of the front seat attracted his attention. Fr. Polanski noted it and reassured him.

"Two bottles of wine. Mrs. Donovan's goodnight gift. Don't worry. They're well wrapped with papers, so they won't break."

Fr. McCarthy took his word for it and silently increased the pressure on the gas pedal. He glanced at the time. It was almost ten o'clock. Traffic was light and he engaged the cruise control button and settled into some quiet rumination. Fr. Polanski reached and turned the radio on. It was playing Luther Vandross's *Here and Now, I Promise to Love Faithfully.* He brought it to a very low cozy volume and reclined back for a joy-filled ride.

# HOUSTON, TEXAS

## NOVEMBER 22, 2012

IT HAD BEEN ALMOST four weeks since Fr. McCarthy ate dinner at the home of Geoffrey and Patricia Donovan, at the behest of his attorney, Stacy. Finding himself going to another dinner made him cagy, not because he did not like socializing, and not because this was his first dinner with his family, because it wasn't. In fact, it was one in a series of the one annual family tradition at which he was always expected to be present to say the grace, as if the grace on this occasion was different from that of any other occasion, which anybody could say. It was Thanksgiving Day. He was cagy because he knew he would be the focus of much of the conversation that day. Everybody in the family had, by now, heard about his lawsuit, thanks to his mother, who excitedly spread the story as though her son's being sued had updated her CV and made her the mother of a celebrity. He knew he would get asked a lot of questions, relevant and irrelevant. And he did not like it. On the other hand, he cherished the uniting value of the celebration. Coming together once a year, apart from the family reunion they had every three years, was something he would give anything to sustain. As dysfunctional and as diverse in outlook and attitude as they were, everyone seemed to tacitly accept that it was better to be family than be autonomous individuals.

He exited the freeway onto Spring Cypress, drove a mile and a half, and turned right onto Saw Tooth Canyon Drive, then right again onto Hollow Wood Circuit, a cul de sac that ended in a spacious circle. The McCarthy family house was the third on the right of the circle. Contrary to what he expected, there were only four cars—three lining the curb and one directly in front of the garage. He knew to whom all four cars belonged. His maternal auntie, Emma Henson, and her husband, Trevor, both retired and dealing in antique furniture as a hobby, drove a junior hummer. John McCarthy, his dad's only younger brother, came in his well-polished black

Corvette as usual. At 52, he was not married, but always had a girl on his arm for every occasion. Fr. McCarthy was almost positive he came to Thanksgiving dinner with a paramour. A sporty red Mustang announced the presence of his half-brother, Josh, who, though nerdy as they come, seemed to have developed an unusual love for fast cars. Josh was adopted when Fr. McCarthy was almost 13 years old. The age gap between them did not help Josh's awkwardness, which was almost robotic. Fr. McCarthy still recalled one incident, years back. Their mother, Hannah McCarthy, was preparing to go to her women's quilting club meeting. Josh protested that she should not leave yet. When asked why, he stated that he was planning to ask her for permission to go with the Buckner kids to read in the nearby community library.

"You have my permission to go read, Josh," their mother said.

"I have not asked for permission yet," Josh replied, confused, as if his mother was encouraging him to break a very important rule.

"Okay, Josh, you can ask for permission now," his mother said, wearily.

"It is not yet time, I still have five minutes," Josh replied, plaintively.

"Josh, I have a club meeting to go to," Hannah said, exasperatingly, piqued at herself for not figuring out a way yet to deal with Josh's robotically programmed ways. "I see now that if I teach you something in one context, I practically have to unteach you the same thing in another context where it doesn't quite fit. I know I said you must always ask for permission five minutes before, but I didn't carve that in marble, Josh."

"So, when you unteach me, what do I do?" Josh asked, looking quite serious.

"You go ahead and unlearn," Fr. McCarthy, just Cletus then, had heard himself interject on that occasion, almost bursting into laughter over his half-brother's awkwardness, except that their parents had forbidden that, years back, to not worsen Josh's gawkiness.

"What do I unlearn now?" pursued Josh.

"Well, Josh, not really unlearning," their mother said, trying to pick the right words that would not prolong the drama. "In this case, you will learn that at any time, you can ask for permission to do what you want to do. You don't have to wait till five minutes before the time. Is that understood?"

"Yes, Mom," Josh replied, dutifully.

"And, remember: that's only for the things that you need to ask permission for." Hannah then remembered to add. "For instance, you don't need to ask for permission to sneeze. Okay?" To everyone's surprise,

Josh broke into a spurt of laughter that ended as abruptly as it had started, making others laugh at his being punch-tickled by the suggestion that he should not need to ask for permission to sneeze. Then as Hannah turned to go, Josh cleared his throat, rearranged his clothes, and stood at attention.

"What are you doing?" she asked.

"Pulling myself together and choosing the right words," Josh answered.

"Of course, Josh," Hannah said, visibly exasperated now. Then, under her breath, she added, "Gosh, another one of my 'silly' lessons."

Josh marched forward and stood before her and asked, "Please, Ma'am, may I go with Freddy and Alyssa to the library?"

"Yes, Josh. You may go with Freddie and Alyssa to the library." For Josh's satisfaction, Hannah decided to match his formal tone.

"Thank you, Mom."

"You're welcome, Josh," she replied. She watched, pouting to stifle a chuckle, as Josh marched awkwardly to his room to change, dress, and wait for Freddie and Alyssa Buckner, his equally nerdy friends and study partners. As she turned to pick up her handbag to walk out, she noticed that her husband was watching the little drama from the staircase landing. She looked at him and shook her head slowly from side to side.

"He'll be alright," he said, casually.

"Yeah, but not without some deconstructing work,"

That was more than fourteen years ago. It was certain that Josh had lost much of his gawkiness over the years, but how much of it, though, he could not tell. The one big thing that was certain, and to Josh's credit, was that what he lacked in social skills, he overcompensated for in academics, acing his way through high school and college. At college, he was first on the President's Honor List and delivered the valedictory speech at graduation.

As Fr. McCarthy was about to park behind Josh's Mustang, he noticed that he would partially block the car in the driveway. He put the gear in reverse and started to clear the entrance, but decided against it and parked, blocking the car, anyway. The car belonged to Jennifer, their feisty and vivacious cousin with whom he took so much delight friendly-fighting whenever and wherever they would meet. He relished the thought that he would make her beg to be let out, and permitted himself a mischievous, toothless smile.

The doorbell sang the usual Westminster chime: *Ti-Te-Tung-Tum, Tum-Te-Ti-Tung*, and Fr. McCarthy had to wait but only a split second and the door flew open.

"Oh, we-el. How nice to see you, Fr. Cletus," his mother, in a beautiful flowery dress with an apron tied around her waist, sang sweetly as she wrapped her arm around him in a mother-bear hug. She reeked of the delicious aroma of home cooking blended with a whiff of her favorite perfume. The blended scent was so sweetly warm and comforting, and so reminiscent of the motherly care that Fr. McCarthy had known over the years that he drew in a lungful of it and held it for a few seconds before exhaling. "Come in Fr. Cletus. I hope you're hungry. Can I give you something to drink?" Then she sang again, almost, "Fr. Cletus is here," to nobody in particular.

"Well, well," John McCarthy said. "If it isn't Fr. McCarthy himself, the loyal son of the Church. I'm so pleased that you could come."

"I'm always delighted to be present at Thanksgiving dinner, Uncle John," Fr. McCarthy replied. "And may I say to you also, 'welcome.' How's life been treating you?"

"Better than I deserve, I would say, Fr. McCarthy," John McCarthy replied with a buccaneer's smile. He was about the only one in the family who addressed Fr. McCarthy by his surname. "Over here, Patrick. Come and meet Fr. McCarthy." A beautiful thirtyish-looking lady attractively sprang over and offered her right hand to Fr. McCarthy, daintily pinching the stem of a wine glass between the thumb and first two fingers of her left hand with two pinkies sticking out. She wore a strapless, body-hugging red dress with a strip of white, edged in sky blue, running diagonally from her left breast down to her right thigh like a sergeant major's stole.

"Hi, I'm Patrick," she said in a sweet soprano kind of voice. "That's my first name. I'm Patrick Darlington, John's friend," she added, noticing that Fr. McCarthy was waiting for her full name. "I know you're familiar with a man answering to Patrick, but that's my name," she concluded with an air of finality, looking straight into Fr. McCarthy's eyes with a pleasant smile, as the latter was still struggling to absorb the jolt of the situation.

"Uhhh, yes, of course…" Fr. McCarthy tried to find his voice. "I almost thought you said Patrick. But…um…You said Patricia?"

"No, Patrick," she confirmed, still smiling pleasantly.

"Oh, yeah. Patrick, of course. Um…a very good name. The Patron Saint of Ireland," Fr. McCarthy said, pointlessly, and smiled inanely, still confused.

"Must sound quite unusual for you, Fr. McCarthy," John said, patronizingly. "My friend Patrick believes everything should be unisex, especially names."

"Oh, I see," Fr. McCarthy said, taking Patrick's handshake. "I'm Fr. Cletus McCarthy. A few intimate friends call me Nick, short for my middle name, Nicholas."

"So nice to meet you, Fr. Cletus," Patrick said.

"Don't worry, Pat," a voice came from behind Fr. McCarthy. "It's going to take him time to process it. He belongs to the patriarchal age. I'm patiently trying to lead him into the age of enlightenment." Fr. McCarthy turned to see Jennifer approaching, clad in a tight denim and a flimsy, see-through, pink blouse that was almost not there. At 32, he thought Jennifer was beginning to show signs of desperation as she dressed more risqué every day. She was a very beautiful lady, which, in Fr. McCarthy's opinion, was sufficient assurance that she could still snag a husband without having to flaunt her female assets too much. She put her arm around him and pecked him on the cheek. "Welcome, Cousin. Don't worry. I'll soon help you come to grips with the new age."

"Hey, do you know this lady?" Fr. McCarthy asked Patrick, indicating Jennifer. "Keep your distance from her. Otherwise, she's gonna mess with your head. She's been trying to mess with mine. She hasn't succeeded yet, though, and she won't."

"You couldn't be more right, Cousin," Jennifer replied, calmly. Then she added rhetorically, "Whoever succeeds in messing up what's already totally messed up?" John and Patrick burst out laughing at Jennifer's witty rebuttal.

"And the two old nemeses meet again, and the third world war soon begins," John said poetically.

"Hi, Fr. Cletus."

"Hi, Pop!" Fr. McCarthy called out. "Happy Thanksgiving."

"Happy Thanksgiving," the elder McCarthy responded as he walked in from the back of the house with a pan-load of carved turkey meat. "I can see Jennifer was waiting for you, so you two can have a ball together, as usual."

"Uncle, you better not talk in metaphors," Jennifer interjected on cue. "Fr. Cletus might fetch a ball from the closet and throw it at me before you say, 'kick it,' thinking you're actually talking about playing ball."

"You know, that wouldn't be a bad idea, Jenny," Fr. McCarthy mused aloud. "Especially if I threw it at your mouth to cut out some of your excessive talkativeness."

"No, Jennifer. That would be Josh, not Fr. Cletus," the elder McCarthy interjected.

"Will y'all quit it and be civil to each other?" Hannah danced in and matronly rebuked the sparring bunch. "And you. Thank God Josh isn't within earshot to hear that," she addressed her husband.

"What's that?" Josh asked from the far end of the room and started inching his way toward the group. "I swear I heard my name."

"Talk about the devil," the elder McCarthy said under his breath. "Thank God, he wasn't within ear-shot," he added, stealing away, to avoid further entanglement.

"He was within eyeshot, though," Jennifer whispered almost. Then she added aloud for Josh's benefit, "Josh, we were filling Fr. Cletus in on your peculiar dot-com job. Isn't that true, cousin?" She edged closer to Fr. McCarthy as she spoke, and pinched him on the elbow, for agreement.

"Ouch!" Fr. McCarthy, unprepared for the discomfiting prompting let out, then quickly caught himself at a scowl from Jennifer, and agreed, "Yes, um… Josh, I was just asking about your job. You know, you dot-comers create and run interesting job portfolios these days. So, really, what is it that you do, exactly?"

"I do systems analyses, computer programming, and I build websites and install applications for companies. Mostly, we do work for oil companies and their subsidiaries, but recently we have started to build programs for research and pharmaceutical companies. The current one we are building now is a database for bioinformatics for the ROCENTRIX Foundation in Kansas City."

"What's that?" Fr. McCarthy asked.

"It's an international research center that is hoping to manufacture personalized medicines for the cure of certain diseases, based on the patient's genetic reading," Josh responded, excitedly, grateful for the opportunity to elaborate on his very important work. He was about warming to the subject when their mother glided back into the group and invited them to be seated for dinner. She had already ushered Trevor and Emma Henson, who had formed a separate discussion group with John and Patrick, to the table.

"If everybody would take a break from getting too curious about what everyone else is up to recently, and take a seat, Fr. Cletus would say the grace, and we would eat before the food goes cold," she announced good-humoredly.

"Thanks for rescuing us from that vice, Hannah," Trevor said, just to make conversation, it seemed. "They say curiosity killed the cat."

"Thanks, Trevor," Hannah responded. "Well, curiosity, in this case, would make your food go cold. Fr. Cletus, would you sit at the head, please," she asked as she pointed to one end of the table. Then as Fr. McCarthy moved to stand by his seat, she noticed that Jennifer also moved to the seat next to him on his right, and she added, "Oh, no, Jenny. Please promise me you're not moving there just to be within combat range of Fr. Cletus." Everyone laughed at Hannah's use of military terminology and at what seemed only too obvious.

"Oh, c'mon, Auntie. You know I can't promise you that," Jennifer responded in her characteristic way of addressing every family member by their relational, instead of proper, name. "I gotta be close to my cousin in case he messes his shirt front with soup. If he does, I can clean it for him. You know very well he still needs me to babysit him."

"And hearing that, you guys may think she's kidding," Fr. McCarthy retorted wittily. "But she's not. Baby sitting's about the only thing she knows how to do. Ask her to cook, and you either starve or force yourself to eat her mistake." Another round of laughter followed his comments.

"I know how to cook," Jennifer protested.

"Since when?" Fr. McCarthy retorted.

"I cooked you broiled snapper and shrimp in pontchartrain on fried rice, with steamed broccoli and spinach, just last month, and you ate and licked the plate with your tongue," Jennifer responded, factually. "Hey, wake up your memory. Too bad for a priest of your age to have senior moments."

"I didn't lick the plate with my tongue. And, oh, by the way, standing over a stove with a book in one hand and a spatula in the other...is that what you call 'knowing how to cook'?" Fr. McCarthy asked dismissively.

"Well, to me, if she was able to assemble such mouth-watering menu as she just recited, even from a cookbook, I would say she knows how to cook." Patrick came to Jennifer's rescue.

"Okay, ladies and gentlemen, combatants and civilians," the elder McCarthy interjected and began to address everybody and managed to draw more laughter using Hannah's words. "It's another Thanksgiving, and we are grateful to God for His many blessings. Though we are few this year, we're still going to have a good time...that is, if Jennifer and Fr. Cletus don't duel each other to the death and end the day on a sad note." He drew still more laughter. "And now, Fr. Cletus, if you don't mind, can you lead us in praying the grace before the meal?"

"Sure," Fr. McCarthy replied. "We give you thanks, Lord God, for bringing bread out of the Earth through human labor…" He continued giving thanks for almost two minutes, and then concluded, "…and now, as we settle down to eat, we pray: bless us, O Lord, and this thy gift which we are about to receive out of thy bounty, through Christ Our Lord. Amen."

"Ooo!" Jennifer cooed a sigh of relief. "Thank you, Dear Lord! He finally remembered to conclude it. He nearly slipped us into Pontifical High Mass." Everybody laughed, as they pulled out their chairs to sit down. Hannah rolled her eyes in longsuffering and busied herself putting the service spoons in the food pans. Then she went over to Fr. McCarthy's side to serve him his salad.

"Well, it's Thanksgiving prayer, I guess," Trevor said, graciously. "So, you got to count your blessings a little bit longer than usual."

"Say that again, Mr. Henson," Fr. McCarthy said, cupping a hand to his ear and cocking his head.

"Don't celebrate the support. Everyone knows your 'grace before a meal' is usually longer than the meal time itself," Jennifer countered, to the cheery laughter of all.

"My goodness," Patrick said in between heaves of laughter. "Are you guys always like this, always pulling each other's leg?"

"Right from the word, 'Go'," Emma responded. "I don't know how my sister manages to endure their constant haggling. It would drive me nuts."

"They have been that way since they met and grew up together," Hannah said. "We adopted Fr. Cletus at one week. Jennifer came to live with us when she was seven and he was five. They took an instant liking to each other."

"Jenny was on and off, though," said the elder McCarthy.

"Yeah, but she has lived with us more than she has with her mom," Hannah reminisced. "If she stayed with her mom for one month, she would stay with us for three or four. And that was good for my friend because she was working two jobs then."

"She always came back to live with us because she couldn't bear to live without me," Fr. McCarthy teased. "She's so dependent on me."

"Oh, give me a break!" Jennifer interjected. "You were the dependent one. Every time I left, you couldn't bear to see me go. He would always ask, so pitiably, 'Are you going to come back soon?'" She mimicked his tearful request. "And I would always assure him not to worry."

"Nah, I didn't look that pitiable," Fr. McCarthy countered. "You're exaggerating. On a few occasions, I might have asked when you would be back. But I don't think I got all weepy, as you make it sound."

"Okay, so all this leg pulling is nothing but cloaked sibling love?" Patrick asked. "How cute!"

"They started that gradually, and now, they can't seem to live without it," Hannah said, resignedly.

"And then I came along, and they used to tease me mercilessly as I grew up," Josh said.

"We adopted Josh when Fr. Cletus was almost 12," Hannah continued her adoption chronology.

"Thirteen," the elder McCarthy corrected. "Fr. Cletus was already 13."

"Well, then, 13," Hannah said, seemingly piqued at being so unceremoniously fact checked. "And he was already...a year old?" she asked, looking at her husband, as if not wanting to be fact checked again.

"Yeah. A day shy of a year to the day he was born."

"Okay, Josh was adopted, too?" Patrick stated, more as an accepting statement than as a question.

"Yeah. We're a bunch of adoptees with adoptive parents," Josh said. "My biological parents died," he added, somewhat facetiously.

Oh. Sorry about your parents," Patrick patronized, genuinely.

The conversation veered to, and continued for some time, on the subject of adoption and stories of abandoned babies. Fr. McCarthy did not like the way the conversation was going. He shifted in his seat and fidgeted slightly. The others proceeded, warily though, and it was obvious that they, too, were uneasy talking about what seemed to touch on a sensitive portion of the McCarthy family history. But, for some reason, they could not seem to get off it, either.

"Adoption is good," Emma Henson said. "I like it. It saves the life of an innocent child who, probably due to circumstances, would otherwise not have a good life. And it saves the life of the adopting parents, too."

"You're right, Emma," her husband concurred. "It's much better than messing with these new technologies they have, trying to create babies... *in vitro*. Is that what they call it?"

"Yes, it's called *in vitro* fertilization," Patrick confirmed. "The male seed and the female egg are put in a test tube and left for fertilization to take place. Then the fertilized egg is transferred into the woman's womb."

"So, the woman gets pregnant that way?" Trevor asked, looking curious.

"That seems to be the idea, Mr. Henson," Jennifer interjected. "Except that it is not always successful unless more than one fertilized egg is transferred into the woman's womb."

"What?!" Trevor inquired, alarmed. "So, what happens if all the eggs get implanted?"

"That is not possible, Mr. Henson," Jennifer replied, warming to what she considered her area of expertise. "Only one gets implanted at a time. But you can have a situation where the fertilized egg gets split in two and you have twins or, even into three or four and you have triplets or quadruplets."

"That was what happened in the case of the Octomom. Remember?" Patrick put in her line, too. "Unfortunately, her own subdivided into octuplets."

"Wasn't that awful?" Emma said, somewhat sneeringly. "I wonder what she was thinking."

"She was craving for attention. She wanted a celebrity status in society," the elder McCarthy responded. "And, boy, did she get it!"

"Yeah, but not in the way she bargained for," John replied. "She got all the negative attention she would have gladly done without. I pitied her, though."

"I would go for adoption any day, rather than mess with all them fertility drugs," Trevor said. "There's lots of babies all over the world waiting to be adopted. And once in a while, we hear or read about some thrown away."

"There's lots of reasons, too, Uncle, why people want to have their babies using the new rep techs," Jennifer came to the defense. "For one, the hoops you have to jump through to adopt a baby can be so daunting that you opt to try having your own. I know Cousin does not agree with me because the Church is against rep tech."

"The Church is not against reproductive technology, as such, if it does not separate the unitive and procreative intents of marriage," Fr. McCarthy offered his opinion, defensively. He felt drawn into the conversation because Jennifer implicated him by her remark. "If the scientific community comes up with a technology that leaves those two areas intact, the Church will support it."

"Cousin, that's unrealistic," Jennifer countered. "The very technique and the process of fertilization must happen outside the womb, but the fertilized egg or embryo is put back into the womb. It is not like the child develops outside the womb throughout all nine months."

"There is a break in the procreative process with mechanical tinkering.

That makes the child a product, not a begotten. And, besides, borrowing the male or female gamete from a different person other than the spouse is a violation of the unitive bond that the spouses vowed to each other and a violation of the child's right to be born in a legitimate union of one father and one mother," Fr. McCarthy concluded, feeling he needed to give the impromptu lecture to correct what he perceived as a misguided point of view.

"I can see the ethical problem you're raising, Fr. McCarthy, but is that a legit problem, or a matter of biased perception, if I may ask, with due respect?" Patrick asked, struggling to conceal the edge in her tone.

"I believe it is a legit ethical problem because, to repeat myself, it entails a violation of human dignity and integrity," Fr. McCarthy continued patiently.

"I think you've lost me, Cousin," Jennifer replied, with some edge to her voice, too. "Medical science has been mechanically tinkering with the human body since anybody cares to remember. So, why is it suddenly sinful in this case? I mean, for instance, pigs' valves have been life savers for those with coronary disease, and the Church has not protested inserting animal parts into humans as a deprecation of human dignity and integrity. I fail to see why sperm and egg, both human parts, put together to result in a new life for a couple or an individual in need of a child should be treated as a horrendous evil."

"Indira Pootanveel, my systems analysis professor, had a kidney transplant a year ago," Josh added his voice, furtively though, to the growing objection to Fr. McCarthy's position. "Would that be considered a violation of her integrity? I'm just asking to be enlightened."

"Family! Family, please. Can we change the topic of the conversation before we spoil an otherwise beautiful Thanksgiving afternoon?" Hannah McCarthy begged for peace, then asked, by way of change to sanitize the conversational atmosphere that was beginning to get putrid, so to speak, "Anybody care for seconds?"

"I think giving away one's body part, doesn't matter which—internal or external—to benefit another person is an act of charity, from the bigger picture perspective," the elder McCarthy said, as though to resurrect the unpopular conversation. "I believe the Church can be somewhat flexible on some of these matters and God will not frown too much."

"Well, Dad! Thank you very much! That's very supportive and very complimentary," Fr. McCarthy interjected with sarcastic ire.

"My apologies, Fr. Cletus," the elder McCarthy quickly offered. "I didn't mean that as a barb, and certainly not one directed at you. I just hope as medical science and technology progress, the Church does not, one day, find herself trapped in her own ethical maze of dos and don'ts."

"Anybody for seconds?" Hannah interjected again, a shade too loud, after trying in vain to catch her husband's eye and the latter studiously avoiding her glare, a ruse unmistakably obvious to others at the table. He kept his gaze on his plate to avoid her scowl.

"I'll have seconds," Trevor announced, struggling to get up.

"I'll have seconds, too," Emma announced and tried getting up, too.

"I'll have seconds, also," the elder McCarthy announced too loudly to the laughter of everyone, now looking straight at his wife and wearing a mischievous toothless smile while pushing back his chair and making as though he was getting up. A longsuffering Hannah rolled her eyes exasperatingly at her husband, getting up to serve him as the dutiful wife she was and loved playing.

Fr. McCarthy was not laughing, though he wasn't scowling, either. He was somewhat piqued at the way the others at the table seemed to gang up on him, but he studiously kept a straight face. It would not do to let them think he was taking it personal. He wished he had an opportunity, a forum where his family wasn't antagonistic, but eager to learn, so he could expound the Church's ethical teaching on the new reproduction technologies that were springing up by the day. Then they would understand. They would not be so defensive. He wondered why Church moral teaching on any topic concerning human sexuality always seemed to touch nerves, even among Catholics themselves. He remembered reading an article by a so-called feminist lady lecturer at a university and coming across a sentence that was undisguisedly vitriolic. She had referred to Church hierarchy as 'clueless male celibates' with no families or children of their own, who pretend to know how families should be run and children reared, and who, arrogating themselves the status of 'experts' on women's reproductive life, relish handing down chauvinistic and sexist moral dictates to subjugate women. She called this the new slavery and condemned it as unworthy of a twenty-first-century Church. Fr. McCarthy thought that was too intense and indicative of someone who, perhaps, had a bone to pick over a past hurt. He had made a mental note to write a rejoinder for publication in the same Journal, but, for some reason, had not yet gotten around to doing it. And what did his father mean by hoping the Church would not, one day, be trapped in her own maze of ethical dos and don'ts? His train of thought was interrupted by his mother putting a saucer of brownies in front of him. He declined and asked for a bowl of fruit instead, a gesture of which Jennifer approved, though still contriving to do that by way of a teaser dart.

"Yeah. Thank God, my efforts have paid off. Cousin is beginning to practice healthy eating style," she said, glancing at Fr. McCarthy from the corner of her eye. The latter kept a straight face and refused to indulge the remark. John and Patrick smiled coyly into the crook of their arms. Jennifer knew Fr. McCarthy was sore from their earlier barrage of disagreements with his moral views, and she decided it was time to ease off teasing him.

The family dinner continued for another one hour with small talk here and there and a discussion of the season's games. Fr. McCarthy was not particularly interested in either football or basketball and didn't watch enough of them to have ample material to immerse himself in the conversation. So, he withdrew with his uncle and Josh to the veranda for a different type of conversation. The elder McCarthy, Trevor, Patrick, and Jennifer retired to the sitting area to continue arguing about touch downs, quarter-backs, and referees' mistaken calls, as well as boast over their favorite teams. Hannah and Emma busied themselves by clearing the table, washing and wiping the dishes while catching up on what new recipes they had discovered or learned since their last discussion about cooking.

Fr. McCarthy glanced at his watch, noticing that the sun had gone down and the evening was getting cooler. It was that time of year when the days began to get shorter while the nights became longer. He knew darkness would soon set in. He excused himself from John and Josh and went back inside to find his mom and instead bumped into Jennifer. He was about to say something when the latter placed a finger over his mouth and spoke first.

"Shsh! I need to apologize to you, Cousin," she began, sort of sweetly. "It wasn't fair the way we ganged up on you. You have a duty to be what you were called to be: an official of the Church. I respect you for being loyal to the Church. That's what you should be…"

"Jennifer, wait," Fr. McCarthy interrupted. "It's not about being an official of the Church. I didn't say those things to be loyal to the Church. I was expressing my convictions, otherwise, that would make me a kind of public relations officer for the Church."

"I didn't say you are a PRO for the Church," Jennifer replied, defensively.

"Not directly," Fr. McCarthy replied. "You probably didn't imply it, either. I'm the one reading it into your statement. Look, I'm just trying to make my point clear that I am convinced about the moral teachings of the Church as far as artificial contraception, in vitro fertilization, preimplantation testing, and intra-fallopian gamete transfers go. All these things are forbidden by the Church because of their moral implications. Our duty as loyal Catholics is to agree with what the Church teaches."

"That's why I apologize, Cousin. Our attitude during that conversation was less than catholic," Jennifer replied, somewhat contrite. Then she quickly remembered to be Jennifer, "But don't expect me to come to you for confession over that, because I won't."

"Too late," Fr. McCarthy said with a tinge of gusto. "You've already confessed. Only I'm denying you absolution until you show evidence of true regret."

"Oh, I'm sorry. I didn't know you were hearing confession," Hannah cooed, having just then run into the tail end of Fr. McCarthy's statement.

"Auntie! Give me a little more credit than that," Jennifer feigned hurt. "You wouldn't expect me to confess to a hardhearted priest like Cousin? I was just letting him know that in spite of our seemingly antagonistic stance during our conversation at dinner, we're very supportive of him. And, by the way, Cousin," she addressed Fr. McCarthy directly. "Let me know when they fix the trial. I intend to be there in court to lend moral support."

"Just what I was going to talk to you about, Fr. Cletus," Hannah said, grateful for the cue. "But, first, could you let Jenny out? That's her car you blocked in the driveway."

Fr. McCarthy turned around, beaming like he had just won the Kentucky Derby. "What did you say, Mom?"

"I said you're blocking Jenny in. Can you let her out?"

"Mom, Jennifer can speak for herself," Fr. McCarthy said, spoiling for a fight with Jennifer. He smiled mischievously at the opportunity to win the battle of the cousins for the evening by making her beg to be let out. "She knows the magic word to utter for me to let her out. Don't you, Jennifer?"

"Oh, sure, Cousin. I'll utter the magic word promptly," Jennifer said with a cocky smile of her own. "At 7:30 tomorrow morning when I'll be leaving for work."

"Oh, goodness! Fr. Cletus, I forgot," Hannah said, contritely. "Jennifer's staying the night. She fixed her old room first thing when she arrived this afternoon," Hannah said to her son, barely holding from laughing, noticing that Fr. McCarthy's mischievous smile faded like light at the realization that he'd have to leave before Jennifer and wouldn't be able to exact a plea from her. "Can I speak to you now, before you go? I know you have to say Mass in the morning."

"You're bluffing, aren't you?" Fr. McCarthy said, feigning disbelief.

"No, Son. I really want to talk to you about your impending court case," Hannah replied.

"No, I meant about Jennifer not going tonight," he corrected.

"Could you, please, sheathe your sword, Son, and let Jennifer win the battle this once?" Hannah pleaded with mock exasperation. "Hmm! Battle of the cousins! I think I'm beginning to get a little tired of it. This way, Fr. Cletus." She led the way as Fr. McCarthy, scratching his head in defeat, followed, pretending chagrin at being made to let go his quarry. Jennifer grinned mischievously, whistled a song, and waltzed a dance step to celebrate her victory, which further piqued him. He had no choice but to follow his mother out to the back of the house where she stopped to have a private conversation with him.

# PART II

*To know your purpose in life you*
*ought to know who you are.*

- ANON

# HOUSTON, TEXAS

## SPRING, 2012

"HEY!" CRYSTAL SANDERS greeted her friend, Edo-Mma Eshiet, insipidly. Both had just gotten off of their respective school buses and walked through the gates of the Christo Rey High School. The late February morning was bright, cool, and crispy, typical of spring time. They were always the early birds. By some coincidence, they almost always seemed to arrive at the school gates at the same time every morning since they had become friends two years earlier. Now in their final year before graduating and moving on to college as they both planned, they were almost like sisters and could read each other's mood change, no matter how slight.

"Hey!" Edo-Mma greeted back. "Morning. You look kinda grouchy this morning. What's up, girl?"

"Nothing," Crystal said, looking at her friend slightly quizzical and defensive. "I'm not grouchy. I'm….okay."

"Okay, as in 'Okay-it's-okay', or okay, as in 'okay-whatever'?" Edo-Mma quizzed further, heaving her backpack into a comfortable position.

"I'm okay! What's wrong with you, girl? You some kind of Guantanamo prison interrogator?" Crystal said, feigning slight vexation. "Watch your skirt. Pull it down before the guys start whistling at you," she added, indicating Edo-Mma's skirt, the back of which was pulled up when she heaved up her backpack, almost revealing her panties. Edo-Mma giggled with embarrassment and tucked at the back of her skirt to pull it down.

"I'm sorry. I'm just concerned about you," Edo-Mma demurred. "You haven't been in the best of moods these past couple of days, you know."

"I stayed up late doing that assignment, you know," Crystal said. "In case I get called up to present first. Mrs. Pivonka always seems to pick on me first."

"Yeah, I know," Edo-Mma concurred grudgingly. "She likes you."

"No. I think she's always trying to catch me off guard, so she can embarrass me," Crystal said plaintively. "You don't know that woman."

"Oh. Come on, Crysie. She gave you an 'A' last semester." Edo-Mma said, as they passed through the scan-fitted doors, nodding and calling 'hi' to their friends and classmates. The scanner emitted a brief turquoise laser light with a beep, indicating they were cleared. "I know she's tough, but I kind of like her style. She makes you work."

"She makes me work my ass off every time," Crystal said, with a faint hint of petulance. "But you're right. I kind of liked the 'A'. But you got an 'A', too."

"Yeah. And I worked my ass off for it, too," Edo-Mma said, nonchalantly. "You sure you don't wanna tell me what's eating your insides before we go in?"

They stopped at their lockers in the hallway, to drop off their sweaters and bags, and get their books for the day. Crystal didn't answer, so Edo-Mma pursued, "Let me guess: Josh is breaking up with you?"

"Edo!" Crystal sounded exasperated. "You are such a doggone, dogged, inquisitive little lady, aren't you?"

"Shall I lend you some more adjectives?" Edo-Mma quipped, not in the least ruffled by Crystal's soured humor.

"Josh would never dream of breaking up with me," Crystal said, somewhat smugly. Then she whispered, darting her eyes this way and that, conspiratorially, "The poor guy is madly in love with me." Then she resumed her voice, "I sometimes feel bad when I don't treat him right. But, as you know, he can't stay mad at me for too long."

"I know," Edo-Mma concurred. "And I envy you."

"Kelechi is a good guy," Crystal said, sensing her friend might not be kidding about the envy part.

"He's hot-tempered and moody," Edo-Mma sounded judgmental. "But he coaches me well in my computer lessons." She found a good point to counter Kelechi's bad side.

"Talk about the wizard, and he shows up," Crystal said, looking in the direction of an approaching young man and fellow student.

The electric bell shrilled, startling the dinning students in the hallway, opening and banging their lockers. It was time to go to class. They closed their lockers and said, "Hi."

"Hi," Kelechi said, taking and kissing Edo-Mma's hand, as much as was allowed in Christo Rey, among coeds. "How are you?" he inquired.

"I'm good," Edo-Mma replied. "And how are you?"

"Good, just the way my mom brought me up," Kelechi replied, drawing a spurt of giggles from the girls.

"Aren't you the lucky one, then?" Crystal quipped.

"I know," Kelechi said, then craned his neck, calling out, "Hey, Josh!" Josh was about to enter his classroom, but turned upon hearing his name. Josh was a handsome mulatto with a sixtyish hairstyle. Edo-Mma noticed that Crystal's mood had brightened at Josh's approach.

"Kelechi, the bell has sounded," Edo-Mma said, squirming visibly.

"I know, but we just need to agree on the time," Kelechi said.

"Time for what?" Edo-Mma asked, confused. "What's going on?"

"Edo, I was going to tell you at the right time," Crystal said, sensing the suspicion in her friend's demeanor. "Okay, let me give you the gist," she whispered in her ear, as they shuffled toward the classroom door. "Kelechi is helping me find my dad. Or, more precisely, my sperm donor dad," she concluded with a faint note of derisiveness.

"What?!" Edo-Mma exclaimed a trifle too loud.

"Shsh!" Crystal said, pushing Edo-Mma through the door. "Twelve-thirty in the basement,"

"Josh, she says, twelve-thirty, in the basement" Kelechi said to Josh, as they exchanged their fist-bumping greeting.

Edo-Mma had no time to process what was going on, as the students scuttled to their seats, killing their din as Evelyn Pivonka might walk in any time.

She was a no-nonsense teacher. Every student knew if you wanted a good grade from Mrs. Pivonka, then you simply had to work hard and behave. Otherwise, you had to prepare yourself to repeat the course, and no student enjoyed repeating courses.

———

The meeting was held underneath the school auditorium, which was a finished basement, a thirty-by-seventeen-feet, box-like space, broken by four sturdy columns that supported the beams holding up the ceiling, which also happened to be almost two-thirds of the auditorium's floor. Four fanlights lined the top of the wall along the ceiling, on one of the longer sides, each measuring eight inches by three feet—narrow window-like openings of translucent glass—which let in enough light during the day to permit comfortable reading without switching on the electric lights. The walls were unprofessionally done with mortar, not sheetrock, though whoever did the painting did such a good job that he/she compensated for its roughness. There was a light socket at each of the far ends of the room, each designed to accommodate four plugs. There was no cooling or heating system, and the fact that it was designated as the approved safe haven for the 600 plus students in case of a hurricane, made the students nick-name it the "tornado tomb." The school authorities banned the nickname, but habits die hard. Officially, it was 'the basement', but among the students, it was mischievously known as the 'tornado tomb'.

A few wooden chairs and desks, mainly of the old batch discarded when the school bought metal ones, were strewn about. Scraps of paper lying around the dusty floor told the story of a large room generally forgotten or just ignored and cheated out of cleaning services until a storm warning would remind the authorities of its existence. Not that the students complained about it, as it was to their advantage that school authorities left that one space inadequately policed. And not a few romantic rendezvous were scheduled there after hours, though it was used mostly by students seeking a quiet spot to catch up on their reading and cramming during finals. There were no exams going on, as it was just two weeks into the spring semester. Kelechi knew that few students, if any, would be in the basement. It was a perfect spot to meet and complete his Internet hacking.

He plugged in the power cord of his laptop, pulled one of the chairs to the table, pressed the power button, and waited for it to boot up.

"I can't believe it's this cold down here," he said, plaintively, rubbing his hands together. "The stupid contractor who put this dump together didn't believe there should be a heating device of any sort down here."

"Not the contractor, moron," Josh chided, pulling two chairs to the table. "It's the architect who forgot to put a doggone heater in his drawings. And why are you complaining anyway? It's not that cold." He pulled a bench to the table with a mad screeching sound as the two turned to watch the girls make their entry.

"Quit that, man! It jars my teeth," Kelechi snarled. "You don't want to draw some inquisitive crowd down here. In any case, if either the architect or the contractor had a nickel worth of sense, they would have figured it's below ground level here and could do with some heating of some sort. I'm from the tropics, man!"

"And I'm from the Arctic," Josh quipped as he sat down.

"Hi, guys," Crystal said, taking her seat beside Kelechi.

"Hi, guys," Edo-Mma called her greeting and took her seat beside Josh opposite Kelechi and Crystal. "So, what's this hush-hush meeting about, and how long is this gonna take? Remember, Kelechi, break time is only thirty minutes."

"Oh! I thought we were gonna stay here till Jesus comes again!" Kelechi teased. He added, "I'm just kidding, Edo," noticing the instant hurt in her eyes. "We should be done in about fifteen minutes."

"Yeah, Edo," Crystal concurred, taking out a diary from her bag. "We should be done in no time. I need to take a pee before the next class."

"You should go and pee, girl," Josh said. "Here, give me that. I can read it." He stretched his hand to take the diary from Crystal.

"I can't let you read my diary, Josh!" Crystal said, holding the diary away from Josh's reach.

"C'mon, I've read it before," Josh said, dismissively.

"You read Crysie's diary?" Edo-Mma asked. "Crysie, you let Josh read your diary?"

"It's just a diary!" Josh said, exasperatingly. "Man! Girls make a lot of fuss about their diaries."

"He was just beginning to read the first page when I caught him," Crystal said. "Yeah, Josh, it is just a diary, but I have some personal stuff inside it that is not meant for your eyes. And you've got to learn to live with that," she concluded pedantically.

"That's not manners, Josh!" Edo-Mma chided.

"Guys! Guys! Can we get on with this thing?" Kelechi called out plaintively.

"Okay, okay," Josh said, raising his hands in mock surrender. "I promise to behave. I won't touch your diary, Crysie. Kelechi, you never read Edo's diary?"

"Josh, I'm not interested in female stuff," Kelechi responded casually. "Besides, I value my peace."

"I would kill him," Edo-Mma interjected, petulantly.

"See what I mean?" Kelechi said, shrugging, like a math wizard proving a theorem QED. "If you guys don't mind, can we please get on with business?"

They all broke out in laughter, more for Kelechi's witty crack than for Edo-Mma's vehemence.

Crystal opened her diary to the required page. Kelechi booted up his laptop, loaded google chrome, clicked up a web page, fed in a password, and made a few other clicks. He proceeded to scroll down a list of names, dates, and coded numbers, as Crystal called out an entry in her diary. Josh and Edo-Mma went around and hunched over Kelechi's and Crystal's shoulders, watching, but hardly making any sense of the array of names which appeared neatly recorded in alphabetical order with numbers and dates arranged beside the names in two neat columns. The ritual went on for almost fifteen minutes, and then, Kelechi stopped abruptly at a page and asked Crystal to call out her diary entry again, which she did.

"We got it!" Kelechi said, with a tinge of subdued excitement. "Write this down: California two four nine."

"California two four nine?" Crystal repeated, looking confused.

"Yes, California two four nine," Kelechi confirmed.

"What the hell is 'California two four nine'?" Edo-Mma asked, confused.

"Yeah, what the hell is that?" Josh parroted.

"We'll find out," Kelechi said, closing the Internet program. "Write it down Crysie, and we'll find out."

As if on cue, the school bell began to shrill off above the basement, summoning students back to class for the short afternoon session. The quartet of hackers headed up the basement stairs back to their classroom, excited. They could hardly wait for the end of the school day to go back and work to find out the actual identity of "California two four nine."

"CALIFORNIA TWO FOUR NINE," Crystal said, looking at her mother, Barbara Sanders, across the dinner table. "That was his name, or pseudonym."

"California two four nine!" Barbara repeated, looking at her daughter, somewhat confused.

"Mom, you look as if you don't know what I'm talking about. Why did he call himself 'California two four nine'?"

"Why did who call himself 'California two four nine'?"

"My real dad, Mom," Crystal raised her voice in near exasperation. "Quit pretending you don't understand me. I'm not talking rocket science. I'm asking you about the man whose sperm formed part of me sitting here and, who, up till three weeks ago, when I asked you, you said you didn't know."

"You found out!" Barbara said, more as a statement than a question.

"Yes, I found out what you were trying to hide from me," Crystal replied, accusingly. "You lied to me all along."

"No, Crysie. I didn't lie to you. It's complicated," Barbara interjected.

"You said you just paid for the sperm," Crystal pursued. "And that you were not allowed to know who the sperm donor was."

"Oh, God. Crysie why?" Barbara was alarmed. "Why did you have to go and dig that up for?"

"Because I need to know who my biological dad is. I need to know who I am, Mom...and you lied to me!" Crystal said, almost yelling.

"Oh, Crysie, honey, don't say it that way," Barbara countered. "I didn't lie to you. It's kind of complicated. I couldn't tell you because you wouldn't understand and I wasn't even sure, and a lot of people would have been hurt."

"Yeah? A lot of people would have been hurt?" Crystal seized upon the slip and, vindictively, bored down on her mother. "So, you couldn't tell me who my biological father is for fear you would hurt 'a lot of people'? Good old Ms. Sanders! Always so sweet and never hurting anybody. Not even a fly! Except me, your daughter. You chose to hurt me so you wouldn't hurt them. You chose them over me. Mom, did you ever love me?"

"Oh, Crysie, please, don't go off that way," Barbara was exasperated at the abruptness of her daughter's anger and offensive remarks. She was on the verge of tears. "Don't say that. I didn't choose anybody over you. I love you, dear. I love you, honey, but it's complicated…"

"Everything is complicated for you, and you think you can make other people's life complicated, too. Guess what? I don't want to hear that word from you again. And I don't want to talk to you again, either…ever. I hate you!" Crystal got up, quickly heading for the stairs.

"No, Crysie, honey, you don't mean that. And you know it," Barbara stood up also, moving around the dinner table toward her daughter who was talking amidst sobs of anger as she ran up the stairs toward her room. "Crysie, I was waiting for the right time. Please, come back. Don't walk away. I can explain everything. Crysie, dear, come back!"

"Don't talk to me! You don't love me and I hate you! Go away! You are not my mom! I hate you!" Crystal yelled, ran inside her room, and slammed the door shut.

"Crysie, come back, please!" Barbara made a last-ditch effort, but couldn't keep up with Crystal. She gave up on the fifth step and, instead, called after her daughter's vanishing figure, "Crysie, I love you! I love you, honey! I'm still your mom and I love you!" She broke down and sat on the fifth step, sobbing loudly. "Oh, God! Please, forgive me! I hurt my daughter! I hurt her badly! Oh, God! Oh, God….!"

Barbara Sanders cried for almost three minutes, sitting and leaning her back on the bannister railing. When she finally calmed down, she permitted herself an excursion into her past, back to when she worked as a nursing assistant to Dr. Josef Horacek at the Norfolk Fertility Clinic in Norfolk, Virginia. Coming from her parents' failed marriage and a broken home, she was the second child of Mark and Crystal Sanders. Her brother, almost six years her senior, had run away from home when he was 17, and her parents had made little effort to find out where he was. Looking back in hindsight, Barbara knew her parents' mutual hatred for each other and constant fighting did not bode well for a loving family. Unable to love themselves, they couldn't love their children, either. Things came to a head when they finally got divorced when she was 13. She had gone to live with her auntie, who was married to a successful stock broker. Through their generosity, she got to continue her schooling. After graduating high school, they put her through nursing school, where she got her associate's degree in nursing. Her father, meanwhile, had vanished from her life entirely, not even communicating with her. Her mother, who had taken to drinking and prostitution after her divorce, eventually got implicated by her boyfriend in a botched robbery attempt and both were sent to prison. She later died in prison. Her mother's death was devastating for Barbara and was instrumental to her stunted student career in nursing. She got a private job with a dentist in downtown Norfolk, but that wasn't to last because of her erratic behavior. She had started smoking and drinking, and would sometimes turn up late for work. Fired from the dentist office, she took up waiting tables at a local restaurant and started hanging out with some drifters after hours.

As she, herself, would later keep saying, it must have been the grace of God that kept following her around, and eventually helped her turn her life around and get back on track. Ironically, Barbara actually found salvation through the bad company she kept. From some of her girlfriends, she got to know about a lucrative, but likely illegal and immoral, business that was becoming popular among young ladies. She learned that she could "donate" her egg to a fertility clinic or hospital that treated infertile couples, for a good sum of money. Barbara needed money to pay her rent and feed her crack cocaine habit which she had picked up. So, she agreed to accompany her roommate, a part-time college student, who did some odd jobs on the side, to the Norfolk General Hospital for "donation," a euphemism that was used to shield the fact that money did exchange hands in the process. As the belief went, it was only reasonable that the donor be compensated for her pains and for the things she needed throughout the duration of taking a drug regimen that would quicken her ovulation. The process was complicated, but when it was finally done and the egg was successfully retrieved via laparoscopy, it was well worth the inconvenience. Barbara found out that it was even better if one negotiated directly with a patron and the patron happened to be wealthy. Fed all this information, she decided it was worth a try. The first egg harvested from her, four weeks after the completion of her regimen, fetched her the cash amount of six thousand dollars, more money than Barbara ever had in her entire life. She quickly opened an account with Chase Bank and was ready for business.

To her disappointment, however, she was not allowed to donate again for six months.

So, six months to the minute after her first donation, Barbara was at the hospital again, but this time, she had done her homework and had found a patron who was willing to pay twelve thousand dollars, not for egg donation, but for surrogacy. Barbara still had to donate the egg, which was fertilized in the laboratory with sperm from another man. The fertilized egg was reinserted into her womb and she carried the baby to a full, nine-month term. The whole process was quite daunting, but the additional benefits that were added to the agreement made her decide to try it. She had to have weekly hospital testing for the first month. Then it was reduced to biweekly visits for two months, and then, to monthly visits. The cost for all the hospital visits and medications were paid by Barbara's patron. Her own side of the bargain was to eat healthily to ensure that the growing fetus had proper nutrition. This was risky, as any mishap that resulted in a malformed baby meant that Barbara would forfeit the twelve thousand dollars. A healthy baby meant that the entire twelve thousand dollars would be hers, in addition to other gratuities. So, Barbara decided to draw upon her experience of the few years she spent in nursing school to make sure everything went right. That became her first salvation, since she voluntarily quit smoking and any drug habits she had, though she constantly worried whether the residual effects of the drugs in her system would affect the baby.

Luck was on her side once more, as Barbara delivered a healthy baby boy weighing seven pounds, nine ounces, by caesarian section, at nine months, three weeks. She walked away from Norfolk General Hospital, two weeks after healing completely, with twelve thousand dollars in her purse, and didn't look back. She knew deep in her heart that one day, she would miss the child, that she would ache for him. Just then, though, she was filled with too many plans for her future—plans she wanted to accomplish with the twelve thousand dollars—to let herself worry over that. Her first thought was to go back and complete her studies and obtain a bachelor's degree in nursing. She knew, however, that she could not accomplish that with only twelve thousand dollars. So, she decided to keep searching for a job. Having been successful in kicking her drug and smoking habits, she knew she could get and keep a job. She had grown wiser in the three years she was wheeling and dealing in the world. Moreover, after the grueling experience of surrogacy, she wasn't sure that was a business she could do on a regular basis, and how many times would she even be able to do that? Another support line in Barbara's life was that she had reestablished contact with her auntie and could call her from time to time for useful advice. Being the only kin Barbara had who actually cared a hoot about her, she was determined to turn her life around to impress her auntie and win back her support.

During her numerous trips to Norfolk General, she had met and established a kind of friendship with a young intern struggling to finish medical school. He was a handsome Bohemian by name, Josef Bernard Horacek, and he became Barbara's heavy crush. Mindful of hospital policy, he kept his distance, and she tried to keep hers, too, but one thing soon became apparent: It soon became a routine for them to run into each other in the hospital cafeteria. It became clear, too, that most of the encounters were not by mere happenstance. The attraction was mutual. Having left the hospital after fulfilling her surrogacy contract, Barbara had no way of meeting him any more on a regular basis, but she kept in touch by phone. For some reason, though, Mr. Horacek did not once ask Barbara out on a date, which worried her increasingly by the day. Not wanting to be pushy and give herself away as being cheap and desperate, Barbara decided to bide her time. Besides, he had a promising future. She would monitor him and wait for his full graduation, then she would set her feminine wiles in motion to get him for herself. She would sometimes catch herself at an unguarded moment dreaming of herself as Mrs. Horacek. Who knows? Dreams sometimes do come true.

Barbara thought hers was coming true when, less than a month before his full graduation, Josef Horacek told her during one of their phone conversations that he had pooled a small fortune together to start and run his own clinic after graduation. Barbara immediately blurted out, "Can I come and work for you?"

"Sure, if you have the qualifications. I don't see why not," he said.

"What qualifications are you looking for," she asked.

"What qualifications do you have," he countered.

"Well," she started haltingly. "I only have an associate's degree in nursing."

"Why, that's good-enough qualification to start with," he replied. Barbara couldn't miss the enthusiasm in his voice. Affected by the contagiousness of it, she chattered excitedly about all the things she would do to help him start off the business. He went on and on, too, on what a great working relationship they would have with each other. That evening, they talked well into the night before saying their 'goodnights', barely able to contain their excitement enough to get a good night's sleep.

The clinic did take off, as planned, after four months and a lot of ground work, especially with City Hall ordinances and building codes for clinics, as well as the National Institute of Health (NIH) policies and protocols, the American Medical Association (AMA) accreditation, and other hoops to jump through. Josef Horacek worked hard to meet all the requirements and the license for running a clinic with a specialty in obstetrics and gynecology (OB/GYN). He had to have mentorship supervision for the first three years. It was here that life threw Barbara a curve she would have gladly done without.

Dr. Josef Horacek's mentor, herself an OB/GYN, happened to be one of his former professors in medical school who had a daughter almost the same age as Barbara. The young lady was also finishing medical school at about the same time that Dr. Horacek was working to get his clinic off the ground. Though she graduated a heart surgeon, her mother's supervisory work with Dr. Horacek, which brought him to her house on numerous occasions, saw her daughter taking more than a mere liking to Dr. Horacek. And this was not without her mother's sly manipulations. Barbara had started noticing it barely six months after beginning work at the clinic. The young heart surgeon had started frequenting the clinic for no purpose at all, and she would be closeted with Barbara's boss in conversation for hours on end. Curiously, still, her boss had not invited her out on a date, which, initially, Barbara put it down as the need for professional distance between boss and employee. But no such protocol was necessary after hours and, besides, it was his private business, not a public institution for him to live by such strict boss-subordinate code of conduct. She had thought of becoming pushy, but, on the advice of her auntie, ruled it out. She needed the job, and she was highly paid, too. She knew Dr. Horacek purposely paid her higher than what her qualification merited because she worked hard and knew her job, and he probably didn't want to lose her. But she had an inkling there was some other reason, which she also could not figure out. She became increasingly worried by the day because her biological clock was ticking in fast forward, not marking time on the same spot. The experience of her parents' failed marriage and the tragic story of her family that ended with her mother's death in prison—a death which she still blamed on her absentee father—had inhibited Barbara from venturing out with men in the hope of possibly getting married and settling down. Dr. Horacek was the only man she felt comfortable with, but from the looks of things, he didn't seem interested in her romantically. He seemed content with the platonic relationship they had. So, Barbara began toying with the idea of getting pregnant by in vitro fertilization (IVF). Although she'd had an occasional one-night stand when she was living a self-destructive life, she hadn't gathered enough confidence to trust in a relationship that tied her to a man only because they shared mutual parentage of a child. So, she had ruled out sleeping with a man just to get pregnant. But it seemed now that she would jump at that opportunity with Dr. Horacek, if he cared enough to ask. The latter, however, just seemed to content himself with being nice to her, paying her a mouth-watering salary, fiendishly clutching to his smug aloofness in the name of professional ethics and pretending not to notice her desperate flirtations. This irritated Barbara to no end, especially when he would make time to sit in his office in an hour-long conversation with his mentor's daughter. She thought it was probably because she was not a doctor. So, in the autumn of 1990, Barbara decided to register in a course to study for her B.Sc. in Nursing. She also became very eager to get pregnant and have a baby of her own.

Barbara threw herself into her studies and lived only for work and study. Two years later, her efforts paid off hugely when, at the end of spring in 1992, she graduated *magna cum laude*. Dr. Horacek promoted her with an even greater mouth-watering salary package, a gesture which Barbara later used against him, accusing him of imprisoning her with money while punitively starving her emotionally. And this came on the occasion when Barbara, by now a very ambitious young lady, was laying out a plan to try killing two birds with one stone. She went on to register for her Masters in Nursing while also intending to get pregnant by IVF at the same time. She figured she could work and study part-time while nursing the pregnancy. She wanted the child to be her graduation gift to herself at the end of her master's program. Her auntie was no less excited when she listened to Barbara's plan. She was very proud of her, especially for turning her life around and, despite family tragedy, setting herself on the road to success in life. And so, she didn't hesitate to encourage her to move ahead with the plan.

Barbara would keep wondering, years later, what imp put such a scheme in her head, except that, for some reason, she had thought it was time for her to become pushy and claim what she thought should belong to her by right. Having laid out her life plan for the next two years with the help of her auntie, she decided to bait her boss for a chance to corner him for a long-overdue date and, who knows, perhaps things might finally move to the next level. So, one night in the summer of 1992, she picked up the phone and broached the subject. She started with her plan for a Master's degree in Nursing, about which her boss was even more excited than herself, and kept saying, "That's great! That's great, Barbs! That's great! I support you fully!" Then she hedged toward the difficult subject.

"Doctor, I was also thinking…" she began.

"Great things happen when people start thinking, Barbs!" Dr. Horacek chimed enthusiastically. "So, what about?"

"About a child," Barbara replied, using her best baiting voice, husky and sexy. "I was thinking it's time I got married and settled down. My biological clock, you know…" she trailed off waiting for Dr. Horacek to respond.

"Oh, you have found a man, then?!" Dr. Horacek replied, with the same level of enthusiasm as before. "So, who IS the lucky SOB?!"

"Yes and no," Barbara replied. "Yes, I found a man more than three years ago, and no, as he doesn't seem to notice me, no matter what I do."

"Well, either the man doesn't know there's a gem at his feet waiting to be picked up, or he's not interested in marriage. Have you discussed it with him?" Dr. Horacek asked, genuinely concerned.

"I am currently in discussion with him, but he seems so obtuse and aloof," Barbara went on. "I don't know how to get him to understand. If he doesn't realize what he's missing and wake up, I'd probably try IVF. I want a child. My experience with surrogacy that time and the feeling I've had since then tell me I need a child of my own. Maybe I CAN try IVF."

"Well, if the man you are talking about isn't interested, then yes, IVF is a good idea," Dr. Horacek concurred.

"What do you mean 'IVF is a good idea'?" Barbara asked, querulously. Her tone caught Dr. Horacek off guard and confused.

"I mean, um…" He stalled and cleared his throat. "I mean that you can get pregnant by IVF if you…"

"I know what you mean, but I just want to know why that is a good idea for you," Barbara warmed to her fight, to the surprise and confusion of Dr. Horacek.

"Goodness, Barbs! I'm just agreeing with you that…"

"How dare you agree with me?" She interjected sounding quite hostile.

"So, if the man whose attention I'm trying to attract pretends not to notice me, then I should go and get pregnant by IVF. And that's a good idea for you?"

"Barbs, I don't understand why you're so upset!" Dr. Horacek sounded distressed. "I don't think I've said anything offensive. You mentioned IVF, not me."

"Yes, I mentioned IVF, not you," Barbara raised the tempo of her fight. "But I wasn't mentioning it for you to agree with me. Guess what? You wanted to know who the lucky sonofabitch is? Well, the lucky SOB, as you call him, is *you*. You are such a smug and a bore, you take refuge under some obsolete code of professionalism and pretend you don't notice my feelings for you, even when I openly flirt with you. It's been more than three years, Doctor!"

"Oh, gosh! Oh, no! I should have known that was where you were heading." Dr. Horacek said, almost to himself. Then he addressed Barbara more directly. "We've been very good friends, Barbs. It's not like I don't notice you."

"I didn't want to be just 'good friends' with you. I wanted more than that. I wanted to be asked out on a date, I wanted to enjoy my first decent kiss by a man with you. I wanted you to sweep me off my feet and take me on a vacation with you. I wanted...." Barbara choked, sobbing loudly over the phone.

"Barbs, please calm down," Dr. Horacek tried a conciliatory tone again. "Calm down. Please, stop crying. It isn't as easy as you think. It's complicated."

"Yeah, I know," Barbara replied, seeming to calm down from her outburst, but still not done with her fight. "Especially with that old haggard mentor of yours breathing down your neck, pretending to be supervising your work when all the time she's busy pushing her bimbo daughter on you."

"Oh, c'mon, Barbs. Will you quit that kind of language?" Dr. Horacek demanded with firmness. "She is not an old haggard and her daughter is not a bimbo. I know I became too eager to get my clinic licensed and I let myself fall too far in, and now I can't seem to be able to get out."

"What do you mean?" Barbara asked, as though with renewed interest. "So, you have made up your mind. You don't want to have anything to do with me?"

"I wish it was a simple matter of making up my mind. It's complicated, Barbs."

"What do you mean 'it's complicated'?" Barbara asked, genuinely confused.

Dr. Horacek heaved a sigh on the other end of the phone and said, "Vivian is pregnant with my child." There was a deafening silence on Barbara's end of the phone. Her voice, when it came back on the line, was intriguingly calm.

"Yeah. I can see what you mean. It's complicated." She broke off again into an uncomfortable silence. Dr. Horacek cleared his throat, but couldn't think of anything else to say. An aeon seemed to pass, and then Barbara spoke.

"Doctor, will you promise to do me one last favor?" Barbara asked.

"What do you mean?" Dr. Horacek asked, disguising his voice to hide his panic. He had heard of people committing suicide over unrequited love. Barbara's voice was menacingly calm, too calm for comfort, considering her previous outburst, just a few minutes earlier.

"Promise that you will give me a good recommendation for my next job, just for old time's sake," Barbara said, still sounding very calm. In his relief, Dr. Horacek gave her a bear hug in his mind. The last thing he needed in his career was a Romeo-and-Juliet scenario.

"I still don't understand what you're talking about, Barbs," he hedged. "Why do you need a recommendation for a 'next job'?"

"You're not going to fire me, after all that outburst and nastiness?"

"Fire you! Okay, Barbs," Dr. Horacek said, chuckling, glad for the opportunity to demonstrate his capacity for magnanimity mixed with humor. "If that's what you were spoiling for, then that was quite a lousy effort and you've failed woefully. I don't fire people for venting their frustration over unrequited love, especially when the culprit happens to be me, as has been factually proven. So, if you don't mind, be at your nursing post and at work next Monday, as usual."

"Well, I have no choice," Barbara replied. "You have me in a stranglehold. I need the money, and you pay well…very well…but I think it's just cruel of you to imprison me with a fat paycheck while starving me of your love. I wish to God it was different. I'll be at work, Monday, but it's going to be hard for me…very hard."

"All I need, Barbs, is for you to understand that it's not easy for me, either. It's complicated, very complicated. Really!"

That was twenty years ago. Dr. Josef Horacek was right. What happened later, in the course of the next three years, proved to be, even much more complicated for all concerned. But little did she know then that she would use the same word, twenty years later, to try and calm her daughter. She smiled, ruefully, at the irony of it all.

A click sound upstairs woke her from her revelry. Looking up at the sound, she caught a furtive movement from her daughter, Crystal, standing at the top of the stairs, looking at her. Barbara got up and looked longingly at her daughter for a few seconds. Then she called out, warily, "Are you hungry?" Then, as Crystal started down the stairs toward her, she continued, "Do you want a banana split? Let me make you one. I know you like a banana split. I can make one fast."

Crystal reached the step where her mother was and said, "Listen, Mom. Don't trip over yourself to please me. You hurt me, but I want to apologize for freaking out on you. I apologize for the stupid things I said. I don't hate you…"

"Oh, Crysie. Come here, honey. I know you didn't mean those things," Barbara said. Reaching out and taking Crystal's hand, she pulled her close for a tight hug. "And I want you to understand that I love you and am very sorry. Very, very sorry."

"I know, Mom. And I'm sorry that I said what I said," Crystal said, hugging her mother.

"It's okay, honey. Everything is alright now. As my only child, I couldn't ever dream of not loving you, Crysie. But it is complicated. I know you don't want to hear that word, I'm sorry to say it again," Barbara said, laughing with tears rolling down her cheek.

"It's okay, Mom. I don't mind," Crystal said, struggling to endure her mother's tight embrace.

"I love you, sweetie," Barbara was so beside herself with relief at having reconciled with her daughter that she hugged her a little too tight, stroking her long hair at the neck region.

"Mom!" Crystal called out. "I can't breathe!"

"Oh, I'm so sorry, dear!" Barbara released her daughter and, holding her hand, led her down the steps to the kitchen. "Come, let me make you your banana split and I'll tell you the story behind that phrase, 'it's complicated'."

Crystal sat down at the breakfast table and was relieved to see her mother recovering so quickly from their row of the previous thirty minutes or so. She knew her mother was a strong woman. Being a single mom, she had to be. She fought for everything good that she wanted her to have, but she wondered why she had to be so secretive about her biological father. She was eager to hear the story she wanted to tell. Maybe it really was complicated, as her mom kept saying. Looking at her mother bobbling about the kitchen, preparing a banana split for her, she almost felt ashamed at her unwarranted outburst.

"There you are. Enjoy your banana split and let me tell you my story." Barbara placed a saucer of banana split in front of Crystal, took a seat opposite her daughter, and began her story.

It was almost 7:30 p.m. when Barbara finished her story. She heaved a sigh of relief and sat staring off into space. Crystal was staring at nothing, too. Eventually, she looked down at her plate and saw that she still had a last piece of banana left, with the ice cream and syrup now melted and looking like milk. She tried to gather as much of the milk-like fluid on the plate as she could, along with the banana piece. Before shoving the scoop in her mouth, she asked, "So, why did you finally decide to ask Dr. Horacek for help?"

"He was the intern who worked with me when I was impregnated with the baby who belonged to that couple," Barbara continued in a somewhat subdued tone. "After I gave them the baby, I missed him so much that I decided to never think about IVF. I just consciously lost interest in researching or reading anything further about IVF other than what I needed for helping the clients who came for treatment in our clinic because I didn't want anything that would remind me of the baby and make me sad that he was not mine to keep." She paused and then continued, "That baby was beautiful. He had blue eyes and tawny-colored hair. And he was so full of life." Barbara smiled toothlessly, with lips clenched. Tears stood in her eyes, evidence that she still missed him.

"Was he the donor?" Crystal asked, looking, not at her mother, but at her plate, and still scouring it with the spoon, as if to clean out the last drop of the sweet cream on it. "Did he tell you who the donor was in my case?"

"No, Crysie. He didn't," Barbara interjected. "You see, we had to adhere to the terms of the contract, which forbade the donor and the beneficiary from knowing each other. We were not to make any claims either way. So, contact was forbidden. He sold his sperm, and that was it…Well, I know we say 'donate' to avoid any semblance of selling body parts. But, what the heck! It's one and the same thing. I paid three thousand dollars, and that was it."

"I didn't know I cost you such a fortune," Crystal quipped. "That was big money then, I guess."

"That's why I named you 'Crystal'," Barbara replied, matter-of-factly.

"I wanted to name you 'Diamond', but it sounded too strange in my ear. So, I settled for 'Crystal'. You know, crystal is precious, don't you? You are precious to me because you are all I have, and you remind me of my mother, and so many things in my life."

"I know," Crystal replied insipidly.

"And you're my only child."

"Okay, Mom. That's crystal clear," she quipped again, and they both chuckled briefly at her intended pun. "How did his wife react? Did she know he was helping you?"

"No, Crysie. That was just between me and Dr. Horacek," Barbara replied. "Now, don't forget, I was still working at his clinic. So, we could pull it off without any third-party knowledge."

"It is interesting that as close as you were, he wouldn't breathe a word of the identity of the sperm seller...."

"Crysie, please call him 'sperm donor'," Barbara interjected, wincing at the way her daughter pronounced the phrase 'sperm seller'.

"Okay, 'sperm donor', whatever," Crystal said, in the characteristically throw-away tones of the young and bored. "Don't you think he could have, at least, whispered a name to you, contract or no contract, just for old time's sake?"

"He probably could have if I had pressed him for it," Barbara conceded. "But I didn't want to give the impression that I was taking advantage of the situation to force him to do something unethical, but, yeah, he could've told me."

They fell silent again, each seemingly mulling over the whole incident. Then, suddenly, Crystal said, "I found his name." She rummaged in her shorts' pocket and brought out a printed piece of paper. "We used his code name of 'California two four nine' to search, and we found him listed under that code name. Surely you remember the man who went by this name and worked at the clinic the same time you worked there?" she asked, with exaggerated irony, shoving the piece of paper in front of an incredulous-looking Barbara, without waiting for an answer.

"No, that can't be true!" Barbara said, a shade too vehemently. She sat back with a start, as if retreating from the sting of some harmful bug.

"Yes, it is true," Crystal said, looking straight at her mother.

"That cannot be true!" Barbara repeated, looking quite alarmed. "I don't think that's the name. No, Dr. Horacek couldn't have pulled that on me! No, no...he could have told me."

"Well, Mom, he PULLED that on you," Crystal said, with a confirmatory tone of voice. "And he didn't tell you because it was policy and part of the contract. You said so, remember?" Crystal said, almost mockingly. "Since I wasn't party to that contract, though, I am DEFINITELY going to find out why."

———

School wasn't the usual big fun for Crystal the following day. Her mother's story of the previous evening had both a depressing and an exciting effect on her. Depressing because she had never known until then how difficult a life her mother had as a teenager and a young adult. She had told her snippets of it in the past, but not in vivid details, as she heard her do that evening. She also realized that, had she known such detailed facts about her mother's life, she would have probably shown her more appreciation and understanding than what she had been showing her before that evening. Again, she surmised that her mother was probably shielding her from the trauma she would have experienced listening to an account of such a difficult life. She kept wondering whether telling her the story before that evening would have been more beneficial for her or more damaging. In the end, she decided that whatever was the case, her mother handled the situation as best she could, and probably couldn't have done any better, given all the circumstances that came into play.

On the other hand, she was so excited that she had discovered, at last, who her biological father was, and it was just a matter of time before she would meet him face to face. Would he acknowledge her as his daughter? Or, would he require DNA testing to confirm or disprove? Crystal began to wonder. However, she did not allow that to worry her so much just then. Whatever his reaction would be when she would meet him, she decided to leave that till that moment. For now, she wanted to enjoy the euphoria of the moment fully. It felt very exhilarating for her, the knowledge that she now had a dad with a name, who was soon going to have a face. It was very healing for Crystal. She felt like other normal kids now, she thought. Most importantly, she had discovered something else. She had discovered what a hard-hitter at life her mother was. Yes, life had hit Barbara Sanders hard since childhood, but she had hit back at life even harder. To have overcome all the difficulties she recounted and still strive to make something respectable of herself, not just scratching through, but living comfortably as a woman of means, all by her effort and hard work, was something Crystal would always admire about her mother. She did graduate with a Master of Science degree in Nursing from the University of Virginia and, a month and two weeks later, had Crystal as the graduation gift she had planned for herself. She resigned from the Norfolk Fertility Clinic and moved to Texas, where she got a job at the Baylor College of Medicine. She was one of the few women at the university to be earning a six-figure salary. It dawned on Crystal what a strong woman and a great achiever her mother was. She made a mental note to write a poem for her mother to celebrate this fact about her on her next birthday.

"Hey, girl. What's up?" It was Edo-Mma. "You look quite bright today, with a smiling face. Tell me, what did Josh do to you?" she asked, looking coyly at her friend.

"Do I?" Crystal replied. She had no idea that her ruminations about her mother had brightened her countenance and made her appear as though she was smiling.

"Yeah, these past few weeks, you have always been very moody," Edo-Mma said. "But I am telling you, Crysie, I am so overjoyed to see you smiling. Josh must have done something right. Now, tell me, what did he do?"

"Must everything be about what Josh has done or not done?" Crystal asked in mock alarm. "Come off it, Edo. Josh is the least thing on my mind right now."

"What an awful thing to say, Crysie!" Edo-Mma chided mildly. "Good thing he is not around to hear that."

"Oh, he wouldn't mind," Crystal dismissed. "Poor guy is purple-sick with love for me. Josh does make me happy, don't get me wrong. I'm just as purple-sick over him, you know that. But something happened last night between me and my mom."

"You confronted her?" Edo-Mma asked warily.

"Not as such," Crystal replied. "Well, you could say it was such at the beginning. But along the way, it turned out that I hadn't known a whole lot about my mom. She opened her entire life to me for the first time, and I tell you, Edo, my mom is a great woman. I have a newfound respect for her. She is a very strong woman!"

"You showed her the name?" Edo-Mma asked, expectantly.

"She recognized it immediately, but she herself was kept in the dark about it until last evening," Crystal said. "Can you believe that?"

"How so?" Edo-Mma asked, getting more interested.

"Let's get to the basement, and I'll tell you," Crystal replied as she steered Edo-Mma in that direction.

"And I will also tell you what I discovered when I told my father about it," Edo-Mma said, with excitement. "You won't believe it, Crysie. The man, your dad…Can I call him your dad?" Edo-Mma asked, self-consciously, confused about how to address the subject of their conversation, who, from all indications, was now discovered to be her friend's flesh and blood.

"Yeah, call him that," Crystal replied. "He's my dad. Even if he denies it, in theory, it's a fact."

"Your dad was a college and frat mate with my father at Berkeley," Edo-Mma said.

"You mean it?" Crystal asked, incredulously.

"Better believe it, Crysie," Edo-Mma replied. "And they had kept contact with each other over these years. My father recognized the name and immediately took out his phone and dialed him up. I tell you, Crysie, they talked and laughed, well into the night."

"Hey, Edo. Remember when I told you that our middle school geography teacher, Mr. Herken, used to say, 'This world is round'?"

"Yes."

"Well, this world IS round," Crystal said, pursing her lips for emphasis.

"It's a small place, too, they say," Edo-Mma concurred. "Come. Let's go sit down, and tell me your mom's story."

Crystal and Edo-Mma almost didn't get to finish regaling each other when the bell rang, signaling the end of break and the beginning of the afternoon session. As they emerged from the basement to get back to their classroom, Kelechi and Josh were also coming out from the auditorium with a group of other boys with whom they were practicing their step rhythm on the stage. They caught up with the girls and continued their chatting into the classrooms. That afternoon, before boarding their rides back to their different homes, Crystal declared her intention to travel to visit her biological dad for the first time. She planned it for the short Spring break, which would end with Easter Sunday.

# NORFOLK, VIRGINIA
## SPRING, 2012

THE BOEING 707 American Airlines Airbus, Flight 56, taxied smoothly into Terminal A at the Norfolk International Airport in Virginia and Barbara stretched and unbuckled her seatbelt. She looked at her daughter, Crystal, who, as she could tell by her facial expression, looked excited and apprehensive at the same time. Barbara knew she was thinking about the impending meeting with her biological father, not knowing how she would be received. Barbara had assured her when they left home in Houston that everything was going to be alright, but now, watching the faint expression on Crystal's face, she could not help wondering if the trip was a foolhardy venture after all. Though Barbara felt a little fluttering in her stomach, also, she decided to muster up her courage and do what needed to be done.

"It's okay, sweetie," she muttered, assuredly. "Everything will be alright. Are you ready for this?" Barbara asked rhetorically.

"Uh huh," Crystal replied, bobbing her head back and forth to show she was determined and there was no going back.

"Okay, baby. Let's do this," Barbara said with a note of finality. Barbara slid out of her seat and opened the carrier compartment to retrieve her carry-on bag. Crystal slid out, too, grabbed her backpack, and followed her mother.

Muttering words of assurance to Crystal was a way for Barbara to beef up her own courage. Neither mother nor daughter knew how their host would receive them, and how he would react to their quest. That, however, did not deter them from making the trip from Houston to Virginia. The worst that could happen might be a flat rejection. In that case, there would be nothing to do but turn back and go home. They had prayed together to prepare their minds to handle the situation with calm resignation, if it came to that. The important thing was that Crystal would have, at last, confirmed the truth which she already learned about her biological father. And Barbara was determined to help her to do just that.

She could not get that evening out of her mind when, three weeks earlier, Crystal, sitting at the table across from her, pushed that piece of paper in front of her. The name on it was all too familiar. For seventeen years, Barbara had thought that she was done with that name, and would never cross paths with its bearer. As it stood, that was not to be. She kept wondering during the short flight to Norfolk, how uncanny destiny's long arm could reach across time to loop a person back into its original design, for better or for worse. She prayed and hoped the path of destiny she now travelled with her daughter would bring something better.

They reached the baggage claim area and waited silently, if uncomfortably, for their luggage. They had not waited two minutes when a series of beeps came through the loudspeaker and a warning to steer clear of the conveyor belt, which started moving with muffled rumbling, squeaking, and screeching. As mother and daughter waited silently for their luggage to appear, each was deep in thought. Crystal went down memory lane to ruminate on why and how she decided to embark on a quest to find her biological father. She had always wondered who her father was and what he looked like. The most her mother could tell her then was that she bought, from a sperm bank, the sperm that she used in the IVF process that resulted in the pregnancy that became Crystal. It was later, when Crystal was probably 15 years old, that her mother revealed that her former boss at the Norfolk Fertility Clinic brokered the process, and that she was not allowed to know the "donor," to legally avoid claims either way. That was alright, as far as her mother and the mystery "donor" were concerned, but Crystal had often wondered where she fitted in in the equation. That both parties—her mother and her sperm "donor" father—seemed nonchalant about her feelings and her sense of self-identity and esteem bothered her to the point of being painful. As the years went by, she began to feel some resentment, first toward her mother for dismissing the matter lightly every time she brought up the subject, and then toward the mystery man whose genes she came from, at least, partly.

The urge to start the quest for her biological father really consumed Crystal one day when Kelechi, Edo-Mma's boyfriend, announced to them jubilantly that he had traced his biological mother and found who she was. Kelechi was adopted at birth because his mother got pregnant with him at 16 by a 19-year old Nigerian man, Kelechi Ugobueze, who was sent to prison on a two-count charge of rape and sexual abuse of a minor, despite her insistence that she consented to the sexual encounter. Her parents, livid that she had to drop out of school, had prevented them from running away and getting married, a tryst which would have made Kelechi Sr. escape prison, since by marriage, she would have assumed the status of an emancipated minor. It was quite obvious that her parents were bent on punishing Kelechi Sr. So, left with no future with the man of her dreams, and under family pressure, she gave up her baby for adoption, after giving birth and naming him after his father. All this had happened years ago, in Louisiana. Little Kelechi's adopted parents first moved to North Carolina, then eventually to Texas. Kelechi Jr. grew up not knowing his mother, much less his father, whose student's visa had long expired as he served time in prison, and he was deported after serving seven years, without a chance to renew it or change his status. Kelechi Jr. had traced his mother to Baton Rouge, and had gotten all the story about his father. His mother had later married a lumberjack and had three children—two girls and a boy—ages eight, six and four. Kelechi Jr. made a promise to himself to, one day, travel to Nigeria to search for his father. Kelechi's success in tracing his birth mother had given Crystal the impetus to enlist his help in tracing her own biological father.

"Crysie, that's your bag there," Barbara's voice jolted Crystal out of her revelry. "Get it." Crystal pursued the bag and got it, snaking her way to avoid colliding with other baggage claimers. They waited for another five minutes before her mother's bag came through. Having retrieved their luggage intact, mother and daughter headed for the car rental desk by the airport exit door. The rental process was quick: five minutes of filling out a form, a show of ID cards, a swipe of a credit card for money to exchange accounts, then a further ten-minute wait, and a BMW SUV pulled up outside. The attendant walked in briskly and handed the keys to the cashier, who invited Barbara to sign on the dotted lines. She did and was promptly handed the keys with a smile and the words, "Thanks, Ma'am, for doing business with us. Enjoy your ride."

"You bet, I will," Barbara said, returning the lady's smile as she walked to the sliding doors, Crystal in tow, feverishly texting on her iPhone. Barbara couldn't quit wondering how the youngsters did it: texting while walking on a crowded sidewalk, mall, or airport concourse without bumping into people or, worse, tripping and falling. She didn't mind Crystal performing the feat, as she was used to it, but she had absolutely forbidden her from trying that while driving. As they reached the car and Barbara remotely opened the trunk, she watched with mixed amusement and vexation that Crystal picked up her bag with her left hand and dropped it in the trunk without even looking, while she continued texting with her right hand. Barbara kept watching Crystal out the corner of her eye as they got into the car. Crystal eventually took note and turned to look at her mother.

"What?" she asked, confused.

"Nothing," Barbara replied, dismissively. "Why?"

"Well, I caught you looking at me," Crystal said. "You're driving. I'm not driving."

"As if that isn't obvious enough," Barbara replied, mockingly.

"Well, you act as though it isn't," Crystal parried. "Mom, you should really learn how to text. It's fun. When we get to the hotel, I'll show you."

"Who says I don't know how to text?"

"I…" Crystal interjected.

"I just don't make a show of it," Barbara replied.

"You don't know how to text. I'll teach you when we get to the hotel," Crystal insisted, annoyingly.

"Alright, Madame Professor," Barbara countered, impatiently. "Have it your way, but quit yapping and let me think." She nosed the car onto the airport main exit and headed out to their hotel reservation, calling out, "Seatbelt."

Crystal clicked the seatbelt to and chuckled quietly at her mother's unease. Whenever they had an argument, she almost always enjoyed brow-beating her mother into giving in to her and would derive a kind of impish pleasure watching her do so with her characteristically mild vexation. She knew her mother doted on her, being an only child, and, although she sometimes pushed the envelope, she also knew when to quit.

The Marriot Hotel, where Barbara had booked their reservation, was barely three miles from the airport hub, but it took them almost ten minutes to get there because of the heavy traffic leaving the airport. When they had settled into their room, Barbara took her phone and quietly disappeared into the bathroom, and pretentiously turned on the shower while placing a call to the Norfolk Fertility Clinic. Within a couple of seconds, a man's voice came on the other end of the line and she engaged him in a brief conversation. When she was done, she took a deep breath, exhaled, and thought to herself, 'It's gonna be alright'. She turned off the shower and went back into the room.

"I thought you were taking a shower?" Crystal inquired.

"Changed my mind," Barbara replied. She noticed that Crystal had changed from the t-shirt and pair of shorts she wore during the flight, into a body-hugging dress that emphasized her blossoming adolescent curves. Barbara permitted herself a faint smile and turned her back toward her daughter to hide it. She knew Crystal was eager to make the best first impression on her father, and she also knew that only an insane man would refuse to acknowledge such a beautiful young lady as his daughter. In that dress, Crystal was a paragon of beauty. Barbara moved closer to the dressing mirror and, looking at the image that stared back at her, knew that she, herself, wasn't ugly, either. She picked up her handbag and moved to the dresser in front of the mirror, emptied the contents onto the dresser, and, for the better part of fifteen minutes, mother and daughter applied themselves diligently to the art of cosmetic make up. When they were done, the results were exquisite. As they later joked about it, they left the hotel lobby headed for their car that late morning, looking like a couple of Hollywood A-list stars on an Oscar awards night.

It was 11:25 a.m. when Barbara Sanders eased the car onto the road heading toward the Norfolk Fertility Clinic. She purposely took a detour to drive past the Norfolk General Sentara Hospital at 600 Gresham Drive. The drive brought back vivid memories of her first pregnancy ordeal as a surrogate mother making countless trips to the hospital Gynecology Department to receive her drug regimen. In hindsight, she felt as though she had been used, but she needed the money back then, and twelve grand was not peanuts at that time. She wondered where the baby—certainly a young man of 30 by now—was and what he was doing with his life. She wondered if the parents were still living and how they looked now in their late 70s. She wondered what her life would have been like if that first pregnancy was her own and she didn't have to give the baby away. As she kept wondering, she realized she was getting farther out of the way. So, she turned into a side street, and made a U-turn to head back and connect to Fairfax Avenue. Crystal was unusually quiet, but very alert. Barbara noticed she was taking in the view of Norfolk with relish. She kept darting her glance this way and that, and didn't seem to notice that her mom was doubling back. Normally, Crystal would have faulted her mother's sense of direction and criticize her for losing her bearings, but she seemed too busy sight-seeing to mind. And Barbara was secretly happy to be spared her daughter's complaining.

As Barbara pulled into the parking lot of the Norfolk Fertility Clinic on Fairfax Avenue, she felt as though she was back again, seventeen years ago, when she would pull up that way as she arrived for work. Everything was very familiar—the dull, light-beige color of the brick walls of the clinic building, the front entrance double glass doors with Dr. Horacek's name and clinic hours embossed on them, the front desk and receptionist post—except for two things: the sign outside had changed from a regular to an electronic LED, displaying and changing information in beautiful characters of assorted fonts and colors, every ten seconds or so; and there was a modest-looking, but beautifully designed, duplex building behind the clinic, occupying not more than eight hundred square feet of space. Barbara noticed all this in one sweeping glance as she and Crystal got out of the car and walked toward the double glass doors.

"This is the clinic where I worked for thirteen years," Barbara said, looking sideways at Crystal.

"Nice-looking place," Crystal complimented. "Did you like working here?"

Barbara nodded, affirmatively, but wordlessly.

As they walked in through the double doors, a young lady, primly dressed in the clinic receptionist uniform, came around the desk to greet them with the bright welcoming smile that Dr. Horacek insisted his receptionist must cultivate as the door opener to patients, guests, and clients coming to do business in his clinic. He was a stickler for good image and excellent first impressions—and Barbara loved that about him.

"Good morning, ladies," the receptionist said, looking first at Crystal, then directly at Barbara, holding her glance with her own smiling eyes. "How can we help you today?"

"We have an appointment with Dr. Horacek," Barbara said.

"And what's your name, please?" the receptionist asked politely.

"Sanders," Barbara replied. "Barbara Sanders. And this is my daughter, Crystal." Crystal and the receptionist shook hands and exchanged their "hi."

"Oh, yes, Ms. Sanders. He is expecting you," the receptionist said. She reached behind her to pick up and present the visitor's register to Barbara. "Please, sign your names and I will take you to the house. Dr. Horacek said I should bring you to the house when you arrive."

"The house?" Barbara asked as she took the pen to sign in.

"Yes, the building behind this clinic," the receptionist replied, noticing the wonder on Barbara's face.

Barbara thought it was a good idea that Dr. Horacek decided to build himself a house behind his clinic so he wouldn't have to keep commuting the long distance in the traffic from where he lived before, off Jefferson Drive, a good twenty miles away. She wrote her name and the time of arrival, and had the urge to ask when the house was built, but she decided against it, not wanting to engage in conversation with the receptionist. Dr. Horacek would probably tell her before their encounter was done. She gave the pen to Crystal, who quickly scribbled her name and handed it back to the receptionist.

A second receptionist was already at hand to cover for the first as they were being ushered out through a side door.

"This way, please," the first receptionist said, taking the lead.

"Quite a busy place!" Crystal commented, almost whispering, for her mother's benefit.

"Yeah, it was always like that," Barbara concurred, spotting a middle-aged nurse coming out of a consulting room with a pregnant woman and making her way to the nurses' station. Barbara recognized her immediately and was thankful that the nurse didn't see her. She was in no mood to waste time on elaborate hugs, greetings, and story-swapping about old times, questions and answers about the present, and whatever else Nurse Jackson would bring up. She was always chatty and friendly, and Barbara liked her very much, not only for her easy, friendly ways, but also because Nurse Janice Jackson—Nurse JJ as they fondly called her—was one true friend who would always have your back, no matter what. Their work partnership was so strong that on the day Barbara left, JJ cried while helping her pack. Barbara made a mental note to seek her out and reconnect for old time's sake if all went well at their meeting with Dr. Horacek.

They took a short thirty-foot walk to the house, which was linked to the clinic by a roof-covered cobblestone pavement. Neatly cultivated flower beds lined the base of the walls outside, breaking the monotonous light-beige motif of the brick house, which was built to match the clinic. Barbara was impressed. She recalled that Dr. Horacek was one person who always strove for the good life. He was hard on himself when it came to working to achieve what he thought he needed to achieve, and Barbara respected this driving force in him. The receptionist pressed the doorbell button and a soft, beautiful chime came from inside. Barbara looked at Crystal, who looked back, smiling very faintly, but nervously. Barbara took a deep breath and exhaled, arranging her apparel and brushing an imaginary lock of hair into place by her right ear.

The door opened with a swish to reveal a tall gentleman in his late 50s, with a broad forehead and receding hairline with a few strands already turning blond. He was wearing a short-sleeved shirt of light-blue color and khaki pants. His lean frame gave him an athletic bearing. Barbara thought Dr. Horacek had not changed much; he was still his usual handsome self with a slight swagger to his demeanor. Crystal took one look at him and was transfixed, not knowing what demeanor she could adopt—formal or informal. He was just rounding up a phone call he had and was trying to unglue his ear from the phone.

"Yeah! Yeah, that's correct," he said to the person on the other end of the phone. "It's left for the Institutional Review Board to come up with some guidelines of their own, if they're not completely satisfied with the protocol, but…listen, let me call you back. I have very important visitors now." He finally unglued the phone from his ear and pressed the 'end call' button as the receptionist quietly retreated.

"Barbara! Barbara!" Dr. Horacek called, smiling warmly and extending his hand for a shake. "It's so good to see you again, after such a long time. But guess what? It's just like it was yesterday. It doesn't feel like fifteen years have passed since we set eyes on each other."

"Sixteen years," Barbara corrected, ignoring the hand and striking a pose, cocking her head slightly to one side and putting on a swag of her own. "And it's good to see you, too, Dr. Horacek. As I can see, things are looking bright for you. The clinic is booming and you have a nice new duplex. Congratulations! I'm happy for you."

"Well, Barbara," Dr. Horacek demurred, "I don't know about things looking bright, but I thank God it's not all bad. It could have been worse, after all. You look great! That's one thing I always liked about you. You know how to take care of yourself. And the young lady with you…, is she the one? My goodness, she has grown into such a gorgeous beauty!"

"Well, Dr. Horacek, I thank God, too. It's not all bad. It could have been worse, as you said," Barbara mimicked his comments. "Yes, Crystal is my daughter, and she is here on a quest with which I hope you can be of some help to her."

"Of course, Barbara. I told you there is nothing to fear," he replied, extending his hand toward Crystal. "Josef Horacek. Nice to meet you, and welcome. Please, come inside."

"Crystal Sanders. Nice to meet you, Sir," Crystal introduced herself, taking the proffered hand. Feeling the warm, friendly grip, she knew it was going to be okay. She followed her mother inside and was awed at the interior furnishings of the house. "You have a very beautiful house."

"Thank you, Crystal," Dr. Horacek replied, pleased that the young lady was impressed. "What can I offer you? There is wine, soda, scotch, bourbon, cognac, and Jamaican rum. Barbara, I remember you used to like Jamaican rum. Can I offer you some?"

"Not anymore," Barbara replied. "You don't seem to recall that I quit drinking after I was pregnant with Crystal."

"Oh, I AM sorry. I did not know you quit," Dr. Horacek replied with candor. "What about you, Crystal? Can I get you something to drink?"

"No, Sir," Crystal replied. "I don't drink."

"Not even soda?"

"No, Sir," Crystal replied, shifting uncomfortably on the settee.

"I think Crysie is nervous because she had a question for you," Barbara said, rummaging in her handbag for something. "She won't be able to drink or eat until she finds out what she came to find out. I think that makes sense, Doctor? Don't you?"

"I do, Barbara," Dr. Horacek concurred, somberly. "But that is no reason to reject every one of my gestures of hospitality. We are not enemies, Barbara, are we? And I don't think you came as enemies."

"No, Dr. Josef Bernard Horacek," Barbara replied, spelling out his name for effect. "We are not enemies. We are not rejecting your hospitality. We are simply a puzzled mother and daughter seeking the truth, and our appetite for food and drink will only be whetted by a true answer to our quest."

"And you will have that answer, today, Barbara," Dr. Horacek continued, gently. "And honestly, too. I did promise you that. Didn't I?"

"You did," Barbara replied. "Admittedly, I am having a hard time trusting that that will be the case, but am ready to gamble. So, Crysie did some research on her own, without my knowledge, and found out that her biological father went by the name of 'California two four nine' and she confronted me with it. I didn't know who 'California two four nine' was, so I brought her here today so that you can help by letting her know the person's name. She wants to know and I don't think there is any need to continue pretending to hide from her what she already knows. So, who is 'California two four nine'?"

"Oh, c'mon, Barbara, quit asking pretentious questions about what you already know."

"No, Doctor, I don't know," Barbara replied, contentiously. "How WOULD I know when you LIED to me? You deceived me and kept me in the dark."

"No, Barbara," Dr. Horacek countered. "I did not lie to you and I did not deceive you. I am positive about that."

"Yes, Doctor, you did," Barbara continued. "Just as you did concerning your marriage to that lady surgeon."

"Mom!" Crystal called out, alarmed that her mother was derailing the whole process that started peacefully. "What are you doing, Mom? This is not about you. This is about me. Can you please just let us approach this peacefully?" She was visibly shaken, feeling that her mother's unjustifiable heckling of Dr. Horacek would make him mad and inflexible.

"No, Crysie, it's not about me," Barbara agreed. "But it is all interlinked, and I am trying to appeal to him to be forthcoming, for your sake."

"You don't make an appeal to someone by heckling and nagging them," Crystal said, becoming more upset with her mother.

"It's okay, Crystal," Dr. Horacek assured her. "I understand where your mother is coming from. She has every right to be angry with me. And she is right, too. It is all interlinked, but I can assure you that it's all going to be well in the end. Barbara, the man who went by the nickname 'California two four nine' is ready to take responsibility. He promises to be forthcoming. That, I can assure you. But first, I think we should all go out and have lunch together before we come back to listen to him. His story might turn out to be a long one. Again, he promises to be forthcoming."

"He had better be," Barbara continued, unrelentingly. "Everything hangs on his being honest. That's what Crysie, here, is looking for. By the way, where is your wife? I hope we will be gone before she returns. The last thing we need is a jealous, angry wife trying to protect her husband. Where is she? At work?"

"Dead," Dr. Horacek said curtly, without emotion.

"What?!" Barbara thought she did not hear correctly.

"She died," Dr. Horacek repeated with the same emotionless demeanor.

"I'm so sorry!" Crystal said, genuinely feeling for Dr. Horacek. "Was she ill?"

"Automobile accident," Dr. Horacek replied, still without emotion. There were several seconds of awkward silence as Barbara continued staring blankly at Dr. Horacek. Crystal looked down at the coffee table top, squirming uncomfortably in her seat. "She died on impact—she AND her boyfriend."

"Boyfriend!" Barbara blurted out. "What do you mean, 'her boyfriend'?"

"Our marriage fell apart, Barbara, five years after you left the clinic and went to Texas. Of course, you know it was a business marriage; it wasn't really founded on love. The good thing is that there were no children involved. So, it was an easy process. She was happy with her new man, and I was happy to be left alone to face work at my clinic. According to the story, they were returning from El Paso, where they went to visit his parents, and apparently, he had had enough to drink, and fell asleep at the wheel at a high rate of speed, veered off the road, hit the ramp of the bridge, and somersaulted, plunging to the road crossing bellow. The wreckage was unbelievable. This happened almost three years to the day after our divorce."

"Dr. Horacek," Barbara called, still staring blankly into space.

"Yes?" he replied.

"I think I will take the Jamaican rum now," she said.

"You are a bundle of surprises, Barbara," he said, getting up to pour her the drink at the bar.

"I am so sorry for your loss, Sir," Crystal said again, unsure of anything else to say at that moment.

"Oh, that's okay," Dr. Horacek said, coming back with the drink for Barbara. "I don't miss her. I'm not callous, and I am not happy that she died that way. I don't think she deserved to die violently as she did. It's just that time had elapsed since we got divorced, and we didn't really click emotionally to the extent that I would miss her so much to consider her death a loss to me. If you understand what I mean." He crossed the room and began to pull down the blinds. "If you ladies don't mind, we can go out to lunch together. It's almost past lunch time. When we come back from lunch, I will explain everything.

"You have a lot of explaining to do," Barbara said as she put down her empty glass and got up.

"I'm sure I do, Barbara," Dr. Horacek replied with a tinge of wry humor.

---

Later that afternoon, at approximately 2:53 p.m., and back at the house, Dr. Josef Bernard Horacek killed the engine of his Toyota Prius, got out, and entered the house through the door connecting the garage to the kitchen. He crossed the kitchen into the siting room and made for the front door to open it for Barbara and Crystal, whom he had dropped off at the front of the house while he drove around to the back of the house, where the garage was located. Before he could turn the knob of the door, the soft music from the doorbell chimed. He opened the door to see Barbara looking straight into his face, her face flushed and pleasant, almost smiling. He knew that the category three purple Margaritas—a.k.a., Bahama Mama—that Barbara had gulped down at the restaurant always had more than a warm effect on her, but the look on her face was not that of a woman tipsy on cherry-tinged rum. He guessed she probably rang it as a prank, but he decided to ask why, anyway.

"You rang the doorbell?"

"Yeah," she replied, looking pleasantly at his face. Then she added, for his benefit, "I like the music. It's soft and celebratory. Happy Birthday, Dr. Josef Bernard Horacek!"

"Oh, gosh! Oh, gosh! Oh, my goodness! You remembered?!" Dr. Horacek exclaimed in disbelief. Barbara thought his eyes were going to pop right out of his head because they bulged with so much excitement. "Barbara, you remembered my birthday, and I forgot it myself! Oh, gosh! Thank you! Thank you so much! Please, come inside!"

"Truthfully, I forgot it myself, but remembered in the restaurant when the waiters gathered around the elderly couple who sat three tables away from us and sang Happy Anniversary for them," Barbara said, taking her seat again on the sofa.

"And that should have been my cue," Dr. Horacek replied in mild self-excoriation. "I stopped celebrating my birthday the year my wife and I got divorced. She always planned and executed it. When she was gone, I saw no need to continue the ritual. Moreover, it would have always been a painful reminder, instead of a pleasant experience."

"Happy Birthday, Dr. Horacek!" Crystal chimed in her felicitations.

"Thank you, Miss Sanders!" he replied, with a slight nod of the head. Then, he looked again, longingly at Barbara. "Barbara, you still remembered my birthday, even after these fifteen years!"

"Sixteen years," Barbara corrected again. She thought Dr. Horacek was on the verge of breaking down. She could see he was struggling to hold back tears. "When I recalled it in the restaurant, my first thought was that you took us out to celebrate it. But as I watched, I realized that that was not the case, and that you had probably forgotten. Your doorbell music sounds like a birthday song. That's why I rang it."

"Thank you, Barbara," Dr. Horacek said, composing himself. "Thank you so much. As it stands, I am indebted to you so much that I need to start paying up. And I will pay by installments." He pulled up a chair and sat directly in front of Barbara and Crystal, instead of sitting on the sofa, as before. He relaxed, crossed one leg over the other, and began to speak. "So, first installment: Miss Crystal Sanders," he addressed himself directly to Crystal. "Where do I start?"

"I have something here to show you, Sir." Crystal reached into her handbag and brought out a piece of paper, the one that she had shoved in front of her mother three weeks earlier, the evening of her outburst, and asked the question, "*Surely you remember the man who went by this name and worked at the clinic the same time you worked there?*" She handed it to Dr. Horacek.

"That's the name of the man whom I discovered to be my biological father," she said, evidently. "And as it stands, the only man I know as the owner of that name is you, Sir. Are you my dad, Sir? My biological father?"

"As sure as daylight follows the night, Miss Sanders, I am Josef Bernard Horacek and, as far as I can tell the code name here, *California 249*, is, or was, my code name." Then he turned to Barbara and asked, "You knew about this and you didn't let me in on it?"

"I didn't know Crysie was doing research to find out her biological father's identity," Barbara protested. "How could I have known when she only confronted me about it three weeks ago?"

"I don't mean the research part," Dr. Horacek replied. "I mean the fact that she already found out and linked my real name to my code name, 'California 249'. You could have told me she already knew that for a fact. Since you called me up last week, we have talked twice over the phone. You could have dropped me a clue."

"You mean the way you dropped me a clue that you were my 'sperm donor' for this past eighteen years?" Barbara asked, mockingly.

"Okay, Barbara. That's very sarcastic." Dr. Horacek said, resignedly. "Now that you've had your revenge, are we even?"

"No, Sir!" Barbara replied, then added, "Not until I give you a thorough whipping for messing with my emotions for these past eighteen years," seemingly spoiling for a fight.

"Mom!" Crystal called out, warily. "You're starting again!"

"I'm so sorry! I got carried away!" Barbara sounded calmer, but suddenly stoked the fire again by addressing Dr. Horacek directly. "I just want to let you know that I would not have made any claims on you if you had told me that I was carrying your child in my womb."

"Mom, why are you doing this?" Crystal asked, visibly irate. She was about to launch into a tirade against her mom, but Dr. Horacek deftly interjected.

"Miss Sanders, please! Don't lose you calm. Your mother means well. I understand where she is coming from and she is right." Then he addressed Barbara directly. "I must say, Barbara, that I am stung to the quick by your last statement. And it's more painful than the poison from a hornet's sting because you and I know that that is not the truth. You know, partly, why I couldn't tell you that I was the so-called 'sperm donor'. The part that you don't know is what I am going to tell you now, if you would please allow me."

"Yeah, that's right. I signed a contract binding myself to a clause forbidding me to make inquiries about the identity of my donor," Barbara acknowledged with a derisive grudge. "But you could have told me later, considering that we were close enough for you to do so. So, what other explanation do you have to show, that you were not deliberately walling me out because you thought I would make demands on you?"

"That is very strange, Barbara," Dr. Horacek replied with a faint smile and a slight squint. "You know the same could be said about you. You were eager to sign that part of the contract because you thought, based on the information you got, that the donor was a financially distressed construction worker. You were eager to wall him out so he wouldn't know the woman who was the recipient of his sperm. You were afraid that being financially distressed, he might try to suck up to you, using the fact of his being the biological father of your child."

"Oh yeah? That's what you think I did, you son of a..." Barbara launched.

"Mom!" Crystal interrupted, almost yelling. "If you continue this, I will walk out and take a taxi back to the hotel." Then she addressed Dr. Horacek. "Sir, is there any way we can change the tone and focus of this conversation? I didn't come here to listen to you two fight with yourselves over each other. Y'all had the opportunity to fall in love with each other, but didn't. Y'all missed it. Can't y'all move on? This was about me, not either of you. It's about MY identity and MY sanity. Is that too much to ask?"

Crystal's vehemence had a calming effect on both of her parents. For several seconds, no one spoke. Then eventually, Dr. Horacek cleared his throat and began to speak.

"Miss Sanders, I must say, that was quite intense, but I loved it." He paused and smiled faintly. "I loved it because that was me coming out of you. I loved the passion…"

"Dr. Horacek, can you please be civil enough and quit claiming credits so early," Barbara said, plaintively. "At least, I never knew you to be that greedy," she added, intending to hurt him with the calculated insult. Instead, her insult had a punchy effect on Dr. Horacek. He cracked up, laughing joyfully.

"I'm not claiming any credits. Miss Sanders is my child, as far as blood is concerned," he said, matter-of-factly.

"I'M her mother," Barbara retorted, petulantly. "I carried her in my womb for nine months, almost ten."

Crystal rolled her eyes exasperatingly and sank back into the sofa. She figured there was nothing she could do, but wait for her combatting parents to either satiate themselves in their fight, or get tired of it, whichever came first. She, too, was riled at the turn of events, but she was grateful that Dr. Horacek DID acknowledge paternity of her. What remained was whether he would agree to be her dad. That part, she intended to find out, if her mother would allow sanity to prevail. The next statement by Dr. Horacek fanned her hopes.

"Barbara, let's not spoil the day by intractable squabbling. You don't know how both of you have made my day today. I can tell you in all honesty that I am one lucky son of a bitch. You called me that many years ago, remember? And you were about to call me that again today, before Miss Sanders interrupted you. Only that you forgot to add the adjective 'lucky'. For me, this is how I see it: What would have been, eighteen years ago, has come full circle to be. You are her mom. I am her father. Whether we like it or not, the three of us in this room are family, even if a loose one. So, I am still a lucky son of a bitch."

"Don't brag about it," Barbara retorted, still defiantly petulant.

"I won't, although I have the right," Dr. Horacek replied, half appeasing and half mocking. "When I finish my story, you will, perhaps, see what I mean and you will count yourself lucky, too, if you can calm down enough to dismount your high horse of righteous anger."

Barbara started to retort, but caught the glare in Crystal's glance and retreated into her corner of the sofa, squirming. She sat back, pouting slightly, crossed her legs, and folded her arms across her chest without a word, seething impotently like a restrained tigress. Dr. Horacek shifted his weight in the chair, sat up, looked straight at Crystal, and began his story.

"My real name is Josef Ezra Ben Murdoch. My ancestry is not strictly Bohemian, but Jewish. My family history is quite a checkered one and I will not bore you with it. Suffice it to say that our family name had to be changed from Murdoch to Horacek for survival reasons. That is how my grandparents escaped the gas chambers and were able to migrate from Bavaria to Schellingwoude in Amsterdam, in the Spring of 1945. In 1955, my parents decided to migrate once more from Amsterdam to the United States of America. Born in Amsterdam in December of 1945, on the Feast of the Holy Family, I was christened Josef Bernard. Although my parents were Jewish, they were influenced more by the cultural milieu of Christendom than by traditional Judaism. So, I was christened and dedicated to the foster father of Jesus and the husband of Mary. I was almost 9 years old at the time we came to the United States. That year, something very tragic happened in our family, and to this day, I am still thinking that that incident may have been the catalyst in my father's decision to migrate. It was also an incident that left an indelible mark on my memory and, perhaps, contributed to my future life and career as an OB/GYN.

My auntie, Susana, my dad's only sister, was nursing a pregnancy. For some reason that nobody could tell, she went into labor on a certain day in the seventh month, and was taken to the hospital. The doctors decided to deliver the child by caesarian section. By the time she was operated upon, the child had already died in her womb. My auntie died of complications five days later. I was seriously scarred by that incident because I was close to my auntie. Though it's fuzzy in my mind now, it must have been then that I decided that I would grow up to be a medical doctor. When I finally entered medical school, my choice of specialty was definitely influenced by the memory of what happened to my auntie."

Dr. Horacek's story was fascinating and Crystal listened with rapt attention. Barbara was enchanted, too, but pretended nonchalance. She didn't want to give him the satisfaction of knowing she enjoyed his story. Dr. Horacek's story was fast-paced. He described his years at Berkeley School of Medicine, where he joined the Theta Kappa Epsilon fraternity, and adopted the code name, California 249. He explained that the code name was a simple way of referencing where he resided in apartment 249 in California Hall on the west side of the campus. He explained that his first cultural awakening occurred at Berkeley, where he met two African members of the fraternity who, according to his honest judgment, were sort of prodigies.

"One of them was Martin Osei Damkwa, from Ghana, and the other was Barnaby Edidiong Eshiet, from Nigeria, the first son of the Chief of the Annang tribe. He was always vain and boastful and hated his first name, which, according to him, was a symbol of European colonization of the mind of the African man. So, he eventually switched the order of his names altogether, and started going by Edidiong Eshiet. They were always impeccably dressed, and Edidiong eventually attached the title 'Prince' to his name and went by Prince Edidiong till we graduated from medical school and dispersed, as it were, for internship. Dr. Damkwa went back to Ghana and, last I heard about him, became the Minster of Health in his country.

"Though Dr. Eshiet was the youngest among us, he always seemed to be ahead of his years. He was always current with political news and very opinionated, very antagonistic toward the white man. He couldn't get over the fact that his people were colonized, and he viewed apartheid in South Africa as the greatest evil of the twentieth century. Academically, he was very intelligent. He was so enamored of genetics that he nearly ditched obstetrics for genetic engineering. He, in fact, got me interested in genetics, too, and that's how we ended up applying to do our internship at Norfolk, which was the university bold enough, at that time, to make forays into uncharted territories of human reproductive technology. The irony of it all was that, with all his vitriolic anger against the white man, Dr. Eshiet applied for and ended up with an internship mentored by the Joneses— Georgeanna and Howard Jones—a couple who had done extensive work on *in vitro fertilization* with a British scientist by the name of Robert Edwards in the late '60s. Though retired then, from Johns Hopkins, the Joneses were still enthusiastic about their work in reproductive technology and, in 1980, succeeded in opening an IVF clinic in the Eastern Virginia School of Medicine in Norfolk, resolutely spurred on, perhaps, by the proven success of their former co-researcher, Robert Edwards, who, in 1978, brought the first IVF-engineered baby, Louise Joy Brown, into the world. The media called her a 'test tube' baby then.

"Telling you honestly, I still remember it as if it was yesterday," Dr. Horacek smiled, as if ruminating to himself. "Reading about it in the London Times before we could get to the Journal of Reproductive Science, everyone went berserk at Berkeley. It was a collective achievement for the scientific world. In fact, I remember trying awkwardly to mimic Neil Armstrong: 'one small test tube for Robert Edwards, one giant engineering feat for mankind'. For me and my fellow students, it was like the scientist could now replicate God's work: create a human being. From that time on, we read up every publication on IVF. Edidiong became insatiably voracious. That is, of course, how he got wind of the Joneses' earlier association with Robert Edwards. And what better couple to get as mentors. He did not waste time writing to them, and he got me—in fact, forced me—to go along with his plan. It was like a dream come true when we arrived at Norfolk in the summer of 1981 to work as interns for Georgeanna and Howard. The Joneses were already working with two clients when we joined them. Unfortunately, they lost nerve during the winter months and dropped out of the program by the first week of February, after three attempts at implantation had failed. Luckily, a third client, who came into the program in the middle of January, stayed. She was a school teacher from Massachusetts by the name of Carr—Julie or Jolie—I can't recall exactly which, but..."

"Judith," Barbara interrupted, to Dr. Horacek's surprise. "Judith Carr. I met her in her third trimester, October of 1981, when I came to register."

"You met her? That's right!" Dr. Horacek concurred, excitedly. You have a photographic memory, Barbara," he complimented genuinely. Then added for Crystal's benefit, "Your mother has a magnetic memory."

"Well, don't labor that too much," Barbara demurred. "I only remember her because of the incident with the pet hamster, remember?"

"Oh, yeah, you're right. We had to do a little bit of hamster chasing. Boy! That was funny!" Dr. Horacek recalled, chuckling.

"What was it about the hamster?" Crystal inquired.

"It got mischievous," Barbara replied.

"Well, Mrs. Carr used to come to the clinic with a pintsize pet hamster tucked away in her handbag," Dr. Horacek filled in the story. "On this particular day, as she got up to go have her vital signs taken, the little trouble maker decided to jump out of the bag and explore the territory. Boy, it took two interns and three nurses to rein the little explorer back into its nest."

"And she kept shrieking with laughter whenever the little animal would duck a hand reaching to catch it and the intern or nurse would nearly fall," Barbara recalled.

"That was the lady. You remember her very well," Dr. Horacek replied, still excited at the memory of it all. "She was a pleasant lady, and determined, too. In fact, I still believe it was her high spirits and positive attitude that made her our first success in a series of experiments. When her child finally came on December 28th that year, it was the crowning glory of the Joneses' life's work, and ourselves, who made up the team. I can't erase from my memory the look on Howard's face after the umbilical cord was cut and the baby gave a healthy cry, protesting a slight whack on the butt by the head nurse. His eyes were huge with excitement as he pulled down his mask below his jawline, smiled from cheek to cheek, and announced, 'well folks. It's a girl'! as if it wasn't already quite obvious."

"I believe, too, that she was the reason why I was determined to go through with the surrogacy," Barbara recalled with conviction. "At the initial stage, I was plagued by fear and numbing doubts. All sorts of questions came to my mind, but listening to her story, and seeing her fully pregnant and counting days, I decided to go ahead with the plan and not look back."

"So, that's when you were trying to have the baby for the couple that you told me about?" Crystal asked, trying not to sound judgmental.

"Yeah," Barbara replied ruefully. "Isn't that strange? Having a baby for someone else?"

"Stranger still, is having a brother whose person or whereabouts I neither know nor imagine," Crystal countered aloud. "Suppose one day I meet him and fall in love with him?"

"Ouch! Crysie!" Barbara bolted upright in her seat. "God forbid!"

"It's possible, Mom," Crystal said, evidently concerned.

"God forbid such things from happening," Barbara replied, forcefully, as if her sheer vehemence could prevent it. "Quit reading that crap from Sophocles and Freud."

"Mom, it's not about Sophocles and Freud. This is something that could happen. In any case, I'm not going to wait for God to forbid it," Crystal replied, almost scandalizing her mom. "I am going to do something to forbid it myself."

Crystal reclined back resolutely in the sofa. Something in the tone of her voice told Barbara and Dr. Horacek that she was proposing using the same method she used to find her biological father to search for her biological brother whom she had never met. Barbara knew that Crystal could, and would, do it. The thought of it awoke a barrage of mixed feelings inside of Barbara: wanting Crystal to pursue this, and not wanting her to. Dr. Horacek became convinced that the story of his life and the lives of the two beautiful women sitting in his drawing room across from him was beginning to fill out like a stack of puzzle pieces falling into place. And he did not know what he should do about it, or if he should do anything about it, but wait to only fill in the details whenever the ball landed squarely in his court, as it did at that moment concerning Crystal. He rooted for the latter.

"Well, Barbara," he began, softly. "The Oedipus scenario is not avoided because one ignores Freud or Sophocles. The opposite might be a wiser course of action and an antidote to Murphy's Law. One doesn't have to wait for something to eventually go wrong because it could go wrong in the first place. Certain situations can always be preempted."

"Well, I don't know." Barbara shifted uncomfortably in her seat. "I don't know. This is getting more complicated and I am getting tired."

"That's why we should let her," Dr. Horacek replied. "You won't be the one to search. You are still ethically bound by your contract. And me, though I was an intern then, and not directly involved in the contract, I am implicated and, as such, ethically bound, too. We don't do anything ethically wrong if a third-party stakeholder who's directly concerned does the digging." Barbara started to respond, but thought the better of it, and kept mum. After all, he was right. Dr. Horacek turned to Crystal again and said, "Whatever plan you have, Miss Sanders, I support you. But, as you can see, we only need to come in when the case has unfolded itself."

"I know," Crystal said in throwaway tones. "All the ethical humbug and contracts. I thank God I have signed nothing with anybody to block my quest. At least I now know who I am and can determine my personality bearings. But I'm still curious to hear the rest of your story, Sir, like how you knocked up my mom and she didn't know."

"He didn't knock me up," Barbara retorted vehemently. "He messed with my uterus with a syringe and a pipette."

"At your consent," Dr. Horacek added, stifling a chuckle.

"Yeah, at my consent," Barbara concurred, sneeringly.

"So, how does that change the fact that you were knocked up, and you didn't know your baby daddy?" Crystal pursued her vengeful humor, to the surprise and amusement of Dr. Horacek.

"I said he didn't knock me up!" Barbara was beginning to get riled. Her voice went a decibel higher. "He did it with a pipette and…Oh gosh! Now… that didn't come out right," Barbara said with embarrassment, holding out a finger to stop anyone from saying anything.

Dr. Horacek cracked up in laughter, "I'm so sorry, Barbara. It's the way you said it…."

"I said, THAT didn't come out right," Barbara retorted, petulantly, sticking out her chin like a defiant teenager.

"Okay, I got you," Dr. Horacek replied, holding out his two hands like he was parrying off an attack. He was even taken aback when, glancing at Crystal, he observed that the latter, looking at her mother coyly from the side of her eyes, and smiling impishly, pursued her vengeful teasing.

"Mom, accept it," she pressured, patronizingly. "You were knocked up with me and, like a clueless teenager, you didn't know your baby daddy. Until I brought you here."

"Alright, alright! Have it your way, spoiled brat," Barbara irritatingly conceded defeat. "I was knocked up using a pipette and a syringe. With you. But I was not a clueless teenager. I consented by signing a contract. The contract prevented me from knowing my...'baby daddy'. And you didn't bring me here. I brought you. At least I bought your ticket. Now, can the two of you please quit amusing yourselves at my expense?"

Dr. Horacek suspected that mother and daughter were engaged in some game familiar to them, but he didn't know if Crystal was kidding or serious. He decided to ask. "Are you upset with her, Miss Sanders?"

"With whom? My mom? Oh, no. No, Sir," Crystal replied. "Don't mind her, Sir. She's not upset, either. She knows I'm just teasing her. Truth is, Mom got knocked up with me, and, like a clueless teenager, she didn't know her baby daddy until I brought her to him. That's my story, and I'm sticking to it," she concluded with a Collin Raye line, sitting up with pride and looking sad and amused at the same time.

"Dr. Horacek, please, continue with your story," Barbara said with measured calmness, rolling her eyes at her impertinent daughter. "Don't mind Crysie. She's a spoiled brat. I know it wasn't ethical for you to tell me you switched places with my donor, but I'm dying to know how you lived with that secret for so long, how switching roles and becoming my sperm donor wasn't unethical, but telling me would have been unethical."

"Switching sperm donors wasn't forbidden in the contract," Dr. Horacek hedged wisely. "But revealing the identity of the donor was." Then he continued with his story. "Fast forward fourteen years. Let's leave the story of your surrogacy years and focus on Miss Sanders. What I did here at my clinic when you worked for me, remember, wasn't just getting women pregnant by IVF. I was secretly experimenting with the new genetic thing that was going to be cutting-edge inOB/GYN practice. I was reading up on, and experimenting with, a new strategy for testing the genes to detect the ones that might be responsible for the early or late onset of certain diseases like Down Syndrome, Tay-Sachs disease, Cystic Fibrosis, Parkinson's Disease, Turner Syndrome, and breast cancer—what is now widely called preimplantation genetic testing. Well, the guy who showed up to donate…we found an aneuploidy condition in his genes, susceptible for Turner Syndrome. His gene had twenty-five chromosomes."

"You're kidding!" Barbara sat up, confused.

"No, I kid you not," Dr. Horacek replied, matter-of-factly. "And considering the time frame and the fact that you wanted the child to be your graduation gift—remember, you told me that—I had to do something fast. I had no time to wait for another donor to show up for me to go through the experimental testing again from the beginning. I felt that you were going to be deeply disappointed if you knew. Believe you me, Barbara, I agonized over that decision for a long time. Since I had already done the test on myself, I decided to donate my sperm. Remember the night you blew up at me and called me…well, 'lucky son of a bitch'?"

"Yes, I remember," Barbara replied, ruefully. "Looks like you still are… because as it stands now, I can't even sue you."

"Yes, Barbara, I still am," Dr. Horacek replied in a tone devoid of triumph. "I realized that night how seriously I had wronged you by becoming blind to your crush and yearning over me, because I was ambitiously pursuing the success of my career and the flourishing of my new clinic. But the damage was already done. I was married, at least legally. So, secretly donating my sperm so I could meet the deadline for your child to be born around your graduation time was my private way of atoning for the emotional injury I had inflicted on you. It was a way of satisfying myself that I had compensated you."

"That was very selfish of you," Barbara responded, without emotion.

"Yes. I realize that now," Dr. Horacek agreed, sincerely. "But I WILL claim credit for two things, though: You have a beautiful young lady who will not suffer the ravages of Turner Syndrome and you had her as your graduation gift, just on time. Those two things were because of my efforts."

"Shall I decorate you with a gold medal?" Barbara quipped, somewhat hurtfully.

"No," Dr. Horacek said. "What I have now, what has come to me—a beautiful, smart, and intelligent young lady who happens to be part of me because I donated that late afternoon in the lab here at my clinic—is worth more than a thousand gold medals. What's more, the woman sitting across from me right now, who doesn't know how right she was when she called me a 'lucky son of a bitch', is worth more than another thousand medals, if she would quit pretending to be mad at me, show some understanding and forgiveness, taking into account that providence in its own time has brought around full circle—360 degrees—what was meant to be." Dr. Horacek paused, got up, and went to the window, peeped outside for a few seconds, and then came back to squat before Barbara Sanders. "Barbara, do you see what I see? You are here, my child's mother. I am here, your child's father. Our child, a beautiful, brilliant young lady is here. All of us in this one room. Isn't that what is called a 'family'? And all of it, on my birthday!" He got up, breathing hard and looking like someone dazed witless.

"Excuse me, Sir," Crystal called in measured tones. "Does that mean you agree to be my dad? That was going to be my last question for you."

"Miss Sanders," Dr. Horacek replied, still looking dazedly happy. "What idiot of a man would say 'No' to being a dad to his exquisitely beautiful blood who has flown more than a thousand miles to seek him out and offer him redemption and forgiveness? Miss Sanders, I…"

"Call me Crysie, then," Crystal interrupted.

"Okay… If you agree to call me 'Dad', Crysie," Dr. Horacek replied.

"Yes, Dad!" Crystal replied excitedly, springing up from her seat.

"Crysie, come here and give your undeserving dad his first hug," Dr. Horacek almost shouted. He extended his arms and Crystal ran into his embrace, sobbing loudly and repeating 'yes, Daddy' over and over again.

Father and daughter held tightly to each other for about a minute. Then Dr. Horacek extended his hand toward Barbara. She hesitated for a second, then noticing Crystal looking expectantly at her, joined them. For a long time, father, mother, and daughter held tightly to one another, sobbing uncontrollably and bathing one another's shoulders with tears. Then they quietly and slowly began to disengage themselves. Dr. Horacek leaned over and kissed Barbara's face several times in quick successions, making sucking sounds with the pecks.

"What are you doing?" she protested, feebly.

"Kissing away your tears, the tears you shed for me over the years," Dr. Horacek said, still kissing her.

"Eew! That must be quite salty," Barbara said, making faces. "Quit licking my face like an overjoyed dog." She moved her face from side to side to evade him, vexingly amused.

"I like the salty taste," Dr. Horacek said, unrepentantly. "Salt preserves, you know. It's the best and first preservative that the primitive man discovered. So, I am redeemed and preserved because I have family." He started shouting and cavorting like a crazy man. "I have family! I have family! I am redeemed!" He cavorted like an amateur trying a foxtrot for the first time.

"Crysie, your dad's gone crazy on us," Barbara said, chuckling with amusement, surprised at this side of Dr. Horacek, which she was seeing for the first time.

"I'm crazy, too, Mom!" Crystal replied, catching her dad's euphoria. "I have family! I have family!" She echoed his shouts.

Daughter and father held hands, chanting, "I have family," prancing and cavorting like two happy stags. Eventually, they grabbed Barbara and forced her to form a triangle with them as they broke into Sister Sledge's *We are Family.*" Laughing and giggling, they sang the song, first skipping to the left, and then to the right, and to the left again. They sang and danced until they eventually fell on the sofa in one happy giggling heap.

THANKSGIVING AT Barbara Sanders's house was sweeter than those of previous years. It was really a Thanksgiving for Barbara, in every sense of the word, because it had a personal context other than just recalling the first Thanksgiving that was celebrated one year after the arrival of the Mayflower on the shores of the New World. Barbara Sanders was celebrating her engagement to Dr. Josef Horacek, and Crystal was celebrating her newfound family in both parents, and she would forever wonder what a lucky year it had been for her. Her first visit to her dad in Norfolk, Virginia was quite dramatic, but it fulfilled her dream beyond her wildest expectations. She had feared that Dr. Horacek would deny paternity and not want to be involved in either her life or her mother's. It turned out that just the opposite was the case. He had tried to prevail on them to stay for a few more days before returning to Texas, but Barbara had to return to work. Before they left to go back, a trade-off deal was struck. They would return to spend the last week of the long summer vacation with him again in Norfolk. That was a fair deal, as Barbara could use her paid time off. Then, Dr. Horacek would spend the Christmas holidays with them in Texas, during which he intended to visit and reconnect with his old friend and medical school colleague, Dr. Edidiong Barnaby Eshiet, so they could catch up on the latest scientific development in the OB/GYN world.

Their one-week summer visit was still too short for Crystal, but it was a very sweet one. She not only had the opportunity to bond with her dad, but she also got to know a few of her dad's connections, chief among whom were the President and the Registrar of the University of Virginia, Norfolk, who had been invited to the dinner that her dad held in her honor—to introduce her, his daughter, to the Norfolk medical science community. She knew her dad was paving a pathway for her to get direct admission into the university come autumn 2013, when she would finish her final year at Christo Rey High School. Crystal couldn't be more pleased with herself. Over and above all these, it was her parents' eventual engagement after nearly twenty-five years of knowing each other that crowned the year for Crystal.

You could say she saw it coming. Shortly after they came back from the first visit, her mother had hit the gym, and it took Crystal almost a week to realize what was happening. She also noticed that her mother invested a lot more money in assorted cosmetic and beauty products and, although she knew why, she couldn't resist teasing her.

"Mom, you are behaving strangely these days," Crystal had said on one occasion when her mom had returned from her usual work-out routine. "Are you alright?"

"What do you mean, Crysie?" Barbara had asked.

"You're wearing out the floors of the county gym, and getting a little too hard on those facial creams and skin toners!" Crystal had responded, then added, "If I catch you with some hunk, I'm gonna tell Dad on you."

"Such disrespect!" Barbara had retorted, petulantly, and stalked away into the bathroom for a shower. Crystal had smiled furtively, knowing her mother wasn't really mad at her for the remark. And she was right. As she turned on the shower and got under it, Barbara also permitted herself a coy little smile because, for one, her daughter's teasing meant that the results of her efforts were showing. She knew Crystal wasn't really thinking she was doing all she did because there was a man she wanted to 'catch'. But she also knew that Crystal was wrong if she thought she did all that to impress Dr. Horacek on their next visit. She did it for him, quite alright, but not to 'catch' him, rather to seduce and reject him to punish him by way of revenge. For the one week they would be together, she planned to tease him incessantly and drive him nuts with her feminine wiles, to make him see what he had been missing and regret the many years he had punitively ignored her. Later on, Barbara would wonder what mischievous imp had put that idea into her head because it didn't work.

It was on the fourth day of their visit and they had just driven two hours back from the Science Museum of Virginia on West Broad Street, Richmond. Barbara was about to go inside the house when Dr. Horacek insisted there was something he needed to show her in the examination room to seek her opinion. Grudgingly, she followed him into the clinic, which was strangely silent. Barbara noticed that a thick curtain divider stretched from one wall to the opposite wall at the east end of the large rectangular exam room, and she was about to inquire whether the staff had a day off when Dr. Horacek spoke and distracted her attention.

"You're going to find it strange because it's not the way you saw it last. I modified it," he said, grabbing her arm and gently propelling her toward the exam bed. "Here. Sit down, pull off your shoes, and slowly lie down."

"Wait," Barbara said, a bit unsure what Dr. Horacek was up to. "Isn't this the same bed…?"

"Yes, it is," Dr. Horacek replied. "My mistake. I'm sorry. I modified the wall structure, not the furniture. I should've said that. It's the same bed you laid on when I did the gametes transfer." Noticing the frown of confusion on Barbara's face, he added, "Don't be afraid. I just want you to perform a simple experiment and then tell me about your feeling. Close your eyes and lie down. Imagine you are back twenty years ago, and I am performing the transfer procedure on you, but with your eyes closed."

Part of Barbara wanted to protest the little charade as childish and ridiculous, and another part convinced her to be adventurous and follow his instructions to see what he was up to. She hesitantly lay down and closed her eyes.

"Relax, breathe deeply, count up to ten, then open your eyes and sit up," Dr. Horacek directed, sounding serious.

"What?" Barbara asked with eyes still closed. "Are you into magic now? I thought scientists didn't believe in magic?"

"Barbs, please, quit talking and keep counting," Dr. Horacek pleaded. He counted ten in his mind and then said, "Sit up and open your eyes."

Barbara slowly sat up and opened her eyes. Dr. Horacek was in a genuflecting posture like a pious pilgrim in front of the statue of a saint famous for granting instant favors. In his left hand, he held out a small black jewelry box with a sparkling diamond ring ensconced in a velvet bed of opal blue. Then he asked, "Barbara Maria Sanders, will you marry me?"

Barbara looked at the sparkling diamond ring in the box, looked at Dr. Horacek's face, looked again at the ring, and then slowly and silently held out her left hand. Dr. Horacek took the gesture as a 'yes' and quickly slipped the ring on Barbara's finger. She looked again at the ring and blurted out, almost breathless, "Yes…" Then aloud, "Yes, I will marry you." Then she slapped him—hard—across the face.

"Ouch! That hurt!" Dr. Horacek yelled in pain. But before he could protest further, she grabbed him and kissed him hard and long on the lips, so hard that he feared he might not come away from the amorous act with his lips intact. As if on cue, the curtain on the east end of the room rolled open and a crowd of three male medical assistants, five nurses, and two receptionists erupted into a loud, merry applause which had been delayed a bit because of the unexpected slap. Barbara was startled and embarrassingly surprised. She now understood the unusual silence when she first walked into the clinic. It was all planned. She felt simultaneously stupid and overjoyed, and started giggling like a silly, gawky teenager. Crystal appeared from nowhere and started singing Isaiah:

*I have loved you, with an everlasting love. I have loved you, and you are mine.*

After the singing, the crowd erupted into one more applause as Dr. Horacek gathered Barbara in his arms and kissed her back. Tears flowed freely. Nurse Jackson, a.k.a. JJ, wept with abandon, and joyfully refused to be consoled. She had been privy to the unrequited love that her friend nursed for their boss over the years, and couldn't believe that Barbara Sanders could finally be engaged to the love of her life, and with a grown child who was their biological daughter. By now it was no longer grapevine gossip, but an open story that Crystal was Dr. Horacek's biological daughter. Since it was 3:30 in the afternoon, and everybody was too excited to behave themselves, Dr. Horacek closed the clinic for the rest of the day and herded everybody into his house behind the clinic for an engagement party. Later that night, after their first-ever love making, which, years later, they jokingly called 'catch-up/ make-up sex', Dr. Horacek wondered aloud, "Barbs, what was that for?"

"What was 'what' for?" Barbara asked in return.

"That slap across my face." he replied. "Did you know that hurt?"

"Thank God it did," she replied. "That was just a small price to pay for still being one lucky SOB."

"Will I be paying for it forever?"

"No, silly," she replied, sweetly. "That was your last installment." She kissed him and rolled onto her side of the bed and went to sleep, wondering if Crystal would tease her the next day for not waiting to sleep with her fiancé.

For the remaining three days, the newly constituted Horacek family spent a lot of time excitedly planning their next time together, which was going to be at Christmas of 2012, in Missouri City, Texas. Everyone walked on air until it was time to say their goodbyes. Tears again flowed freely and when Barbara and her daughter finally boarded their plane back to Texas, it was with the consolation that their Christmas holidays together would be even sweeter.

So, it was that, instead of teasing and punishing Dr. Horacek, Barbara got wooed, won, and engaged. She would wonder why a woman's heart always betrayed her and made her fall for the man who rejected her, in the first place, and later went back to reclaim her. 'Must be the reason why the ancients referred to women as the "weaker sex,"' she thought. 'Or, maybe it is naturally designed just that way by providence, so Hollywood can make movies with the ending: "And they lived happily ever after".'

---

When school resumed in the fall of 2012, Crystal Sanders had told her friends about her newfound identity. She wasted no time after coming back from her summer bonding with her dad, in having all her official documents redone to bear her new name. She, in fact, dropped Sanders as her surname and adopted Horacek, a decision which pleased her dad so much that he promised her a big Christmas gift which he didn't reveal. Crystal was agog with expectant excitement at the prospect of the 'big gift'. Although she would have given anything to know what it was that her father was planning to give her, she decided to wallow in the suspense and did not even dare to guess so as not to take the fun out of it. Altogether, it would have been a perfect beginning to the school year, except for one thing, which, though they saw it coming, no one actually thought about how they would handle it: Kelechi Okubueze Jr. had graduated in May of that year, and as he had planned, travelled to Nigeria to embark on a search for his biological dad. He knew it wasn't going to be a long, drawn-out adventure, having been armed by his mother with all the information he needed. For one, that meant that Edo-Mma would feel the absence of her boyfriend, and Crystal thought she and Josh would not know how to sympathize with her or whether to sympathize at all. Second, it meant that Crystal would have nobody to help her in her quest to track down her brother, the first child whom Barbara Sanders bore for a couple by surrogacy.

As far as computer wizardry was concerned, Kelechi was their eye and champion. He had revealed to them that he got all his training from belonging to a group of freelance prodigies who called themselves the "Geek Squad". He had warned Josh and Crystal, even Edo-Mma, to keep their mouths shut about his hacking activities because, apart from being illegal, it was against the *Geek Squad* code of behavior, as they strictly discouraged members from using their skill in that direction. The big disappointment was that although Kelechi had said he would be back from Nigeria by the end of the summer, it turned out that nobody was sure if he would ever come back to the States. Crystal Horacek did not know whether to worry about her friend, Edo-Mma's loneliness, or her stalled project. There, again, fate seemed to deal her a lucky card. The solution to the situation came from Edo-Mma herself.

So, it was, that on a certain day, sitting on the wooden bench of the school football pit and munching on their usual break-time snacks of peanut chocolate bars and chips, wondering what their final year at Christo Rey was going to look like and bemoaning the situation of things, an idea suddenly occurred to Edo-Mma.

"Wait a minute, Crysie," Edo-Mma said. "Why can't we ask your dad to do the tracking himself?"

"Well, Edo, I don't know," Crystal replied, with measured skepticism. "He might start giving me his usual lectures on the ethics of confidentiality."

"Crysie, you've got to ask him," Edo-Mma persuaded. "After all, it's not like there's a whole lot of secrecy about it now."

"Yeah, Crysie," Josh interjected. "If he told your mama he was the father of the first child, as well as you, there isn't no more confidentiality there, man. Just ask him. The worst he can say would be 'No'."

"My dad can possibly help, too," Edo-Mma pressed on, beginning to get excited. "They worked together and, good thing, your dad is coming to Houston in December."

"Well, I'll try," Crystal finally gave in. "I'll mention it when I call him tonight. Or, should I wait till he comes?"

As Josh and Edo-Mma unanimously disagreed and urged her not to wait till December, Edo-Mma's phone gave a text message signal. It was Kelechi. Edo-Mma swiped her finger across the LED screen of her phone to reveal a picture of Kelechi swathed in local Nigerian attire, sitting among other young men of his age, similarly dressed, and holding up what seemed like animal horns. Edo-Mma knew it was the horn used for drinking the local palm wine. They sat around a table with plates and bowls which seemed to have food remains in them. Underneath the picture was the short inscription: *Yam Festival.* Kelechi seemed to be laughing hard and having a good time, like one who'd had too much food and wine.

"Oh, my God!" Edo-Mma exclaimed, exasperated. "This boy is no longer coming back to the States!"

Josh and Crystal rushed and huddled over Edo-Mma's shoulder to look at Kelechi's picture.

"Boy!" Josh exclaimed. "The guy's having a good time. Look at him laughing with his mouth wide like a yawning crock."

"Yeah, looks like they've had plenty to eat and drink," Crystal remarked, woefully. More worried now about her friend, she added, "He'll come back. He can't just up and quit like that."

"He graduated," Edo-Mma said, a shade too loud.

"Sorry, I didn't mean coming back to Christo Rey," Crystal said, conscious that her first statement of assurance fell flat and, instead of consoling, irritated her friend. "You could go to Nigeria to visit him. Couldn't you?"

"That can only happen after I graduate, and only if I still have feelings for him then," Edo-Mma said resolutely. Then added, "And I probably will still love him if he keeps in touch the way he does now. He calls every other day and sends an occasional text as he just did."

"See, the guy's big-time interested in you," Josh said with an air of final proof.

"He'll come back," Crystal repeated.

"He had better," Edo-Mma replied, menacingly, as the bell shrilled, signaling the end of break. "If I have to go to him, I will whip him, pinch him by the ear, and drag him back here."

Crystal and Josh cracked up at the thought of Kelechi, almost a giant, being flogged, pinched on the ear, and dragged back to the States by a girl half his size. They put their trash into the dumpster and trooped back to class, still laughing. Edo-Mma knew why they were laughing. She tried gallantly to stifle her own laughter and only ended up pouting and looking amused at the same time.

# PART III

*Then Nathan said to David:*
*"Thou art the man."*

2 SAMUEL 12:7

"ALL RISE! First circuit court in session. Honorable Justice Anieno Montgomery presiding." The bailiff, a tall and sturdily built gentleman, in a well-pressed khaki uniform spoke in a booming, but flat, baritone voice laced with a hint of boredom, indicative of an *ad nauseam* repetition of the same speech over the years. All in court stood to attention as Judge Montgomery, an equally tall and stately middle-aged woman in black gown, stepped up to the bench amidst the fading din that pervaded the court prior to her arrival. She sat down, raised her face, and swept the court sternly through her thick glasses, almost the size of aviation goggles, as judges do when about to start the business of the day. She had an almost square face with strong cheek bones. Her glasses rested on the ridge of a broad nose indicative of her African heritage. Her hair was combed Afro-style, too. She looked every inch a no-nonsense, learned, dispenser of justice. She oozed power, or at least tried to look it since, in spite of her veneer of sternness, there was something innately compassionate about her bearing. Having determined that the level of comportment in court was satisfactory, she nodded to the bailiff, who said curtly, "All sit."

No small shuffling followed the order as the court audience and jury took their seats, as though it were a long-yearned-for reprieve from holding their breath while they stood. The seating arrangement was adversarial, as was customary, with a central isle running from the front of the bench to the back of the court, effectively separating Fr. McCarthy and Stacy Donovan, his attorney, sitting by the desk on one side, from Edidiong and Ima Eshiet sitting behind another desk with Patrick Turner, their attorney. The jury of nine—four men and two women, all white, and one man and two women, all black—sat on pews on the left side of the judge's bench, all with businesslike demeanors. The rest of the audience consisted of family members and friends sitting behind their respective litigants. A handful of reporters, pressmen and women, with cameras swarmed the back of the court, ready to report on the proceedings of what, from all indications, was a high-profile case of discrimination in the Catholic Church.

Not that it was the first case of discrimination alleged in the Catholic Church, nor was the substance of it extraordinarily important, as others in the past were probably denied Holy Communion by their priests and acquiesced under the sanction. But it was the first time highly learned members of the Church dared to take it up as a court case. The sheer mettle of the couple who dared to drag such a powerful entity as the Catholic Church to court over such a seemingly light matter was novel, and the press, running pre-trial articles and opinion editorials, tended to lean heavily on the side of the couple, thus whipping up popular sympathy for them. Excitement filled the courtroom and, in fact the whole city of Houston, as people waited to read about or watch the big trial.

Inside the courthouse, the two attorneys—Turner on one side and Donovan on the other—silently flexed their legal muscles as they brought out papers from briefcases, arranging and shuffling them, putting some back or rummaging again for more, conferring in whispers with their respective clients and bobbing heads like victory was already a done deal for their side.

"Bailiff, call the case of the day," Judge Montgomery ordered.

"In the case of Eshiet and Eshiet versus the Reverend Cletus McCarthy and the Catholic Archdiocese of Galveston-Houston, will the plaintiffs indicate their presence in court?" the bailiff called out.

"We are present and ready, Your Honor," Patrick Turner responded, stood, and sat again.

"Will the defendants indicate their presence in court?" the bailiff called again.

"Your Honor, we are present," Stacy stood to respond, and sat down again.

"Thank you," Judge Montgomery acknowledged their presence. "Prosecuting counsel may proceed with the first witness."

Patrick Turner stood up, adjusted his tie and his pin-striped, custom-made grey suit, cleared his throat, and walked out from behind the desk.

"Your Honor, prosecution calls Dr. Ima Eshiet to the stand," he announced with a flourish. Ima Eshiet, who was sitting beside her husband behind the prosecuting counsel's desk, stood up and moved to stand in the dock. The bailiff approached and, holding a Holy Bible, invited her to place her left hand on it and raise the right.

"Do you solemnly swear by this holy book to tell the truth, the whole truth, and nothing but the truth, so help you God?" He rattled through the formula.

"I do," Ima Eshiet responded. The bailiff retired to his corner.

"For the record, Ma'am, could you state your name once more?" Patrick Turner asked, approaching her dock with measured steps.

"Ima Eshiet," she responded.

"Your profession?" he asked again, as a matter of red tape.

"I am a pediatrician by profession," she responded.

"From the facts of this case, I assume you are Catholic and a member of the Our Lady Queen of Peace Catholic Church. Am I correct in my assumption?"

"Yes, I have been a member of the Our Lady Queen of Peace Catholic Church for fifteen years," Ima Eshiet responded with a tinge of pride.

"And for those number of years you have been a good and practicing Catholic…"

"Objection," Stacy interrupted with a strong voice. "Counsel is leading the witness."

"Sustained," Judge Montgomery ruled, in the flat, boring tone that is characteristic of judges in that circumstance,

"I'll rephrase the question," Patrick Turner conceded. "Ma'am, would you describe your life as a Church member at Our Lady Queen of Peace for those fifteen years, please?"

"I have been a good practicing Catholic all these years," Ima Eshiet responded on cue, to the gladness of her attorney, who smiled faintly and nodded as she proceeded. "I am a member of the Gospel Choir, the Samaritan Ministry that caters to the bereaved, and the St. Vincent de Paul Society, where I contribute substantial amounts of food and clothing for the Society to reach out to the poor. I pay a monthly tithe of one thousand dollars every month."

"And for fifteen years, that must be quite an amount," Patrick Turner interjected.

"Yes," Ima Eshiet concurred. "Five years ago, I and my husband, we donated a set of cassocks for use by the altar servers. We also bought and donated the statue of Our Lady of Peace, made to order, for the Church's grotto."

"Are there any more …"

"Objection, Your Honor," Stacy shot up again. "The litany of Mrs. Eshiet's good works in the Church do not seem to be relevant to this case."

"Your Honor, I am trying to show the good will and love that the Eshiets have for their Church, and even their Pastor," Patrick Turner pled.

"Overruled," Judge Montgomery replied in the same flat tone.

"Are there any more things you remember, that you...?"

"Yes," Ima Eshiet, interjected before Patrick Turner could finish his question. "When Fr. McCarthy, our Pastor's house was renovated last year, we bought all the furniture in the sitting room from Gallery Furniture, and paid Hobby Lobby to decorate the sitting room, though we did these things anonymously." Ima Eshiet continued, beginning to sound maudlin and sentimental.

Fr. McCarthy fidgeted slightly in his seat and frowned at learning for the first time that the anonymous donors of his sitting room furniture and furnishings were the Eshiets. He did not like the way the case was proceeding and communicated his misgivings to Stacy in whispers.

"Any more to say, Dr. Eshiet?" Patrick Turner asked gently and ever more reverently.

"No," Ima Eshiet replied, softly blowing her nose into her handkerchief, more for effect than the need to do so. Then she continued with pathos, "I could go on, but I'm not here to toot my own horn."

"Ma'am, could you describe in detail what happened on the day you attended church and went up to receive Holy Communion and were denied?" Patrick Turner solicited, gently.

"I attended church, as usual, like any other parishioner," Ima Eshiet began her story. "When it was time for Communion, I walked up with other Communicants, as usual." She continued, sniffling a little. She told of how she approached Fr. McCarthy, stretched out her hand to receive Communion, and he asked her to move on because she was not in a state of grace to receive Communion. She recounted how she was shocked and for a moment stood stupefied until an usher came and directed her back to her seat. She was too stunned to notice that her husband was subjected to the same humiliation, but she later learned of it. By the end of her story, she was sobbing quietly into her handkerchief and expressing how emotionally scarred and ashamed she had been since then, so ashamed, in fact, that she couldn't even bear to face her friends to explain because, of course, she was still unable to make sense of such a disgracing experience at the hands of Fr. McCarthy.

Curiously, Patrick Turner did not ask her any further questions. He turned to Stacy and called out in the customary way, "Your witness," and took his seat.

"Ma'am, are you pregnant right now?" Stacy threw the question straight at Ima Eshiet.

"Yes," she responded curtly, feeling a bit caught off guard.

"How did you get pregnant?"

"By conception," Ima Eshiet responded, feigning surprise at being asked about what should be quite obvious. A spate of laughter broke out in the audience.

"Silence in the court!" Judge Montgomery ordered sternly, banging her gavel at the same time. Then she addressed Ima Eshiet directly, "Ma'am, answer questions as you are asked. We are not here in court to play games with words."

"I'm answering as I am asked, Your Honor," Ima Eshiet responded, matter-of-factly. Patrick Turner smiled toothlessly and smugly.

"Of course, silly me. I had forgotten that people get pregnant by conception," Stacy continued unruffled. "Fair enough, Ma'am. As I can see, for a person of your educational standard, everything must be spelled out in simple terms for you to understand. I will do that now."

There was another round of laughter as Stacy smartly turned the tables on Ima Eshiet, who scowled slightly, but decided to eat the insult.

"Silence!" Judge Montgomery hammered the gavel again.

"Ma'am, what procedure did you use to conceive the baby?" Stacy proceeded, carefully this time. "Was it through normal sexual intercourse with your husband or through a procedure whereby your egg was fertilized in a petri dish outside your womb, and the fertilized egg reinserted in your womb?"

There was silence in the court. Ima Eshiet was silent, too, for a few seconds until the judge's voice prodded her. She glanced at Patrick Turner, who, himself, looked stunned, but decided not to object to the line of questioning Stacy had chosen to follow.

"Answer the question, Ma'am," Judge Montgomery ordered.

"It was through a procedure of external fertilization of my egg and reinsertion," Ima Eshiet replied.

"What do you call that procedure in medical terms, Ma'am?" Stacy pursued.

"It is called in vitro fertilization," Ima Eshiet responded, still wary.

"Now, you said the procedure involved fertilizing *your* egg," Stacy repeated Ima's statement for emphasis, then asked, "Was the egg really your own egg?"

"Objection!" Patrick Turner stood, raising his hand in protest. "Counsel is asking for sordid details that have no relevance to the case at hand."

"Your Honor, I am trying to let the court understand the nature of the procedure which constituted an offense in Catholic teaching and which led to the sanction for which the plaintiff is suing my client."

"Overruled," Judge Montgomery said. "Proceed carefully," she addressed Stacy.

"Thank you, Your Honor. I will," Stacy resumed her line of questioning.

"Ma'am, did you at any time solicit and pay for a donor egg from a certain Miss Kylie Gardner, a former graduate student of yours, to use in your bid to get pregnant?" Stacy was merciless in her questions. Even the court audience sat spellbound and very silent, wondering where all of this was leading. Ima Eshiet looked a bit unsettled. She glanced again at Patrick Turner, who nodded for her to answer in the affirmative.

"Yes, I did," she responded, still uncertain whether she should refuse to answer some of the questions. Her attorney had nodded his blessing. So, she decided to keep answering Stacy's questions until she couldn't really do so.

"So, the egg which was fertilized and implanted in your uterus, and which is the fetus growing inside of you now, thereby rendering you pregnant, was, indeed, NOT *your* egg?"

"Well..." Ima Eshiet hesitated. "Yes and no." There was muted murmuring and Judge Montgomery banged her gavel.

"Can you explain what you mean by 'yes and no'?"

"When my egg was screened and found to contain weak elements in the mitochondria, the yolk from Kylie's egg was removed and the yolk from my egg was injected into her albumen by a process called *ooplasmic* transfer. Then the redesigned egg was fertilized by Edy's sperm, that is, my husband's sperm."

There was a confused murmuring in court. Even Judge Montgomery sat forward a little to listen with rapt attention to Ima Eshiet describing how she got pregnant.

"So, Dr. Eshiet, if the egg that was fertilized by your husband's sperm carried the yolk from you and what you call the mitochondria from Miss Kylie, would I be correct in asserting that the fetus you are carrying in your womb when born as a child will technically have THREE parents, instead of the traditional two?"

"Yes," Ima Eshiet answered curtly, without adding any other statements. The audience gasped. This was a novel issue. Although pregnancy by in vitro fertilization was widespread and taken for granted by many, as a form of reproduction technology that had come to stay, conceiving a child that would literally have three parents was not yet a common occurrence. It came as a shock to the court audience. Reporters kept darting out to call information to their paper or TV headquarters and sneaking in again to cover the proceedings as the case progressed. Patrick Turner was feverishly taking notes on his pad, occasionally glancing up to assure his client that all was still okay. He kept exchanging words in fierce whispers with Dr. Edidiong Eshiet, who seemed agitated at his wife being subjected to such ruthless grilling by the defense counsel. Stacy continued pacing menacingly as she bored down on her quarry.

"Dr. Ima Eshiet," Stacy addressed her with a formality that indicated she was about to deliver the death knell. "You have been a member of Our Lady of Peace Catholic Church for fifteen years, but for how long have you been a Catholic?"

"I have been a faithful Catholic all my life," she answered, adopting a stance of superiority that failed to hold.

"I thought so," Stacy concurred, patronizingly. "As one who has been a faithful Catholic all your life, would you say that your action—that is, the procedure that you used to get pregnant—is acceptable in Catholic moral teaching?"

"Objection!" Patrick Turner interjected. "Catholic moral teaching is not my client's area of expertise, nor is the morality of my client's action the point in question here. Discrimination is."

"Sustained," Judge Montgomery concurred.

"Let me rephrase my question," Stacy stood her ground. "Dr. Eshiet, was there ever a time when your Pastor, the Reverend McCarthy, discussed the morality of in vitro fertilization in Catholic teaching with you and your husband?"

"Yes, but…"

"Did he explain to you that it was not morally acceptable?"

"But he…"

"Yes or no, did he explain to you that such procedures as you have described were morally unacceptable?" Stacy insisted.

"But he…."

"Yes or no, did he?" Stacy bored down unrelentingly.

"Objection, Your Honor!" Patrick Turner started.

"Overruled. Answer the question, Ma'am," Judge Montgomery ruled.

"Yes," Ima Eshiet finally responded, grudgingly. She was upset at being rattled that way by a woman whom, given a different context, she would have put in her place.

"No more questions," Stacy announced, walking back to her desk with such power and self-confidence that made the audience murmur in approval. They had never witnessed a more ruthless cross examination. Dr. Ima Eshiet stood down and proceeded to her place beside her husband. Both husband and wife were visibly fuming. Fr. McCarthy sat still and gave away no emotions. He reached out, furtively, and shook Stacy's hand on the sly as the latter resumed her seat beside him.

"Mr. Turner, your next witness?" Judge Montgomery called out.

"Your Honor, Counsel calls Dr. Edidiong Eshiet," Patrick Turner announced again with a flourish, but without a smile this time.

Dr. Edidiong Eshiet was a tall gentleman, an inch or two above six feet. He had the physique of a wrestler, with broad chest and bulky shoulders, and walked straight like an army general marching on parade ground. He stood and walked into the dock, carrying his entire six feet two inches effortlessly. The bailiff administered the usual oath and he took his seat, leaning back haughtily, as though he was the one about to ask the questions. He sported a well-trimmed mustache that gave his broad visage a stern look. His hair was well-trimmed, too. He wore a well-starched white shirt with cufflinks and a tie, and looked every inch a prosperous medical VIP and someone who commanded power. Even Patrick Turner, with his custom-made suit, paled in comparison. As Dr. Edidiong Eshiet sat waiting for the first question from his attorney, it was obvious that he wasn't amused at the way his wife was rattled by the defense counsel. The court was silent.

"Once more, Sir, would you please state your name for the record," Patrick Turner said, with his usual smarmy air.

"My name is Edidiong Barnaby Eshiet," he replied in a strong, clear voice laced with an African accent.

"And your profession, Sir?"

"I am an obstetrician and gynecologist by profession," he replied.

"How long have you been a member of Our Lady Queen of Peace Catholic Church?"

"I have been a member of the Church for fifteen years. My wife and I joined the parish at the same time, shortly after we moved here from Norfolk, Virginia."

"And how long have you been a Catholic?" Patrick Turner continued needlessly.

"I was converted to Catholicism from my African traditional religion when I was 17 years old. Since then, I have been a practicing Catholic up till now," Edidiong continued.

"Dr. Eshiet, on a certain day in September of this year, Sunday the ninth of September, to be exact, you attended church and walked up to receive Holy Communion, as usual, but was openly denied. Can you please tell the court what happened?" Patrick Turner demanded, as though the details were going to add any novel information to his summary.

Dr. Edidiong Eshiet straightened up and gave the details of the events of September 9, 2012, at Our Lady Queen of Peace Catholic Church, where he and his wife, Ima, were denied Holy Communion. He conceded that if Fr. McCarthy had informed him before Mass to stay back, he, probably, would have understood and obliged. But letting them walk up and then humiliating them in front of the whole church was unacceptable. He concluded by stating that it was a very embarrassing and humiliating experience for him and, especially, his wife.

"Dr. Eshiet, Sir," Patrick Turner picked up his line of questioning. "Did you ask the Reverend gentleman why he singled you out for this public disgrace?"

"Objection! Counsel is proposing ideas and words for the witness," Stacy called out.

"Overruled," the judge replied. Then she addressed Edidiong, "Answer the question."

"My wife and I went to him immediately after Mass to express our disappointment at such treatment," Edidiong responded.

"What did he say?" Patrick Turner prodded.

"He was very arrogant," Edidiong continued. "First, he told us that we had broken Church law by conceiving a child in vitro, thereby disobeying him. I pointed out that that was the only way we could effectively conceive a child after twelve years of struggling. He said he had asked us to adopt a child, but we badly needed a child of our own, and, besides, the red tape of adopting a child, coupled with all the hoops we were required to jump through, as well as the uncertainty about the health and personality of the child we would have adopted, were not worth the trouble when we had an easier and cost-effective means at our disposal."

"Continue," Patrick Turner prompted. "Did he agree with you?"

"No, Sir," Edidiong replied. "He said we had done something immoral and that we were not worthy enough to receive Holy Communion. I asked him why my wife and I were the only ones who were branded immoral when there have been others who have used the same method we used to conceive and have not been so treated."

"Did he ask to know who these others were?" Patrick Turner asked.

"No, Sir. He said I was just making assumptions, that he did not know anybody in the parish who openly flouted Church teaching as my wife and I did. He said that ours was public knowledge, and that when he comes across a case similar to ours, he would put the couple under the same sanctions."

"Did he challenge you to name the couples you alleged were in the same position as you and your wife, but were not sanctioned the way you were?" Patrick Turner continued very methodically.

"No, he dismissed us and would not even listen to us again."

"And do you, in fact, know any such couple who conceived a child using the same IVF method you used, but was allowed and, in fact, is still allowed to receive Holy Communion in the same Church?"

"Yes, Sir," Edidiong answered, confidently.

"Dr. Eshiet," Patrick Turner called, turning and facing away from his witness in the usual way that lawyers sometimes do to put a dramatic effect into their interrogation when they are about to nail the point of victory. He paced a couple of feet and stood facing the jury box, not looking at any of them in particular. "How, if I may ask, did you come by this knowledge about the couple in question?"

"I was part of the team that worked with the specimen gametes that were used to conceive the child," Edidiong replied, somewhat proudly, looking straight at the jury box, also. "In fact, the couple is here in court and that child, a grown man, is here, also."

"What did you say?" Patrick Turner turned abruptly and faced Edidiong. "Can you repeat that again? You are quite sure the couple is here inside this court right now?"

"The couple is here in court with the son they conceived using IVF," Edidiong replied firmly, sitting up and looking straight at his attorney.

"And they are members of the same church you attend, Our Lady Queen of Peace Catholic Church?"

"Yes, Sir. They are," Edidiong replied, bobbing his head to and fro for emphasis.

"And they are still receiving Holy Communion and are not sanctioned the way you and your wife were?"

"Yes, Sir. They are still receiving Holy Communion and, no, they have not been subjected to the same treatment."

"Dr. Eshiet," Patrick Turner called, putting more drama into his movements as he turned on the balls of his feet to face the full court. "Can you point out this couple to the court, so that the court may know the special couple that receives this privileged treatment?"

Everybody shuffled excitedly with eyes darting about in expectation. Stacy frowned and vacillated between objecting and letting the process continue. She realized his opponent was not under any obligation to reveal his star witness. All he was required to do was share evidence. Fr. McCarthy was equally alarmed. He looked around at the audience, looked at Edidiong, and then back at the audience. He looked at Stacy and both looked at the audience behind the prosecution desk, expecting to catch a tell-tale clue of the mystery couple that was about to be the prosecution's star witness. Everyone sitting on that side of the court looked the same as everyone else, shuffling and expectant. Stacy was about to ask Fr. McCarthy if he actually did not know about such a couple, but decided to keep calm. After all, she had grilled him on that before, and even asked Greg to do some behind-the-scenes research for her. He came up with no information about any other parishioner who used IVF to conceive and managed to escape being sanctioned by Fr. McCarthy. But looking at the plaintiff in the dock stating with absolute confidence that such a couple was indeed in the courtroom at that material moment was not a comfortable experience for Stacy.

"Yes, Dr. Eshiet. The court is waiting," Patrick Turner prompted again, looking as though he was about to burst with the expected excitement.

"That's the couple," Edidiong pointed to the defense desk. "Stephen and Hannah McCarthy, sitting behind their IVF-conceived son and priest, the Reverend Cletus McCarthy."

"No! No!" Everyone turned to the single figure who shouted. Hannah McCarthy had fallen from her seat and fainted. A stampede of helpers rushed to help. The whole court broke into one big noisy confusion. Fr. Cletus McCarthy stood up, dazed and confused. He protested, unheeded, and to nobody in particular, "No! I was adopted. I was not conceived by IVF." But even to him, his protestations sounded hollow and unconvincing.

The din that erupted in the courthouse threw the court into such pandemonium that it was almost impossible to control. Pressmen and their cameras struggled frantically to get a good shot of the McCarthys, especially Fr. McCarthy, while reporters stampeded over each other to get to the lobby of the court to call in the latest development to their papers, TV, and radio stations. Judge Anieno Montgomery broke two hammers and split a gavel, banging furiously and several times, shouting, "Order in the court!" The bailiff disappeared into the judge's chambers to fetch her a fresh set of hammers and gavel. For almost two minutes, the commotion continued, and, as is the case with such situations, started dying down on its own. Judge Montgomery was finally able to assert her authority and reclaim her court. A handful of security policemen that were called in to arrest the situation finally got the reporters and their camera crews under control. The group of sympathizers that rushed to help a fainting Mrs. McCarthy reluctantly dispersed back to their seats while the latter continued to sob and snivel, with her face buried in her husband's chest. Stephen McCarthy was still trying to console his wife, rocking her gently and assuring her that everything was going to be okay. Judge Montgomery reminded Edidiong to maintain his seat in the dock for cross examination.

"Miss, Donovan," Judge Montgomery called. "The plaintiff is still in the dock. Do you wish to cross examine him?" She banged the gavel for the final time to achieve absolute silence.

"Yes, Your Honor," Stacy replied, trying her utmost best to look composed, though inside, she was rattled to her core. "I just have one question."

"Dr. Eshiet," She looked straight at Edidiong and asked, "How much money are you asking and looking forward to receiving in this case?"

"Objection!" Patrick Turner said, "Counsel is arguing beside the point. My client is suing for equal treatment, not for money."

"Overruled," Judge Montgomery ruled.

"I am suing because I was discriminated against," Edidiong replied with an edge to his voice that he barely controlled. "I am well established and my interest in this case is not money, but fairness and equality."

"Great values, Dr. Eshiet," Stacy patronized. "Fairness and equality. Great values! May I remind you, though, that in the statement of your suit you are asking for five million dollars in damages, but since, according to you now, in the full hearing of the court, you assert that you are well established and your interest in this case, quote, is not money, unquote, we take it that your statement in the hearing of the jury supersedes your earlier demand. Since you have used privileged information that was supposed to be confidential, to expose the reverend gentleman to ridicule and get even, can you give your word that in fairness you will walk away from the case without asking for any monetary payment, since your interest in the case is not money?"

"Objection!" Patrick Turner bolted upright again in protest. "Your Honor, it is not clear where Counsel's line of questioning is leading."

"Your Honor, information about a person's process of conception is supposed to be privileged and confidential," Stacy rejoined. "The plaintiff having been privy to such information by virtue of his having been part of the team that, quote, worked with the gametes used to conceive the child, unquote, has decided to blatantly and very unethically violate that privilege and use that information to his advantage, and without permission from the couple or the child in question. The motive for that can be nothing else except money. Since he denies that that is his motive, the question is: Who is asking for the five million dollars?"

"Your Honor, Counsel is introducing confusion into the matter of the case. Such information is not privileged or confidential when needed to prove a case of injustice such as my client suffered," Patrick Turner rebutted.

"Says who and stated in which penal code?" Stacy countered.

Judge Montgomery banged her gavel, "Enough! Both of you!" She commanded with authority. "Approach! Immediately!"

The two combatant counsels approached the bench, and Judge Montgomery proceeded to scold them, "I will not have any unruly altercations in my courtroom. You must proceed in this case with civility or I will find both of you in contempt of court. Is that clear?"

"Your Honor..." Patrick Turner began and was cut short.

"Is that clear?" Judge Montgomery addressed him directly.

"Yes, Your Honor," he replied grudgingly.

"Your Honor, in light of the claim by the plaintiff, may I request an adjournment of this case?" Stacy prayed. "I need time to gather more evidence to be able to answer that novel claim that has been sprung on us."

"Go back to your desks!" Judge Montgomery ordered. She banged her gavel one more time to quiet down the muted din that had broken out again. It was evident that the court audience was still agog with excitement after the bold statement of Dr. Edidiong Eshiet. Some were still craning their necks to catch the reaction of the McCarthys, and a good look at Fr. McCarthy himself.

"This court will now go into recess for ten minutes," Judge Montgomery announced. She left the bench to go into her chambers, inviting Stacy and Patrick to follow. "Come into my chambers, both of you."

The rest of the court erupted again into raucous excitement. Stephen McCarthy escorted his wife out. Fr. McCarthy watched Stacy go into the judge's chambers and decided he needed to be with his family during that short break. He was still dazed at the turn of events, and refused to give deep thought to his plight just immediately. He knew that what had just happened in the courtroom that late morning was an event of great impact, not only for him, but for the Church, as well. It was a jolting revelation, that he was conceived via IVF. And there he was, a Catholic priest, stoutly defending Church teaching and opposing the very method by which he came into the world. Was it true? Was he conceived via IVF? Why did his parents hide this information from him? Why would they hide it from him? Why did they keep telling him over the years that he was adopted?

As he got up from his seat to make his way to the door, he was swarmed by a pack of reporters asking harsh questions and training microphones at his face. The flashlight from cameras snapping him almost blinded him. He felt vulnerable and betrayed. With Stacy not at his side, he responded to every question with, "no comment" or "ask my attorney." The reporters wouldn't let off, but dogged his steps all the way out of the courthouse to the veranda. He looked up and saw that his father and mother were suffering the same mobbing treatment. He noticed that they were heading toward a car that had pulled up. Someone grabbed him by the shoulder and forcefully turned him around, walking him in the opposite direction. It was Fr. Brady Callahan. As they descended the few steps to the curb, he saw Fr. Polanski waiting in the open door of the driver's side of his car. A look of genuine concern was written all over his face. Fr. Brady opened the back door and all but pushed him inside.

"Get in, Fr. Nick. Let's get out of here before they lynch you." He went over to the opposite side and got in beside Fr. McCarthy. Fr. Polanski eased the car into traffic and drove away with a swarm of reporters falling off behind them. "The Cardinal sent us to …well, kind of rescue you. Sister Caroline Ellis, OP, was sent to monitor the process incognito. She was the one who called the Cardinal as soon as that infamous allegation was made," Fr. Brady announced, somewhat gushingly. Fr. McCarthy made no comments. He was still stunned as they turned out of Congress Street onto Dallas, from where they headed for Fannin and San Jacinto.

The court convened again after ten minutes. Everyone took their seat and the bailiff called the court to order as the judge walked to the bench. She sat and everyone sat down. Stacy remained standing, but the seat where her client sat was vacant. His parents were also conspicuously missing from their seats. Dr. Edidiong was escorted back to the dock and reminded that he was still under oath.

"Counsel may proceed with cross examination," Judge Montgomery called, her voice slightly trailing on looking up to see that two pews behind Stacy were empty. The entire McCarthy clan had decided not to come back into court, but to head home to sort out what had happened. Stacy was reading a text message from her phone. She eventually looked up and made a request.

"Your Honor, may I approach?"

"Certainly," Judge Montgomery granted.

Patrick Turner watched unperturbed. He knew why Stacy requested to approach, and waited for the inevitable pronouncement which he was sure Judge Montgomery would make in deference to the defense counsel's request. He would do the same in that situation.

"Your Honor, I think Mrs. McCarthy is in very bad shape. I just got a text message that she is running a temperature. As you can see, the entire family, including my client, are absent right now. I request for adjournment until I find out what is happening with my client, and his mother. I guess the sudden and cruel disclosure of the plaintiff caught them off guard, as it did everyone. I request, if it pleases the court, for an adjournment," Stacy prayed the judge.

Judge Montgomery beckoned to Patrick Turner and informed him of Stacy's request and asked, "What is your comment?" more for his acceptance rather than his objection. Patrick Turner shrugged and replied that he had no objection. "Alright, Miss Donovan. I will grant your request. Both of you can go back to your desks." She banged her gavel to quiet the muted din and announced that due to the trauma of the situation for the defendant and his inability to continue for the day, the court stood adjourned until after the Holidays, precisely, January 8, 2013.

In the Chancery conference room, on the second floor, where Fr. Brady, Fr. Polanski, and Fr. McCarthy were waiting for the Cardinal, everyone was too excited to sit down. Fr. Polanski tried to make small talk to cheer his friend, but failed, as the latter stood very introverted and quietly looking through the west window at the fleet of vehicles crowding the BMW dealership parking lot below. He was still virtually blank and seemed to be contented to remain in that mental twilight zone till he could be by himself. Fr. Brady, nervous and fidgety as usual, and not knowing what to do or say while waiting, stood by the coffee urn pretending to make coffee. Then he called out, "anybody for coffee?" The others both declined with a curt 'no,' not really having any appetite for victuals or snacks at that moment. Sr. Caroline Ellis walked in, having followed them from the courthouse five minutes after they drove away. She announced that the Cardinal would be in with them any minute. She went to the coffee urn and poured herself the stale dregs of lukewarm black coffee, which she held more as a comforting prop than for something to drink.

What happened was so abruptly novel that nobody knew how to react, let alone what to say to support or console Fr. McCarthy, who was at the center of it all. They had thought the suit's discrimination claim was a non-issue since the thorough background inquiry Stacy conducted had produced no other couple who claimed they had used IVF, but escaped Church sanctions. Everyone believed Stacy was going to 'walk through' this case, as with two previous cases which involved workplace discrimination, and she led the Church to victory. This one was different. The defendant himself was the *evidence* against himself. If it turned out to be true that he *himself* was conceived via *in vitro* and his parents were not denied Communion, then he was guilty of discrimination of the nepotistic kind. What was Stacy going to do? How was she going to handle it? Would she somehow produce a white furry rabbit from her defense attorney's hat, and lead the Church to victory again, to the surprise and cheers of everyone?

"Good morning, everyone," the Cardinal greeted them in his usual booming baritone, walking in with a flourish of authority, with the Seminary Rector and moral theologian, Fr. Paul Tram Tung, in tow. "Please, take a seat, and don't look so woebegone, as though Jesus had been crucified again," he added, drawing an uneasy laughter from everyone. "I know in a certain way, this is a crucifixion, and a very intriguing one at that, given the novelty of it all." He took the seat at the head of the desk. "But the good Lord will provide the way out. He instructed the apostles to not worry about what to say when brought before the Sanhedrin. 'It will be the Spirit of your Father speaking through you.' Our faith is being tested here, and certainly, Fr. Cletus's faith, but I am confident that God will vindicate His Church as He has already given a sign. I was about to place a call to Fr. Tung to meet with me, and as I reached for the phone, there he was at my door. Isn't that a miracle?" The Cardinal asked rhetorically. "And Bishop Montano, the Chancellor, is due back today from his visit with Cardinal Dolan in New York. As a matter of fact, he may be here any minute. So...." He looked around at the faces present at the table, smiled and added, "This, too, shall pass. Fr. Tung, you look like you want to say something?"

"When I heard about the case, I decided to sneak in and sit in court to watch the proceedings so I can use it as material for my moral theology class at the seminary," Fr. Tung put in edgewise, excited at being asked. "I did not expect the shocking turn it took."

"It looks like you now have more than sufficient material, not only for your moral theology class, Fr. Tung, but also for quick research to help us here at the Chancery," the Cardinal replied on cue. "So, how do we handle what has happened? But before we go on," he turned to Fr. McCarthy, "how are you taking all this, Fr. Cletus? I am not going to ask whether you are okay, because I know you are not. You are probably shaken and more confused than the rest of us since you are the subject of attention here."

"I don't know how to take this, Your Eminence," Fr. McCarthy replied, visibly angry. "I am still in shock."

"You are, Fr. Cletus, and I thought you would be," the Cardinal concurred, in a fatherly tone. "Do you want to take the rest of the week off to be with your family while we sort this out? Of course, we will keep in daily contact with you."

Stacy appeared just then, stood by the door of the conference room, and surveyed the scene. She did not look very pleased.

"Here she is," the Cardinal announced. "Please, sit down Ms. Donovan. I already know what has happened. You know, of course, that Sister Ellis was in the courtroom, as well as Fr. Tung. The question we are trying to answer is, where do we go from here? What do we do?"

"Your Eminence, with the new turn of events, I do not yet know how the case will play out," Stacy replied, taking the seat beside Fr. McCarthy. "But the first thing I intend to do is interview Fr. McCarthy's parents, if that is okay with you, Father, and get the truth from them. After that, I will plot my next move."

"My parents certainly have a story to tell me, too," Fr. McCarthy replied. "Not just to you, Ms. Donovan. I think that's where to begin."

"From the moral theology angle, if I may add," Fr. Tung interjected, wriggling in his chair as though he had discovered an academic goldmine, "We might even get the case to play in our favor. Invincible ignorance takes away culpability, and as it appears, Fr. Cletus here was kept invincibly ignorant of the circumstances of his conception."

"Canonically, too, I… I think this is a new case that calls for, um…a new norm," Fr. Callahan nervously added.

"Fathers, please, shall we skip trying to take this case first to the surgery tables of moral theology and canon law, and focus, instead, on how we can help Fr. McCarthy come to grips about this embarrassing allegation sprung on him from nowhere?" Fr. Polanski interjected, riled at his brother priests for failing to notice that Fr. McCarthy was in a state of distressing confusion, but, rather, behaving as though protecting the canonical and theological systems of the Church was paramount at that moment, and superseded the solidarity and compassion that should be accorded his young friend. "I think, as His Eminence suggested earlier, that Fr. McCarthy should take the rest of the week off, his parishioners should be informed to respect his privacy, as he must be with his family to sort things out before the next court date. Before then, as Ms. Donovan intends, she should be able to legally counsel the family while at the same time gathering necessary information to prepare her defense."

Everyone agreed with Fr. Polanski. After more discussion of duties and strategies, the meeting adjourned. As Fr. McCarthy headed for the elevator doors, Stacy touched him lightly on the shoulder and said, "Just try to stay calm. Don't over agitate yourself, please. Just give me time. I will call and set up an appointment with your parents. I am quite positive that with the additional information I will get from them, I will be able to have the case under wraps."

"But why do you think my parents deceived me all these years?" Fr. McCarthy asked in fierce whispers, letting out his thought for the first time.

"'Deceive' is a harsh word, Father," Stacy cautioned. "People do certain things for certain reasons. I am quite sure that your parents had a reason for not telling you that you were conceived via IVF, but, rather, leading you to believe you were adopted."

"Do you think my being ignorant of the circumstances of my conception will excuse me from the accusation of discrimination?" Fr.

McCarthy inquired, wedging himself between the elevator doors to prevent them from closing.

"No, Father," Stacy replied, honestly. "Ignorance of the circumstances of your conception does not exonerate you because, at least, your parents knew the facts full well. I will try and argue the case along other lines, but I need to talk to your parents first in order to see those other lines clearly."

"Guess what, Ms. Donovan?" Fr. McCarthy said, as he entered the elevator. "Don't take this personal because it is not you, but whoever drafted the principle that ignorance of the law is no excuse for breaking it…if he stood here before me at this very moment, I'd punch him right in the mouth."

With that, the elevator doors closed. Stacy smiled ruefully and stood still for a second or two pondering Fr. McCarthy's anger. She felt deep empathy for him and wondered what it felt like to be caught in the trap of the very system you are charged with upholding and propagating. She turned to head to her office, taking out her cell phone to call her mother.

———

Fr. Polanski eased his car into the traffic on San Jacinto, and drove for five uneasy minutes before finding his voice to start a conversation, since Fr. McCarthy was certainly not going to say anything voluntarily.

"Do you want me to take you to Hollow Wood Circuit directly, or do you have anything you want to pick up from the rectory, like toiletries, or anything?"

"Take me to the courthouse parking lot," Fr. McCarthy said. "My car is still there, remember? You guys whisked me off so fast that I forgot I drove to court myself."

"Oh, yes. I forgot," Fr. Polanski said. He turned onto Travis and, one block later, turned again onto Dallas and headed for Congress Street. "But I can still accompany you to your parents' place."

"Thanks, Charlie. You're very kind," Fr. McCarthy replied, exaggeratedly. "Just drop me off at the parking lot opposite the courthouse and, if you don't mind, from then on, I prefer to enjoy my 'unaccompanied minor' status undisturbed."

"Just trying to help," Fr. Polanski replied, feigning a hurt. "But I can see that you intend to do better on your own. So, I won't push." He slowed considerably as he pulled up to the curb and stopped for a split second. Fr.

McCarthy swung the car door open too fast and put out his leg to get out. The dull thud to his knee, as the door bounced back, made him hiss and swear under his breath from the pain, as he limped along the pavement, heading for his car.

"Minors need adult company!" Fr. Polanski called after him in mock humor. "To teach them how to exit cars without incurring injuries." He said the latter part almost to himself and grinned furtively at his friend's receding back, still slowly driving close to the curb to make sure Fr. McCarthy got to his car before driving off. The latter remote opened his car, walked to the driver's side, and turned around to wave before getting in and heading for the parking lot exit with his paid parking ticket still on the dashboard. As Fr. Polanski finally drove off, Fr. McCarthy headed in the opposite direction toward Main Street to get back to the rectory. Three blocks after that, he changed his mind, turned onto Fannin and headed for Highway 59 South. He had a sudden urge to see his parents before returning to the sanctuary of the rectory. He started mulling it over in his mind whether to spend the rest of the week off in the rectory, or with his parents, who, probably, were afraid and bracing themselves for his confrontation, which was inevitable.

He again wondered what made his parents lie to him for thirty-one years, or, at least, for twenty-four, judging from when he had attained the age of reason and would have understood a simple explanation of how he was conceived. He also wondered how the seminary authorities were not able to discover this about him, with their sophisticated system of background checks before recommending a candidate for ordination. Apart from facing a sure conviction on counts of discrimination and emotional battery, he wondered what the impact would be on Church teaching about the validity of ordination. Would the Church defrock him, citing his conception via IVF as invalidating his ordination? But there was no precedence on which to base such a decision, and there was no norm in either canon law or moral theology to support that line of action, as far as he had fulfilled all necessary requirements for a valid ordination, and was consequently ordained. If the Church did not invalidate his ordination and defrock him, it would have to write a new Catechism and a new canon to take into account his situation, which, from all indications, was the first of its kind. It scared him to think about the impact of his circumstances. On the one hand, he was fast garnering an unwanted celebrity status. He was sure the airwaves were already inundated with news of him, the first IVF-conceived

Catholic priest. The next morning all the papers in the country and beyond would carry his photograph and news. He was certain that he would be the front-page news in every paper. On the other hand, he was becoming an embarrassing albatross around the Church's doctrinal neck, morally speaking. Was Pope Benedict XVI going to publish a corrigendum or an addendum to *Donum Vitae*, and *Dignitatis Personae*, to accommodate or explain away his peculiar case? What about Pope John Paul II's *Catechism of the Catholic Church*? Would the entire section on human reproductive technology be revised to explain away or accommodate his case? Above all, what was his future going to be like?

He was so consumed with his thoughts that he nearly drove into another harsh confusion in front of his parents' house. It took a split second for his mind to register what the pile of vehicles in front of the house meant. If not for the TV dishes and antennae protruding from two of the vans, he would not have recognized what was happening until it was too late. The vans all had fixed TV cameras trained at the windows and doors of his parents' house, and the crowd milling around noisily was a pack of reporters and pressmen, some with hand-held video cameras. Others were brandishing cordless microphones. A few reporters were standing in front of cameras still relaying news to their stations for later broadcasting.

Suddenly feeling like a hunted game, he swung his car onto the next street and doubled back out of the area as fast as he could. "Gracious God!" he muttered to himself. "This is worse than I thought." He drove fast, but mindful of his speed, so as to not attract attention. He was going to head back to the rectory of Our Lady Queen of Peace, but realized that the same scenario might be awaiting him there. So, he decided to drive to the only place he thought might offer him a safe haven till the stormy situation died down.

Fr. Polanski came out to welcome him. He got the keys from Fr. McCarthy and got into the car. "Get inside the house before anybody notices you are here," he said, almost snarling. Fr. McCarthy strutted into the house, closed the door behind him, and sighed relief while Fr. Polanski drove to the back of the house to park the car. He came back into the house through the kitchen, and called out to Fr. McCarthy, whose back faced him as he peeped through the window blinds at nothing in particular, "drinks?"

"Screwdriver," he responded, without turning around. "Make it stiff. I need to calm my nerves."

"You ordered the right cocktail, boy," Fr. Polanski responded, supportively. He handed Fr. McCarthy a glass of the spiked juice and dropped his bulk into his favorite spot on the settee. "Goes without saying, Nick. I would give anything in the world not to be you right now. But whatever happens, please, you must admit that when situations force you to become like a 'minor', you need 'adult' company for support. I thank God you came back."

"I appreciate the daggering humor, Charlie. No contest," Fr. McCarthy responded, also taking a seat, clasping his screwdriver glass with both hands, like he could use all the comfort it could offer. "You could have seen the speed with which I made my one-eighty-degrees U-turn to scuttle out of Hollow Wood Circuit."

"Why? What happened?" Fr. Polanski asked, confused.

"The front of my parents' house is a bee hive," Fr. McCarthy replied. "The entirety of the media in the state is camping out there. Charlie, my parents are practically under the worst siege since the Greco-Trojan fallout over Helen. I am at my wit's end right now. I don't know what to do because, right now, I'm like a hunted rat myself. I ran because I was not prepared to face the media's unending questions." He paused to sip his screwdriver, then continued, looking distantly, "I cut and ran like a child. An adult would probably have barged right through the thick of them all with the simple defense weapon of 'no comment,' and gone into the house. That's what I should have done, Charlie!" Fr. McCarthy said, looking energized, like he was about to spring into action.

"Hold on to your breeches, Nick!" Fr. Polanski interjected, raising his hand to emphasize his restraint. "You're right. An adult would have acted that way, but that would have been acting impulsively, and that's why adults frequently say the wrong thing. There would be no way that your 'simple defense weapon' would have sufficed without your making a slip. Believe you, me, Nick, news reporters are sharks, and they crave the scent of blood in the water." He paused and Fr. McCarthy looked at his friend quietly and was forced by the logic of his comment to agree with him for the umpteenth time. Fr. Polanski continued conspiratorially, leaning forward with both of his elbows on his knees and speaking almost in whispers, "Just so you know, when I dropped you off at the public parking on Congress, I doubled back to the Chancery to find out from Fr. Brady what the Cardinal's next line of action is going to be."

"So, what's next?" Fr. McCarthy asked, with lukewarm curiosity.

"What is he going to do next, except wait for Stacy's advice and the next court date?"

"By the time Stacy gets behind her desk tomorrow morning, the Cardinal will already be on a plane heading for the Vatican," Fr. Polanski replied matter-of-factly.

"To..." Fr. McCarthy started to say something.

"Yes, to discuss your case with the Holy Father," Fr. Polanski interjected. "I don't think you understand the far-reaching impact of your case, Nick. And, by 'your case', I don't mean the allegation of discrimination, but the circumstances of your conception and the validity of your ordination. The Church is going to have no valid canonical reason to annul your ordination because there is no canon impeding a person conceived through IVF from receiving Holy Orders. There may be one impeding anyone who uses or aids and counsels the use of it for conception, but *in materia conceptus per fecundationem in vitro, canonici tacet.*"

"Which is to say?" Fr. McCarthy inquired, cynically.

"About the product of IVF, canon law is silent," Fr. Polanski offered the English translation. "On the other hand, the Church is not going to be in a hurry to revise the existing canons or re-write existing *Congregation for the Doctrine of the Faith* documents to accommodate your situation."

"So, then, what are they going to do? Sacrifice me for the system? The least they can do is work for my acquittal from the charges of discrimination. I don't care which doctrine they want to write or not write. Defending a doctrine is what got me in this situation in the first place. If I can get out this once, I will not care a jut about doctrines." Fr. McCarthy was beginning to show signs of cracking under pressure, Fr. Polanski thought.

"Yes, unfortunately," he replied. "The Church might choose doctrinal cohesion of the system over your plight, sort of letting one man take the plunge for the good of the whole system."

"Thank you, Sir," Fr. McCarthy said, starting to rise from his seat. "I have no wish to be Jesus Christ right now. If you don't mind, I am going in to have a nap."

"That's a bit scandalous for an *alter Christus*, Nick. Thank God nobody is within earshot!"

"And thank God that you are not Caiaphas, Charlie," Fr. McCarthy replied, heading for the guest room.

"On the bright side, you are becoming an important figure, Nick," Fr.

Polanski said, somewhat excitedly. "You are rewriting the history of the Church without even knowing it."

"Would you like to take my place?" Fr. McCarthy turned to inquire from the guest room door.

"Oh, no. We already settled that, Nick," Fr. Polanski said, shrugging and shaking his head from side to side to buttress his point. "I said, I would give anything not to be you right now."

"Wake me up at five." With that Fr. McCarthy disappeared into the guest room and shut the door.

The thing of it was that Fr. McCarthy did not take the nap he went in to take because, of course, he couldn't sleep. Too much adrenaline was coursing through his veins and boiling his brains to let him savor the peaceful embrace of Morpheus. He did not like it, either, that his friend was chattering flippantly in the hope of brightening up his humor. But he felt that Fr. Polanski was, perhaps, more scared, though not so much about him as about what his case might mean for the Church in the long run. The reproductive technology of IVF was already mainstream medical practice used as a remedy for infertile couples, and more than just a few so-called Christians having difficulty conceiving a child the natural way had embraced it. For those faced with the prospect of having a child of their own, traditional Church arguments about the act being immoral because it involves the separation of the unitive and procreative purposes of the sexual act, or because the child born thereof is a *product* and not a *begotten,* were no longer impressive. He wondered what specific harm persons conceived in the glass walls of a test tube would incur that those conceived in the membranous walls of a womb would be spared of. Or, what advantage those conceived normally *in utero* had over those conceived via IVF, for that matter.

Here he was, Cletus Nicholas McCarthy, a vibrant and brilliant young man, a fine young priest, well-read with a Master of Divinity degree, well beloved by his parishioners, in his priesthood, pastorally effective as that goes—touching and spiritually healing more lives as any other priest and, perhaps, more than most priests who were conceived normally—and, yet, facing a crisis of that magnitude because of the manner of his conception. Did the separation of the unitive and procreative purposes of the sexual act in the process of his conception and the fact that he was conceived in a petri dish and not in his mother's uterus invalidate his normalcy as a person and the evident effectiveness of his pastoral work as a priest? Was a criminal—say a serial killer—who was conceived through a normal sexual act and in a woman's uterus a much better child of God than he, Cletus Nicholas McCarthy? If not, then who was the better bang for society's buck: a serial killer who was *begotten* through normal sexual intercourse, or a spirit-filled priest who has touched and healed many lives, though *produced* in the petri dish?

As a Catholic priest, he was expected to uphold and defend Church teaching on the issue. He did just that, and did so loyally until it backfired, as it just did. Suddenly finding himself on the receiving end made all the difference in the way he now perceived the issue. And just as suddenly, he also felt drained of any anger he had previously nursed against the Eshiets for dragging him into court. He thought he would have probably done the same if he were in their situation. He remembered the humorous anecdote of the philosophers of Plato's academy who were so sure their definition of the human person as a featherless biped was the final say on the matter, until Diogenes, the cynic, threw a plucked chicken over the wall of the academy. Well! There it was before them: a featherless biped that certainly wasn't human.

Fr. McCarthy felt like Diogenes's plucked chicken. There he was before Church authorities, a healthy human being and a validly ordained priest who was not begotten, but, rather, produced in a petri dish. Plato's scholars promptly modified their definition of the human person to escape Diogenes's mockery. Would the Church modify her view about the technology of IVF? How would the Church hope to convince the world of the immorality of IVF when the only basis of argument is that it separates the unitive and procreative purposes of sex and makes the child a product? What does it mean, for that matter, to say that one person is a product and the other isn't, when it can equally be said that the child conceived *in vitro* and the one conceived *in utero* are both produced by their parents, without infringing on any grammatical rule or the logic of thought? What discernible moral advantage would the regular conception of, say, a serial killer, have over his IVF conception? The barrage of hypothetical questions was making Fr. McCarthy's head swirl. He caught himself getting angry at the Church for fiendishly and nostalgically clutching impractical doctrines and symbols instead of honestly opening her mind to new realities through research and deep thought. He was even angrier at himself, feeling betrayed that he was made to zealously preach against the very process by which he came into being. He recalled his father's remark at the Thanksgiving dinner table about the Church one day finding herself trapped in her own ethical maze of *dos* and *don'ts*. The very thought that all along, he was defending what was eventually going to crumble under powerful logical scrutiny and overwhelming evidence to the contrary smarted relentlessly. Worst of all, knowing that he was going to be the accidental catalyst of that dissembling was most unnerving. He kicked off his shoes furiously and pulled himself into bed and was beginning to tuck himself in for a forced siesta when he suddenly thought it would be very cruel not to call his parents to see how they were doing.

He pulled out his phone to call his parents, only to discover that they had called several times. Jennifer called about five times and even Uncle John called twice. He had switched off his phone while in the courthouse and in the aftermath of the confusion and commotion, he'd forgotten to switch it on again. He touched one of the missed calls from his parents and touched the one-dial button. The phone rang once and was picked up in the middle of the second ring.

"Fr. Cletus!" His adopted father's voice came through, strong, confident, and warm. "Are you alright? Are you safe? Please, tell me you are…."

"I'm okay, Dad," Fr. McCarthy responded, effortful in checking himself not to come across as alarmed. He surmised that his parents may have panicked, worrying about him. That explained the frantic calls. "I'm just resting somewhere and trying to make sense out of what has just happened. Other than that, everything is okay. Don't worry about me. How's Mom?"

"Thank God, you're okay," his father replied with such relief that he could feel it himself from his end of the phone line. "Your mother was trying very hard to reach you. I know you want to talk to her. Please hold while I give her the phone." Then he called aloud, "Hannah! It's Fr. Cletus."

Fr. McCarthy knew his mother would be upstairs in such circumstances and would take his call there. So, he braced himself for the phone encounter with her.

"Hey, Cousin, are you okay?" It was Jennifer. It didn't surprise him. She would grab the nearest receiver on hearing he was on the line, beating his mother to it.

"I'm okay, Jennifer," He replied with a longsuffering sigh.

"Good! Stay where you are. I'm coming to you," she replied, like the team captain of a rescue mission. "I'll bring some food. I know you haven't eaten and it's past lunch time."

*Trust Jennifer!* Fr. McCarthy thought. Though they were (or were supposed to be) cousins, he wondered where their intense love for each other would have landed them, had it not been that he was a priest. He knew that their mutual sparring whenever they met was simultaneously cathartic in diffusing that intensity, as well as a defense mechanism that prevented them from crossing the line. He often mused that they were like two naughty adolescents madly in love with each other while also chaperoning each other. He could have welcomed no other comforting presence with him at that moment than Jennifer's, except for one thing.

"Jennifer, I'm not in the rectory just now," he said, apologetically.

"You're not?" Jennifer asked, disappointed. "Well then, where are you?

"I'm sorry, Jennifer. I can't tell you. Please, just let me talk to Mom."

"Okay, here she is," Jennifer said, still with a note of disappointment. "I'll talk to you after she's done."

If Fr. McCarthy, in self-righteous anger, was going to have a confrontational phone conversation with his mother, and if he was going to press her for answers to questions he thought he had the right to ask, all that fizzled like a raging flame under the powerful hose of a fire hydrant, within ten seconds of hearing his mother's voice.

"Fr. Cletus!" his mother's high-pitch voice came through. "Fr. Cletus, my son, are you alright?"

"I'm okay, Mom," Fr. McCarthy spelled out his condition. "I need to talk to you."

"I know, my son," his mother interjected. "I know, I have a lot to explain to you, even if it doesn't make sense. And I don't expect you to forgive me because I do not deserve it. I have wronged you terribly in my selfishness, my son."

"Mom, hold on," Fr. McCarthy tried to cut in. "I need to know the truth…"

"The truth is what you heard," Hannah McCarthy sobbed, brokenly. "I had you through a surrogate and you were conceived in a test tube. When you grew up and started to develop interest in seminary education, I didn't think it was necessary to bring up the details of your conception. More so, when you transitioned to the major seminary and was well on your way to becoming a priest, I didn't want to hurt your chances at realizing the calling of your life by bringing up such a trivial issue as the manner of your conception. At least, it seemed trivial then, but I see now that I was wrong. Maybe it was more my selfish ambition to see my son become a priest…"

"Mom, I know you wanted to shield me," Fr. McCarthy interjected.

"I don't fault you over that, but you could have told me after I'd become a priest."

"That's why I blame myself, Fr. Cletus," his mother replied, sobbing even louder. "That is why I think I've hurt you so badly, my son. I thought, foolishly, that what you didn't know couldn't hurt you. Oh, how can I ever make it right? What I've done to you, I am so sorry, my son. I didn't intend to hurt you that way. And now, I've unintentionally sold you to the public, to become fodder for the media and the ridicule of society. How can I ever be forgiven for what I've done…"

Hannah McCarthy wept so bitterly and so loudly on the phone that Fr. Cletus was forced to stop listening. He dropped the receiver on the bed beside him and sat still in a moment of stupor. Though he could still hear the muffled sound of her weeping coming through, he had lost the drive to continue talking to her. For one thing, the tone of her self-excoriating wailing was a wrenching cry that he could swear came from deep down in her soul. For another, he had never heard her weep so bitterly and inconsolably. He rapidly ran down memory lane, over the years when he was in the seminary. He recalled how proud and happy his mother was that he was studying to become a priest, and how she celebrated with unfettered joy on his ordination day. He couldn't forget the love that his mom had always lavished on him. Even when Josh came into the family, he was always given preferential treatment in everything, as though he was the only child. Was it right to forget all that because he was upset that he was made to believe that he was adopted, instead of being informed he was conceived through IVF and birthed by a surrogate mother?

Fr. McCarthy went into his utilitarian calculus mode of thinking. Were his parents right in deciding to shield him from the knowledge of the manner of his conception, and the decision turned out to be an unfortunate idea only because he was outed by his angry parishioners? What would have been the benefit of knowing about it anyway? Or would it have been a disadvantage to know about it? Would that knowledge have influenced his self-perception positively or negatively? Depending on the age at which he was given such information, he was, somehow, certain that he would probably have spent a good chunk of his life worrying whether he was typical or different than the other children conceived in the supposedly 'normal' way. And so, what was happening to him was whose fault? Certainly not his, since he only grew up to find himself in that situation. Was it his parents' fault? From what he was told, it took them seven years to make the decision to "adopt" him, meaning they had struggled for seven years as a childless couple. What was the pain and anxiety of those seven years like? The Eshiets had struggled longer, for twelve years! He could not believe that for all the time he was counselling and dissuading them from choosing that option, it had never occurred to him to think deeply about their twelve years of pain and anxiety. He was always so focused on maintaining purity of doctrine and making sure that defaulters were duly punished. He felt ashamed, in hindsight, that he could have been that callous. It crushed him to think that instead of being a compassionate *alter Christus*, he had all along been a heartless juridical *alter Christus* who was more concerned with the administration of justice. The last words he had heard his mother utter before he put the phone down was a prayer asking God to heal him. "Dear Lord, please, heal my son, Fr. Cletus, from the hurt and anger of this cruel revelation," she had petitioned. And he thought it was the prayer of a true penitent. If so, what would Jesus do? The story of the prodigal son and the merciful father flashed through his mind.

"That's it!" Fr. McCarthy shouted suddenly and bolted to his feet. "That's what I should do. I should run toward my mom." He slipped into his shoes with fury and nearly sprained his fingers trying to stretch the back of the shoes to accommodate his heels. He picked up the phone and was glad to find that his mother had stopped weeping and was only breathing heavily. "Mom," he called, curtly.

"Yes, Father," Hannah answered with a voice so meek and respectful. Fr. McCarthy's heart broke. Tears welled up in his eyes and ran down his cheek. "Father, were you going to say something?" she inquired, somewhat shakily.

"Mom, I am coming to you," Fr. McCarthy replied, realizing that her trembling voice was that of a truly sorry woman desperately nursing the last thread of hope for forgiveness. If ever he was going to redeem himself and become a more compassionate person, his parents were his last hope and the best opportunity to launch that new side of him. He thought it was uncanny how the forgiven and the forgiver both needed each other. "Mom, I'll be there in a few minutes."

"No, Fr. Cletus," his mother called in a slightly panicky voice. "Don't come. They're still here. The media is…"

"I don't care who's there, Mom," he replied, resolutely. "I am coming to be with you." With that, he dropped the receiver into its cradle, swung open the door, and marched out, nearly bumping into Fr. Polansky, who had inched his way to the door when he heard the first shout.

"Are you okay, Nick?"

"I'm a coward." Fr. McCarthy accused himself so abruptly and vehemently that it left his friend almost speechless.

"Well, of that, I'm not sure," Fr. Polanski replied, haltingly.

"I should be with my parents right now. I suddenly realized that this isn't all about me," Fr. McCarthy continued, suddenly possessed of good spirits. "I mean, this whole thing must be equally as painful for them as it is for me. And they've been under siege since morning, while I ran here to hide like a coward. I'm going down to Hollow Wood Circuit to be with my parents."

"That's a good idea…and I'm coming with you," Fr. Polanski said, also beginning to catch the high spirits.

"No, you're not coming," Fr. McCarthy replied with bravado. "This is my fight. I'm going to walk straight through that zoo in front of my parents' house and if anyone blocks my way with stupid questions, I'll punch him right in the face."

"Now, that is NOT a good idea," Fr. Polanski said. "You can ill afford a second suit. If you're so in need of a face to punch, I'll tell you whose face to punch."

"Whose?"

"Mine," Fr. Polanski replied without humor. "If you keep insisting that I cannot come with you, you'll have to punch me in the face, and punch hard enough to knock me out and prevent me from tagging along."

"You know I wouldn't do that to you, Charlie," Fr. McCarthy responded, somewhat mellowed. "Here's the key to my car, since you so desperately need something to do," Fr. Cletus said, as he tossed the key in the air to Fr. Polanski.

Fr. Polanski caught the key in midair as it flew toward him, threw on his tank top and tennis cap, and was hot on Fr. McCarthy's heels. The two marched stoutly around to the back of the house to get into Fr. McCarthy's car and drive to his parents' place, media or no media.

———

When Frs. McCarthy and Polanski left the Chancery, the Cardinal had convened another meeting in which duties were assigned. Fr. Brady was to call a press conference for the Cardinal to address the city and the Archdiocese on the new development before it got wildly out of hand. It was important to control the Church's end of the information from the Chancery. Sr. Ellis was to quickly send out an email letter to all pastors of parishes, instructing them to never field any questions from any media agent, but to refer all such questions to the Chancery spokesperson, Fr. Brady Callahan. She was to call the airlines and book the Cardinal on an early flight to Rome. Stacy volunteered to visit with the McCarthys and get their own side of the story ready for the next court date. Though not at the meeting, Dr. Regis Murphy of the University of Houston's Faculty of Law, a legal consultant at large to the Archdiocese, was saddled with the unenviable duty of calling to see the possibility of negotiating with Turner and Stendhal for a settlement with their client, if worse came to worst. He promised to do his best, but gave no guarantees, having been an old foe of Turner and Stendhal on a previous tort litigation during which he vanquished the firm. The firm directors did not smile at him then and, probably, would not do so now. The Chancellor, Bishop Mario Montano— Marmon, he humorously nick-named himself, playing on the sound of the word, mammon—walked in just before the meeting ended.

"There you are, Marmon," the Cardinal said, as Bishop Montano walked in. "I hope your flight back wasn't as tumultuous as our workday has been here at the Chancery today?" He added rhetorically.

"No, Your Eminence. On the contrary, I had an odd day: A peaceful flight with a tumultuous mind," Bishop Montano quipped, then became serious. "I received news of the new development just as I was about to board the flight back. So, what is the next line of action?"

"Not certain yet," Cardinal Felice responded. "We are just playing fire brigade right now with the aim of getting the situation under control. And, if it is not placing too much on you, you're hitting the ground running. You and Fr. Brady will field all calls from the media. Assure them that they will get answers to their questions at the press conference I intend to give in about two hours." With that, Cardinal Felice dismissed the meeting. "Everyone to your oars," he called out in mixed humor and seriousness. "The bark of Peter must scale over the waves and get into peaceful waters."

Everyone dispersed to go about their assigned duties. The Vice Chancellor, Sister Ellis, followed Bishop Montano into his office to fill him in on the details of the day. Stacy gave instructions to her secretary, packed her briefcase, and headed out for Hollow Wood Circuit. She ran into Fr.

Polanski in the foyer and they walked out to the Chancery parking lot. She answered a couple of questions from Fr. Polanski, freely sharing what transpired at the meeting, bearing the fact that, as Fr. McCarthy's buddy, he wasn't really breaching any confidential barrier.

————

As Frs. McCarthy and Polanski wheeled onto Hollow Wood Circuit from Saw Tooth Canyon Drive, they were surprised to see the cull de sac almost empty, except for three cars. Stacy's convertible was unmistakable. There was Jennifer's SUV and John McCarthy's Corvette. The door was opened by Stephen McCarthy himself. He pulled in Fr. McCarthy and silently embraced him tight for a few seconds before releasing him. Fr. McCarthy looked at his father and knew he was touched by what had happened in a way he had never been before; he could not recall the last time he gave him such a tight hug. Tears stood in his eyes and he swallowed hard with tight lips, trying to keep from sobbing.

"Come in, son," he said, eventually finding his voice. "Thank God you're okay. Everything will be alright. Come in, Fr. Charles," he said, addressing Fr. Polanski by his first name. "And thank you for keeping him company. He needs the support."

The big dining table had been converted into a conference table, and seated around it were Stacy, who from all indication was presiding, John McCarthy, and Hannah McCarthy. On the opposite side sat Jennifer in between two empty chairs. Stephen McCarthy assumed his position in one and motioned Fr. McCarthy to the other. The latter sidled to where his mother had stood up and was moving with unsure steps toward him, head hung in penitent shame. Her face had sagged and she looked five years older. She looked at Fr. McCarthy, practically pleading for mercy with her big, teary eyes. Fr. McCarthy knew she was going to break into another bout of weeping. He all but dashed toward her, swept her up in a tight embrace, felt the heaving of her chubby torso, and coaxed her as she was about to break into babbling sobs.

"I so desperately needed a child," she sobbed.

"There, there, Mom," Fr. McCarthy coaxed. "It's okay. You didn't do anything wrong by desiring to have a child."

"I did something wrong and tried to hide it."

"That's okay, Mom," Fr. McCarthy said, rocking her gently from side to side. "To err is human, to forgive is divine. I'm quite sure you had a reason for going about it that way. Calm down, Mom. I forgive you for everything."

The rest of the people at the table sat out the mother-and-son emotional moment in respectful silence. Then Stephen McCarthy went over and extricated his wife and son from their mutual embrace and led her back to her seat. Jennifer got up to serve fresh rounds of coffee. Fr. Polanski took a seat also and the meeting resumed with Stacy taking the lead in laying out the plan of action. She coached the McCarthys on what pieces of information to share with the press and neighbors, and what to reserve for her, their attorney. She revealed her plan to dispute the alleged discrimination as a technical error and to discredit it as litigation-worthy. After all, the McCarthys were still right in calling the parentage of their son, Fr. McCarthy, an adoption since Hannah McCarthy was not the gestational mother and the egg wasn't hers.

"And I did give my sperm," Stephen McCarthy said, in a somewhat hedging tone, "But…and this is the first time I am going to reveal this…it wasn't my sperm that was used in the process of conception. I had a very low count and it was not going to work. So, it was substituted."

Everyone at the table looked up, surprised at the new revelation by the elder McCarthy. Hannah McCarthy herself was taken aback that her husband had kept this from her all along.

"It was substituted?" she asked, more out of surprise than hurt.

"Yes, it was," Stephen McCarthy replied, ruefully. "That young doctor, I can't remember his name, assured me that the substitute was from a very strong and very healthy young donor."

"And he didn't tell you who the donor was?" Stacy asked, hopelessly. She knew the answer was negative.

"The contract forbade that," Stephen McCarthy replied. "Unless the donor wished to reveal himself, which would be after he signed an undertaking not to lay any clams to the offspring or demand money."

"You say you can't recall the name of the doctor," Stacy asked. "But wasn't that Dr. Eshiet who revealed himself in court today as having full participatory knowledge of the procedure at the time in question?"

"No. I think I now remember him as one of the four doctors whom we met on various occasions. But the one who met with us more frequently and directed the whole process was a doctor Erik…or Jared…Honey, do you remember his full name?" He solicited his wife's aid.

"I think it was Dr. Harick," Hannah tried to recall. "Oh gosh! It's been thirty years. His name is in the papers we signed. I still have those papers and I can fetch them." Hannah struggled to her feet to go upstairs for the papers.

"Mom, tell me where the papers are. I can fetch them," Fr. McCarthy offered.

"No, let me go. It'll take you time to dig them out. I know exactly where they are," she declined help. "I'll be back."

"I'll help you, Auntie," Jennifer was already on her feet and heading for the stairs before Hannah could reject her offer.

As both women went upstairs to fetch the papers that contained the name of the doctor who, in Stacy's reckoning, might hold the break or damage to her case, John McCarthy decided to make small talk with Stacy. He had never been one to endure awkward silence. He started to ask her about her work at the Chancery, but before he could pose his question, the doorbell chimed the Westminster melody, so he answered it.

Greg Sullivan was at the door. He inquired about Stephen and Hannah McCarthy and was told they were in. The elder McCarthy recognized Greg's voice and invited him in.

"Come in, Greg," he called. "We're all here, like prisoners in a fortress. Just trying to recover from the jolt." He rose to his feet to receive the Parish Council Chairman of Our Lady Queen of Peace.

"Well, I just wanted to stop by and see how you guys are doing," Greg said, somewhat gawkily. He took the elder McCarthy's proffered hand and pumped it. "We're behind you and we support you a hundred percent with our prayers. We realize this is a very trying time for you."

Stephen McCarthy thanked him profusely, as well as the parishioners of Our Lady Queen of Peace, some of whom had already called to offer their friendship and support. Greg exchanged greetings with Fr. Polanski and Stacy and expressed his satisfaction that the two were already there to support Fr. McCarthy. He shook Fr. McCarthy's hand and took the seat beside him, mumbling the same assurances of solidarity and support which the latter thought he had probably rehearsed over and over again as he drove out there. John McCarthy resumed his seat and inquired about Greg's family and work. Greg told him he had retired, and was about to give him a rundown of the state of his family members when he was interrupted by Hannah and Jennifer coming down the stairs.

"I was quite sure he had a Bohemian name," Hannah said from the top of the stairs, and then stopped short as he spotted Greg at the table. "Oh, hi, Mr. Sullivan. How are you?" She greeted in her warm singsong voice, perfectly disguising her distress of the earlier half hour, to the impression of Fr. McCarthy. If there was one thing that he loved about his mother, it was her gracious bearing. She had a way of making friends even with total strangers within the first five minutes of encounter. As he observed her slipping into her gracious hostess' mood, offering this and that to Greg to make him feel welcome, Fr. McCarthy concluded that his mother was one of those rare women who, no matter how big a blunder they committed, you could not *not* forgive them. Her hearty graciousness was such an atoning character in her that it was impossible to stay mad at her for very long. He resolved to forgive her completely and not hold her accountable for keeping him in the dark all these years.

His dreamy rumination was interrupted by Stacy tapping him on the shoulder and asking to confer with him privately outside. She had the large brown envelope that Jennifer had handed her on the sly because they couldn't talk about it in Greg's presence. She announced her exit on the excuse that the Cardinal's press conference was due in half an hour and she needed to make it there before it started.

"You plan to stay with your parents, right?" Stacy inquired of Fr. McCarthy once they were outside.

"Yes, of course," Fr. McCarthy replied. "For the time being, but I don't intend making myself a prisoner because of anyone."

"Certainly not," Stacy concurred. "I was going to recommend that after today, you should take off and go somewhere to rest. Go about your normal life, but don't talk about your case with anybody. I'm going to find that doctor and have a conversation with him. I'm quite sure you don't have a case to answer. The next court date isn't until January 8. That's enough time for me to prepare a solid defense. Any questions?"

"When do we have the next tennis tournament so I can beat you?"

"You *are* an enigma, Fr. McCarthy!" Stacy said, laughing. "You always puncture the mood, don't you?"

"That's how I cope, Ms. Donovan," Fr. McCarthy replied, smiling apologetically.

"It's a good strategy," Stacy replied and added, "Hey! You've given me the best metaphor to guide my work. It's been a long time since anybody beat me on the court playing singles. Patrick Turner seems to be handling his racket well so far, but let's see how long he's going to last. I can assure you, I don't intend to let him last very long."

"I believe you, Serena Williams," Fr. McCarthy quipped.

"I'm Stacy Sally Donovan, not Serena Williams," Stacy replied, graciously. "And I intend to win this tournament. Now, run inside and keep your parents company. I'll call you if I need your opinion on my legal proficiency." With that, she turned and walked toward her convertible, wiggling gracefully.

"Miss Donovan," John McCarthy called, having just emerged from the house at that moment. "May I have your business card, if you please?" he requested, taking out his wallet and extracting his own card to exchange with hers.

"Sure. I apologize," Stacy replied, ruminating in her handbag. "I almost forgot I had promised you one."

Fr. McCarthy watched for a minute as his uncle put on his wiles to ingratiate himself to Stacy. He smiled and turned to go inside, wondering where Patrick Darlington was, and when Uncle John would quit his game of collecting paramours.

———

The Cardinal's press conference was brief and terse. It was set on the front steps of the Co-Cathedral of the Sacred Heart. At exactly five o'clock, and on the last toll of the tower bell announcing the hour, the double doors of the Co-Cathedral opened and Cardinal Umberto Pacino Felice, followed by a train of the Chancery officials, walked out and stood behind the podium decked with microphones. He looked up, sweeping the crowd of media men and women and other curious bystanders with sparkling eyes, and spoke in his rich baritone voice.

"Ladies and gentlemen, on behalf of myself, the clergy, and the faithful of the Catholic Archdiocese of Galveston-Houston, I stand here to address these few words to you about the events that took place in the First Circuit Court of Houston this morning. One of my priests, a faithful and loyal servant of the Church, a very compassionate pastor of the people of God at Our Lady Queen of Peace Catholic Church, Fr. Cletus Nicholas McCarthy, was taken to court by a couple in his parish, on the allegation of discrimination and emotional battery. Fr. McCarthy had temporarily stopped said couple from receiving Holy Communion as a sanction for the scandal of using a method not approved by the Catholic Church for its members, to conceive a child. By using the method of in vitro fertilization, the couple in question not only knowingly disobeyed Church doctrine, but also went against their pastor's good advice and best judgment.

"As indicated in court this morning, the couple alleged they did so, not because they did nothing wrong, but because Fr. McCarthy, himself conceived by the process of in vitro fertilization, did not stop his own parents from Holy Communion. At this juncture, it must be borne in mind that this is only an allegation that has yet to be substantiated. Fr. McCarthy's birth documents state clearly that he was legally adopted at birth, and, hence, is the legitimate son of Mr. Stephen and Mrs. Hannah McCarthy. A court date has been set for when this allegation will either be proved or disproved. Until then, I ask, in the interest of truth and fairness, that you desist from disseminating wild and unsubstantiated rumors. I also ask that you keep all concerned, both the litigating couple and Fr. McCarthy and his family, in your prayers. I also request that you please respect Fr. McCarthy's privacy and integrity. Please direct all questions to his attorney and Counsel, Ms. Stacy Donovan, or to the Chancellor, Bishop Mario Montano. Thank you and God bless you all."

A barrage of questions, not unexpected, followed the Cardinal's address. The first came from a bald gentleman who sported a moustache that made him look like a clone of Lenin.

"Why is the Catholic Church so much against science? Does the Church believe it can succeed in taking everyone back to the age of superstition?"

"The Church is not against science, as long as it is good science" Cardinal Felice responded with a fatherly smile. "The Church is against bad science that degrades man and vitiates his human dignity as a person created in the image of God."

"Do you deny that the Reverend McCarthy was conceived through in vitro fertilization?"

"That is just an allegation at this stage. It needs to be substantiated."

"Popular belief is that the Catholic doctrine against all forms of reproductive technology is harsh and intentionally directed against women. What is you comment on that?"

"No Church doctrine is directed against women. The Church respects and gives a unique place to women in deference to the Blessed Virgin Mary, the mother of Jesus. Church doctrine is directed against the type of scientific pursuit that degrades women and their reproductive vocation."

"If it is eventually proven that Fr. McCarthy was indeed conceived by in vitro fertilization, will the Church change its view and doctrine on reproductive technology?"

"Church teaching on reproductive technology is based on scientific truth about human reproductive vocation and what is morally in accord with right reason.

*"So, the Church will change its doctrine then, on the evidence of scientific truth?"*

"The Church will continue to teach about reproductive technology based on scientific truth about human reproductive vocation and what is morally in accord with right reason."

*"Why does the Catholic Church refuse to ordain women? Don't you think that is discrimination?*

"That question is not germane to the issue under discussion. Next," the Cardinal responded firmly, but patiently.

*"What is the Catholic Church doing about all the pedophile priests and the victims of their abuse?*

"Question not germane to the issue under discussion…"the Cardinal again responded with grace, and then added, "Ladies and gentlemen, I think that is it for now. God bless you all."

———

Fr. Polanski and Greg Sullivan watched the Cardinal's press conference, broadcast live, at the McCarthys' place. Stephen McCarthy said he thought the Cardinal gave the best press conference under the circumstances. Jennifer eventually succeeded in persuading Fr. McCarthy to eat. Then she went upstairs to clean and arrange his old room for him. The discussion went from the press conference to the games of the season which the men watched on TV and made noise as usual. Hannah and Jennifer retired to the kitchen to prepare the evening meal. Fr. McCarthy, having been practically forced to eat a very late lunch, gave instructions not to wake him up till he had slept his fill. Fr. Polanski and Greg stayed for dinner and left shortly after. John McCarthy was the last to leave, and he promised to visit Stephen and Hannah every other day to keep them company. The McCarthys retired to bed before nine o'clock, thankful that they could finally get some rest from what had turned out to be the longest day of their lives.

# PART IV

*Some are born great, some have
greatness thrust upon them.*

— WILLIAM SHAKESPEARE

# PART IV

# HOUSTON, TEXAS

## DECEMBER 11, 2012

IT WAS 11:30 a. m. in Houston when Dr. Horacek took the escalator down to the baggage claims area of the George W. Bush Intercontinental Airport. He waited with other passengers who had disembarked from the same flight from Atlanta where they had connected from Norfolk, Virginia. It was the first day of his vacation in Houston with his newfound family. He felt like a man who had been given a million-dollar chance at life, to begin it all over again. The air was nice and crispy, and, lacking the early snow of Norfolk, it wasn't too cold. He felt somewhat exhilarated and genuinely looked forward to his time with Barbara and Crystal. He was still incredulous at his luck of coming full circle to be father and "dad" to Crystal, whom he had thought he would neither ever see again nor have any paternal relationship with. The last time he set eyes on Crystal was when she was born. Soon after, Barbara had unceremoniously moved from Norfolk to Houston, without so much as a farewell conversation. He knew she was quite angry at him then. As it stood, it looked as though the years had healed some of that anger. Their first lovemaking together during her second visit to Norfolk indicated that she had, most probably, decided to forgive and receive him back into her life, not knowing what else to do with him. After all, there was Crystal, not just in between, but linking them. And she had grown into such a gorgeous young lady. Feeling blessed more than he deserved, Dr. Horacek smiled ruefully and reached out for his suitcase and grabbed it off the conveyor belt.

As he emerged from the glass doors of the terminal, he nearly bumped into Crystal, who was sent by her mom to look inside for him.

"Oh, hi, Dad," Crystal said and extended her arms for a hug. "We had circled the terminal twice, so I decided to come inside while Mom waited."

"Hi, Crysie," Dr. Horacek responded, gathering Crystal into a warm bear hug. "Baggage claim is always a bore. I guess it's meant to school one in the virtue of patience. How's your mom?"

"She's right there, in the car," Crystal replied, pointing to a Mercedes 350 Sedan with her mom inside, waving to attract their attention. The trunk of the car was remote-open as he approached and stuffed his luggage inside and closed it. He sidled to the front passenger seat, as Crystal was settling into the back, and was about to sit when he hesitated. A copy of the Houston Chronicle was on the seat and Barbara, all apologies, reached for it, but he beat her to it. He settled into the seat with his eyes glued to the front page of the newspaper, at the headline that caught his attention read in bold: **FIRST IVF-CONCEIVED CATHOLIC PRIEST OUTED.** The portrait of a handsome young man in suit and collar, probably in his late twenties, Dr. Horacek thought, appeared under the heading. He was intrigued, and before he could comment on it, Barbara began filling him in.

"All Houston is agog with the news since yesterday," she said with a note of excitement in her tone. "All the TV and radio stations couldn't give enough news about the court proceedings that ended in the priest being exposed as having been conceived by IVF. I bought the paper on the way to the airport because I knew you might be interested in reading about it because Crysie and I were debating whether the doctor who sued the priest is the same as your colleague who worked with you during your internship with Georgeanna and Howard."

"I keep telling Mom that that is the same guy," Crystal interjected. "His daughter, Edo-Mma, is my friend and classmate, and she has talked a lot about her dad, who is an obstetrician and gynecologist."

"I know everything seems to pan out that way," Barbara continued, not really being tenaciously incredulous. "Being conceived at the Norfolk Hospital, and Dr. Eshiet claiming to have been part of the team that was responsible for the pregnancy, and…."

"…in the year 1981!" Dr. Horacek, who was silently reading through the paper, suddenly interjected, sitting up. "Barbara, pull into that gas station. Pull in, please," he all but ordered her. Barbara eased off the gas pedal and swung the car into the CITGO gas station, just before they were about to hit the junction where Airport Boulevard emptied into Sam Houston Tollway. "We did not work with anyone else at that period, at the Clinic, other than Elizabeth Carr, and *you*, Barbara Sanders!" Dr. Horacek said, a shade too emphatically.

"What are you trying to say?" Barbara asked, creasing her forehead in disbelief and almost visibly shaking.

"Mom, I told you," Crystal said, barely able to suppress the excitement in her tone. "We may have found my brother without even having to search for him."

"Barbara, the couple mentioned here, the parents of the young priest, are the couple whose baby you gave birth to: Stephen and Hannah McCarthy."

"Well, I didn't know their names," Barbara responded, plaintively.

"You were not supposed to know. Remember?" Dr. Horacek explained, "The deal was not directly between you and the couple. It was between you and the hospital and between the hospital and the couple."

"So, you mean…" Barbara said, haltingly. "This young man…I mean, the young priest…might be my biological child?"

"All the arrows seem to point in that direction, Barbs," Dr. Horacek said, looking distantly into space as someone stunned and lost in thought.

"But…a priest?" Barbara asked rhetorically, still creasing her forehead, incredulously.

"You are the biological mother of a priest?" Crystal followed the cue, also sounding incredulous. "And I have a brother who is a priest?"

Barbara looked at Crystal, then at Dr. Horacek. Crystal looked at her mom, then at her dad. Dr. Horacek looked from Barbara to Crystal and back to Barbara, then started chuckling humorlessly, wearing the inane expression of someone stunned stupid. Crystal and her mom joined her dad, and, all three, looking stunned and stupid in the face, broke out into a silly, almost hysterical, laughter that lasted almost a whole minute. Then they calmed down and no one spoke for another minute. Then Dr. Horacek broke the silence.

"And that is not all."

"What else?" Barbara asked, looking straight into Dr. Horacek's face.

"Never mind. Just drive. Let's get to the house and I will tell you," Dr. Horacek said and picked up the paper again to continue reading, still looking stunned. As they drove on, Crystal kept wondering whether other commuters on the road realized that the three of them in the car were the hidden, but big, part of the news dominating the Houston airwaves and print media just then. It was an uncanny experience to be simultaneously famous and incognito. She wondered, too, when and how she would meet her brother, and what that meeting would be like. She took out her phone and started a text message to Edo-Mma.

The same day, the same time as Dr. Horacek was descending on the escalator to the baggage claims area to wait for his luggage, Fr. McCarthy rolled over on his side, in his bed, in his room, in his parents' house on Hollow Wood Circuit, opened his eyes and squinted at the bedside clock. It was 11:30 a.m. It took him several seconds to be fully awake and realize that he wasn't at the rectory at Our Lady Queen of Peace Catholic Church. He surveyed the room and noted that, being his old room before he left to study for the priesthood, and became a priest, nothing changed that much, except for a new chest of drawers that his parents had purchased a few months back, in case Fr. Cletus ever had occasion to stay for a few days. As he sat by the edge of the bed, as yet undecided whether to get up or lie back down, he knew that he would not use the drawers on that occasion because, of course, he was beginning to hatch other ideas in his head. He started to play back the events of the previous day, especially the courthouse session during which Dr. Eshiet pointed to their section of the court to indicate that his parents had conceived him via IVF, and the fact that he now knew from his mother that he was birthed by a surrogate mother. He wondered who his biological mother was, where she was just then, what she looked like, and to what ethnic background she belonged. He made a mental note to search for her in the near future, just to know who she was, once his life had calmed down.

It was very quiet in the house. He got up and donned his bath robe to go downstairs, but decided against it and, instead, went to take a shower and get dressed. He remembered the Dean of Affairs' instructions to seminarians: "As a priest, never be caught not well dressed." He smiled, turned on the shower knobs, and tested the water for the right temperature.

When Fr. McCarthy went downstairs to the kitchen, he realized that the quietness in the house was not for lack of other people's presence. His dad was at the dining room table, quietly reading the day's papers. His mother was in the laundry room, ironing kitchen linens and some clothes. He knew they were subdued, almost to the point of depression, due to the events of the previous day, so he decided to perk up the mood by being enthusiastic himself.

"Good morning!" he called to his parents from the foot of the stairs. "Do I look handsome enough for a celebrity in that paper? I know I'm on the front page of the Chronicle and any other paper that looks to make money off of me."

"What else would you look like, if not handsome, Fr. Cletus?" his dad asked rhetorically, impressed at his son's sense of humor. Then he added, "Seeing as you have enough offers stacked up to make you a millionaire, if only you tell your story, or, more accurately, allow them to tell it and make it sellable."

"You know, that's not a bad idea," Fr. McCarthy replied, half joking and half serious. "Who knows how much my litigation cost will amount to? Where are the offers?" he asked, picking up the Houston Chronicle to look at his portrait staring back at him. Above it was the bold caption, **FIRST IVF-CONCEIVED CATHOLIC PRIEST OUTED.**

"Check the voicemail," Stephen McCarthy said as he nodded toward the telephone in the corner. "You probably have the same number of offers, if not more, on your rectory phone." Fr. McCarthy threw down the paper and headed for the phone, as its accompanying answering machine was blinking furiously. There were nine messages on it and he was about to press the play button to listen when his mother interrupted.

"Good morning, Fr. Cletus." Hannah appeared from the laundry room with a hamper of freshly washed and ironed linens and hand towels. "Are you hungry? I made you breakfast. It should still be warm because I put it in the oven." She put the hamper on the kitchen table and proceeded to bring out plates and cups. Fr. McCarthy returned his mother's greeting, but declined the brunch and opted for a cup of coffee, instead.

"It's almost lunch time, Mom," he said. "I'll just wait and have lunch. Jennifer left for work?"

"Of course," Stephen McCarthy responded, looking up with a smile. "Otherwise, she would've appeared from nowhere the moment you came downstairs. She can sniff every movement you make and track you down, you know?"

"Yeah," Fr. McCarthy replied wearily. "And heckle my poor life to death, for sport." Deciding to play the voicemail later, he sat down and picked up the Chronicle again and began to read. Though he knew there wouldn't be anything in it that he didn't know firsthand, it was good to know how the media portrayed the story about him and what spin they were putting on it.

"Fr. Cletus, what would you like to have for lunch?" Hannah interrupted.

"Mom, you know my favorite. Just go ahead and cook it, please?"

"Alright. Chicken alfredo with Caesar's salad," Hannah announced, as if to assure herself she hadn't forgotten. She started moving about in the kitchen, getting items for lunch ready. The house fell silent again, as father and son sat quietly reading the papers and tabloids.

Just as Fr. McCarthy suspected, the article had very little to say about him beyond the bare facts: the names of his parents, the clinic where he was conceived, and the fact that acting on the authority of the Church, he had denied Holy Communion to the Eshiets, sanctioning them for using the very method by which he himself was conceived, to conceive their child. The rest of the write-up was a poorly veiled excoriation of the Catholic Church for always being anti-science, and being too strict on issues of women's reproductive rights. He read the article with disgust, but he couldn't decide if he was disgusted with the media, the Church, or himself.

After lunch, he announced his decision to go on a two-week vacation. His first choice was to visit the Holy Land and spend some time visiting the holy sites. But that evening when the discussion came up again at the supper table, Jennifer swayed him to let her take him to Rome and Venice. She had been there before and describe the enticements those places held well enough to get Fr. McCarthy to change his mind. Moreover, she had accumulated more than enough paid time-off to be away from work for two weeks and still have two weeks left to take later. Hannah and Stephen McCarthy forgot their sorrow and mused aloud on how the perennial battle between Fr. Cletus and Jennifer would play out without either of them on hand to make sure they were fighting fair. Getting the two to quit their mutual heckling of each other whenever they met was an impossible task. So, the elder McCarthy and his wife resolved to be content just playing referees. Jennifer and Fr. McCarthy, for their parts, were too excited and too busy taking inventory of all the places they would visit to give any thought to whether they would be fighting their usual fight or not. They talked far into the night. In the end, Jennifer took over the duty of calling and booking their flight first thing in the morning.

## DECEMBER 13, 2012

CARDINAL FELICE WAS ushered into Pope Benedict's private library by the pope's private secretary, Monsignor Georg Ganswein, a young, sprite, and slender Bavarian, with piercing blue eyes, who was quickly rising through the ranks in the Vatican Curia. The pope was sitting at his desk, in front of a massive bookshelf full of books of assorted sizes and binds. A few papers lay to the left and right corners of the desk. At the center, slightly to the right, was a bronze crucifix, black with age, which had probably stood guard over many of the popes down the ages. Cardinal Felice remembered that it was there in the same spot that he last had entered the library to meet with the late Pope St. John Paul II. He had an errand to run for the then Prefect of the Congregation for the Doctrine of the Faith (CDF), Joseph Cardinal Ratzinger, when he was the acting personal assistant to the pope. That was before Cardinal Felice was made the Archbishop of Galveston-Houston Archdiocese in the United States. Then, shortly thereafter, he was elevated to Cardinal. He thought the crucifix, though cleaned every day, was purposely left unpolished to darken with age so as to command reverence as an antique religious relic. The pope himself seemed to be staring at it as Msgr. Ganswein announced the Cardinal's presence.

"Felice. Umberto Pacino Cardinal, Your Holiness," Msgr. Ganswein announced, then gave a slight bow and moved out of the way, slightly to the left.

"*Ah! Mio fratello, Umberto. Benvenuto. Mi aspettavo,*" the pope, with a full smile, said in Italian as he rose and extended his arms in fraternal embrace of his former aid. Then he inquired, "How is Galveston-Houston?"

"*Grazie, Santita. Sono lieto di essere in vostra presenza,*" Cardinal Felice responded in Italian to match the pope's greeting. Then he replied, "Galveston-Houston archdiocese is doing fine at the moment, Your

Holiness. But I must say, my coming before you indicates that we have an unusual problem for which we need immediate guidance. And I am happy to see my brother Cardinal and the Bishops present. I know I will benefit tremendously from their collective wisdom."

"Well, brother Cardinal, don't raise your hopes too high," Cardinal Bertone, the Vatican Secretary of State, said, rising to greet their guest. "You may be disappointed to learn that we are at a loss, as are you. What we have heard is a novelty. Welcome." He gave the fraternal embrace to Cardinal Felice. "But rest assured that we will work with you to arrive at a solution."

"Yes, Your Eminence. I am strengthened by the presence of the two pillars of the Pontifical Academy for Life," the pope chipped in again. "Their research experience will certainly be of immense help."

"Thank you, Your Holiness. I couldn't be more encouraged myself," Cardinal Felice assented to the pope's upbeat tone.

The other five men in the library followed on cue, each taking turns to offer his fraternal welcome. Selected pillars of the Curia, so to speak, were present: Bishop Bernhard Fuller, the incumbent Prefect of the CDF; Bishop Jose Ignacio Paulo Borelli de Alonzo, Secretary of the Pontifical Council for Legislative Texts and, perhaps, the only guy with the longest name in the Vatican Curia, also referred to as the Vatican Canonist, or Vatican lawyer for short and, of course, the Vatican Spokesman; Fr. Federico Lombardi; Bishop Ignacio Caravaggio de Pietro, head of the Pontifical Academy for Life (*Pontificia Academia per la Vita*, PAV); and the Chancellor of the Academy, Monsignor Dagoberto Renzo. Each man went forward to extend his fraternal welcome to Cardinal Felice. All present were fully dressed in their official regalia. When they had taken their turns to give a warm welcome to Cardinal Felice, Msgr. Gänswein ushered him to the only empty chair in the room. They were all seated, and Cardinal Felice thought the pope looked slightly more aged than the last time he saw him. Of course, the stress of the office would have taken its toll over the years. The pope rose and began pacing the floor with slow, measured steps as he spoke.

"This is indeed something very new and unique. Though it was a possibility all along, the surprising thing is that we didn't see it coming," Pope Benedict said. "If this scenario had come within the purview of the planners of the 2012 General Assembly of the PAV, it would have been thoroughly discussed during the 'Management of Infertility Today' session of the Assembly's deliberations. So, it is very good that you have come, Eminence, so that you can have a voice in the solution to the problem. As you can see, I have all my advisers in the different offices here so that we can discuss the matter together and come up with the right directive for the people of God."

"Your Holiness, if I am not speaking out of turn," Bishop Fuller said. "What this indicates is that the young man's ordination was invalid. It means the very foundation of it was spurious. I think there should be an investigation to determine how the vetting process was done at the seminary he attended. How was it that the situation was not known before calling him to Sacred Orders? Maybe his ordination should be annulled, though it will be the first of its kind."

"You have a point, Bernhard," the pope replied. "But let us look into those issues after things have calmed down and we are back to normal. Right now, the question is: What do we tell the faithful?"

"That's a pastoral question, Your Holiness," Bishop Jose de Alonzo responded, raising his hand as though seeking permission to talk, but already presuming the permission by speaking, anyway. "But it is also, and primarily, a canonical one. Maybe we need to answer some questions first: Can the young man's ordination be validly annulled? How do you annul an ordination?"

"Probably the same way you annul a marriage," Cardinal Bertone replied, suggestively. "Analogically speaking, an ordination is a marriage of the priest to the Church. Maybe it could be annulled on the grounds that all the conditions for a valid ordination were not met?" He ended on a rhetorical note.

"And is the manner of conception of the candidate one of those conditions?" the Pope asked, pensively. "What was the manner of his conception? What did you find out from your inquiry?" Pope Benedict addressed Bishop Caravaggio de Pietro.

"Your Holiness, the process of the young man's conception was as irregular as the rest of them using the new technologies go," Bishop Caravaggio de Pietro responded, lugubriously. "First of all, the gametes, that is, the sperm and the egg, were from different persons other than the couple who later became his father and mother. The egg was fertilized in a petri dish and then put back into the womb of the woman who gestated him."

"That would be the surrogate?" Bishop Fuller asked.

"Yes, My Lord Bishop," Bishop Caravaggio de Pietro replied,

emphatically. "After he was born, the McCarthys signed papers and adopted him at birth."

"Hold on, My Lord Bishop," Bishop Fuller interjected. "Did the McCarthys have full knowledge of the procedure that took place right from the start, or did they simply receive news about a newborn baby who needed to be adopted?"

"From all indications, My Lord, it seems that they solicited the surrogate," Msgr. Renzo responded before Bishop Caravaggio de Paula could. "Although the papers they signed as indicated to us by the Director of the Hospital Clinic state that they adopted the baby."

"There is full evidence of complicity as it stands," Bishop Jose de Alonzo said.

"And a clear act of deviance from Catholic teaching on the matter," Cardinal Bertone concurred.

"So, the facts of the case lined up are as follows: The gametes were harvested from a man and a woman who were not married to each other," Bishop Caravaggio de Pietro stated. "They were merged together for fertilization in a petri dish, and then implanted in the womb of the surrogate mother, who carried it to term and gave birth to the male child who would later be Fr. Cletus Nicholas McCarthy."

"And the Church's moral teaching flouted are those concerned with the right of the child to be conceived by two parents who are validly married," Bishop Fuller said, as though briefing the gathering. "As well as the right of the child to be conceived through the natural process of intercourse that does not separate the unitive and procreative purposes of marriage," he concluded, somewhat professorially.

"There is information which indicates that the surrogate was paid for her 'services'," Msgr. Renzo iterated.

"If so, would that mean that the McCarthys bought the child, instead of adopting him? Because that is what it sounds like," Cardinal Bertone said, looking around the group, astonished at the extent to which the McCarthys' action seemed to flout all the Church's moral dictates against the reproductive technology of IVF. "I know that is always referred to as compensation, but when does a sum of money constitute compensation and when is it a purchase price?"

"Brothers, I understand all the analytical angles of the case," Pope Benedict, who had stopped pacing and had taken his seat behind his desk, said in a more somber, but fraternal, tone. "What we are now facing is the fact that the die is cast. The deed is done. How do we clean it up?"

"I suggest an overhaul of the seminary faculty where the young man attended," Bishop Fuller visited his first point. "And, a laicization process…"

"Your Excellency, with due respect," Cardinal Felice, who, all along had sat silently, while listening to the serious discussion, interrupted Bishop Fuller. "I do not feel that we have to be unduly hard on the seminary authorities or call into question their judgment on the vetting of candidates for ordination. The seminary authorities acted on all the information available to them at the time, and I think that my predecessor accepted Cletus McCarthy to Holy Orders in good faith. What they did not know, they could not judge. I would rather suggest that we respond to the Holy Father's question on what to do and how to proceed from here."

At this juncture, four nuns came into the library bearing a tray of cookies, two pots of hot water, and a basket of assorted teas and coffee bags. They began silently serving the victuals. Cardinal Bertone conferred with the pope and then announced a fifteen-minute break in the discussion. The members of the ad hoc advisory group sat munching their snacks and sipping their tea or coffee, filling the library with a low din of small talk. They finished their unofficial snack break in no time and resumed their deliberations.

"Brothers, the option of an annulment came up earlier," Cardinal Bertone was the first to speak. "Maybe the young man's ordination could be annulled and he could be returned to the lay state of life."

"And what grounds could we cite to back that up, Eminence?" Cardinal Felice asked.

"The grounds that all the conditions for a valid ordination were not met," Cardinal Bertone replied, tendentiously.

"It is difficult to pinpoint what exactly that condition is in this context," Bishop Caravaggio de Pietro interjected. "Being conceived by validly married parents is not stated as such a condition."

"Neither is being conceived, say, irregularly as by a surrogate mother or a single parent, a sufficient condition for denial of ordination. To say it in the official way, canon law is silent on the matter," Bishop Jose de Alonzo interjected.

"Then, in that case, the pope must give an authoritative ruling," Cardinal Bertone said. "I think the ruling should be in favor of an annulment because of other implications."

"Yes. I can see one of those implications very clearly," Bishop Fuller replied. "I agree with you, Eminence, though we need to make sure that an annulment will be the appropriate correction of the situation."

"On the other hand, brothers, annulling the ordination of a priest who, on his merits, had fulfilled all the other conditions for a valid ordination, and is discharging his priestly duties well, would be like punishing that priest for the sins of his parents," Cardinal Felice observed matter-of-factly. The room was silent. He had offered a different perspective. Up till then, the attention was not on Fr. McCarthy himself, but on the moral dictates breached and what to do to fix the situation.

"Cardinal Bertone had likened a priest's ordination to a marriage. Maybe we can pursue the problem along that line," the pope said, pensively. "What are the different kinds of dispensations that we give in situations of irregular marriage? How can we explain the situation to the faithful?" He addressed the question directly to Bishop Jose de Alonzo.

"Your Holiness, I think the best principle to apply in this case would be a *sanatio in radice*." Bishop Jose de Alonzo offered what he perceived as a reasonable compromise. "We do that in marriage to avoid scandal, when a union is already consummated, but it is later found that there had been an impediment."

"Based on what we know about the circumstances of his conception and birth, was the young man factually impeded?" Bishop Fuller asked, raising a quandary. "Whenever that happens in marriage, it is always directly concerned with the married couple and the case is always confidential, known only to the pastor and the couple. A widely publicized case of the ordination of a young man conceived via IVF is a different situation altogether. In any case, does the world understand radical sanation? On the other hand, to uphold his ordination would mean that the Church implicitly endorses IVF as a method of reproduction for Catholics. I am just playing the devil's advocate here."

"Thank God you're not playing the devil himself, Bernhard," the pope jabbed humorously. "Only his advocate. That's a big relief. Thank you," Everyone laughed at the Holy Father's unexpected jocularity.

"Don't mention it, You Holiness. Just doing my duty, helping in any way I can," Bishop Fuller replied, gracefully lapping up the Holy Father's humorous jab with his own quip. He drew brief laughter, too.

"If I may come in here. Whether we annul or dispense Fr. McCarthy's ordination, in my opinion, is not the immediate solution to the issue," Fr.

Lombardi interjected, speaking for the first time, also raising his hand for permission, but assuming the permission by speaking, anyway. "I think His Holiness is asking for an interim measure to give assurance to the faithful and, to some extent, as it falls within my area, to protect the image of the Church from the media. I need to relay the official position of the Church in the matter before the media hijack the situation and project all sorts of wild conjectures on the Church."

"An interim measure, Federico, an interim measure," the pope echoed. "But we will still have to face the substantial question of doctrine and pastoral directive to the Bishops and the people of God. Let us first help Federico to craft a statement to send to the press, and then we can discuss how this new development affects doctrine and morals in the Church. But before that, pardon me Umberto, I should have asked how the young man himself is doing."

"Under the circumstances, he is doing fine, Your Holiness," Cardinal Felice replied, glad that the focus was eventually shifted to the truly pastoral, rather than still battling to dissect how the problem was affecting the Church doctrinally. He believed there should be some concern about how it was affecting the person at the center of it all. "Realizing how stressful the situation may be for him, I advised him to take a vacation while we sort things out."

"Good. Good idea, Umberto," the pope said, and straightened up, pushing against the back of his seat, apparently tired of hunching. He looked frail and drained. And Cardinal Felice thought he knew why. Benedict XVI had a lot on his plate, so to speak. Barring the fact that he was not very popular with the progressive phalanx of the Church, who always portrayed him as a kill-joy, ultra-conservative, especially when he headed the CDF. On assumption of office, he barely stepped into the Fisherman's Shoes when he was beset with extremely controversial issues which demanded pressing answers. He inherited the pedophile scandal that caused a moral quake in the whole of the Western Church. Then there was the vexed issue of recalcitrant nuns fighting to be called to Holy Orders. A gay lobby clique in the Vatican's rank and file posed a thorny problem and a tinderbox scandal. Then there was the massive corruption and financial irregularities, both in the Vatican Bank and some of the offices. His sensitive official and personal documents had been stolen and leaked by his butler, Paolo Gabriel, and a host of other very irksome, and not in the least minor, problems existed, which exacerbated issues further.

Families were crumbling with the astronomical increase of divorced and remarried Catholics falling away from the Sacraments. Combining all this with the day-to-day administration of the Vatican, as well as problems of poverty and social injustice everywhere, indeed made being the pope a difficult role to fulfill. It seemed to have been too much for one person to handle and, being primarily an academician, he, most often, took refuge in his private library and his books. There were times when he would confide in Cardinal Bertone regarding his personal doubts about his ability to lead the Church through these problems. There were simply too many forces pulling him every which way. And besides, he wasn't getting any younger. He wished for the mettle and courage of his predecessor and, sometimes wondered how he managed to handle it all. He recalled that when he was Prefect for the Congregation for the Doctrine of the Faith, John Paul II would sometimes confide in him and seek his opinion on difficult issues. Yet, he thought the pope really drew his strength from some mysterious source in making decisions, rather than from whatever pittance of advice he presumed to offer.

The thing of it was that Pope Benedict was anxious to reform and give the world an image of himself as a pastoral pope, rather than the harsh doctrinal bureaucrat who, at least in his opinion, he had been unfairly judged to be. But perceptions, like habits, die hard and it became increasingly obvious each day that that was going to be a tough act to pull off. And there he was, faced with having to sort through conflicts in reproductive technology and the validity of the ordination of the product of that technology. He had no other option, but to reach into the storehouse of Catholic moral teachings over the years, some of which he was the primary architect for. He stretched out his hand and stroked the bronze crucifix, as if to draw inspiration and comfort from doing so. "Good, idea, Umberto," he reiterated. "When you go, reach out to the family, too. Let the parents know of my solicitousness for their wellbeing and that of Fr. McCarthy. Though they have fallen short of the Church's moral expectations, they could not have foreseen what God would do with their son, who he would be. Perhaps this is one more case in which God may be teaching us that He can bring good from evil."

"Yes, Your Holiness," Cardinal Felice responded, touched by the pastoral tone the pope was using. "I will surely let them know how concerned you are for them. I am quite sure they will genuinely appreciate it."

"We could take a cue from your press conference, too," the pope continued. "I watched it transmitted live on BBC America." Then the pope turned to address Federico. "You know, sometimes calming down the people may not necessarily be due to the fact that you have anything of substance to say. Rather, it may just be a matter of assuring them that you are on top of the situation. So, since the next court date is in January, you might like to let the press know that the matter is under investigation by the Vatican, and a statement of clarification will be made soon."

"Is Your Holiness then moving in the direction of annulment?" Bishop Fuller inquired, ambiguously.

"No, Lord Bishop," the pope replied with indulgent patience. "I am moving in the direction of Psalm 51, *Ecce in peccatis meis. Peccator homo sum*, and the Genesis creation story. Everyone is created in the image and likeness of God. If everyone is born a sinner because they were conceived in sin, then no one is qualified to judge the other. We have all sinned and fallen short of the grace of God, according to the Apostle Paul. And if everyone is created in the image and likeness of God, then no one is to be deprived of that to which God calls him, provided that he responds from deep down in his very being. I think Fr. McCarthy responded to God's call in his heart. And as I wrote in *Donum Vitae*, many years ago, and reaffirmed in *Dignitatis Personae*, 'Every human being is always to be accepted as a gift and blessing from God', even when conceived in a manner that is morally culpable."

"*Sanatio in radice* is what Your Holiness advises then?" Bishop Jose de Alonzo inquired, hopefully.

"No, Bishop. There is nothing to purify or sanitize," the pope said, again disappointing the council. "Fr. McCarthy is not responsible for his manner of conception. He had no say in the matter and, thus, incurred no impediment. As *imago dei*, he is to be respected for himself because his human dignity is not contingent upon his manner of conception. We do uphold that in all three documents that deal with the issue: *The Catechism of the Catholic Church, Donum Vitae*, and *Dignitatis Personae*. Therefore, he is entitled to the vocation to which he responded. He cannot be punished for the impropriety of his parents. His parents breached the Church's moral teaching on conception, not him. So, Umberto, I advise that you call Fr. McCarthy's parents and the grieving party and absolve them in the internal forum after they have acknowledged their error with due penitence. Return the grieving party to the reception of Holy Communion and initiate a dialogue with them for a settlement out of court. The end does not justify the means. But both sides erred in their moral obligation. They are the ones who need the *sanatio*, not Fr. Cletus. The Legislative Council must soon sit to address the novel situation and develop an appropriate canon for guiding the Church. God works in manifold ways. What has happened is probably meant to wake us up to new realities. So, my brothers, let us get to work. The Church must go on bearing authentic witness to the world in an uncompromising, but compassionate, way."

The standing applause he received caught the pope off guard. Started by Cardinal Bertone, all the bishops stood and joined in the clapping with cheers of *"Bravo, Papa Benedito,"* and, *"Petreus locuta est* – Peter has spoken." Pope Benedict was almost overwhelmed by the show of solidarity and stood up, waving his hands in a gesture of acceptance and nodding his gratitude. Achieving such a consensus of agreement on a ruling was very rare within the Curia. For Benedict XVI, it was most significant and he was determined from then on to always approach issues from an earthy pastoral standpoint, rather than allow doctrinal constraints or demands to continue to mar his image and that of the Church as being heartless and cold.

———

The Cardinal was true to his name, Felice, as he deplaned from the American Airlines Airbus at the George Bush Intercontinental Airport in Houston. He looked happy and contented. It was December 18, four days after the meeting with Pope Benedict. He was particularly happy about the way things were going, and caught himself a couple of times smiling at nothing in particular. Nothing pleased him more than coming home from a meeting with the pope and the Curia, armed, not only with a credible policy idea, but also with a solution that was going to be pastorally effective. The concerned parties were not irreparably condemned, as the sanction on the Eshiets was to be lifted and they and the McCarthys would be absolved and returned to the Sacrament. Fr. McCarthy was not going to lose his priesthood, and the Church was not going to have to embark on a face-losing revision of its doctrines, but would hold that Fr. McCarthy was adopted. His manner of conception prior to his adoption by Catholic parents—the McCarthys—did not detract from his person or his ministry as an effective pastor of souls.

There was a spring in his step as he walked the airport concourse to the exit where Fr. Brady Callahan was waiting to pick him up. On the way to the Chancery, he filled Fr. Brady in on the meeting at the Vatican. He called Bishop Montano to apprise him of his success and to set up a brief meeting with him and Stacy before heading back to his residence to rest and get ready for the usual annual Priests' Christmas Party that evening. The following day, Fr. Brady would set up a meeting of the entire Chancery staff so that the Cardinal could address everyone. Thereafter, letters would be sent to pastors of all the parishes to be read to the congregation after Mass. It was a carefully laid-out plan.

Fr. Callahan took his turn to brief the Cardinal on the previous six days since he had left for Rome. Dr. Regis Murphy had continued his negotiations with Turner and Stendhal for an out-of-court settlement of the suit and, according to him, there was a silver lining on the horizon. Stacy had already done a substantial job looking into the background of the case, especially cataloguing the nuts and bolts of the conception process of the child who would later become Fr. Cletus Nicholas McCarthy. The papers which Hannah and Jennifer gave her, as well as a few phone calls, had yielded incredible results and she was building up a formidable defense for January 8, should the Murphy negotiation fail. The Cardinal was pleased that everything pointed to success of the case in favor of the Church and Fr. McCarthy. He looked forward to a nice wrap-up that would, hopefully, hurt no one very much. He wondered how Fr. McCarthy was doing, if he had indeed taken a vacation and how he was coping. He made a mental note to go on a vacation himself as soon as everything calmed down.

They soon arrived at the Chancery and Fr. Callahan eased his car into his usual parking spot in the back lot of the Chancery and let the Cardinal out. He helped him transfer his briefcase into the trunk of his car, which was two slots away from his own. Then the Cardinal went into the Chancery and boarded the elevator to go to his office. He took out his phone and called Bishop Montano to meet him in his office for his own briefing. As the elevator doors opened, he ran into Stacy, who was waiting to take the elevator down and go home for the day.

"Ah, Ms. Donovan," the Cardinal greeted. "How's your day?" The Cardinal always greeted every Chancery staff he met with the same inquiry, 'how's your day', to which he would get the usual response, 'good so far, Eminence'.

"Good so far, Your Eminence," Stacy replied, catching the Cardinal's infectious smile. "You're back. How was the trip? Or, more precisely, the meeting?"

"Fine, Ms. Donovan. Just fine," the Cardinal replied, nodding his head to emphasize the veracity of his word. "The good Lord always protects His Church. And this time? I think He's going to do it again." Then he switched his attention to Bishop Montana, who had just emerged from his office, heading toward them. "There you are, Marmon. Let's go to my office for a brief update of events," he said, moving stoutly in that direction. Stacy and Bishop Montano fell in behind him, glancing at each other and wondering what good news the Cardinal bore that put such a radiance in his demeanor.

"Welcome back, Eminence," Bishop Montano greeted, expectantly. "Had a peaceful flight?"

"You bet, I did, Bishop," the Cardinal replied. "And I believe the good Lord is hearing our prayers. We will soon achieve peace of mind again in the not-too-distant future."

The briefing session was indeed brief. Each person took turns updating the others. Stacy spoke last, and, after updating the men on her next strategy, actually asked the Cardinal to call off Dr. Murphy's negotiation, as it turned out that it was a waste of time. She assured them that as she thought from the beginning, she was now quite sure Fr. McCarthy had no case to answer. Cardinal Umberto and Bishop Montano were not quite swayed yet to call off the negotiation. Rather, they settled for asking Dr. Murphy to go somewhat easy on it and talk only once a week with Turner and Stendhal, as opposed to calling them every other day, as he was currently doing. Fr. Callahan was asked to call and set up an appointment for Fr. McCarthy to meet with the Cardinal before leaving for his vacation, if he had not yet left. By the time they came out of the briefing, the Cardinal had just a little over three hours to rush home, shower, and take a nap, to be refreshed for the evening Vespers and Christmas party with the priests.

Stacy made a call to Fr. McCarthy and relayed all they had discussed and the plan of action. She told Fr. McCarthy that she was trying to talk to someone in Norfolk, Virginia, who, she surmised, might be a star witness to testify at the January 8 hearing, and whose testimony she thought would be in his favor. She told him that the Cardinal and Bishop Montano were not ruling out an out-of-court settlement, if it came to that. Then she assured him that he would not need to be in court after Bishop Montano told her he might still be away on vacation by January 8. After inquiring and ascertaining that Fr. McCarthy's parents were doing well, she turned off her phone, opened the passenger-side door of the black Corvette that pulled up and slid inside, and smiled back at the well-shaven face of John McCarthy that was smiling at her.

---

Stacy and John McCarthy started seeing each other after they met at the McCarthys. John was surprised at himself. He had never felt for any of the numerous ladies he had dated previously what he felt for Stacy. And there was no doubt in his mind that he would like to settle down with her and start a family, bearing the blessing of Fr. McCarthy, of course. He wondered when he would have the right opportunity to break the news about his intention to Fr. McCarthy, as he would never go beyond just dating Stacy without letting Fr. McCarthy know.

"Had a nice day at work, honey?" he inquired, sort of sweetly.

"Whoever has a nice day at work, John? C'mon!" Stacy responded, giggling and presenting her cheek for a peck, a gesture that was becoming routine for them whenever they would meet. "It wasn't bad, though. Things are beginning to shape up pretty well for your nephew."

"Well, if it ain't bad, then it's nice," John quipped, in the raw jargon of the farmers of the plains. "That's my adopted philosophy. And if things are shaping up pretty well for Fr. Cletus, as you say, then, I guess, you had a nice day at work," he concluded, syllogistically.

"Non sequitur," Stacy replied, with a coy, toothless smile that John had come to like about her because, as he thought, it made her look prettier and sexier. "Keep praying for your nephew."

"Gosh! Of all the things you should demand from a poor sinner like me," John replied with fake exasperation. She glanced at him and gave a spurt of cheerless laugh, rolling her eyes prettily at him for his phony self-deprecation.

All the way to South Post Oak, they talked and laughed like teenagers in love. Stacy giggled at every one of John's jokes and he felt good inside. 'Get a lady laughing, and you are more than half way into her heart', John recalled the time-tested cliché and delighted himself testing it out on Stacy. As he dropped her off at her parents' place, he promised to swing by that evening and take her out for dinner. Patricia Donovan had noticed the blossoming relationship and secretly encouraged it, longing for her daughter to marry and get out of the house and out of her embarrassing spinster status. Geoffrey Sr. couldn't agree more. He had begun feeling awkward with his daughter still living with them, even though he was the one who insisted on her not wasting money to rent an apartment when he had plenty of rooms in the house. Stacy had resisted initially and went ahead to negotiate with a realtor to buy a house of her own, but after a month or two of the deal not really coming through and the economic benefits she had, she caved in to her dad's idea. After all, they didn't bother her. She could come and go as she pleased and, in the past, had brought a couple of dates to the house without their so much as asking who it was, but none of them had worked out.

John McCarthy was different, probably because he was more mature than Stacy's previous prospects. He treated her with the utmost dignity and respected her views and opinions. Working on Fr. McCarthy's case was a surefire way for Stacy to study John from close up, and she seemed to like what she saw so far. So, like her parents, she was anxious to keep him, though not desperately so. As John dropped her off to pick her up later, she made up her mind that if he again asked her to stay over at his place, she would accept, just to test the waters.

She waved to John as he revved the Corvette into full speed and disappeared down the road within seconds. That was the one thing that intrigued her about her beau. At 52, he had the spirit of a 30-year old and exuberantly embraced life with verve. And Stacy loved that about him because whenever they were together, there was never a dull moment. But she had reservations about his uncanny love for driving fast, and she made a mental note to remind him to always go easy on the gas pedal since life had no duplicate.

She entered the house through the corridor door and went straight to her rooms, a self-contained apartment in the house. Her father and Geoffrey, Jr., were watching some game on TV and making so much noise that they didn't hear her sneak into the house. She dropped her coat on the settee and went over to the answering machine, which was blinking. There were two messages on it and the first one happened to be from a Doctor Horacek. She quickly sat down and played it in full, wondering how on Earth he got her home phone number. Then she quickly remembered that she, herself, had mentioned it as one of the numbers to contact her by. When she traced him to a clinic in Norfolk, Virginia, from the information she gleaned from the papers Hannah gave her, she was anxious not to miss his call if he made the effort to reach out to her at her request. It was crucial that she talk to him, since he was the resident attending when Fr.

McCarthy was conceived at the hospital in Norfolk. So, she had left all her contact numbers on his voicemail, including her home number. She now thought that was a bad idea. It demonstrated how desperate she had been to get firmly back in the saddle, so to speak, after being rattled by the sudden disclosure made by the plaintiff, Dr. Eshiet. The message gave Saturday, December 22nd as the possible and earliest date that she could visit and speak with Dr. Horacek. In his message, Dr. Horacek clearly spelled out the address and the Houston number at which she could reach him. She was surprised to see that the address was not very far from their home. It was on the west side of Missouri City. She wondered if she should visit Dr. Horacek with John or go alone. Eventually, she decided she would go alone, but she would leave a message with the address for John, just for his information. The second message was just a reminder that the single young adults group she belonged to at Ascension Church was due to meet Saturday after the morning Mass. She deleted the message and mulled it over in her mind whether she should continue to consider herself as single. She quickly answered her own question in the affirmative, seeing as John had not yet proposed. She sighed and got up to shower and change before he came back for her, making a mental note to pray a novena for their relationship.

## THURSDAY, DECEMBER 20, 2012

TWO DAYS AFTER the Cardinal had come back from the Vatican, Fr. McCarthy stopped by his office to say hello and to get the latest information before flying out on his vacation. Just as he did two months back, on the fateful day he was first informed of his infamous suit, the Cardinal came out from his seat to greet him. This time he gave him a hug, rather than the usual official handshake. The Cardinal looked straight into Fr. McCarthy's eyes as he spoke.

"Good morning, Fr. Cletus. How are you coping so far?" the Cardinal inquired, somewhat more solicitous than usual. "Are your parents doing alright?

"I'm doing fine, Your Eminence," Fr. McCarthy replied, hesitantly. "But it's hard. I'm still struggling to come to grips with the whole issue, but I'm alright and my parents are doing fine, too."

"As you know, I met with the pope and am glad to inform you that the outcome was very positive," the Cardinal said, hoping to raise Fr. McCarthy's spirits. "So, you can proceed on your much-needed vacation with less worry. I have assigned Fr. Paschal Egbuna to stand in for you while you are gone."

"Is there a particular reason behind that assignment, Your Eminence?" Fr. McCarthy asked, looking quizzically at the Cardinal. "I mean...Fr. Paschal is Nigerian. Of course, the Eshiets will be pleased to have one of their own performing the pastoral duties, as opposed to me."

"You are very smart, Fr. Cletus," the Cardinal said, looking straight at Fr. McCarthy in return. "Yes, and no. Yes, Fr. Paschal has served at Our Lady Queen of Peace as a Parochial Vicar for two years, and the peopled like him, across all cultures—Caucasians, Africans, Hispanics, etc. He is our best bet to hold the fort while you are gone. And no, his assignment is not to appease your legal opponents, although there is a substantial presence of Nigerians in the parish, I am also privy to the fact that not all of them are in support of the legal action taken by the Eshiets. We have got to look at issues objectively, Fr. Cletus," the Cardinal concluded, putting his left hand on Fr. McCarthy's shoulder in a fatherly gesture.

"I understand your point, Your Eminence, and I accept your decision totally," Fr. McCarthy said. "Though I had hoped for a more neutral person. I'm not saying that Fr. Paschal is biased. I was just referring to the fact that his racial background might give the wrong message to others, but, then again, it may not."

"No, Fr. Cletus, it won't," the Cardinal assured. "Rest assured that by the time you come back from your vacation, you'll meet a relatively peaceful parish and a welcoming one. We have Dr. Murphy working on an out-of-court settlement of the case. Stacy is building up a formidable defense, in case that fails. Fr. Brady and Sister Ellis will visit your parents while you are gone and keep them abreast of the Archdiocese's plan of action. From the canonical point of view, your priestly ordination and faculties are not affected in any way...." The phone rang, interrupting Cardinal Felice. He excused himself to pick up the receiver, stating at the same time, for Fr. McCarthy's benefit, "That must be Cardinal Dolan, the President of the United States Conference of Catholic Bishops. We have been going back and forth about your case since I came back from Rome."

"I beg to take my leave, Your Eminence," Fr. McCarthy seized the hiatus to make his exit. "I will keep in touch."

"Please, do. And have a grace-filled vacation," the Cardinal replied, waved good-bye to Fr. McCarthy, and proceeded to take the call from Cardinal Timothy Dolan, who basically wanted to offer his ongoing fraternal support and to state that he was available for fraternal advice if Cardinal Felice needed any. He also assured Cardinal Felice that he would raise the case at the next Bishops' Conference so that an interim policy could be drafted to cover situations in which children born via IVF who express a genuine desire to study and become priests, could be accommodated without being punished by rejection for the sins if their parents. Cardinal Felice informed him that the pope, during his meeting with him, seemed to lean toward such a policy, since he decided in favor of Fr. McCarthy's ordination not being annulled. The two Cardinals agreed that the final statement in the form of a decree would still have to come from Rome. Then they hung up.

The next morning, at precisely 10:10 a.m. Italian time and 5: 10 a.m. Central (Houston) Time, Jennifer's and Fr. McCarthy's flight touched down at the FCO, Fiumicino, Leonardo Da Vinci Airport in Rome. It was a chilly morning as they emerged into the sunlight and waited their turn to board a taxi to their hotel, the Hotel Sant'Angelo on the east side of the Vatican. Snow lay thick and heavy on the ground. 'A very ungodly time to take a vacation in God's city', Fr. McCarthy thought, ruefully. Though it was beginning to get cold in Houston as they left, winter time in Rome was not to be compared to Houston weather. Fr. McCarthy thanked God that Jennifer had insisted they bring heavy winter clothes

They missed two taxis before they realized what was happening. In Rome, you had to hustle to grab a taxi, otherwise, if you were not fast enough, you could spend the whole day waiting to be given your turn, which nobody was very willing to do.

"I guess, as they say, when in Rome, behave like the Romans," Fr. McCarthy said as he secured a taxi for himself and Jennifer. He put their luggage in the trunk and went around to his side of the passenger's seat. Of course, he noticed another peculiar thing about them which could make them stand out. Their luggage pieces were the largest, and, moreover, they had two apiece in addition to their carry-ons. He recalled hearing in a conversation many years back that Americans were the only people in the world who did not know how to travel light. When they left Houston, he had worried whether he had packed enough clothing and toiletries to last him for the more-than-two-weeks' vacation he was embarking on. Now he realized that they were the most encumbered visitors to Rome. He shrugged resignedly and wondered how others managed it. As they rode along, they could see that on some side streets, snow plows were still at work. A few people were shoveling the white fluffy stuff from their driveways, but most of the driveways were still thickly covered. Rome, during winter time, was a city that woke up gradually in the mornings, but went to bed abruptly in the evenings, so to speak.

Fr. McCarthy was thankful again for the watchful Jennifer, who noticed in time that the driver was going to take a longer route in order to charge more. She gave him the directions and threatened to notify the police if he tried to go out of the way to prolong the commute. It worked, as they made it to the hotel in less than ten minutes.

"Well, that's the best part of having you on this trip," Fr. McCarthy gushed. "I would have been had, and mercilessly so, if I'd come alone. I would've just relaxed in the backseat, thinking I was being taken straight to my hotel."

"I did that the first time I was here a few years ago," Jennifer said. "And I paid dearly for it. So, my being that alert was due to that experience. They say '*va bene*' to everything you say and before you know what's happening, it's no longer *va bene*, but *che peccato*."

"Ok. I've learned two Italian phrases now: *va bene* and *che peccato*," Fr. McCarthy said. "Do you speak fluent Italian? I forgot to ask."

"No, Cousin. I know a few words and I get by with those. Don't worry. Most Italians speak English, even if a little awkwardly. We'll get by."

They started talking about the places they wanted to visit while in Rome, chief among which, of course, was the Basilica di San Pietro. For Fr. McCarthy, everything in Rome looked ancient and drab. He thought the same thing about their hotel when they got out of the taxi and he looked up at the hotel building, which was dull brown and of an architectural style that could have been from the sixteenth century. A concierge appeared from the foyer to help them carry in their luggage and babbling some Italian phrases, which Fr. McCarthy thought was meant to assure them that they would enjoy their stay. They checked in at the front desk and the concierge carried their luggage to their rooms. Jennifer's room was next to Fr. McCarthy's, as they had requested. They wanted to stay close since it was his first time in Rome.

Fr. Cletus was taken aback by the inside of the hotel. Contrary to the outside of the building, the inside was neat and clean, furnished to high taste with antique, but solid, furniture, and the curtains were brocade fabric lined with white, almost transparent, lace material. There was a plasma TV on the wall and the concierge gestured to him, indicating the various plug outlets for his electronics. The concierge also pointed to a set of printed numbers on the dresser which Fr. McCarthy understood was the Wi-Fi pass key. Fr. Cletus thanked and tipped the concierge. Watching the concierge smile and repeat *grazie, signore* many times, Fr. McCarthy knew he'd given him a generous tip. Later that day, Fr. Cletus and Jennifer went out to lunch alfresco under an umbrella-covered patio at a nearby bistro. It wasn't very warm, but it wasn't terribly cold, either. So, they'd make do because they wanted to savor the street view of the environment. Since they were not due to visit St. Peter's Basilica for two days, they decided to pay a short visit to the Borghese Gallery and Gardens, where an expert tour guide entertained them with a detailed history of every piece of artwork, ranging from Bernini's *Apollo, Daphne and David*, to Caravaggio's *Sacred and Profane Love, John the Baptist*, etc., in perfect English, which Fr. Cletus appreciated and admired.

At the end of the day, Fr. Cletus and Jennifer were tired, so they decided to grab a quick supper and head back to the hotel. They needed to get a good night's sleep since they had more places thy wanted to visit the next day, including the Colosseum, the Quo Vadis Church, and the live theater. As Fr. Cletus got ready for bed after exchanging good-nights with Jennifer, he thought it had been a good day, a good start to their trip. He had thoroughly enjoyed himself and, for the first time in two weeks, felt relaxed and safe. He was grateful that Jennifer had convinced him to take the vacation, and to Rome, no less! As he reached to turn off his bedside light, he wondered what was going on back home in Houston. It was 9:20 p.m. Roman time, and 4:20 p.m. Houston time. He reached for his phone to check on his parents, but hesitated. Then he decided against it, pulled the comforter over his head, turned over as he closed his eyes, and, in slow motion, dove into a very restful sleep.

## DECEMBER 21, 2012

BACK IN HOUSTON, it was a great reunion for Dr. Josef Horacek and Dr. Edidiong Eshiet. It seemed like ages since they parted ways after completing their residency with the Jones's at Norfolk General Hospital. At Dr. Eshiet's insistence, Dr. Horacek had gone with Barbara and Crystal to visit him, partly because Dr. Eshiet was consumed with curiosity about the woman who had finally captured Dr. Horacek's heart. He knew his friend and former colleague had not remarried after his wife's death. Most importantly, Dr. Horacek had told him in their phone conversation that he knew how to trace the surrogate mother of the priest he was suing. If he could connect with her again, quite apart from having a corroborating witness in his suit, it would satisfy his curiosity to set eyes again on the woman who was part of their success story after Elizabeth Jordan Carr. Carr's conception and birth was not their project, but that of their mentors, Georgeanna and Howard. The young woman who came in to be a surrogate was their project, under the supervision of the Jones's. And because Carr's case was the first success story of an IVF baby in the United States, it overshadowed the second of such cases that followed on February 27th, just barely two months after her birth. Because of the peculiar legal circumstances surrounding their project and the prospective parents requesting absolute anonymity and protection from the media, the birth of baby Doe, who would grow up to be Fr. Cletus Nicholas McCarthy, was not publicized. Nobody knew what the parents named him after claiming him and paying the agreed contract charges for surrogacy. They had whisked him away from his birth mother and disappeared without looking back.

If Dr. Horacek did, indeed, know her whereabouts, Dr. Eshiet was curious and excited at the prospect of seeing her again. He surmised that she would be in her fifties now and wondered how she would feel when he would tell her that he had discovered who her biological son had grown up to become. He did not permit himself to agonize too much about the ethical implications of his actions, given that thirty years had passed and nobody would really mind the ethicalities of the issue that much. Although he felt like he had been unduly vindictive since he litigated his public humiliation from being denied Holy Communion, he had no regrets about it. For him, it was a matter of principle, in keeping with his longstanding personal decision not to suffer any injustice silently from anyone, especially the white man. So, he felt justified in his action. He brushed aside the thought of the litigation and braced himself to welcome his visitor and former colleague for an evening of camaraderie and catching up on the latest developments in OB/GYN. He stepped on the gas pedal to make sure he got to his house on time. Unfortunately, he ran into an accident scene on Highway 59 and was stuck in backed-up traffic for nearly forty minutes.

Luck was on his side. He got to the house just at the nick of time and, as he parked his car in the garage and entered the sitting room, he spotted a black Mercedes Benz sedan wheel into his driveway. He had no doubt it was the Horaceks.

"Honey, they're here," he announced to his wife, who was also emerging at that time from her room where she had been grooming herself, getting ready for the meeting.

To Dr. Eshiet's surprise, watching Dr. Horacek through the open curtain of his window, he thought Dr. Horacek had not aged much, as he had expected that he would have. Apart from a few white hairs around the base and a considerable thinning on the crown of his head, Dr. Horacek looked quite fit and handsome. Two beautiful ladies also got out of the car with him, one slightly younger looking than the other. Dr. Eshiet surmised that the older of the two would be Dr. Horacek's wife. She, too, looked younger than he had expected her to. Dr. Eshiet wondered if he himself was the one growing old. His doorbell rang as he reached and grabbed the knob, turned and pulled it open.

"Behold the eminent California 249!" Dr. Eshiet announced with obsequious ado. "You son-of-a-gun. You look great! Welcome to my home, my little piece of God's own terra firma. Come in, please," Dr. Eshiet said as he ushered them in to the sitting room.

"Well, well! If it isn't the Crown Prince himself. The highly favored son of Annangland," Dr. Horacek replied, trying to match his host's giddy exuberance. "You're living well, my friend. What a mansion you have!"

"God's handiwork, my brother," Dr. Eshiet demurred. "I feel He has blessed me in many ways. Welcome, ladies! I am Edidiong Eshiet and this is my wife, Ima. Welcome to our home. Please, make yourselves comfortable."

Dr. Eshiet and Dr. Horacek shook hands, held on, and bumped shoulders with each other in their old frat style. Then they shook hands with the ladies, pecking them on the cheek in gentlemanly gestures. The ladies shyly and half-heartedly hugged one another, exchanging their names and hellos.

"Please, have a seat," Dr. Ima Eshiet showed Barbara and Crystal to their seats and asked graciously, "Can I offer you something to drink? Soda, juice, lemonade…"

"Oh, water is fine. Thank you," Barbara replied.

"Are you sure you want just water," Ima felt slightly disappointed at Barbara's choice. "And you, young lady. What can I offer you?"

"Yes, water will be fine for me," Barbara confirmed.

Crystal declined the offer and was going to ask about her friend and classmate, Edo-Mma, but changed her mind and decided to wait for the right moment. She had notified her by text massage that she and her parents were visiting.

"What about you, Doctor?" Ima inquired of Dr. Horacek. "What can I offer you?"

"I'll settle for a glass of water, too," he replied, taking a seat beside Barbara.

"Hold on! Hold on!" Dr. Edidiong Eshiet interjected. "Nobody settles for just a glass of water at my house. Certainly not you, Doctor. Let's start again. This time, I'm going to offer you something exotic: African palm wine," he announced and then called out, "Edo-Mma! Bring the palm wine from the fridge in the pantry room."

"Honey, Edo-Mma went on an errand. She'll be back soon, though," Ima Eshiet replied. "I'll fetch the wine myself," she added and glided gracefully out the door, heedless of the token protests of their guests. Barbara thought she looked elegant in the embroidered African maxi dress she wore. She spotted a slight bump, too, a tell-tale sign of a woman halfway through her second trimester of pregnancy.

"I've heard so much about you, Doctor," Barbara said, approvingly. "Patients who have passed through your hands cannot hold back praising your unique style of care. And now, I'm so pleased to finally meet you in person."

"Don't believe everything they say, Barbara," Dr. Eshiet demurred.

"Sometimes patients exaggerate, especially when the outcome of an intervention exceeds their expectations. We do our best, though. I'm quite sure Dr. Horacek does a lot of great things up in Norfolk. After all, that's the seat of cutting-edge tech in OB/GYN."

"More like the cradle than the seat, Doctor Eshiet," Dr. Horacek demurred in his turn. "You guys are probably doing more down here than we do up there. And besides, I work in my private clinic most of the time, not in the mega-arena of Norfolk General. I do get to work there once in a while, though, when I need to use their facility and equipment."

Ima emerged at this juncture bearing a tray with bottled drinks. And in tow was Edo-Mma bearing a similar tray with wine glasses. Both set down their burdens on the coffee table and Crystal and Edo-Mma proceeded to hug and greet each other boisterously, as classmates and bosom friends often do. Then without wasting any time, Edo-Mma gave a decisive excuse for why she and Crystal would disappear and then dragged her friend in the direction of her room, where they could have their girl talk away from the curious ears of the adults. Dr. Ima, who was about to send Edo-Mma on another errand, got cut short by Edo-Mma's excuse and unceremonious departure. Dr. Ima rolled her eyes and sighed exasperatedly.

"Well, I used to do that when I was their age, too," Ima said, vexed and amused at the same time.

"The excitement of seeing each other outside of school," Barbara said. "But you're right. It's an adolescent thing."

"Honey, what do you need? I can help," Dr. Eshiet offered and then threw in some humor. "I am available for honey dos, remember?"

They all laughed at Dr. Eshiet's attempt at humor.

"Get the opener for the bottles, please, honey," Dr. Ima said, and proceeded to pitch her items of hospitality to her guests. "Try our African palm wine. You'll like it. Some of our friends here in Houston are all but addicted to it."

"And you still insist we try it?" Dr. Horacek asked, making a joke of it to the ladies' enjoyment.

"Oh, no! I didn't mean it that way," Dr. Ima said, sweetly embarrassed. "I meant that it is so good, you would want to drink it often."

"Don't mind, him, Doctor Eshiet," Barbara interjected, sounding formal.

"Call me 'Ima'," Ima corrected.

"Oh, thank you, Ima," Barbara replied graciously. "And please call me

'Barbara'. He's just pulling your leg. That's what his daughter, Crysie, does to me. She puts a joking twist on every little slip of the tongue I make."

"Well, I guess the acorn doesn't fall far from the tree," Dr. Horacek said, glancing at Barbara with a mischievously knowing smile.

Dr. Eshiet came in from the kitchen with a bottle opener and proceeded to open the bottles of palm wine and, after inquiring what the conversation was about, and being filled in, he joined his wife in praising the salutary benefits of the African palm wine, saying he would stake his stethoscope on proving that it was rich in yeast and good for the eyes.

He didn't have to stake his stethoscope, after all. Dr. Horacek was the first to praise what a good drink the African palm juice was. Barbara concurred and they almost got lost in small talk about wine, cheese, gourmet coffee, and cookies. Then, without even realizing that it had happened, the conversation wound its way back to the subject of their profession and the latest innovations in rep tech. Dr. Eshiet described for the benefit of his guests how he finally decided to use Preimplantation Genetic Screening (PGS) in the process of conceiving a child with Dr. Ima.

Being a "good catholic," Dr. Eshiet had agonized over the issue for a long time, and had had sessions with his pastor, the Rev. Cletus McCarthy. Then, during one of their conversations, the Reverend had advised him to consider adoption. He went so far as to indicate that he himself was adopted and that Catholic morality accepts adoption.

"When he mentioned Norfolk General as the hospital where he was adopted," Dr. Eshiet continued his story, "something rang a bell in my memory. His family name, his age, and the place of adoption all sounded quite familiar. That was when I decided to make a few phone calls and search my personal notes and records of the clients we served and the patients we worked with during the two years within which he would have been born and put up for adoption. I recalled that there was no information about any male child who was born and put up for adoption within that period during when he could have been born. I recalled, too, that there was a young lady we worked with, who was a surrogate for a young couple by the last name of McCarthy. But the young couple, being shy, did not want to deal directly with the surrogate. You can recall, Doctor, that as soon as we delivered the baby and the hospital management closed the deal between the couple and the surrogate mother, they vanished, as it were, and we were strictly forbidden from following up or maintaining contact with the receiving parents because they had requested in their contract to remain anonymous."

"Yeah. I can quite remember," Dr. Horacek concurred. "But we had the address and phone number of the McCarthys, remember? And we thought we would follow up privately, despite the injunction. But I lost mine and then I lost interest in them because after we completed residency, I was fighting to get my clinic off the ground. I don't know which I lost first, their contact information or the interest in following up."

"That's where I'm heading," Dr. Eshiet interjected to resume his story. "Fortunately, I had saved the information on my old laptop. I retrieved it and read through my notes. As I said, everything checked out. I traced their movement from Norfolk, through a friend who worked in the post office there, and their migration ended here in Houston, Texas, in 1988. When I looked into the matter and was satisfied that there was no other McCarthy couple who moved from Norfolk to Houston in 1988, and no other McCarthy couple who joined Our Lady Queen of Peace Catholic Church in 1988, except the McCarthy couple I have been seeing in church, I asked our priest casually during one of our conversations and he confirmed that they had, indeed, lived in Norfolk, but had moved to Houston when the boy child was about seven years. I confronted him with the information that he himself was conceived through IVF, and by a surrogate. I asked him why it was acceptable for his parents to use that method, but it wasn't acceptable for us."

"What did he say?" Dr. Horacek seized the pause in Dr. Eshiet's story to pitch the question.

"He vehemently denied it and kept insisting that he was born the normal way and was adopted at birth by his present parents," Dr. Eshiet replied. "He got very upset with us that we should even think of challenging his pastoral authority by daring to make such unfounded assertions. He literally warned us that if we went ahead with our plan to conceive a child using IVF, he would stop us from receiving Holy Communion in church."

"Oh, God!" Dr. Horacek exclaimed. "That must have aroused the ire of the African lion!"

"You know me well," Dr. Eshiet said, affirmatively. "As a matter of principle, I wasn't going to let anyone, most especially a priest who is supposed to be the embodiment of justice and fairness, bully me around. As I used to say when we were at Berkeley, I had had enough of that with the white missionary priests back home."

"There you go," Dr. Horacek said.

"Nope, you don't understand, Doctor," Dr. Eshiet countered. "Years ago, while I was still at home, I had a conversation with a peer of my dad who used to be an elementary school teacher and also doubled as the Church station catechist. He was fired from his job by the parish priest because he attended the African traditional moonlight dance. Friends of my dad got excommunicated from the Church because they took part in the traditional masquerade play of the people's culture. When I grew older and travelled to Europe, I saw priests attend ballroom dances and still said Mass the following morning. In Europe and here, I have witnessed the Church celebrate Halloween with masquerades and nobody gets excommunicated from the Church. In those days, back home, under the missionary priests, if your marriage fell apart, you were not given the chance to have that marriage dissolved so you could be free to marry again. You were condemned to the 'dead' marriage in perpetuity and stopped from receiving Holy Communion, and if you died during such a time, the priest would deny you a Church funeral service. Here in the U.S., I've lost count of people who were divorced, lived with another spouse in a common-law marriage, and, at the time of death for one member of the couple, the Church buried them as a matter of compassion. My maternal uncle sacrificed almost everything he had for the Church for twenty-seven years. When he died, he was denied a Church funeral service and burial rites because, according to the white priest, he did not do his Easter duty shortly before his death. And this was someone who had been very sick in the previous two years of his life and could not even walk, and never once did the priest visit him...."

"What is Easter duty," Dr. Horacek inquired, confused.

"Doing manual labor at the church grounds during Lent and, for the womenfolk, donating eggs and bundles of firewood, then confessing your sins to a priest so you can receive Holy Communion on Easter Sunday," Dr. Eshiet explained, almost sneering. "That is the one that got me the most. I cannot get over the treatment that was meted out to my uncle, when in Europe and here in the United States, every Tom, Dick, and Harry is buried by the Church. The term, 'Easter Duty', is absent from Catholic vocabulary in the white man's land. Three years ago, a young man who committed suicide was buried with full liturgical rites here in one of the churches, as a matter of compassion. But back home, we were taught that anybody who committed suicide was damned to Hell for all eternity and it was a mortal sin for any Church member to attend his funeral, let alone allow his corpse see the inside of a church. Now, tell me, Doctor: Why is compassion germane in such cases in the white man's land and a mortal sin in the black man's land, within the same context?"

"Well, Doctor," Dr. Horacek said, shifting uncomfortably in his seat, "that's quite an intense tirade, I must say. I can see you feel very hurt by these things, but seeing as I am not Catholic, and not even a practicing evangelical, to my shame, I must admit that I am bankrupt for an answer to your question."

"That's the reason why I had to sue, as a matter of principle," Dr. Eshiet said, almost self-righteously. "I still smart over that fateful Sunday when I walked up to receive Holy Communion, and Fr. McCarthy asked me to get back to my seat. My first impulse was to punch him in the face and knock him out flat. But in doing that, the consecrated hosts would have been spilled. You see, Doctor, I *am* a good Catholic. I revere the real presence of Christ in the Eucharist. And besides, the issue was between me and Fr. McCarthy, not the good Lord. It wouldn't do to knock the Lord Jesus to the ground for the folly of His priest. That would be transferred aggression, like crucifying Him again. He didn't deserve that then and He certainly doesn't deserve it again now," Dr. Eshiet concluded, to the cheerful laughter of his guests.

"The Crown Prince, himself!" Dr. Horacek cheered humorously, rocking with laughter.

"The same as ever," Dr. Eshiet acknowledged and sipped his palm wine, joining in the laughter at his own humorous digression. "I am the true son of my dad, man. I can't suffer in silence. *Haba!*"

Barbara laughed guardedly, but couldn't help liking the way their host cracked them up to ease the tension of his long, angry rant. A brief silence followed their cathartic laughter. Everyone sipped their wine and Dr. Horacek and Barbara mulled over Dr. Eshiet's gripe. Eventually, Dr. Horacek spoke, somewhat abruptly, catching his host midway as he got up to open and serve another bottle of palm wine.

"Drop your suit, Doctor. Let's work as a team to figure this out together, as in the good old days at Norfolk."

"What?" Dr. Eshiet asked, confused. For almost a minute, he thought Dr. Horacek was referring to his jacket, which he was still wearing. Then he got the meaning of it and, chuckling dismissively, replied, "I am trying to make a valuable point here, Doctor Horacek. Someone has to do something radical to wake the institution from stupor and get folks thinking outside of the box."

"I couldn't agree with you more. With all the media attention on the case, I would think you've made your point. But as valuable a point as you have made with your suit, it's like suing God!" Dr. Horacek sparred. "I mean, c'mon, you are the Catholic here and I am the supposed infidel. If that is how it appears to me, then…I wonder at your audaciousness."

"That's the point, Doctor. If my legal opponent is God, which he isn't, then I am suing him for his hypocrisy and pretense," Dr. Eshiet replied, incisively, and added, "Why should he judge and sanction me for the same act that he himself is implicated in?"

Dr. Horacek looked hard and long at his host and realized he was dealing with the same stubborn, pig-headed Edidiong Barnaby Eshiet as during their days together at Berkeley Medical School, a man who swore he would never take any nonsense from any white man. Sensing he would not sway Dr. Eshiet otherwise, Dr. Horacek decided to cut straight to the heart of the matter and come clean.

"Again, to my shame, I have no answer to your question. I'm only requesting that you drop your suit because of a vested interest *I* have in it," Dr. Horacek said, firmly, looking straight at his host.

"What vested interest could *you* possibly have in the case, Doctor?" Dr. Eshiet asked, looking quizzically at his guest.

"You are suing my son," Dr. Horacek replied, matter-of-factly.

"Say…I am not sure I got you," Dr. Eshiet said, straightening up and looking confused. "Can you…please…repeat what you were saying?"

"You are suing my son, Doctor. And the woman sitting beside me now and across from you is his biological mother, the surrogate who gave birth to the Reverend McCarthy."

Dr. Edidiong Barnaby Eshiet sat down before he fell down. He put down his wine glass before it slipped out of his fingers. "You son-of-a-gun!" he said, looking at his guest with bulging eyes and a shark smile.

"Son-of-a-bitch," Dr. Horacek corrected, smiling toothlessly. "I've been called that many times," he added, and earned an elbow jab in the ribs from Barbara. "I donated the sperm that we used to fertilize the surrogate's egg. The man's sperm was defective for the purpose, remember? And we had to substitute it."

"You said you bought the sperm from one of the residents," Dr. Eshiet said, nostalgically, recalling the events.

"I did," Dr. Horacek replied, looking honest. "I *was* 'one of the residents', and I needed the money."

"I'll be damned! You two-faced, double-crossing, slick-talking…!" He paused.

"Shall I lend you some more negative hyphenated adjectives?" Dr. Horacek interjected humorously.

"No. I'm not done yet," Dr. Eshiet replied and resumed his expletive-filled tongue lashing. "You're a real fast-handed, loop-hole-exploiting, smartass of a lucky guy!"

"Wait!" Dr. Horacek, said. "I can understand all the other expletives but…Why 'lucky', all of a sudden?"

"Because you outsmarted everybody and got away with it," Dr. Eshiet replied, to the amusement of his guests. "Although, the fact that you were smart about how you went about it didn't make it right. You do know that?"

"I know," Dr. Horacek replied. "I was young and wild then. I wouldn't do that now." It was difficult to tell if Dr. Eshiet was upset because he was beaten to it by his friend or because his friend did something unethical and got away with it.

"So, you and Barbara are Reverend McCarthy's biological parents?" Dr. Ima Eshiet asked, having sat quietly through her husband's rant until then.

"That is what it means, Ma'am," Dr. Horacek replied, affirmatively. "And for old time's sake, that's why I am asking your husband to drop the suit against my son. We can work out something satisfactory to both of you, I'm quite sure."

"Well, I may be willing to consider your request, but quit repeating the phrase, 'my son', ever so proudly, as if we need to decorate you with a medal," Dr. Eshiet carped bitingly. "You broke every ethical rule in the book, man! You should be sued!"

"Darling, don't be so hard on him," Dr. Ima rebuked her husband eventually. "I am so sorry, Doctor, for my husband's unfriendly behavior. He doesn't know how to be a gracious host."

"Not when the guest is a former colleague who unfairly corners everything, He gets the beautiful lady surrogate and her handsome young priest son, and he's not even Catholic! That's the irksome part. For that, he can take a few beatings from me as the price for his unwarranted good fortune."

"Sorry about that," Dr. Horacek said, jesting. "But I assure you, it's not my fault. Believe me, I just woke up to see myself undeservedly blessed."

The ladies had another round of laughter at Dr. Eshiet's acrid humor and his friend's mock apology. The phone rang and Dr. Ima got it. She listened for a few minutes and then said, "Yes. My husband is here. You can talk to him." She handed the phone to her husband announcing, "Dr. Murphy."

Dr. Edidiong Eshiet stayed on the phone for about two minutes, then hung up, and returned to his seat, announcing, for the benefit of his guests, that it was Dr. Regis Murphy of the University of Houston's Law Department, drafted by the Archdiocese to negotiate for an out-of-court settlement of the case.

"He's been talking with my lawyer, and just called to let me know that my lawyer has left the final decision to me."

"So?" Dr. Horacek inquired, expectantly.

"Let me sleep on your request, Doctor," Dr. Eshiet hedged. "I can't give any guarantees now. There are still other things to consider. Let me think about it." With that, he turned his attention to Barbara and continued the conversation. "Tell me all the good things that have happened in your life, miss, since you left Norfolk General. Don't tell me the sad ones. When you handed the baby to the legal parents and left the hospital, it must have been very difficult, in spite of everything. So, I don't want you to relive that. How was the journey of your life which ended with the success story of being one of the top Professors of Nursing at Baylor University?"

"Yes. I would like to hear it too, Barbara," Dr. Ima Eshiet concurred with her husband. A sneaky movement and a tripping noise behind the wall of the connecting passage to the dining area annexing the sitting room caused a distraction. "What's that?" she asked.

"Oh. I'm sorry," Edo-Mma said, coming out of the shadows. "We were just trying to go outside through the garage."

"No, Edo-Mma, you were not trying to go outside," Dr. Ima said with patient forbearance. "You have been eavesdropping behind that wall since you pretended to go to your room, and I have been watching your reflection on that TV screen. If you are tired of standing, you can come and sit down. Miss Crystal, you come and sit down, too."

Edo-Mma and Crystal looked at the telltale TV screen, then looked at each other and broke into girlish giggles, embarrassed at being caught in an awkward lie. They came out from behind the wall still giggling with hands over their mouths.

"Come out, girls. Come and sit down," Dr. Eshiet called out. "Edo-Mma, why did you make your friend stand all that while? We were not discussing classified information."

Edo-Mma went and sat beside her step-mom, Dr. Ima, and Crystal sat beside her mom, who looked at her with a toothless, disapproving smile. She knew her mom would lecture her at length on the etiquette of being a good guest when they got home.

"By the way, Edo-Mma is my daughter, from my first wife, God rest her soul," Dr Eshiet said, sounding doleful at the memory of his deceased wife. "I lost her to cancer fifteen years ago. My son, her brother, is now in Nigeria, volunteering during his internship year with Roesche, a German pharmaceutical company operating there in partnership with Welcome Nigeria, plc. He graduated as a pharmacist last June. He is due back here in the States in three months.

"Looks like you've been quite lucky, too, Doctor?" Barbara quipped in veiled critique of her host.

"Let's not go there, Barbs," Dr. Horacek said, baiting his friend. He put a hand beside his mouth, as if to shut out Dr. Eshiet. Dr. Horacek mockingly leaned over and whispered loudly, "His own luck was warranted."

"I heard that," Dr. Eshiet called out, looking morose and amused at the same time, and refusing to take the bait. His wife chuckled silently and signaled Barbara to continue with her story.

---

On December 22, at 4:30 p.m., prompt, Stacy Donovan rang the doorbell at Barbara Sander's house on East Westheimer Missouri City. The door opened to reveal a beautiful, shapely young lady whom Stacy surmised might be Dr. Horacek's daughter, since she looked too young to be his wife. She was right.

"You must be Ms. Donovan," Crystal inquired, and without waiting for an answer, invited Stacy in. "Come in. My dad is expecting you." She led the way into the sitting room and offered her a seat. "Dad, Ms. Donovan is here," she called out. "Can I offer you something to drink, Ma'am?" she asked, politely. Stacy requested a diet soda and sat on the single settee, which felt quite comfortable and almost swallowed her. She thought whoever furnished the house had good taste. She had learned a lot from her mother about interior décor. Judging from the choice of fabric and matching color combinations, she thought the whole thing must have been the work of a professional. She had barely enough time to savor the beautifully furnished sitting room when Dr. Horacek appeared from behind an adjoining door. He looked intelligent and stately, and she quickly took a liking to him.

"Hello. Doctor Horacek?" Stacy stood up and greeted him, stretching out her hand for a shake.

"Yes, Ma'am. I'm Dr. Josef Horacek." He took the proffered hand.

"I'm Stacy Donovan, Attorney at Law. I'm the Defense Counsel for the Reverend gentleman you read about and watched on TV being sued by a former colleague of yours, I believe, a Doctor Eshiet."

"Yes, Ma'am. Please be seated. I am fully aware of the case and I spoke with Dr. Eshiet yesterday," he replied.

"Oh, you did?"

"Yes, and I think I might be able to persuade him to drop the case," Dr. Horacek said, sounding somewhat confident. "He's not yet convinced, but we may soon be there."

"I don't doubt you, Sir," Stacy complimented. "I appreciate your invaluable help, but there is still a possibility of a last-minute refusal, knowing very well the Counsel who is representing him. In that case, I need to have a back-up plan, and that's why I want to get the story from you first hand, Sir, to have a good handle on the process that resulted in the Reverend gentleman's conception."

"Your diet soda, Ma'am," Crystal said, placing a saucer with a diet soda can on the table and a drinking glass and some napkins. "Dad, do you want something to drink?"

"No, sweetie pie. I'm ok," Dr. Horacek said. Then he continued with Stacy, "It's a long story, but I'm happy to tell you everything, if you have that kind of patience."

"Patience is my second name right now, Doctor," Stacy quipped.

Dr. Horacek chuckled briefly at her humor and settled down to tell his story.

It wasn't a long story, as he had indicated it would be, but Stacy thought it was an interesting one. Nothing gave her more satisfaction than learning the intricate process of how Fr. McCarthy was conceived. In the end, she thought she could still argue his case, proving that he was indeed adopted. To crown it all, Dr. Horacek had offered to extend his vacation to attend and testify during the second hearing on January 8, if it came to that.

Stacy was quite excited as she drove back to John McCarthy's place that evening. She couldn't wait to give him the news. She had, of late, taken to discussing her legal strategies with him, not only because he was a willing ear and showed a lot of interest, but also because he offered useful suggestions, too. He had worked as a paralegal for some years before quitting to join a pharmaceutical company as a regional sales executive, a job which he was still doing, but using the new and popular style of working mostly from home. Stacy thought that the computer age was making a lot of things possible, but, at the same time, teaching people to be lazy, and she teased her boyfriend mercilessly about that. John took it all with good grace.

Stacy couldn't understand why John decided to have a doorbell with the sound of a barking dog and a cooing pigeon. The *Bark! Bark! Coo! Coo!* sound was irritating, but she endured it and waited for the door to open. She had stopped arguing with him about changing it, making a mental note that if things came to a head, that that would be her first project done on her own authority with no need to consult him. The door flew open, revealing the form of John McCarthy swathed in his satin-lined velvet robe. Holding a glass of scotch in one hand, he swept Stacy with the other into a tight hug and kissed her. Stacy couldn't help feeling the bulge pressing against her, below the navel. She grinned and asked coyly, "Is that the scotch or are you just happy to see me?"

"I guess it's the latter," John replied, looking unabashed as he followed her into the sitting room.

"Well then, hold on to your breeches for a couple more hours. I have good news to tell you first." With that, she wriggled to duck his hand, which reached out for another amorous grab, and wiggled her way into the adjoining room. "Gotta change first."

# VENICE, ITALY

## JANUARY 1, 2013

A WASH OF DULL light enveloped the room and tickled Fr. McCarthy's face to complete wakefulness. Jennifer was at the window, pulling the curtains open and silhouetting her killer, slim figure-eight form against the dull white scenery that was the Venetian winter morning of the first day of the New Year. Fr. McCarthy could see from the hotel window that it had stopped snowing. The white fluffy matter covered the rooftops, and hid the water and boats below in thick blanket-like layers. He took a minute to muse at the human ingenuity of building an entire city on top of water. Venice was cold, dull, and slow in winter, but, for him, it wasn't as depressing as he was told it would be. The dull and calm of the city held a beauty of its own that was more captivating than alienating. He thought he understood why many of the world's great artists were from Venice and its surrounding areas—from Giorgione with his famous depictions of the goddess, *Venus*, from whom Venice takes its name, to Michelangelo with his opus magnum, *The Last Judgment*.

"Good morning." Jennifer's cooing voice woke Fr. McCarthy from his brief revelry. "Or should I say, '*Buongiorno, Padre*', as they say here. Aren't you going to get up?"

Fr. McCarthy turned over and hugged the warmth of the cotton-insulated comforter of the brocade-canopied bed. He felt like he could wallow in its warm fluffiness forever. Moreover, he thought they had no plans for the morning and it was going to be a dull day, coupled with the fact that he needed time to think and make sense of what had happened the previous evening.

"No. I plan to get lost in the folds of these bed sheets," he protested, feebly, like a difficult child irritated at his mom's trying to wake him up to get ready for school. He purposely restrained himself from looking a second time at Jennifer's body silhouetted against the window because he was confused about what had happened. Curiously, though, he felt no pangs of guilt, which accentuated his need to take time and sort things out and get a good handle on what was going on in his life. And Jennifer, standing with arms crossed under her bosom, head cocked slightly to one side, and in a short nightgown that was so flimsy and transparent that he wondered why she bothered to wear it at all, was a paragon of beauty, 'the kind that Michelangelo would like to paint', he thought. Perhaps, some day, he himself might like to try his hand at painting. "I need a few minutes to think and get my thoughts together. I feel like I'm falling apart."

"You're not falling apart," Jennifer countered, and went to sit on the bed. "You're unfolding out."

"I don't know why I don't feel guilty. That's not right!" Fr. McCarthy said, abruptly, suddenly bolting upright on the bed. "I did something wrong; we did something wrong. I should be feeling guilty." He looked at Jennifer, creasing his forehead in a mood of seriousness.

"I don't feel guilty, either," Jennifer said, looking calm and almost amused at his vehemence. "If I don't feel guilty and you don't feel guilty, then I refuse to share your sentiments that what happened between us last night was wrong."

"But we're related!" Fr. McCarthy pursued his self-excoriation.

"Correction," Jennifer interjected. "We're family, but we're not related in the sense you're talking about. *My* mom is *your* mom's adopted—not blood—niece, remember?"

"Yeah. Such is the sordid history of the McCarthys—a bunch of hopeless adopters and adoptees," he sneered.

"If I were you, I'd go easy on myself," Jennifer said, patronizingly. "But knowing you as well as I do, you're probably going to judge, condemn, and banish yourself to Hell before God Himself knows you're gone."

"I'm a priest!" Fr. McCarthy protested, against nobody in particular.

"Not news," Jennifer mocked, mildly. "Even so, maybe what happened was necessary to get you in touch with your human side. You know, it's always intrigued me that Jesus had to die in order to conquer death. Maybe you had to do what you did to rediscover your humanity. If I were you, I'd calm down. What happened between us is called 'love'. It might have been a little inappropriate, but that was it: L-O-V-E."

"False theology," Fr. McCarthy smirked.

"It could be a springboard to the true one. And if you don't mind, Cousin, while you are busy flogging yourself, I'm gonna take a warm, comfortable shower," Jennifer said and wiggled gracefully in the direction of the bathroom.

"Don't call me 'Cousin'," Fr. McCarthy protested, slightly edgy. "I'm not your cousin."

"See? Now you agree with me that we're not related." Jennifer put a spin on his protest and then disappeared behind the bathroom door.

"I agree with you over nothing," he called after her, vexed. Then he said stiffly, under his breath, "Always putting a spin on my words to your advantage." He sat on the edge of the bed, wondering why he permitted himself to get so agitated. He reached and grabbed his bathrobe from the side of the bed, put it on, lapped it over, and tied it. He moved to the window and stood looking out at the slowly waking city of Venice. Again, he wondered at the curious feeling of not feeling guilty about the previous night. He rather felt calm and relaxed. He knew his pretended outburst was a ruse for time and space to think. He knew that Jennifer saw through it, too, since she kept teasing him and didn't get riled at his crankiness.

Fr. McCarthy could have blamed the seductive Venetian evening, the movie they watched at the theater, and the wine and gourmet seafood and pasta they enjoyed together before returning to the hotel that fateful New Year's Eve. He recalled that, despite the cold and the fact that it was snowing lightly as they arrived back at the hotel, they felt good, all bundled up and milling with the few people who could brave the cold evening. He had felt a substantial measure of freedom from the stress of the previous two weeks. They had arrived in Venice early in the afternoon of December 30th, and checked in at the *Ai Cavalieri di Venecia*. It was a difficult decision to make because of the prospect of its being too cold in Venice at that time of the year for them to enjoy a part of their vacation there. In the end, they decided by tossing a coin, and going to Venice for three days won. They didn't regret the decision too much because, even though the atmosphere was somewhat dreary, there had been a break in snowfall for two days before they arrived. Fr. McCarthy was happy because it allowed them to visit the great Basilica di San Marco, and the Museum—Doge's Palace right across the plaza of San Marco—and the Church of St. Mary of Salvation (*Chiesa di Santa Maria di Salute*), so named because the natives believed a devotion to Mary in the 17th century had saved the city from a plague that had decimated almost one-third of the population. They couldn't take a gondola ride, though, since parts of the Great Canal were still frozen, although some boat owners could be seen plying short distances, deftly navigating between frozen portions of the water in small boats, probably for errands rather than entertainment. Due to the inclement weather, there were not a lot of tourists in Venice at that time of the year. The Venetians were nice and easy-going people and Fr. McCarthy thought they knew they had better be nice, since a chunk of their economy depended on tourism. It wouldn't help matters if people stayed away from Venice because the locals were mean-spirited.

Their New Year's Eve outing on December 31ˢᵗ took them to the *Theatro la Fenice*, where assorted opera and concert performances were given to celebrate the death of a year and the birth of a new one. Then it ended at one of the numerous taverns that lined the Rialto Bridge, for a gourmet sandwich of trout fillet and hot Venetian wine. Fr. McCarthy couldn't tell whether it was the warm tipsy feeling from the wine, or the romantic euphoria that clung to them after watching a superb performance of *Venus and Adonis*, by local artistes, or even the need to just exercise some rebellious freedom, but things began to change as soon as they got back to the hotel. Again, he would forever wonder, later, why they had settled, in the first place, for a suite with a master bedroom and a guestroom instead of separate rooms as they had done in Rome. Apparently, most things that create a turn of events usually don't make sense. So, he quit wondering and started dreaming back, replaying in his mind the events of the previous evening.

After their supper of trout fillet sandwich, they had decided to walk the short distance from the tavern to the hotel because they wanted to enjoy the fluffiness of the falling snowflakes, which, washed in the streetlights, created a scenery that looked like a zillion fireflies gently descending on the city. From the Rialto Bridge loft, the Canal Grande was exquisite to behold. It reflected lights of assorted colors from the esplanade lamps and the windows of the tall buildings lining the esplanade. It was such a night that made free hearts and minds wax poetic. And that was what Fr. McCarthy and Jennifer did.

"It is such a beautiful winter night," Jennifer said, feeling euphoric. "With the hazy light from the moon washing the misty clouds in the sky."

"In such a night, young Jessica and Lorenzo prattled with each other about their everlasting love," Fr. McCarthy said. Then noticing Jennifer throwing him a sideways glance, he added, "*The Merchant of Venice*. Act 1, Scene V, in Florence."

"Correction," Jennifer replied. "Act V, Scene 1. And it was not in Florence. You're mixing up your Shakespeare."

"Where was it then?" Fr. McCarthy asked, somewhat querulously. "I bet you don't know."

"Belmont, along the avenue of Portia's house," Jennifer replied. Then she continued with a teasing jab, "In such a night, did Cousin Cletus try to impress poor Jennifer with his knowledge of Shakespeare and botched it."

Fr. McCarthy stopped and looked at Jennifer and she stopped and looked back with a challenging smile. "In such a night did arrogant Jennifer, forgetting I acted Antonio, the Merchant of Venice, in high school pretend to challenge my knowledge of Shakespeare."

"In such a night did an ungrateful Cousin, forgetting I paid for his meal and wine, call me arrogant without any qualms," Jennifer replied, warming to the fight.

They entered the narrow foyer of the hotel and headed for the elevator to get to their suite on the third floor. Once in the elevator, they held their 'fire' because an elderly couple and another man rode it with them. Then the doors opened and they got out and turned right, heading down the hallway toward the fifth door on the right, which opened into their suite.

"And in such a night did the self-styled do-gooder, Jennifer, call me ungrateful, even though I had wanted to pay for my meal and wine and she insisted on picking up the tab."

They got inside and started removing their coats and garments. The suite was warm and Fr. McCarthy was already looking forward to a good night's sleep. Jennifer also went into her bedroom, but quickly emerged again for one more counter jab. She had removed all her clothing, except for her long-sleeved blouse, which looked more like a man's shirt than a lady's blouse. She headed straight for Fr. McCarthy's coat hanging in the open closet and pulled it off the hanger.

"In such a night, did self-willed, independent Cousin Cletus eventually pay for his meal and wine so he can quit whining as if he had lost his manhood because a lady paid for him," she said, proceeding to extract Fr. McCarthy's wallet from the coat pocket and pinching a wad from it.

"Hey! What are you doing?" he asked, abruptly, coming around from the opposite side of the bed. "Give me that. Put back that money. Thief!"

"That's not very poetic, Cousin," Jennifer said and ducked him, moving briskly to the opposite side. "Not very gentlemanly, either, calling a lady 'thief'."

"If the lady is stealing, it's appropriate to call a spade a spade. Put back the money and give me the wallet. You insisted on paying, so you can't turn around and rob me in broad...well, night light," Fr. McCarthy concluded, lamely, and made another dash for his wallet, which Jennifer artfully dodged, giggling.

"Daylight, Cousin," Jennifer replied. "The phrase is 'broad daylight'. I see I still have to teach you everything. Pay for your meal and wine first so you can quit lamenting." She fisted the wad of notes and, putting the wallet back in the coat pocket, threw it on Fr. McCarthy's bed and scuttled toward her room.

Fr. McCarthy jumped, hand first, on the bed and did a baseball-batter slide that brought him to a standing position on the other side, straight in front of Jennifer, blocking her way to her bedroom door. She gasped in surprise and broke out laughing, mesmerized by his unexpected acrobatic feat. She tried to duck and run into her room, but he blocked her and reached to grab her hand.

"Where do you think you're going, Ms. Bonnie Parker, robbing me in broad nightlight?" Fr. McCarthy asked, mixing humor with seriousness and throwing Jennifer into jubilant laughter as she kept trying to dodge him. Eventually they tangled, Fr. McCarthy trying to retrieve his wad of money, Jennifer trying to duck her way into her room and shut the door. The struggle moved, of its own accord, back into the center of Fr. McCarthy's bedroom and, eventually, amidst the laughter and exuberant abandon, they fell into the bed still struggling and laughing. If a spectator had been in the room, it would have been very confusing and difficult to tell if it was still a struggle for the money or whether, by an unplanned consensus, both had given in to just savoring the body rubbing and grappling. It would seem it was the latter, since at one point, Fr. McCarthy was making only half-hearted attempts to retrieve his money while Jennifer was making an equally half-hearted attempt to prevent him from taking it. The only earnest thing that went on between them was the grappling and rubbing and rolling over, with Fr. McCarthy repeatedly chanting, almost, "Give it to me," and Jennifer responding on cue each time, "Try and get it if you can," in between giggles.

Nobody knew who initiated it—though years later, each would argue vociferously to own the blame and claim the credit—but their lips were locked in a wet kiss that ignited a point of no return. And, again, nobody knew how and when it happened, but whatever remnants of clothing were left on their bodies were either lying on the floor or strewn across the bed. Reason disappeared faster than a comet and caution flew out the window as their bodies wrapped and entwined each other, and Fr. McCarthy and Jennifer passionately ravaged each other, powerlessly surrendering to the charming magic of Aphrodite as they tested the sweetest taboo they had ever experienced. Capped off, at last, by the most ecstatic and prodigal distribution of the flesh, they had sunk helplessly together into the cozy bosom of Morpheus.

"Mass is at 9 a.m. at the Chapel of San Marcos," Jennifer's voice woke him from his revelry. "If we get there early enough, we can go to confession."

"Confession?" Fr. McCarthy asked, confused. Then he quickly caught a hold of his thoughts. He had not considered the possibility of confessing his sin of the previous night so he could receive Holy Communion at the Mass, as that was a Solemnity of Mary the Mother of God, a Holy Day of Obligation. "Yes. I think I need to make my confession. Do you think we can make it in time for it?"

"Well, if you shower and dress right away," Jennifer replied, "then yes, we can make it in time."

"I can do that," Fr. McCarthy replied as he headed toward the bathroom. "It's you and your lady's way of taking time to dress that I'm worried about—lipstick, powder, perfume, hair, and God knows what else."

Jennifer started to respond, but decided to ignore it and just get dressed. That was not the time to stoke their usual fight. Moreover, she was emotionally disturbed about what had taken place the previous evening, not because she thought what happened was sinful, but because she realized that what had happened was real: she was in love with her beloved 'cousin', Fr. McCarthy. And that was scary. Again, it wasn't as though she suddenly woke up to the reality of it, rather, what happened was like a climax, a pivotal point, confirming what she had suspected all along with their unrelenting verbal sparring and teasing of each other. It was not strictly a breaking of any taboo since they were not related by blood. Her mom was only loosely adopted by Fr. McCarthy's grandmother, Bernicia. She was an orphan and had struck up a high school friendship with Hannah, Fr. McCarthy's mom. Soon, an occasional sleepover turned into acceptance into the family. Later, after graduating high school, Jennifer's mom found herself pregnant, but when her boyfriend refused to marry her, Bernicia took her in fully as family. Jennifer was born a year and four months before Fr. McCarthy. They grew up together and came to refer to themselves as cousins. Again, Jennifer was not so much worried about herself for what had happened, as about Fr. McCarthy and how he would take it, especially given what he was going through at that moment. She started feeling that she may have added to his worries with her uninhibited vivaciousness that led to their passionate lovemaking. That really seemed to be the main reason why she needed to confess and seek advice.

Fr. McCarthy, for his part, wondered at the two sides of Jennifer. The January 1st, New Year's Day Jennifer was a somber, pious, responsible woman, whereas the December 31st, New Year's Eve Jennifer was a garrulous, tipsy, flirty provocateur with whom he made love. He didn't understand. He philosophized briefly, trying vainly to hit on a theory to explain this uncanny ability in women to switch, in a blink, from being the worst sinner to being the holiest angel ever. He ran down his biblical memory lane, from Rachel to Rahab, and from Ruth to the nameless woman who wept at the feet of Jesus and anointed him with a costly perfume. He made a mental note to look into the matter. Women were indeed a species to be studied. After all, one of his seminary friends had flippantly pointed out the curious fact that no university in the United States had any *Department of Men's Studies*, but most universities had a *Department of Women's Studies*. He thought, too, that the peculiar change in her demeanor was the result of what he would call a 'post-fall calming syndrome'. She, perhaps, calmed down at the realization that she had seduced him into sleeping with her. He again made a mental note to assure her that they were equally to blame for their unconscionable tryst, with him perhaps even more so. The sound of Jennifer banging her shoes together—a habit she had—before putting them on woke him from the revelry and he turned on the water for a quick shower. He was determined to make the time for their confession.

# HOUSTON, TEXAS

## JANUARY 8, 2013

"ALL RISE! FIRST Circuit Court in Session. Honorable Judge Anieno Montgomery presiding," the bailiff pronounced his usual line as Judge Montgomery climbed a couple of steps to her position at the bench. "All sit." The courthouse was packed to capacity, almost double the number of people who attended the first day. The media had dissected the case, analyzed it, sifted it, deconstructed and reconstructed it from many different angles over the course of three weeks until scarcely anybody in the nation, let alone in the state of Texas and the city of Houston, was a stranger to it. It became a subject of debate in families by the fireplace, in pubs among those drinking their beers, in academic common rooms at universities, and just about everywhere: Now that a priest had been conceived via IVF, would the Catholic Church review its position and retract its teachings opposing the tech procedure as immoral? Would the Church permit couples to legitimately use it to conceive or dig its feet in? Such, and other puzzling questions, made the court session of January 8, 2013, a crucial event in the annals of litigation in Houston and the state of Texas, and the sundry media personnel present were poised to let the people know either way.

"Call the case of the day," Judge Montgomery spoke her command with professional ado, without even looking at the bailiff.

"In the matter of discrimination and emotional battery, in the case of Eshiet and Eshiet versus Cletus McCarthy and the Catholic Archdiocese of Galveston-Houston, will the litigants indicate their presence in court," the bailiff called out. Each Counsel responded present.

"We shall begin the proceedings of the day with the Defense," Judge Montgomery said. "Counsel may call its witness to the dock."

"Counsel would like to call Mrs. Hannah McCarthy," Stacy announced. Hannah McCarthy moved to the dock and the bailiff administered the usual oath.

"Ma'am, you may be seated," Stacy said, politely. "And, for the record, state your full name please."

"Hannah Therese McCarthy," Hannah said in her singsong voice.

"Ma'am, you are the adoptive mother of the Reverend Cletus Nicholas McCarthy of Our Lady Queen of Peace Catholic Church, am I correct?" Stacy queried.

"Objection," Patrick Turner said, somewhat disinterestedly. "Counsel is leading witness."

"Sustained," Judge Montgomery cued in her customary call.

"I will put the question another way," Stacy said, not really seeing what her opponent was objecting to. "Do you know the Reverend Cletus Nicholas McCarthy of Our Lady Queen of Peace Catholic Church? If you do. What is your relationship with him?"

"Yes, I do know him," Hannah affirmed. "He is my adopted son and I am his adopted mother."

"Can you tell the court how you came to be his adopted mother?" Stacy said, facing the jury box and away from the witness, in that characteristically dramatic way lawyers use to create an impression when they know their question is going to elicit a cardinal point from the witness. "What did you go through; what was the whole process like?"

Hannah McCarthy shifted in her seat, adjusted her clothing, and, striking the pose of a gone-through-a-lot mother misunderstood, she told her story. After she was done, Stacy turned and asked, "Did you sign any papers indicating that you were adopting the newborn baby?"

"Yes," Hannah answered curtly.

"Are these the papers? Can you recognize your signature?" Stacy said, spreading a handful of copy-size typed documents in front of Hannah. She squinted slightly at the papers as though she was seeing them for the first time.

"Yes," Hannah said, resolutely. "That's the contract document that the hospital gave me, and those are my signatures."

"Your Honor, Defense submits documents as evidence," Stacy said.

"Does Prosecution agree?" Judge Montgomery asked as Stacy moved to show the papers to Patrick Turner.

"Yes, Your Honor." Patrick Turner said, a shade too fast and a fraction of a second too soon, before even looking at the papers, nearly giving away the charade. Stacy placed the documents on the judge's desk.

"Did you at any time have any conversation with the biological mother of your adopted son, either before or after the adoption was finalized?" Stacy asked.

"No, Ma'am. I was not allowed that," Hannah replied resolutely.

"Your witness," Stacy said, looking at the prosecution desk and smiling only with her eyes.

Patrick Turner got up, adjusted his tie, and, slightly backing away from the witness, leaned on the witness railing with one hand and the other on his hip, all red tape and boredom. He did not even look at Hannah, but proceeded with his brief cross examination.

"Ma'am would you recognize the biological mother of your adopted son if she appeared now in court?"

"No, Sir," Hannah replied curtly.

"If she appeared now in court and made a motion to claim her biological son back, what would be your reaction?"

"Well, I had the best part of him as my son for thirty years. Now that he has become a problem child with a lawsuit on his head, she can have him back; all of him, with the lawsuit,"

Hannah replied, throwing the court into a raucous guffaw. Hannah sat still, maintaining a stone face. Patrick Turner was greatly tickled at the wry humor and Judge Montgomery permitted herself a chuckle even as she banged on her gavel for order in court.

"No further questions, Your Honor," Patrick Turner said, moving to his seat still chuckling quietly.

"Ma'am, you may stand down," Judge Montgomery said, watching with amusement as Hannah walked the short distance to her seat beside her husband at the Defense Counsel desk. "Counsel may call her next witness."

"Counsel would like to call Dr. Josef Horacek to the stand," Stacy announced, and after the usual oath and stating of name in full, she proceeded to examine the witness with the same set of questions. Then she asked him to recount the events that took place at Norfolk General Hospital thirty-one years ago, which resulted in the adoption of Cletus Nicholas McCarthy. The entire courtroom was spellbound as they listened to Dr. Horacek's story. From time to time, Patrick Turner and his client, Dr. Eshiet, conferred in whispers and nodded their agreement on some point of issue. Everything seemed to go fine, and his story even began to bore the court. But as he mentioned the part when he substituted the donor sperm with his own, the whole court broke into pandemonium, as had happened on the first day when Fr. McCarthy was outed as having been conceived via IVF. Reporters and camera crews stampeded one another while trying to get to the lobby of the court to call in the breaking news to their different newsrooms. Fr. McCarthy was not only conceived via IVF, but also happened to be the biological child of a prominent Norfolk Fertility Clinic owner, Dr. Josef Bernard Horacek, whose story turned out as the background to set the case straight. Legally, it meant that Fr. McCarthy was the adopted son of Stephen and Hannah McCarthy, but the biological son of Dr. Josef and Barbara Horacek. The documents of adoption exonerated the McCarthys from any direct involvement or complicity in the IVF conception process of Fr. McCarthy. And Fr. McCarthy, himself, was not to blame because it wasn't his fault that he was conceived that way. The Horaceks not being Catholic, the Church was bereft of the power to impose on them the doctrine on the immorality of IVF as a binding article of faith and morals. As such, they had no case to answer. In the end, Dr. Edidiong and Dr. Ima Eshiet were left with only one charge to pursue in their case: emotional battery. That was the part of the settlement that merited the legal fees as due from the Archdiocese because, from all indications, Stacy would have lost on that score. There would have been no way to prove that publicly shaming the Eshiets by denying them Holy Communion in full view of other parishioners was not emotional battery, a category of tort litigations that is always difficult to disprove. So, Stacy was only too glad to stage the drama of putting her witnesses on the stand to bring the case to the point where Patrick Turner would declare prosecution's agreement to an out-of-court settlement.

Judge Montgomery regained order in her court after incessantly banging on the gavel. "Counsel may continue," she called.

"Dr. Horacek, on the adoption contract, who signed for the father of the baby?"

"The hospital management signed. Technically, the baby had no father, so the hospital signed *in loco patris*."

"Your Honor, defense rests," Stacy announced with formal ado, turned to Patrick Turner and added, "Your witness." Then she walked back to her seat.

"Dr. Horacek when the sperm from the first donor was found to be unfit for use in fertilizing the egg of the surrogate mother, because of aneuploidy as you said, what did the hospital do?"

"The hospital management asked me to find another donor and I found one," Dr. Horacek replied.

"You found one?" Patrick Turner asked, looking confused.

"Yes," Dr. Horacek replied, resolutely.

"Who?" he asked, creasing his forehead.

"Me," Dr. Horacek responded, matter-of-factly.

"Oh! I see," Patrick Turner said, looking like one who has in fact gotten it, finally.

The court broke into another round of laughter. He turned and faced the audience with a shark's smile. Scratching his head and looking stunned, he admitted, "He threw me off," exacerbating the laughter. Then, turning theatrically on the balls of his feet to face the bench, he announced, "Prosecution rests," bowing obsequiously.

"Mr. Turner, is this a charade?" Judge Montgomery asked.

"No, Your Honor. It is not," he replied, getting serious again.

"Good," Judge Montgomery said with a slight edge to her voice. "Because, if I can recall well, at *Turner and Stendhal*, you don't kid around." She parroted Patrick Turner's statement on the day of the preliminary hearing.

As it turned out, the court session of January 8 was, in fact, a charade. The background negotiations that Dr. Murphy and Dr. Horacek had participated in had resulted in Dr. Eshiet agreeing to an out-of-court settlement. Dr. Eshiet had even agreed to drop the claims to damages for emotional battery except for the legal fees that the Archdiocese would pay to *Turner and Stendhal*, to cover costs and time spent. In turn, Dr. Edidiong and Dr. Ima Eshiet would be restored to the Sacrament of Holy Communion after they would have been duly absolved. In lieu of this, they would do the mild penance of bagging relief material for two days, for needy clients at the St. Vincent de Paul Food Pantry, a job at which Dr. Ima Eshiet was already a regular volunteer for two days a week, and a cause which was already a pet project for both husband and wife, as they had donated huge sums of money and material toward it. They gleefully embraced the penance and even finished it before the court date. They even continued donating their time and money to the Food Pantry, as they did so almost weekly prior to their penance. Thus, their penance was also a charade, to give the parishioners of Queen of Peace the impression that the Eshiets were punished for their insubordination. And both husband and wife made a big splash of finally giving in to the authority of the Church, by doing their "penance" in the limelight, with reporters and cameras all over the place. But Dr. Edidiong Eshiet kept insisting that he and his wife were contented they had made their point by forcing the Church to review its record of justice and fair treatment of its members. So, all parties concerned knew ahead of time what was going to happen in court, and were, to a certain extent, coached on how they would respond to certain questions. So, the edge in the judge's voice was a cue for Patrick Turner to do what he had agreed to do to bring a close to the matter.

"Your Honor!" he called, raising his forefinger like a town council voter. "One minute, please." He bent over his desk and conferred in whispers with the Eshiets, then straightened up, adjusted his suit, cleared his throat and intoned in a powerful baritone voice, "Your Honor. Given all the submissions by the witnesses, especially the testimony of Dr. Horacek, and in consultation with my client, prosecution has decided to drop the charge of discrimination against the Reverend Cletus McCarthy and the Catholic Archdiocese of Galveston-Houston. On the Charge of emotional battery, prosecution, in consultation and after due negotiations with all stakeholders, has agreed to an out-of-court settlement with the defense counsel." He gave a slight bow and sat down.

"The discrimination charge against the defendant is hereby declared dropped," Judge Montgomery said and banged her gavel. "On the charge of emotional battery, litigants are hereby advised to settle their grievances out of court. Court is dismissed." She banged the gavel one more time and walked out from the bench into her chambers, as if she couldn't wait to get out of there. The crowd rose and started for the door in a raucous din, looking a bit disappointed at the seemingly anticlimactic ending to such an explosive case. Not in the least disappointed was the Houston KHOU TV Channel that had obtained the streaming rights to air the proceedings of the day. It announced, somewhat unenthusiastically, that the discrimination case against the Catholic Archdiocese had been dropped after a high-powered negotiation had forced the prosecutor's hand.

---

In the Chancery office on San Jacinto Street, Cardinal Umberto Felice punched the air in a gesture of victory and said, "Yes!" Bishop Montano and Sister Ellis, who were watching the procedure together on the conference room TV, abruptly stood up, hugged, and kissed each other. Then, suddenly self-conscious, they quickly disengaged and scuttled out of the room before anyone noticed. Fr. Callahan and Fr. Tung, who were also watching the procedure on Fr. Callahan's office TV, high-fived each other, and Fr. Tung waxed scriptural, "And the powers of the netherworld will not prevail against it."

"The bark of Peter is, once more, on safe waters," Fr. Callahan concurred.

At the courthouse, Stacy escorted the McCarthys into their vehicles to drive home. She promised to call Fr. McCarthy and bring him up to date, then turned to walk to her car in the parking lot behind the courthouse where John McCarthy was waiting for her. Fr. Charles Polanski was on his cell phone pacing on the steps of the courthouse. He waved to Stacy and she waved back, suspecting he had beaten her to it, updating Fr. McCarthy. She hoped he was giving him the message the right way, though it didn't matter a whole lot as she would still call him to advise him on the next steps to follow.

She was just coming level with her BMW convertible when she heard her name. Turning around she saw Dr. Horacek walking briskly toward her. In tow was a stately middle-aged lady whom she surmised was his wife Barbara. She had never met her. The day she visited Dr. Horacek, Barbara was out, she was told. Stacy was struck by her beauty and felt secretly happy for Fr. McCarthy, though, technically, Barbara wasn't his mother.

"Ms. Donovan, I want to thank you so much for a wonderful job," Dr. Horacek said, almost swooning. "You don't know how much it means to us for Reverend Cletus to finally be exonerated."

"Yes, thank you so much, Ms. Donovan, for representing our son so well," Barbara concurred. Then, realizing she might be misunderstood, she quickly added, with a tinge of embarrassment, "Well, technically speaking, not our son. But, you know the sense in which I am saying that. He came from…, well, my womb, you know." She chuckled, awkwardly. "We love him and we're proud of him."

"You're welcome, Dr. Horacek," Stacy replied, shaking his proffered hand. Then she gave Barbara a hug. "Don't make too much of it, Mrs. Horacek. I am sure he will be glad to welcome you to be part of his life, as his 'other mom'."

"Oh, that is such a sweet thing to say," Barbara cooed, hugging Stacy again. "I can't wait to meet him when he comes back from vacation."

"Yes, please, Let us know as soon as he is back," Dr. Horacek said. "We would like to meet him and offer him our support and encouragement. We would like for him to know that even though we are not his parents, still we do love him."

"No problem I'll let you know," Stacy assured. "Have a nice day," she said, waving as she walked on and grabbed the car door thrown open for her by John McCarthy. They waved back with smiles and gratitude.

"What a fine young lady," Barbara said.

"Yes," Dr. Horacek agreed. "And well at home in her profession."

———

It was an unusual Saturday afternoon on January 12, 2013, at the McCarthy residence on Hollow Wood Circuit. It felt like it was Thanksgiving again. The food, the guests, the camaraderie, the stories, and the fellowship were all typical, except that the gathering was for a different reason. Fr. McCarthy had come back from his vacation almost a week earlier and, having met with his biological parents, Barbara and Josef, and his sister, Crystal, at Barbara's house, he insisted on arranging a meeting during which both his adopted family and biological family would meet and get to know each other. As he put it, there was no reason why both families could not relate together in mutual friendship. After all, it wasn't a "new normal" as the popular phrase went, that he had adopted parents and biological parents. Having four parents had always been the lot of any adoptee since ever the first child was adopted, whenever and wherever that was. So, it was one big celebration at the McCarthy residence, despite the stories in the media about them which came in all slants and angles, depending on the paper and the TV station, and the intent of the publishers. Even their neighbors came to visit and share in the euphoria, but most probably to see Fr. McCarthy, the first IVF-conceived Catholic priest, as the media had put it.

Fr. McCarthy felt like a celebrity. As a matter of fact, his parishioners treated him that way at the reception they held after Mass, the previous Sunday, to welcome him back to the parish. Not that it was unusual to welcome a pastor back from a short vacation with a reception ceremony. Just that it was appropriate to do so as a matter of solidarity, considering the situation of things. And Greg Sullivan and his wife openly rejoiced, almost tripping over themselves to show how much they and the parishioners supported him 'in these trying times', as he put it in his brief speech. There was more than enough food and drinks, music and dancing, and brief speeches here and there—some exaggerated—to show how much Fr. McCarthy had touched their lives. It was a good ceremony, but, through it all, Fr. McCarthy could not help feeling that something had changed in their relationship with him. On the general level, the normal pastor-parishioners relationship was still in place, but beyond that veneer, the dynamics had changed. In fact, without actually saying so, some parishioners exhibited an unintended curiosity in the way they looked at him, probably wondering whether a 'test tube-conceived' person was just like any other normal person.

It was both fun and unnervingly embarrassing to be an object of curiosity in that sense, and Fr. McCarthy could not decide if he liked the experience or hated it. But the most worrisome thing for him was that his peculiar situation had confused most parishioners and warped their image of him as a channel of God's grace for them, despite their bravado at political correctness whenever they ran into him or talked about him with others. He thought this was going to greatly affect his ministry on a deeper level. His sacramental theology professor at the seminary used to painstakingly explain how the person of the priest was impacted by his ministry and vice versa. And if, in the minds of the people, there was a disconnection between the message and the messenger, there was no ministry. Fr. McCarthy thought his current situation vividly illustrated the scenario and, for the few days he was in the parish at Our Lady Queen of Peace after his vacation, he experienced increased inner turmoil. He knew that unless he took care of his inner turmoil, he would gradually become ineffectual in his ministry. But was he really interested any more in ministry as a priest? That was the primary question he needed to answer and he thought he would do that best if he went on retreat in solitude. This would afford him the time and space to sort things out in his mind.

"May I have everyone's attention, please," he called, rapping his wine glass several times with his fork and raising his voice to supersede the din. "Attention, please."

"Fr. Cletus is calling our attention," Hannah McCarthy announced, fervidly. "Listen, he wants to address us."

Everyone stopped talking and all eyes were trained in Fr. McCarthy's direction. He stood up and cleared his throat and began to speak in measured tones.

"First, I want to thank God for making this gathering possible, especially for the two sides of my family—my adopted parents and my biological parents—to meet in celebration of a common linkage: me, their son. As I reflect on what has happened in the past few weeks and what is happening now, I cannot help but think about the wonderful way that

God is always uniting seemingly impossible factors and situations, all for His good purpose. He did it at the incarnation. Whoever would believe that the divinely spiritual could be married to sinful flesh? But there He was, the Son of Man, walking the Earth in human form and yet bearing in Himself the fullness of God's glory. The more I think about my situation, the more I am inclined to think that God's hand is still controlling what is happening to me. Catholic moral teaching totally condemns using *in vitro* fertilization to conceive a child, and for good reason. But here I am, a man who was conceived via *in vitro* fertilization, yet ordained a priest in the Roman Catholic Church, to propagate that same teaching, unknowingly judging and condemning the very method by which I was conceived. My priesthood is as if the test tube met and married the altar, the altar having stolen the test tube's heart, because as I am standing here. I love being priest, in spite of everything."

He drew a brief, rousing applause for his analogy.

"But the function of the test tube and the function of the altar are seemingly incompatible as far as human reproduction is concerned. At least, so the Catholic Church, of which I am a servant and a teacher, teaches. And since I find myself in this unique, unenviable position of being simultaneously the law-giver and the law-breaker, albeit indirectly so, I have been plagued by more questions than I have answers for. But I am going to do one thing. I am not going to dwell on the past, trying to agonize over the reason why what happened did happen. I am going to try and figure out what it is God is trying to tell me here, and how best to sort out my unique case. While on vacation in Venice, something odd, but interesting, happened to me, on which I still need time to reflect and determine what it really meant."

Jennifer started slightly but unnoticed, at the mention of the incident in Venice. She was thankful that Fr. McCarthy didn't go into details. Not that it mattered, but it would have been a very inauspicious time to bring up such a topic. She too had been pondering about the incident since ever they came back, though, like Fr. McCarthy, not yet able to make sense of it.

"So, for that reason," Fr. McCarthy continued. "I am taking another one week off from pastoral duties, to reflect on my situation and to plot my next move forward. All things being equal, which is a rare occurrence...."

"I will pray for all things to be equal in your case," Hannah McCarthy interjected, looking warily at her son, as though he was about to pronounce an unfavorable omen. Barbara drew her closer with a sideways hug and rocked her very gently from side to side as if comforting a frightened child. Fr. McCarthy was pleased to see how fast the two women – his two mothers – bonded. He decided to put Hannah at ease with a little humor.

"Well, Mom, you should have let me finish the sentence so you don't pray for the wrong equation," he carped, humorously, to another brief bout of uneasy laughter. "As they say: be careful what you pray for, so that you don't get it."

"Because you might get it," Jennifer interjected, correcting Fr. McCarthy.

"I mangled that on purpose because I knew you would jump in; can't stand to be quiet for too long, can ye?" Fr. McCarthy replied, to the merry laughter of everyone who knew them. Jennifer rolled her eyes at him and looked away, pouting beautifully. "As I said," he continued, "all things being equal, I will probably get reassigned in a new direction. I do not know which, but I have a feeling that it will be good for me. Once again, thank you all for coming. Thank you, Dr. and Mrs. Horacek, my parents in the natural order of things, and my beautiful sister, Crystal. Thank you, Mr. and Mrs. McCarthy, my parents in the legal order of things, for hosting everyone. Thank you, my extended family—Uncle John, Josh, Jennifer, Mr. and Mrs. Henson. Thank you, Mr. and Mrs. Sheridan, and Mr. Wong. You guys are wonderful neighbors. Thanks so much for your support and good will. God bless you all."

A resounding applause followed his speech as he sat down and took a sip from his almost empty glass.

"Where will you be going this time, Father?" Crystal asked with bland curiosity.

"Oh, not too far this time," Fr. McCarthy replied. "I'll take a week at the Passionists' Retreat Center. It is a nice and quiet place for individual retreat and meditation."

"Reverend, do you have any idea what your next assignment will be when you come back," Dr. Horacek inquired, just for the interest of it. "Or, do you think you will continue as pastor of Our Lady Queen of Peace?"

"I would advise a change of parish," Stephen McCarthy interjected before Fr. McCarthy responded. "Nothing like a fresh start in a fresh environment."

"Actually, I did apply to be transferred once I get back," Fr. McCarthy replied. "But a whole lot depends on my state of mind after my one week retreat."

He fielded a couple more questions before he was left to enjoy the rest of the afternoon's party with no mention of his situation. Though they didn't sit down to plot it out, the Horaceks and the McCarthys, by tacit agreement, decided to just focus on bonding and providing each other the friendship and support they needed. Brief speeches and expressions were made, each side assuring the other of unflinching support for the sake of their mutual link in the person of Fr. McCarthy. The Horaceks assured the McCarthys that they would totally eschew meddling in the McCarthys' parenting rights and privileges, and would leave it to Fr. McCarthy, himself, to feel free to either relate with them or not. Fr. McCarthy dismissed that as 'nonsense' and reiterated that as far as he was concerned, all four of them were his parents; he would love them equally…and be a nuisance to them equally. His remark drew brief laughter and Hannah and Barbara assured him that he would be a very welcome nuisance to both of them. Perhaps the most touching statement of all was a question from Crystal.

"When you come back, will I be permitted to visit and hang out with you as my brother, as often as I want to?" she asked with a whining lilt in her voice, like a kid who makes a difficult request, but, nonetheless, wants to pressure the parent to not refuse it. Fr. McCarthy quickly got up and went over and gathered Crystal into a tight bear hug, to the applause of everybody.

"Yes, my dear little sister," Fr. McCarthy replied. "You will have unlimited visitation rights, 24/7, to hang out with me. Only one thing: I will not permit you to say Mass. So, don't even dream of asking."

Everyone laughed again. His remark and the vehemence of his tone tickled Crystal so much that she giggled with abandon, looking simultaneously radiant and silly. She was so beside herself with joy that throughout the gathering, she looked longingly at Fr. McCarthy. She had confided in Edo-Mma earlier that it gave her a higher self-esteem and sense of fulfillment that she had a brother who was a priest. Jennifer wasted no time bonding with Crystal that afternoon. They became great friends and promised to chat, call, or email each other as often as possible. Altogether, Fr. McCarthy was happy that he organized the gathering that afternoon. The solidarity and healing that took place was tremendous. When the time came to disperse, tears of joy flowed freely down every cheek, good-bye hugs were extra generous, and Barbara and Dr. Horacek had to exert extra effort to tear Crystal away from her newfound brother. She cried all the way to their vehicle and promised to be the first person to visit him when he would come back from his retreat. Fr. McCarthy assured her that that would be most welcome, though he knew who would be the first to welcome him back. As the taillights of the last guest's vehicle disappeared from view, he smiled contentedly and turned to go inside and stay with his adopted parents for a couple more hours before heading back. He thought life wasn't totally bad for him, despite everything.

# PART V

*When the self is just a shell,*
*and the business of living so untrue*
*Strain and reach beyond the spell,*
*to reinvent yourself anew.*

- ANON

# HOUSTON, TEXAS

## JANUARY 21, 2013

F R. MCCARTHY'S THREE-DAY intensive retreat or 'time away', as he loosely called it, was, by all accounts, a very important hiatus in his work life and, you could add, his litigation life. It not only afforded him the solitude he needed to reflect on and be at peace with his newfound identity as an IVF-conceived Roman Catholic priest, but, also, the much-needed personal space to do so while restructuring and projecting a vision of himself in the future and what role he would comfortably assume in the scheme of things. The two-week vacation in Rome and Venice was just that: a vacation. Throughout that period, his mind was virtually vacuous. He focused on no thought-engaging issues, but just on the things that would help to unwind him, relax his nerves, and bring him to a state of calmness of spirit and mind. This time around, without Jennifer at his side, he could meditate for long periods without the luxury of her distracting interruptions. Not that he resented those mood-puncturing moments; they had their usefulness. Only that, as some smart aleck sang, *With a beautiful lady in your arms, it's kind of hard to think straight.*

Fr. McCarthy came away from his partly self-imposed retreat very much at peace with himself. The Retreat Father who helped direct the process was very friendly and quite resourceful. He took him on a soul-searching journey that was a novelty to Fr. McCarthy, and he came away satisfied that he had achieved more interior healing and reconciliation than at any other time in his life. Yet, one thing that he was still unable to come to terms with was how his new identity would fit into his pastoral ministry, and what image of him his congregation would carry. Would that enhance his ministerial effectiveness or detract from it? Would they "click" with the image of him as a priest conceived by the same process which the Catholic Church condemns as 'intrinsically evil', or would they find that to be a stumbling block? Nothing scared him more than finding himself to be a spiritually ineffectual priest. He would be no more than a social functionary going through the mechanics of the trade with no inward commitment. And that was not Fr. McCarthy's understanding of who a priest should be.

Upon speaking with the Cardinal two days after he returned from his retreat, Fr. McCarthy asked for and was transferred from Our Lady Queen of Peace to St. Monica Catholic Church, northwest of the city. This was a multi-cultural church, with the majority of congregants being African American. The next most-dominant population was Hispanic. There were a few Caucasian families, but they could be counted on the fingers of one hand. Fr. McCarthy wondered whether that was a good choice for him. St. Monica was a church mainly populated by converts from non-Catholic denominations who knew or made little about Catholic hardline doctrines on reproductive technology. For them, Fr. McCarthy's birth origin was not a big deal. Even the Hispanic community did not raise any outcry. For them, as long as a priest was validly ordained and touching lives in his ministerial duties, it didn't matter how he was conceived. What was not taken into consideration, or, perhaps, even imagined, was the reaction that would come from the few white parishioners, and the damaging effect it would have on Fr. McCarthy's spirit. As soon as he arrived in the parish, four of the six white families left the parish, citing the fact that they could not belong to a parish under a priest who had been conceived via IVF. When Fr. McCarthy learned of their intention to leave, he was despondent.

"What is more painful, Charlie, is that these are people of my own race and color," he had riled to his friend, Fr. Polanski. "They practically disowned me. And do you know who have been my comforters so far?"

"I could guess," Fr. Polanski said. "But I will let you tell me."

"My Black parishioners, Charlie," Fr. McCarthy said, vehemently. "They visited me on two occasions and virtually forced me to let them pray for me and with me. After each prayer session, they stayed to offer words of solidarity and comfort."

"They *forced* you?" Fr. Polanski asked, dubiously.

"Well, bad choice of word," Fr. McCarthy recanted. "They prevailed over me to let them pray for me…. Well, Charlie, you know what I mean… the 'white pride' thing: I mean I should be the one to pray over them and comfort them, not they over me. That's why I was reluctant to accept their sodality ministrations."

Fr. Polanski looked at his young friend curiously for a fraction of a second longer than normal, then he broke out in a merry guffaw, causing Fr. McCarthy to also look at him, confused.

"What...what is tickling you?"

"You, Nick," Fr. Polanski replied, in between heaves of laughter.

"What did I say funny?"

"Not what you said," Fr. Polanski replied, reigning himself in. "It's the whole situation. Remember, two months and few weeks back, you could have given anything not to have any Black person involved in your case because, generally speaking, you didn't believe a Black person could wish you well?"

"I was sued by a Black man, for crying out loud," Fr. McCarthy said, plaintively.

"And you had a fair hearing by a Black lady, for crying out loud," Fr. Polanski countered. "Don't get me wrong, Nick. I am probably more into the 'white pride, white privilege' thing than you are. And, candidly speaking, if I found myself in your situation I would be more chagrinned than you are now, except that I have learned a lot over the years and I am beginning to accept the hard, albeit, uncomfortable truth."

"Which is?" Fr. McCarthy interjected, anticipating one of his friend's hackneyed theories.

"Read through the Bible, Nick. The Black man has this peculiar thing going for him; call it the spirituality of the helper. A few instances: remember when Jeremiah was thrown into a well to die? Who interceded and had him pulled out?"

"Ebedmelek, the Cushite?"

"Yeah, the land of Cush is modern day Ethiopia in East Africa," Fr. Polanski expounded, gleefully. "When Herod sought the life of the infant Jesus, didn't his parents run with him to the land of Egypt in Africa? And who helped Jesus carry his cross, but Simon of Cyrene, a North African? So, as an *alter Christus*, if a Black sodality offers you comfort at this time in your life, take it. Our Lord took it when he needed it."

"Well, I always considered those instances you mentioned as coincidences," Fr. McCarthy said, dismissively. "And not really gave a thought it could be interpreted that way."

"It's my own interpretation, Nick," Fr. Polanski replied. "You are not bound to agree with me. There are a few more instances than I have mentioned, and they are simply too many to be coincidences, all. I seem to see some kind of design."

"You going to publish a book on it?" Fr. McCarthy asked, half serious and half facetious.

"I might," Fr. Polanski replied, curtly. "My point, though, is that you shouldn't be so chagrinned at being ministered to by your lay Black congregation. As things stand, the future might see a Church of reciprocal ministrations between the clergy and the laity, and I think that would be very healing."

Fr. McCarthy sat pensively for a few seconds, mulling over his friend's unpopular theology. He was always impressed by the way Fr. Polanski seemed to read meaning out of, and sometimes into, seemingly innocuous events to create a new way of looking at the same issue. He grudgingly thought he might be right again about the spirituality of the Black man, but he was not going to openly admit or begin a ministry on that.

"Remember that time I had a brief missionary stint in the Sudan, three years ago?" Fr. Polanski's voice jolted him slightly. "I always enjoyed the company of the young people there, especially the teenagers. They always had anecdotes and tales about the animal kingdom. On one such occasion, one of them asked, as the usual openers go, 'Do you know what the coyote said to the fox'? I said, 'no'. Of course, that's what you are supposed to say to get the story teller going. He said, 'the coyote said to the fox: *If I fall down for you and you fall down for me, I will know we are playing. But if I fall down for you and you stay standing over me, then you are spoiling for a fight. When I get up, we'll duel.*'"

"What was their interpretation of that?" Fr. McCarthy asked, genuinely curious.

"They had no interpretation for it," Fr. Polanski replied. "I read my own interpretation into it. You see, what I came to learn about the Black man was that if you rub him the right way, he can be the best of friends, but if you rub him the wrong way, he is the worst of enemies because he reacts from the basis of his historical perception of the white man as an oppressor of his race. So, if your Black parishioners have reached out to you, accept their friendship. Who knows? They might be the harbingers of the healing and peace that you need."

Fr. McCarthy sat for a while ruminating over his friend's advice and his unconventional theology of the Black man. He didn't know whether to believe him or dismiss his views as that of a self-flogging white man becoming too sympathetic to the Black man's cause. But one thing was apparent: he was consoled and relieved from his previous angry frustration. He looked at his watch and stood up to call his exit.

"Feel like tennis, tomorrow evening?" Fr. Polanski asked as he escorted him to the door.

"No, I have an appointment with the *Movimiento Familia Catolica* group. Let's do it some other time," he declined. "I'll call, though."

As he drove back to St. Monica Church that evening, he wondered again whether he would ever put behind him the trauma of what he was going through. It seemed to be deepening as the days went by. Like Job, he felt like cursing the day he was outed in court, firmly convinced that he was functioning well when he didn't know that he had been conceived via IVF. He thought whoever invented the saying that 'what you don't know cannot hurt you', had hit the fact spot on. The evening was cool and breezy, typical of Spring nights, and since it wasn't even 8 o'clock yet, he decided to stop by Jennifer's apartment, hoping to leave a note if she was at work. And that was another bad idea.

———

Jennifer was home, in bed. Fr. McCarthy was surprised because it was unusual for Jennifer to be in bed before 8 p.m., unless she was working night shifts, during when she had to leave for work by 9 p.m., so then, and only then, would she go to bed at 6 p.m. for a two-hour nap. She came to the door after Fr. McCarthy had waited for almost a full minute since he heard her voice inside, acknowledging the doorbell. She was in her pajamas, practically dragging herself along.

"Come in," she invited Fr. McCarthy in, sniffling.

"What's the matter, Jenny?" he asked. "Are you alright?"

"Yes…I mean, no," she replied, haltingly. "No, I'm not alright now. Yes, I will be when I'm fully rested." She pointed Fr. McCarthy to a chair by her writing desk, then, noticing that he was still looking at her inquiringly, she added, "I lost a five-year-old girl this morning."

Fr. McCarthy sat down. Under normal circumstances, he would have jokingly teased her about that by saying he didn't know she'd had a baby, but watching Jennifer at that moment, he knew the circumstance was not normal. He just called out his sympathy.

"I am so sorry. Was she very sick?"

"She was, but she didn't deserve to die that way," she said with a tinge of anger in her voice. "She had acute leukemia and we were lucky to get a bone marrow donor who we thought was a match. The marrow transplant was successful, but for no apparent reason, her autoimmune system rejected the tissue. She died in my arms at 5:37 a.m. this morning. We battled for more than two hours to save her life. It's unfair…It just seems so unfair. She was such a sweet angel, and we all loved her. It's just not fair for children to die like that for no fault of theirs…It's not fair!" Jennifer broke down and practically fell into Fr. McCarthy's arms as he rose to hold and console her. She cried openly for several minutes before Fr. McCarthy could coax her back to some semblance of calmness. He implicitly agreed with her that it wasn't fair. 'But was life, in general, ever fair to anyone'? he thought.

"There, there," he coaxed, rocking her from side to side. "Calm down, calm down. It wasn't your fault. Don't cry. You did all you could. You did everything there was to be done."

"I know. And that's why it isn't fair," Jennifer interjected, defiantly. "Why does God refuse to answer little children's prayers? We prayed for her and with her; all the nurses in the unit, we prayed for God to spare her life. After she had the transplant, she kept expressing the hope that she would soon go home. She even said she would be a nurse when she would grow up. Why didn't God answer her prayers?"

Fr. McCarthy swallowed hard and scrambled mentally for some consoling response, but coming up with none, he decided to remain silent. He had learned in his pastoral theology class years back that sometimes silent witnessing to suffering may heal faster than risking a bland answer that hurts even more because it's just the usual cheap cliché. He continued holding her tight and rocking her gently from side to side for another minute. Then he started to let her go, but Jennifer grabbed him and pleaded with him to hold her a little longer.

"I am sorry to put you on the spot," she said, seemingly calm. "I guess such questions have no answers. I know, too, she wasn't my child but I had no idea how much I had bonded with her until she breathed her last and went limp in my arms. I was her primary nurse, you know."

"Yeah, I can understand why it weighs so much on your spirit," Fr. McCarthy said with deep sympathy. "But take consolation in the fact that you did all that was within your power to do for her. She is at rest and she is at peace…"

"Say that again," Jennifer started in his arm and looked at his face as he repeated the sentence.

"She is at rest, she is at peace," she repeated it herself, pensively, then added, "That makes sense. She had suffered for a long time. You are right, Cousin. May she rest in peace."

"Amen," Fr. McCarthy responded, for want of any other sensible thing to say.

"Let's sit down, Cousin. But hold me for a few more minutes till my distressed spirit finds peace too," Jennifer said as she led Fr. McCarthy to the sofa. They sat down and she snuggled against him very tightly so much that he could feel all the soft curves of her torso. "Did you have supper?"

No," he replied.

"Hold me a little longer," she pleaded, snuggling deeper into him. "I have some food I could warm up. You'd like it." She snuggled and wriggled. Fr. McCarthy could feel her nipples hardening against his side, but she had her arms around him so tightly that he would have to practically push her to tear himself away. He had no time to figure out the best way to disentangle himself because Jennifer started kissing him on the cheek, first furtively, then, boldly. He vacillated between gently pushing her away and cooperating. He would have done the former, but Jennifer's body was so seductively soft and deliciously warm, and the pleasure current coursing through their bodies was so overpowering that he lost all willpower to resist. He rather felt himself sweetly responding by kissing her back. Soon their lips locked and their bodies entwined each other on the sofa as they sank together, once more, into the abyss of forbidden pleasure.

---

As Fr. McCarthy drove back to St. Monica Church that evening, he knew that he had reached the point when he must make a critical decision. He looked at his watch and it was almost 9:45 p.m. Although he hadn't been to spiritual direction in more than six months, he decided to do so first thing in the morning after Mass. Then instead of driving straight back to his parish, he made a detour and knocked on the rectory door of St. Leo Church. He knew that his confessor, an old Vietnamese priest in residence, was not in the habit of going to bed early. So, he decided to catch him for a quick confession since he needed to say Mass in the morning. As usual, the old priest did not show the slightest surprise or curiosity at Fr. McCarthy's confessing to sacrilegious fornication. He just casually 'fatigued' him with three Our Father s, three Hail Mary s, and three Glory to the Fathers, and went back to watching his basketball game on TV. Fr. McCarthy was almost amused at the old man's perfunctory style. Yet he believed in the juridical efficacy, *ex opera operantis*, of the sacrament.

Just as it happened after their first shared sexual experience in Venice, Fr. McCarthy did not feel guilty. On the contrary, he felt healed and peaceful interiorly after the intense orgasm he experienced with Jennifer. He could see on Jennifer's face that she, too, was experiencing the same wholeness of spirit as they ate their supper. She was back to her usual exuberant and chatty self. Fr. McCarthy accepted, inwardly, that he went to confession only to fulfill the juridical requirement to be in a state of grace to celebrate Mass, and kept wondering whether such imperfect contrition, in fact, the lack of it, which he experienced, had nullified the sacrament. He became somewhat conflicted, and absent-mindedly drove over a flower bed in his driveway as he wheeled his vehicle toward his garage. Was he, in fact, losing it? For one, he knew that his second fall had caused any residual willpower he had for resisting Jennifer to vaporize. Secondly, the curious phenomenon of guiltless euphoria he always had after intercourse with her was anomalous. He thought such anomaly could only spell one thing, and he resolved to act accordingly, resolutely convinced that it was the right course for him to follow.

# HOUSTON, TEXAS

## THURSDAY, JANUARY 24, 2013

FR. BRADY CALLAHAN finished reading Fr. McCarthy's petition letter and looked up, heaving a sigh of defeat. For almost two weeks, he had tried to dissuade Fr. McCarthy from his decision. He had asked him to discuss his decision with his spiritual director, which he did. He had consulted with Bishop Montano and the Cardinal. The latter had asked Fr. Polanski to try and dissuade Fr. McCarthy from taking the drastic decision he was about to take, all to no avail.

Fr. Callahan sighed again, folded the letter and put it back in the envelope.

"Well, I will mail it for you first thing this afternoon," he said, unconvincingly. "It should be there in a few days' time."

"That won't be necessary," Fr. McCarthy replied, casually. "I already sent it Tuesday morning of last week by currier service. It is probably in discussion this week."

Fr. Callahan looked at Fr. McCarthy with incredulity and said, "You meant business, didn't you?"

"I need to move on, Father," Fr. McCarthy replied. "That is your copy, for the records."

He stood up and Fr. Callahan, not knowing what else to do or say, stood up too, and escorted him to the door. He was still bereft of words as he shook Fr. McCarthy's hand, nodding quietly as though he understood why the former took the decision he took.

"Pray for me, Father. I need all the prayers I can get now, but I think I am heading in the right direction" Fr. McCarthy said as he turned to go. He stepped into the hallway walking briskly toward the elevator.

"I will pray for you," Fr. Callahan, finally finding his voice, called after him, feebly.

Cardinal Felice presided over the brief meeting in the conference room, after Fr. McCarthy left Fr. Callahan's office and was gone from the Chancery. They had been in dialogue with him for more than a week, trying to prevail on him to change his mind, but to no avail. With the information from Fr. Callahan that Fr. McCarthy had already dispatched his petition by currier to the Holy See, everyone knew the die was cast. So, the meeting was not going to be about Fr. McCarthy as such, but about what message the Cardinal would send to all the parishes, and how that was going to be viewed. They surmised that conservatives would breathe relief, liberals would rile in protest, and moderates would remain ambivalently calm.

The job of the Chancery was to have an official statement for the faithful before the press fed them with dubious and wild versions of the issue.

"Good morning everyone," the Cardinal began, somberly. "I guess it's no longer news that Fr. Cletus Nicholas McCarthy has petitioned the Holy See for his own laicization. We had spoken with him about this for almost two weeks, and he had also been in intense discussion with his spiritual director. As it stands now, he has concluded that to be returned to the lay state of life would be good for him. It may, perhaps, be good for the Church, too, but I do not know. Only God knows. If we had prevailed on him to stay on in the priesthood, perhaps, with time, everyone would get over the fact of his IVF birth and life would go on. I do not know, however, whether he himself would be able to get over it and move on. Having believed, because of Church teaching, that IVF as a technology for human reproduction is intrinsically evil, and having convincingly taught the same for many years, to the extent of sanctioning members of his Church who used it to conceive, only to, suddenly, be proved beyond reasonable doubt that he himself was born by the same process, is enough to destroy a person psychologically."

"Gosh! Akin to being caught in your own trap," Bishop Montano interjected, almost under his breath.

"Yes, Marmon," the Cardinal confirmed. "It is easy to sort things out when you contradict yourself about an object outside of yourself. It's a different ball game, altogether, when you yourself are the walking contradiction, in person. That's the situation that Fr. McCarthy finds himself, and it is not a very enviable situation either."

"A sign of contradiction," Bishop Mario Montano chipped in again, looking sagacious. "Very Christological. I wish he had considered things along those lines."

"He talked about it with me," Fr. Callahan said. "He said his spiritual director had offered him that angle, but his take of that was that it is easier said than done. Moreover, he dismissed that line of thinking by saying it was not becoming of him, a mere human, to contest for that title with the Lord."

"A typical Father-McCarthy response," the Cardinal said, with mild exasperation. "However, we need to preempt the press by getting a statement out to the parishes. Marmon, if you could handle that I would be most grateful. Just let the faithful know that due to the situation of things, Fr. McCarthy has decided to ask Rome to be returned to the lay state of life. That's all."

"It will be done, Your Eminence," Bishop Montano said, looking at Sister Ellis who nodded consent and took down some notes.

## WEDNESDAY, JANUARY 30, 2013

FR. MCCARTHY HAD just finished reading through the drafts of his prepared homily and his statement of farewell to the parish for the weekend, when his cell phone rang. It was Fr. Charles Polanski. He hesitated before answering, since he suspected the reason why he called.

"Why did you go and do that for, you shelfish, shelf-centered coward?" Fr. Polanski shouted from the other end, catching Fr. McCarthy off guard with his bellicose tone and diction. "Yes, you heard me, Nick. You are one helluva shelfish coward."

"Hold on! Hold it, Charlie! I don't know what is going on over there but, you sound hurt," Fr. McCarthy said.

"The hell, you know what's goin' on. And ya'll know am 'urt."

"Charlie! Charlie, you are slurring your words," Fr. McCarthy said, genuinely concerned. "Are you sure you're alright?"

"What the 'ell d'ya'll care if am a'right?" Fr. Polanski continued, practically ranting and slurring. "Ya'll wanna know if am a'right? Yeah, am a'right. Ish yu that's not a'right. Yu perfidiash coward."

Fr. McCarthy had had enough to conclude that that was not a conversation he wanted to have on the phone. Fr. Polanski was in very bad shape, and he couldn't recall any time recently when he heard him sound like that. He knew he had been drinking and was drunk. He also suspected the reason why he hit the bottle. There was nothing else he could do just then than to drive out to wrestle his friend and mentor out of the bottle before he drank himself to damage point. He arrived at the rectory at precisely 4:50 p.m. When Fr. Polanski refused to answer the doorbell, he went around to the back and entered through the garage door, which was always open. Fr. Polanski was conked out on the couch, a bottle of vodka in one hand and a glass in the other.

"Ger' rout of me 'ouse, I don't register ex-priestsh in ma parish," He slurred the words, trying unsuccessfully to lift himself from the couch and get up. "I won't accept you in ma parish. I don wan no ex-priestsh as me p'rishioner."

"How long have you been drinking, Charlie?" Fr. McCarthy asked, moving in to help his friend up. Fr. Polanski tried to shun his help and, still holding his bottle and glass aloft, tried to use his bottom as the only fulcrum for catapulting himself into a standing position and kept falling back into the couch. "Here, let me help you. You can't get up if you don't drop the bottle and glass and use your hands for leverage."

"Don't 'elp me," Fr. Polanski said, trying futilely to resist as Fr. McCarthy wrested the vodka bottle and glass from his hands. "I don need yar'elp, I say," he yelled feebly and ineffectually. "You went and resigned ya priestshood without ma permission."

"Sorry about that, Charlie," Fr. McCarthy replied, trying to humor his drunk friend. "I didn't know I needed your permission. But I had to move on. And, by the way, I told you I was going to do it."

"And I told 'ou, 'No,' givit tam," Fr. Polanski was now in a standing position but was a bit unsteady on his feet as he rocked back and forth. "Yo see, tam 'eals a lot. Always givit tam when sonthing happens, and it will 'eal." His eyes were glazed and bids of perspiration dotted his forehead and rolled down his temples in rivulets.

Fr. McCarthy looked hard at his friend and knew he had quaffed a huge quantity of vodka. He was drunk in a way he hadn't seen him drunk before. He went and put down the vodka bottle and glass on the decanter and went back to coax Fr. Polanski to a chair.

"Here, sit down and I will make you a strong cup of coffee."

"I said, I don wan none o yar 'elp," Fr. Polanski protested, still feebly.

"Well, friends need friends to help when situations make them no better than unaccompanied minors," Fr. McCarthy teased, using Fr. Polanski's words he spoke on the court day when he dropped him off the court parking lot. "I'll make you some coffee now."

"I ain' no companied minor, and ya not my friend," Fr. Polanski kept on his feeble truculence. "Leave me alone. I got no friensh in the priestshood. Yo were ma friend, then yo went to resign from the priestshood. I got no more friendsh. Yo acted like a perfidiash coward. I pray Pope Benedette don't grant yu laity statush. Don brew me no caffee. I don need ya gad-forsaken brew."

"Benedict," Fr. McCarthy interjected, stifling his guffaw. "Try Pope

Benedict. By the way, God doesn't hear the prayer of drunks. That's why you should drink my brew to sober up before you pray."

"He's gonna 'ear mine. Gad 'earsh the cry a the poor," Fr. Polanski iterated with vehemence, bobbing his head for emphasis.

"Ah, c'mon, Charlie," Fr. McCarthy continued to chat him up to keep him awake for the coffee. "You own a duplex and an antique Bentley. And you drive an Acura TLX and run a fairly affluent parish."

"Am poor 'cause a gat no friendsh."

"How many times do I have to remind you that I am your friend?" Fr. McCarthy chided, pointlessly, just to keep his friend talking.

"Ya not ma friend. Friendsh don 'urt friendsh," Fr. Polanski said, pouting defiantly.

"Well, I'm sorry, Charlie, if my action hurt you," Fr. McCarthy said, demurely. "Here drink this and you will be as strong as an ox. What's more, you will be able to convince God to hear your prayer."

"Don't 'umor me. He'll 'ear ma pr'yer," Fr. Polanski replied, looked at Fr. McCarthy's outstretched hand with the mug of coffee for several seconds, then he took it and held it for a few more seconds, still pouting and looking simultaneously morose and bellicose.

"Drink it, Charlie, and you will be fine," Fr. McCarthy coaxed. "I am sorry that you got affected so much by my resignation. But it is a decision that I must make now. And as you have said, time will heal everything, I hope."

Fr. Polanski looked with rheumy eyes at his younger friend for a few silent seconds more and then took his first sip of the black brew that would bring him sobriety in the next one hour.

Fr. McCarthy sat down on the couch, waiting on Fr. Polanski to finish his coffee. He felt deeply sorry to discover that his decision to apply for laicization could hurt his friend so much, to the point of sending him to the bottle. He began to weigh in his mind whose action was selfish: his own resignation to fate and the resolve to move on in a different mode of living, or his friend's anger because he couldn't prevail on him to stay on in the priesthood so he could have a friend. He wondered what kind of friendship that would be, if he stayed on to battle forever, his crisis of identity, and of what use that would be to Fr. Polanski, or himself, for that matter. He felt no regrets for his action. On the contrary, he thought he would live to regret staying on. The constant, daily battle to try and feel comfortable with the idea of being a walking contradiction, teaching a doctrine that judges and condemns the very origin from which he came as 'intrinsically evil' would have destroyed him psychologically. Life was going to be simpler for him now that he would not be the teacher, but the hearer of the teaching. He would not be living a conflicted life, being a contradiction to himself. He believed that in time, Fr. Polanski would get over his anger and disappointment. They would continue to be friends, except that the dynamics of their friendship was going to change drastically. What the new configuration was going to be or how it would play out was not yet clear. The one thing he was sure about was that he would still be a good friend to Fr. Polanski. He hoped that Fr. Polanski would try to be the same to him.

Fr. Polanski finished his coffee as fatigue and boredom were getting the better of him. He started dozing. Fr. McCarthy gently pried open his fingers, took the coffee mug from his hand, and put it on the table. Then he asked whether he wanted to go sleep on his bed. Fr. Polanski declined and trudged dreamily to the couch, sank in, and lay down. Fr. McCarthy brought a pillow and a blanket. He propped Fr. Polanski's head up and covered him with the blanket. Soon, Fr. Polanski started purring like a giant cat. Fr. McCarthy sneaked out the back door and placed a call to Julio, the yard maintenance man, to go over and sit watch over his boss till he woke up. Then Fr. McCarthy got in his car and drove home. He resolved to call at hourly intervals to check on Fr. Polanski.

TWO DOCUMENTS ARRIVED on Fr. McCarthy's desk the same day: a very ironical coincidence, but through different routes. The one came by courier from the Holy See, while the other was an email forwarded to him by Sister Ellis, which he printed out. He laid the two documents side by side and read through them each two times. Then he sighed and reclined back. The Holy See courier document was not unexpected because he had initiated a process that needed a response which, in fact, he was glad to receive. The email printout was from the Holy See, as well, but not directly. It was a declaration sent to the Bishops by the Holy Father about persons born of IVF, preempting the official canonical formulation of it. The courier document was terse and formal in the way that juridical documents from the Holy See are usually cast.

> *Dear Father Cletus Nicholas McCarthy,*
>
> *Grace and peace to you from the Lord Jesus Christ, our Great High Priest, who, in His great mercy has called us to a life of service in holiness. Blessings from me, the unworthy successor of Peter. In response to your formal request for laicization and in consultation with the office of the Congregation for the Clergy, after a prayerful reflection, I have decided to grant your request. You are hereby released from the clerical state of life and all the duties pertaining to that state of life. You can no longer perform the priestly duties by public administration of the sacraments of the Church, effective Thursday, February 14, 2013. Bear in mind that this ruling does not remove the mark of the priestly ordination from you which may efficaciously be used at the*

*service of any person in danger of death. I pray that you find*
*peace and healing in your new state of life.*
    *Yours in Christ,*
    *Benedict XVI*

The second document was equally terse and formal.

*To my Brother Bishops,*
    *Grace and peace to you in Christ, our Lord and Master.*
*In light of the new things happening at jet speed in the*
*scientific world of today, especially in the area of human*
*reproduction, it has become necessary to issue an interim*
*declaration to take care of emergent situations, pending*
*a formal canonical decree. I hereby declare, by the power*
*vested in me as the Supreme Pontiff, that persons born of*
*the process of conception known as in vitro fertilization*
*(IVF), whether of recalcitrant Catholic parents or received*
*into the Church by conversion and profession of faith, are*
*not to be denied or excluded from any of the sacraments of*
*the Church, provided they request for such sacraments with*
*sufficient evidence of faith and determination to lead a life*
*of holiness and moral rectitude, their manner of conception*
*notwithstanding.*
    *Fraternally yours in Christ,*
    *Benedict XVI, Successor of Peter.*
*Given this day of the Presentation of the Lord, February 2,*
*in the year of our Lord, 2013.*

For some reason that baffled Fr. McCarthy himself, he felt simultaneously relieved and depressed after he had read both documents. He sat at his desk for several minutes, pondering the implications of his actions of the past few weeks. His life had become a roller coaster of unpredictable events since he was outed in court: his cold winter vacation in Rome and Venice; his three-day retreat of self-exploration which, though very relaxing and very healing, did not produce solid answers to questions perplexing his mind; his meeting with his biological parents and sibling which padded him, so to speak, with very positive feelings of support and wellbeing; and, of course, his twice sexual indulgence with Jennifer, who, he could no longer pretend, was the love of his life. Then there was what lay immediately before him: the answer to his request for laicization. He had refused to endorse Fr. Polanski's opinion that he was becoming schizophrenic because of the trauma of being outed as the fruit of the very act he was preaching against and condemning. Fr. Polanski had insistently urged him to go for extended psychological counseling and rehabilitation instead of trying desperately, like a drowning person, to claw his way out of a suffocating identity crisis back to normalcy, all by himself. Was Fr. Polanski right after all? He began questioning himself. Was he beginning to feel despondent because he had passed the point of no return by requesting for laicization against all dissuasions from his bishop and friends? Was he acting rashly by opting for laicization instead of sticking it out in the priesthood, with the uncomfortable stigma of being the first exposed IVF-conceived Catholic clergy who judged and punished others who used the same method to beget children?

The document that lay before him on his desk was a formal vindication of all Catholic children born, theretofore, of IVF, and an exoneration from the 'sins' of their parents in that aspect, he knew. But it was one thing being born into and growing up in a situation where such ruling was already in place. It was quite another thing to be presumed as being born normally, and growing up to condemn the IVF procedure, only to be exposed as the fruit of what you judged and condemned. Mentally and spiritually, it was a distressing situation to find oneself in. Maybe he was destined to be the one to draw the Church's attention to provide the moral and psychological cushion for those not yet born, in an area of life that the Church hadn't thought of providing such services. He felt like Moses, leading a generation toward the promise land, but not setting foot in it himself.

The Mosaic paradigm cheered Fr. McCarthy and lifted his spirit. He still felt he had made a good decision. He knew that as a lay person, he could move from the State of Texas to another state and start his life all over. He could remain a good Catholic, living out of the public glare. Moreover, there was the conviction he felt deep inside him: the fact that he did not feel guilty about his amoral relationship with Jennifer, but, rather, felt liberated and healed every time he slept with her.

The phone rang, startling him from his revelry. He heaved a sigh and stretched, getting up to answer the phone while assuring himself aloud at the same time. "Hey, Cletus "Nick" McCarthy, hold yourself together. It's going to be alright."

"Hey, Nick," Fr. Polanski's voice came on. "You got the email I forwarded to you?"

"What happened?" Fr. McCarthy inquired.

"Oh. You haven't got it then," Fr. Polanski said.

"Yes, I got the email, Charlie. I'm wondering why you opted to call on the house line instead of calling my cell phone as usual," Fr. McCarthy replied. "And, also, I got the laicization document. It's a bit uncanny that both documents came in on the same day."

"So, you have actually been laicized?" Fr. Polanski asked with a lilt of incredulity and disappointment in his voice. "Well, Nick, I suppose I have to deal with it. But make no mistake, I am heart-broken. I had no way of knowing how much I bonded with your priestly persona until now. But, hey! You gotta do what you gotta do."

"I don't know what to say, Charlie," Fr. McCarthy spoke dolefully. "I think I need to find myself. Or, better, I need to reinvent myself. I cannot prove anything at the moment, but I have a gut feeling everything will be alright."

"Do you have time for dinner tomorrow?"

"Only on one condition, Charlie," Fr. McCarthy replied.

"What's that?" Fr. Polanski inquired.

"If you promise not to freak out and get drunk on me," Fr. McCarthy said, without jesting. "Remember, this will be the first time of having dinner with me as a lay man."

"Don't flatter yourself, Nick," Fr. Polanski replied, dismissively. "I'm over your rash impetuousness. Oh, by the way, don't forget to meet with the Cardinal and tell him you have been granted the lay status. He knows about it, but it's a matter of courtesy if you go and meet him and get his blessing before you disappear into the outside world."

"Okay, Charlie," Fr. McCarthy replied. "I will do as you say. But don't sound like it's the end of the world. For me it is not the end. My world will end when I breathe my last. Besides, I am still a priest with faculties until February 14th."

His cell phone rang and Fr. McCarthy quickly ended his conversation with Fr. Polanski. Dr. Josef Horacek was on the line. He sounded very warm and polite, inquiring how Fr. McCarthy was doing. Fr. McCarthy, in turn, inquired about his surrogate mom, Barbara, and his sister, Crystal. He was told Barbara was still in Houston because the transfer from her job was going to take some time. Crystal was in Norfolk for the week and would go back to Houston in a couple of days. They exchanged more pleasantries and Dr. Horacek invited Fr. McCarthy to consider spending his next vacation in Norfolk, a proposal to which Fr. McCarthy agreed enthusiastically.

They went on to lay out the plans. He would travel to Norfolk before Palm Sunday. That way, he could attend the Holy Week and Easter ceremonies in a nearby church, *incognito*, for the first time as a lay man. The time away from Houston could be another grace time for him to plot the course of his future life. He exchanged small talk with Crystal and after almost thirty minutes of chatting, begged Crystal to get off the phone. Later that night, Fr. McCarthy began nursing the thought of making Norfolk his and Jennifer's future home, but wondered how he would be able to convince his parents without making them feel abandoned.

"YOUR HOLINESS, this is a cruel irony," Bishop Ignacio Caravaggio de Pietro said, shaking his head gently from side to side, exhaling sharply in exasperation. "It is the rusted-bucket syndrome: just as you are pulling the bucket of water out of the well, the bottom falls out. Just as we were thinking we have finally hit the solution to the problem, the press messes things up for everyone."

"How did the media get the documents so quick?" Pope Benedict XVI asked, confused, creasing his forehead in obvious mental anguish. "I just assented to the document with my signature last Saturday!" The pope wondered aloud.

"And I sent it by Courier Service to Fr. McCarthy first thing Monday morning for overnight delivery," Bishop Caravaggio de Pietro replied. "And today it is published in a very twisted format and given a very different interpretation by the press."

"We don't know how they got the document, Your Holiness. Perhaps they got it from Fr. McCarthy himself or someone close to him," Fr. Lombardi said, looking equally somber. On second thought, he quickly acquitted Fr. McCarthy as the culprit. "But I don't believe he had the time and the eagerness to do that. Normally priests who get laicized on their own request are very shy of the limelight. They usually prefer to go quietly with no fanfare." There was a brief silence. Then he spoke again. "With your permission, Holiness, I am going to issue a counter statement in article form to try to disabuse the minds of the people. Not that that is going to undo the damage, but it will present the Church's side of the story, at least."

"Another option, Your Holiness, might be to refrain from giving any response to the inglorious headlines," Bishop Jose de Alonzo opined, looking hurt by the turn of events. "Sometimes silence may be the best answer to a mischief."

"My Lord, Bishop, that would probably be misconstrued as confirmation of the misinformation," Fr. Lombardi objected. "Most of the times when you refrain from addressing a situation, your silence is taken as assent. I will not respond to the misinformation of the media, I will simply come out with a statement detailing the procedure the Church has taken at the behest of the young man himself."

"I think I agree with Federico," Bishop Caravaggio de Pietro said.

"I, too, think that Federico is right," the pope concurred. He turned and addressed Bishop Jose de Alonzo: "Furnish Federico with the details of the procedure, and he will go from there. It is very puzzling to me that the secular social media should be so much at war with the Church. They are always eager to present the Church in a bad light, as heartless, and run by vindictive bureaucrats who delight in making life difficult for the people. But that is far from who we are!" The pope sounded exasperated.

"Your Holiness, our way of life and our values constitute a reproach to the world," Bishop Jose de Alonzo said. "I take consolation in Wisdom: Chapter two, verses twelve to nineteen"

"When a priest requests for laicization with good reason, it is usually given. Fr. McCarthy himself made the request and gave good reasons for his decision. I think it is unfair that the media has put a spin on the whole issue just to have an excuse to bash me and the Church," the pope interjected, plaintively. He went behind his desk and sat down, gazing pensively into space. It was obvious to the others that he was very distraught with the turn of events. He pulled toward him the papers that were brought into his office that morning: *The Times* had on the front page, in bold letters: **Pope Benedict XVI Defrocks First U.S. IVF-Conceived Priest**. The second paper, *Agenzia Nazional Stampa Associata* (ANSA), was a bit milder: **First U.S. IVF-Conceived Priest Laicized by Benedict XVI**. The third paper, the *Corriere della Sera* was in Italian and carried the headline, **Papa Benedetto XVI Chiude il Primo IVF-Concepito U.S. Sacerdote**. The tone of the headlines, the slant and content of the write-up that followed each headline did not exactly agree in details, but their collective message did not cast the pope in a very favorable light, either. The stories all gave the impression that the pope dismissed Fr. McCarthy from the priesthood as punishment for being IVF-conceived. The one thing they had in common was their detailed description of how the Catholic Church has always been against the new human reproductive technology procedure known as IVF.

"The old rusted bucket syndrome," Bishop Caravaggio de Pietro muttered again, looking downcast. "The bottom always falls out without warning."

"The bottom didn't fall out. It was knocked out," the pope said, looking straight at Bishop Caravaggio de Pietro. Then he added. "Well, I think the time might be now, for me to make the long-delayed decision I had always considered making. The wolves have won for now, but not for long." He stopped abruptly and did not say more, leaving the Bishops wondering what the long-delayed decision might be, and who he referred to as the wolves. But none of them had the courage to ask him to explain.

Both bishops stood silently for several seconds, not knowing what to say. Eventually the pope looked up and indicated by a nod of the head that his meeting with them was over. They started slowly toward the door, looking a bit disappointed that he had not said much, or made any concrete decision beyond the mandate for Father Lombardi to issue an explanatory statement about what the Church's decision had been regarding Fr. McCarthy's request. They could see that he was in a state of mental anguish. The pain was visible on his face. Yet, not knowing what else to do, they decided to leave him alone to battle with his thoughts.

As if he was eavesdropping by the door, Archbishop Ganswein, recently raised to that position, appeared on cue from nowhere and walked past them into the office as they were going. The pope looked up and beckoned him to get closer.

"Georg, I think I may need to take a rest for the weekend. I have a very big decision to make, and it is weighing on me very heavily because it is a decision that will impact the current administration of the Church," the pope said in one breath. "I am due to address the Consistory in a few days. With a whole lot of pressing issues to make decisions on, I need to be rested and prepared."

"Yes, Your Holiness," Archbishop Ganswein replied, wondering what the pope meant by his words. There was talk of a shake-up in the Curia for a long time and he wondered whether the Holy Father was going to make the changes during that Consistory. He wondered who was going to get the boot and who was going to retain his portfolio.

"Make an appointment for Cardinal Bertone to see me tomorrow morning."

"Yes, Your Holiness," Archbishop Ganswein replied, dutifully and then inquired, "at the library or here in the office?" The pope hesitated for a few seconds.

"The library is a relatively quiet and safe place. Don't you think so?" he asked genuinely.

"I think so, Your Holiness," Archbishop Ganswein concurred.

"Then inform him I will meet him in the library."

"It will be done, Your Holiness."

Pope Benedict stood up, perhaps too quickly because what took place happened so quickly, also. Archbishop Ganswein thought he tripped on the leg of his chair and moved in quickly to help. His alert reflexes saved the day as the pope wobbled, then lunged forward, and his full weight dropped into his arms. He staggered a bit, but quickly regained his balance and moved the pope back to his seat, gently and slowly.

"Are you alright, Holiness?" Archbishop Ganswein inquired, squinting as he looked at the Holy Father's face as though he was trying to find a clue to the cause of his sudden loss of balance. "Are you alright?"

"I think so, but..." the pope replied, not quite firmly. Beads of perspiration were already forming on his forehead. "I feel a little dizzy. I may have gotten up too quickly."

"Breathe, Your Holiness," Archbishop Gasper urged. "Breathe faster and deep. Keep breathing." He grabbed the desk phone and dialed a number that was all too familiar to him. The pope's primary doctor, Patrizio Polisca, came on at the second ring and Archbishop Ganswein rattled through his summons and the description of what happened in one breath. Then he urged the doctor to make it to the office on the double because he suspected the Holy Father may have been on the verge of a heart attack or a stroke. He dropped the phone after extracting the assurance from the doctor that he was, in fact, making his way to the papal office right away. Then he went back to his job of coaching the Holy Father to maintain a fast pace of deep breathing until the doctor arrived.

## FEBRUARY 11, 2013

POPE BENEDICT XVI did rest for the weekend. Dr. Polisca had prescribed a two-week rest for him, only permitting him to come out to address the Consistory and then go back to rest. Although the pope had wanted to be present throughout the entire Consistory, his doctor would have none of it. He jokingly, but seriously, put him under obedience, as he told the pope to stay in bed for the good of his life, an order which the pope found amusing, yet ironic. Being the one who was used to preaching obedience to others, it amused him to realize he could only reluctantly bring himself to obey his doctor's orders.

"I guess I have to take my own pill," he said ruefully, chuckling mirthlessly.

"Yes. Your Holiness, you have to," Dr. Polisca replied, firmly. "It is for your own good. And, I would add, for the good of the Church."

So, the pope stayed in bed in the papal quarters, in obedience to his doctor's orders. He had the time to pray and reflect deeply on a very personal level. And those few days were also very crucial, not only for him but for the whole Church.

There were so many pressing issues that he suspected some of the Cardinals might ask for direct answers to: the demand for women priests; for recognition of the right of gay people to contract same-sex marriage; pressure to admit the divorced and remarried to Holy Communion, etc. There were also numerous and very-pressing bioethical issues ranging from human cloning, prenatal genetic screening with its eugenic tendencies, to the long-standing dispute over surrogacy and IVF procedures, of which the recent case of Fr. McCarthy happened to fall into. There was the request from some third-world bishops for permission for married couples in their countries to use condoms to reduce instances of HIV/AIDS infection. Even from Europe and America, the pope expected considerable pressure in support of the distribution of condoms to teenagers for the same purpose. The big paradox here was that as ultra conservative as the Holy See was, or, was reputed to be, the tendency toward liberalizing views also had quite a considerable number of supporters, though mostly from outside the Roman Curia. He had already preempted the solution to Fr. McCarthy's case, but he was prepared to defend his decision on that issue if it was brought up again.

It was not that the solutions to these problems were difficult to arrive at. Some, if not all, were already fully addressed in the moral teachings of the Church. But those doctrines were being increasingly and vehemently opposed by pressure and lobby groups both within and outside the Vatican. And there were even a few in the Curia who critically observed that the Church was more than 200 years behind in certain aspects. Pope Benedict had constantly agonized over these issues, trying to figure out the best way to handle those oppositions which sometimes got so shrill that he would think about the good old days when the 'hammer' of excommunication was a ready solution for curing stubborn dissent. Alas! Imposed excommunication had not only become obsolete as a papal administrative instrument, but also had been somewhat denounced. Only automatic excommunication—incurred without imposition, but by the very nature of the circumstance into which one has put oneself—was still applied in the Church. And merely opposing papal teachings without action would not be enough to attract that penalty, as there was no canon to that effect. Moreover, the few instances that it had happened in the past, it proved to be counter-productive, as the excommunicated individuals gleefully accepted to stay excommunicated, defeating the purpose in an era when the Church, through ecumenical efforts, would rather see the fruits of Jesus's unity prayer in John's Gospel, Chapter 17, come forth. Pope Benedict's yearning was to present himself as a pastoral leader of the Church, rather than a despotic autocrat. But with the vindictive bashing of him by the media over Fr. McCarthy's case, it seemed that that hope was doomed. He wasn't faring very well with the cream of the Curia, and did even worse on the international stage, image-wise.

Then there were the internal problems of the Vatican City-State itself, and the very personal problem of his confidential documents always being leaked out of his control. Vatican finances were in shambles, and material decadence had eaten so deep into the clerical ranks that it seemed practically impossible to do anything about it. He sometimes thought he would prefer to bear a wooden cross on his shoulder and walk up the Lateran hills, than continue to carry the immense weight of the problems of the Church that he was carrying then. But he didn't have that choice. And since it was getting practically impossible by the day for him to meet the demands of office in adjudicating on all these issues, he came to one conclusion which he was going to announce to the Cardinals at the Consistory.

He felt very peaceful as he dressed, prepared to join the Cardinals for midday prayer. He had prayed a lot during the night and had come to a final decision. As soon as he had resolved to act on that decision, he had experienced so much relief that he slept well the rest of the night. The Church of Christ would go on despite all the problems, and the gates of Hell would never prevail against it, as the Master Himself had promised.

A gentle knock on the door woke him from his revelry.

"Yes, come in," he called out.

The door opened and Archbishop Ganswein walked in with Dr. Polisca in tow.

"Your Holiness," he announced. "The doctor wants to check your vitals before you go into the Consistory."

"How did His Holiness do last night, and this morning?" Dr. Polisca inquired, sort of airily.

"I think I did much better," the pope replied. "Thank you for ordering me to rest. I slept like a log and my appetite is good. I feel more energy inside me."

"*Certamente, Santo Padre!*" Dr. Polisca approbated in Italian. "*Bravo! Bravo, Santito!* It is good for you and for the Church. Now let's take your temperature," he said, sticking an oral thermometer into the Holy Father's mouth, presuming the permission to do so. He read aloud the number and proceeded to check his blood pressure and take his pulse. He pronounced every one of the numbers *bene*. "You are ready to take on the world, Holy Father."

"If the world is ready to take me on," the pope quipped, and Archbishop Ganswein and Dr. Polisca chuckled politely. "They are in for a surprise, I bet you."

"Good, ready to battle the forces of evil!" Dr. Polisca pursued, humorously. "All your vitals have checked out good."

"Battle! What an ominous word," the pope replied. "Unfortunately, a very appropriate word for the life of a pope. Let's go, Georg," he said, leading the way out of the room with measured steps. Archbishop Ganswein and

Dr. Polisca followed closely. In the hallway, on their way to the elevator, they ran into Angelo Cardinal Amato, the Prefect of the Congregation for the Causes of Saints, and Msgr. Alfred Xuereb, Pope Benedict's second personal secretary. Cardinal Amato had an open folder which he brandished in front of the pope, falling into step with him and his entourage.

"Good morning, Your Holiness," he greeted, hurriedly. "Just to let you see the names of the *beati* before I present them in the Consistory."

The pope stopped for a brief second and looked at the three names and nodded his assent. "After midday prayer, you will proceed as usual."

"Yes, Your Holiness," the Cardinal replied.

Dr. Polisca took his leave with permission, followed by Cardinal Amato, while the pope and his two Secretaries got into his private elevator.

As the pope entered the hallway to the Chapel of the Consistory, all the Cardinals, draped in scarlet cassocks, birettas, and capes over white surplices, killed their raucous din and stood ready. Someone started to clap and others joined gradually, swelling the applause as the Holy Father walked to the front, acknowledging the applause with the usual gesture of a smile and a wave of the hand in fraternal welcome. Then the Cardinals followed the pope into the Consistory hall and took their places.

Sext, as the midday prayer—a relic of the monastic tradition—was officially called, proceeded as usual, with the Cardinals all chanting gustily, after which the Holy Father took his seat on a high-backed chair of purple fabric framed in ornately carved wood. The chair was placed on a miniature stage raised three steps at the center front, against the wall, facing the rest of the Cardinals. He himself wore a gothic, embroidered, stole of deep violet with a cape of the same color over his white surplice and white cassock, underscored by the red "fisherman's shoes," with his usual white zucchetto on his head. He was flanked by his two secretaries, Archbishop Ganswein and Msgr. Xuereb, both in white surplices draped over their purple cassocks. The gathering was solemn and very impressive. The Prefect of the Congregation for the Causes of Saints, Angelo Cardinal Amato, stood up, cleared his throat, and began to announce the names of the *beati*—the blessed—who would be raised to sainthood later. The whole Chapel was very quiet, though this was not an unusual ceremony. In fact, the Cardinals were very familiar with the process, but the silence had an ominous foreboding that was quite palpable.

There had been significant grapevine gossip about a couple of changes that the Holy Father was going to make. But, again, the pope making changes during a Consistory was not unusual, except that this time, the Cardinals all thought the changes—usually consisting of a few transfers, promotions, and the creation of new offices and portfolios—were going to include a formal pronouncement of the doctrinal stance already taken about the situation of the U.S. priest, Fr. McCarthy, who was outed as the fruit of IVF, and who they were informed had applied for and been granted the lay status. They had all received the preliminary and informal document a few days back, stating the pope's doctrinal stance on the matter. Most of the Cardinals irksomely wondered why the pope decided to use an open medium like email to communicate to them a document of such importance. But the stormy reports from the press across the Western world which came out simultaneously with the email, exacerbating an already complex situation, made it clear to them that the document had already leaked, and that the pope preferred the email as an instant way to reach them. However, not all the Cardinals agreed with the pope's decision, though it was doubtful whether they would seek to breech protocol and pressure him to reverse the process since it had not been discussed by the plenary Session of the Curia before a decision was made on it. Some of them wondered if Benedict XVI was subtly applying the age-old principle of *ex cathedra* pronouncement in such a minor case that was not a *de fide* doctrine. And so, a few of them were still vacillating, mentally, on whether to call for a review or, at least, for more explanation on it.

The Prefect of the Congregation for the Causes of Saints finished announcing the *beati*, and it was greeted by a very brief and low-keyed applause. Then the Chapel became silent again. The Holy Father, Pope Benedict XVI, took out a sheet of paper from his cassock pocket and started reading in Latin. This slight and unusually deviant act was noticed only by a few of the Cardinals on the front row, who did not wonder too long why it wasn't Archbishop Ganswein or Msgr. Xuereb who opened and presented a folder to the Holy Father, with the document to be read neatly clipped inside it, as they tended to do on such solemn occasions. They quickly absolved the Holy Father for being so private. The "Vatileaks" machine, as it was now called, was still very active.

*Dear Brothers,*

The Holy Father started addressing the Cardinals, reading in Latin.

*I have convoked this Consistory, not only for the three canonizations, but also to communicate to you a decision of great importance for the life of the Church. After repeatedly examining my conscience before God, I have come to the certainty that my strengths, due to an advanced age, are no longer suited to an adequate exercise of the Petrine ministry.*

An unexpected shuffle suddenly erupted as the Cardinals all raised their heads, shifted in their seats and glanced at one another, alarmed. The pope's language was confusing. Instead of talking about issues in the Church, and the likely course of action he was going to propose, he seemed to be talking about his person. What did he mean by "my strengths ... are no longer suited to an adequate exercise of the Petrine ministry?" Greatly taken by surprise, some of the Cardinals instinctively put a hand over their mouths, as if to prevent them from exclaiming aloud involuntarily. Others looked somewhat quizzically at the Holy Father, as if to ascertain that he still had all his faculties intact. A few unconsciously suffered dropped jaws. But all looked on alarmed at what they thought they were hearing, but which did not make much sense. The Holy Father continued.

*I am well aware that this ministry, due to its essential spiritual nature, must be carried out not only with words and deeds, but also with prayer and suffering. However, in today's world, subject to so many rapid changes and shaken by questions of deep relevance for the life of faith, to steer the barque of Saint Peter and proclaim the Gospel, strength of both mind and body are necessary, strength, which in the last few months, has deteriorated in me to the extent that I have had to recognize my incapacity to adequately fulfill the ministry entrusted to me.*

The Cardinals were still sitting on the edges of their chairs, straining to hear the pope as his voice was low and somewhat weak, perhaps intentionally so, to accentuate his point. And the silence was still very unnerving. And, besides, he was reading in Latin.

*For this reason, and well aware of the seriousness of this act, with full freedom, I declare that I renounce the ministry of the Bishop of Rome, Successor of Saint Peter, entrusted to me by the Cardinals on 19 April 2005, in such a way that as from 28 February 2013, at 20:00 hours, the See of Rome, the See of Saint Peter, will be vacant and a Conclave to elect the new Supreme Pontiff will have to be convoked by those who have the competence to do so.*

Msgr. Xuereb choked, looked down, and sniffled loudly. Archbishop Ganswein looked down sorrowfully, with drooped shoulders. There was more shuffling, as some of the Cardinals whispered subdued utterances: *Oh my God! Goodness gracious! Lord have mercy on us!* Or: *This is not happening!*

But it was happening, as the Holy Father continued in his doleful, almost high-pitch, nasal tone.

> *Dear Brothers, I thank you most sincerely for all the love and work with which you have supported me in my ministry and I ask pardon for all my defects. And now, let us entrust the Holy Church to the care of Our Supreme Shepherd, Our Lord Jesus Christ, and implore his Holy Mother Mary, so that she may assist the Cardinal Fathers with her maternal solicitude, in electing a new Supreme Pontiff.*

Cardinal Bertone seemed to have recovered a bit from his initial shock and was furiously taking notes.

> *Regarding myself, I wish to also devotedly serve the Holy Church of God in the future through a life dedicated to prayer.*
>
> *Given this eleventh day of February, 2013, the memorial of Our Lady of Lourdes, and signed by me, Benedict XVI, Successor of Peter and Bishop of Rome until 28 February 2013.*

The pope finished his announcement, folded the paper and put it back in his cassock pocket. There was no applause. Nobody moved for several seconds. Taken by surprise, the Cardinals were shocked in a manner more gripping than if the pope had died. The time was 1:10 p.m. in Rome.

The time was 8:08 p.m. in Houston, Texas, the following day, a few minutes shy of twenty-four hours since Pope Benedict renounced his papacy. Newly laicized Fr. Cletus "Nick" McCarthy had just finished a very sumptuous dinner at his parents' place, and gone back to his room upstairs. He got out his hymnal and made ready for nighttime prayers. He usually had his night prayers early, that way he could feel free to engage in other pressing activities or watch a movie, and drop into bed any time he felt drowsy, without having to worry about forgetting it. Praying could be a chore when done in a state of drowsiness. His iPhone gave the elephant trumpet ring. Fr. Polanski had found the sound eerily annoying and had talked to Fr. McCarthy about changing it, but to no avail. He simply gave up and would endure it patiently whenever it went off in his presence. He thanked God that nobody was with him in his room. His parents were still downstairs: his mother, Hannah, was busy clearing the kitchen and packing away the dishes for the night; and his father, Stephen, was watching his favorite sports on the sitting room big screen TV.

Cletus McCarthy took the call on the third ring. "Hey, Charlie, what's up?" sounding upbeat. He had consciously started responding to people, whether face-to-face or on the phone, with an upbeat tone to prevent them from thinking it was a big loss for him to be laicized and, therefore, talking to him with maudlin and pitiful tone. "Watching your favorite game?"

"No. I thought you might be watching the news," Fr. Polanski said.

"What news?" Cletus McCarthy asked, confused.

"Pope Benedict has resigned his papacy."

"What!" Cletus McCarthy shouted, involuntarily. "What did you just say?"

"Benedict XVI resigned his office as the Universal Pontiff of the Holy Roman Catholic Church," Fr. Polanski spelled out in one breath. "Tune into CNN or BBC America. They are still giving the news now. He announced it yesterday."

Cletus McCarthy threw his phone on the bed and scrambled to put on his small bedroom TV. He did not bother to scroll on to CNN as the first channel that came on, MSNBC, was on the news. He watched with mouth ajar as a news reporter in St. Peter's square in Rome was giving the update about the pope's resignation. He could see a lot of people milling around aimlessly and pigeons flying about in the background and, from the daytime look of St. Peter's Square on the screen, he knew it was a replay, since it would have been about 3 a.m. in Rome. He repeatedly pressed the channel button on the remote control to get to the CNN channel. They had finished giving the main news and anchormen with call-in and studio panels were engaged in a back-and-forth analysis of the impact of the Supreme Pontiff's resignation for the Catholic Church, and the long-term implications for the Christian world as a whole, having been an event not witnessed in the Church for nearly 600 years. Cletus McCarthy slowly inched himself backward toward the bed and sat down gingerly, still watching the analyses with jaw-dropping shock. He wondered what could have made the pope resign. Picking up his phone to dial Fr. Polanski back, he noticed that it was still on. Fr. Polanski had not hung up.

"Hello," he called, expectantly.

Fr. Polanski replied, "Yes, I knew you would need a few seconds to absorb the shock," He said, assuredly. "Everyone is probably in shock. I am in shock myself. First, you. Then the Holy Father. Tell me, Nick, why are you guys quitting the Church so abruptly? Is there something I am missing?" His attempt at humor fell flat as his young friend sat silently, trying to absorb the situation.

"Charlie, do you think it might have something to do with my case? I read all the cruel bashings in the papers and watched some on TV"

"Nick, I don't know," Fr. Polanski replied, genuinely. "The pope has a million issues in the Church to treat, and none of those is famously lightweight. But I would wager there is a possibility your case may have been his last straw."

"Well, that ain't too consoling. Is it?"

"Dude, you asked for my opinion," Fr. Polanski replied. "I'm just conjecturing. And when I say your case, I don't mean your birth circumstance, but the media presentation of your resignation. You said you read the papers, and you saw it was made to sound like you were canned because your parents got you by IVF."

"Yeah, poor Benedict," Cletus McCarthy said, ruefully. "They say he said he resigned because of age and an enormous work stress. Well, that makes two of us."

"Yeah, that makes two of you quitters," Fr. Polanski threw in his barbed humor.

Cletus McCarthy chuckled and said, "Don't start, Charlie."

"Don't start what?" Fr. Polanski asked. "Get off the phone, quitter. I called you just to let you know you are not alone, if that is a consolation."

"Oh, thanks so much, Fr. Self-Righteous," Cletus sparred with a barb of his own. "I don't know what I would do without you."

"You would still do well, especially as you now have an ally in no less a personality than the pope himself. By the way, you should make plans to join him and, together, form 'The New Contemplative Life for Quitters'."

"Alright. Alright, Fr. Self-Righteous," Cletus said, aggressively. "I think you're beginning to cross the line here. Perhaps, it might do you good to go to bed as you proposed. So, good night," Cletus said trenchantly, then added in a low tone, "Fr. Self-Righteous."

"I heard that," Fr. Polanski yelled from the other end of the phone, then added also in a low tone, "Mr. Quitter."

"I heard that," Cletus yelled back from his side of the phone, then added in a harsh and loud whisper, "Fr. Self-Righteous."

"Mr. Quitter," Fr. Polanski whispered back, harshly, too, and switched off his line before Cletus had the chance to rebut. Cletus McCarthy chuckled to himself wryly and said under his breath, "Gosh! Poor Charlie is still smarting because I resigned. Well, Charlie. There is nothing I can do to help you. With time, you will get over it, as I hope to do."

Knowing his older friend as he did, Cletus knew Fr. Polanski would continue those mock fights until he got tired of it and quit on his own. So, he resolved in his mind to always bear him out whenever he would break into such a moment, since it would also be very healing to let him fight his way through the shock as he himself was doing already. He put down the phone and went downstairs again to break the news to Stephen and Hannah McCarthy. 'There have been laicized priests before me. But…the pope resigning!' he thought. For him, the shock was a considerable one.

# HOUSTON, TEXAS
## WEDNESDAY, FEBRUARY 13, 2013

THE ASH WEDNESDAY Mass at the Co-Cathedral of the Sacred Heart was uncommonly glum. The news had reached everyone and there was an added aura of sadness. The faithful felt as though they had lost their dad. Cardinal Felice offered petitions for the good health of the Supreme Pontiff and prayed that when the Conclave would be convened after February 28, the Holy Spirit might direct the election process so that a worthy successor may be chosen to continue the work of the Holy Father. He suggested in his homily that what happened was, perhaps, at a very good time—coinciding with the beginning of the Lenten Season—so that the faithful might pray intensely for the Church in this age of uncertainties. At the end of Mass, not a few of the older Catholics left with teary eyes, wondering what the future of the Church was going to look like.

The work atmosphere at the Chancery was equally melancholic. As the clergy were all out for the Ash Wednesday Masses in the parishes, seminary, and convents, the lay workers found themselves in the grip of sadness, partly because, as it was clear, the resignation of a pope was extremely rare in history. Popes used to die in office, and the faithful had come to accept that as normal. For a pope to resign meant there was something more ominous, if not sinister, going on. Conspiracy theories were already rife in the air that Pope Benedict was forced to resign by the Vatican Mafia, though nobody could say exactly who constituted the Mafiosi. And the fact that nobody knew who they were and what it really was about, added to the heightened sense of curiosity and suspicion concerning what it might mean. Thus, in the grip of such excitement and curiosity, Chancery personnel took to consoling one another by swapping gossips and conjectures along the corridors and in the offices. They permitted themselves more coffee breaks than usual, so they could have the excuse to chat up one another on the novel experience.

There were assumptions, too, that the pope's resignation might have had something to do with Fr. McCarthy's case, though, in what sense, nobody could say. Some even believed that Cardinal Felice would be among the eligible Candidates for the papacy. Others quickly pointed out that Fr. McCarthy's case happening on his watch was not very flattering to the Cardinal's image and stewardship profile, and, therefore, would not merit him being considered for the papacy. Others, especially the single ladies, spent time wondering what Fr. McCarthy was going to do with himself and what his next line of life was going to be now that he was a lay person and, perhaps, the most eligible bachelor around. There was already a lot of buzz in the Chancery grapevine that his attorney, Stacy Donovan, had cornered him, and was probably going to seduce him into marrying her. A few others had already crafted a conspiracy theory to the effect that she may have been the one who actually pressured him into resigning from the priesthood so she could marry him, pointing to the fact that they were getting too close, almost always seen together since the start of the case. Stacy, herself, was not deaf to all the wild rumors, but she just ignored them, deciding to keep all her detractors guessing.

By close of work that Ash Wednesday, the total volume of deskwork done by Chancery personnel for the day was considerably less, if anything at all was done. Everyone was too excited by the recent events to sit quietly working behind a desk.

# HOUSTON, TEXAS

## THURSDAY, MARCH 7, 2013

CLETUS "NICK" MCCARTHY felt good inside as he drove back from Barbara's place. Crystal Horacek was with him and chattered non-stop about this, that, and the other. And Cletus Horacek bore it out with the patient indulgence of a big brother. He had taken to shuttling between his birth mother's house and his adopted parents' house where he had always lived and had now returned to, with Jennifer's apartment completing the triangle. He was gradually settling into his newfound layman's life faster than he thought, and was even beginning to enjoy it. The ordinary everyday people who now constituted his circle of friends brought him a new experience and a new perspective on life in a way quite different than when he was a priest. He couldn't figure out why he felt that way, except that the invisible, but intimidating, line that separated people from his priestly persona had dissolved and was no longer there. He was now one of them, or, they had now accepted him fully as one of them, and no longer as an authority figure.

The freedom to go into certain places where he would not go previously as a priest was exhilarating. For instance, at her insistence, a few days back, he had followed Jennifer to a topless bar where she said she suspected that the father of the young girl she was treating at the hospital, for a drug overdose that nearly took her life, would be found. Her purpose was to talk him into giving more care and attention to the girl, making sure, at least, that she did not get back on dope. Sure enough, the man was there in the front seat by the dance table, living large with friends, rocking and laughing raucously, cheering and peering between naked dancing girls' legs and sticking dollar bills in their G-strings. Jennifer had tapped him on the shoulder and the man had turned around, looking like he was going to get angry at being interrupted during the high point of his enjoyment. When he saw and recognized who she was, and the way she demanded with authority to talk to him about his daughter, the man mellowed. Moreover, the sight of Cletus McCarthy standing there, a good three inches taller than him, with weight-lifter's shoulders, and looking menacingly at the scene, may have prompted him to behave. He had followed Jennifer to a corner where, for almost thirty minutes, she lectured him on why he should be responsible for the good care of his daughter. She only let him off after extracting a promise from him to visit the young lady in hospital the very next day.

Cletus McCarthy had been impressed at Jennifer's solicitousness and had started believing that ordinary people like Jennifer were, in fact, doing a better job of morally rehabilitating people than priests preaching behind pulpits. He resolved that night to be involved in advocacy work wherever his new life would take him, since doing so did not require him to be a priest. But first he needed to decide where he would settle and get a job. Staying in Houston was not possible for him. If he was going to start a new chapter in his life, then it had to be in a new environment free from the hang-ups of his former way of life.

He slammed on his brakes before he ran down a pedestrian. Crystal shrieked, caught her breath, and then started giggling as she realized everything was alright.

"Oh, you young lady of little faith!" Cletus McCarthy teased.

"I was almost sure you had run him over," she said, breathing heavily.

"That's why when you drive you have to be alert," he replied, feeling a tinge of guilt because he actually wasn't alert himself. He just saw the man at the nick of time by some stroke of luck. "How often do you drive?"

"Not very often, am afraid," Crystal replied. "I don't get to go out very often either. "Mom is very strict and very particular about my education. I spend almost all my free time purring over pages of books because she wants her daughter to be Alberta Einstein."

"Is that like the female counterpart of Albert Einstein?"

"Uh hum," Crystal replied, bobbing her head up and down. "Once I leave for college by August ending, I will be free of her. I think Mom's a control freak."

"She means well," he replied, trying to defend their mother.

"I know. And I know she doesn't want me to go through what she went through. But I think she's paranoid about childhood suffering. She's scared that if I flunked my grades and dropped out of school, I might wind up where she came from."

"But that's not what you want," he affirmed her.

"No, and I keep assuring her, you know," Crystal replied. "I'm like, I know what is good! Having listened to the story of her life, I am very wise now. Father, don't you think I'm smart?"

"You are a very smart young lady, Crysie," he assured her. "And you can quit calling me 'Father'."

"Oh, I'm sorry," she replied, slightly embarrassed. "I don't know what..."

"Call me 'Nick'," he interrupted her.

"I'll try. But it'll take some time before I'm used to it," she replied, her voice devoid of conviction. Then she deftly changed the subject again. "Has Mom told you the full story of her life?"

"She did, and I'm proud of her. I'm very proud of my two moms. They're very brave women," he replied, with some emotion. "Now quit talking," he added, more as a defense against getting emotional than for needing quiet.

Jennifer was home. She came to the door at the second ring of the bell.

"Come on in," she said, smiling beautifully. "Hey, look at you, Crysie!"

Cletus McCarthy hugged her lightly and they touched their pouting lips together making the sucking sound of a kiss.

"Good evening, Auntie Jenny," Crystal greeted.

"We're lucky," Cletus said. "I was not sure about your work schedule this week. I just decided to take a chance."

"I leave for work in thirty minutes," Jennifer replied, putting her freshly ironed scrubs in a hanger on the wall. "Yes, you are lucky. If it were other days when I leave early, you would have missed me. Crysie, get to the kitchen and the fridge. You are no longer a stranger in my house. Ask your brother what he wants to drink."

"What do you want to drink, Father...I meant to say, 'Nick'," Crystal stuttered, giggling awkwardly with embarrassment. "Auntie Jenny, he wants me to call him 'Nick,' but...it's a little awkward for me. I mean I still feel him like a priest."

"Don't beat yourself on the head, Crysie, if you catch yourself still calling him 'Father'. He's only just escaped being one type of a father, but he may soon become a father in a different sense," Jennifer said, looking coyly at Cletus McCarthy.

"What do you mean?" he asked, startled.

"Nothing," Jennifer replied, slyly putting a finger on her lips to sign him to be quiet, while darting a glance in Crystal's direction. She then rubbed her stomach gently to give a nonverbal meaning of her statement to Cletus McCarthy and, then, quickly changed the subject at the same time. "He usually drinks a Coke, Crysie. Bring him a Coke."

"No, Crysie. Don't bring any drinks. I'm still full from the late lunch we had," he said, looking at Jennifer with mixed emotions.

"Auntie Jennifer, can I turn on the TV?" Crystal asked, turning it on without waiting for permission.

"Oh, sure, Crysie," Jennifer indulged her. "A *Harry Potter* DVD's in the drive, if you wanna watch it."

"Crysie, give us a few minutes," Cletus McCarthy said, beckoning Jennifer, who followed him into her bedroom. He was glad that Crystal had the TV volume loud enough to give them privacy.

"Okay, I know what you want to know," Jennifer said, preemptively. "I'm pregnant. I should have had my period three weeks ago. I missed it. When I tested it this morning, it was positive, but don't worry. I'm not putting it on you. I want the baby, and I'm very happy and so excited about it. I promise I won't let anybody know it's yours. I'll…"

"Shshsh! Can you just shut up for a minute?" Cletus McCarthy whispered fiercely. "Don't give yourself verbal diarrhea. I'm so happy to hear the good news! I'm so excited to learn I can, and will, be a father. Do you know what that would mean for me and my family? It would mean the cycle of infertility is broken, and we can quit being a family of hopeless adopters and adoptees, and that would mean that even though I came from a test tube…."

"Okay, hold on, Cletus Nicholas McCarthy," Jennifer interrupted, amused at his childlike excitement. "Who's suffering now from verbal diarrhea?"

Cletus McCarthy pulled himself together, realizing he was carried away, and replied, "Certain things are contagious. As a nurse, you should know about these things. And, by the way, don't you conceive any devious plans to steal my baby by letting on that I am not the father."

"Alright, take a hold of yourself," Jennifer said, herself too excited to stand still. "I thought you would be mad at me for taking in, and would be embarrassed about what people might say if they knew about it, having just resigned from the priesthood."

"Fuck people!" Cletus replied, mildly startling Jennifer, who thought his first curse words were both so awkward and so cute at the same time. "The couple who sued me had tried to have a baby for twelve years. And here I am, tripping on it without expending any effort. What blessing could be better than that?" He looked so excited his eyes were almost sparkling in the dim light of the bedroom.

Jennifer was so excited, too, and, cocking her head slightly to one side, looked straight at him, drinking in his joy with every fiber of her being. She resolved there and then that if he should ask to marry her, she would give him her all. Oblivious of the current moment, she was about to throw her arms around him and drown him in kisses when Crystal saved the situation.

"Auntie, Jenny, it's not *Harry Potter*. It's a video of a training class on CPR," she shouted from the sitting room.

"Oh, I'm sorry," she replied, moving in that direction. "I forgot I took it out and put in the CPR demo CD. *Harry Potter* should be on the coffee table."

They trooped out of the bedroom, poker-faced, barely succeeding in hiding their excitement. Jennifer retrieved the elusive DVD from a stack on the coffee table and handed it to Crystal.

"Oh, there it is," Crystal said, taking the DVD to put it in the player.

"Are you sure you want to watch that right now?" Cletus McCarthy asked, drawing her attention to the time. "Jenny's leaving for work. Unless you want to stay behind and house sit for her."

"I'm taking it. I won't watch it now. Auntie Jenny, can I take it? I'll return it, I swear."

"Okay, Crysie. Just return it when you've watched it," Jennifer said. "Don't swear an oath. It's unbecoming of a lady. You are a young lady now, remember?"

"I'm so sorry, Auntie."

"Crysie, if I were you, I wouldn't take that DVD," Cletus McCarthy dissuaded. "Your finals start in a couple of weeks."

"I know," Crystal replied, with a whine. "Can I just watch it one time?"

"You know, I never even thought of that," Jennifer said. "Don't take it, Crysie. I promise to give it to you immediately after your exam.'

"Oh, man!" Crystal whined, then grudgingly dropped the DVD on the table and trudged to the door in silent protest.

"Mom would have taken it from you anyways," Cletus McCarthy said. And turned to follow her out. He stopped and kissed Jennifer on the cheek. The latter reciprocated and held for a fraction of a second longer than necessary.

"Oh, by the way," he said, turning around at the door. "I am visiting Dr. Horacek on Friday the 22$^{nd}$, for three weeks. I promised to spend the Easter with him. But Sunday, March 17, I am taking you on a trip to Galveston for the day. You are not working Sunday, are you?"

"Nope," Jennifer replied. "Am all yours on Sunday, the seventeenth."

"I asked him to wait till school is out in June so I can go with him, he refused," Crystal said, plaintively. "And now, he'll be going to Galveston Bay without me. Nobody pays attention to me anymore. Every one of my requests is always turned down."

"Oh, Crysie," Jennifer replied. "Don't say that. We all pay attention to you. We just want you to give a final push on your academic work so you graduate in the top of your class."

"Crysie, you can't just idle away precious study time," Cletus said.

"I'm not idling away time. I just want to hang out with you," she whined.

"Okay, just face your finals and graduate tops, and you can hang out with me as you like. You can even hang down my neck and swing like a koala," Cletus threw in some bit of humor to cheer her up.

A spurt of laughter escaped Crystal. "Funny," she said.

"You will hang out with me until you are nauseated," Cletus McCarthy pursued.

"Then I will puke, clean it up, and hang out with you again," Crystal retorted, impertinently.

"Funny," Cletus McCarthy said in turn, and watched his younger sister stalk defiantly toward the car. Her worship of him was beginning to be a nuisance, and he didn't want to encourage it to the extent that it would make her dependent and needy. He resolved to devise a way to forestall that.

"Jenny, I'll talk to you later," he said, moving toward the car also. "Let me drop off this cranky lass for her mom before she becomes uncontrollable. I'm not practiced in handling adolescent tantrums."

Jennifer chuckled quietly and watched brother and sister drive off. Then she turned into the house to dress up for work. She understood Crystal perfectly well. Believing oneself to be alone, and then suddenly having a brother who had attained such a high status in society, and still has a higher prospect, was a lot for her to handle. She wanted to bask in the euphoria of it all as fully as she could. She wanted to enjoy her brother so much that she would sometimes act spoiled. It was very uncanny how Cletus McCarthy turned out to be such a controversial figure, but at the same time, such a star in the family that every person naturally felt drawn to him.

Hannah and Stephen McCarthy doted on him, Barbara and Dr. Horacek swooned over him with awe and wonder, Crystal Horacek worshipped her big brother to delirium, and Fr. Charles Polanski was almost driven nuts by the thought that he was losing a friend. Then, Jennifer, herself....

Jennifer shook her head to dislodge the revelry from her mind. She didn't want to think about the nature of her relationship with him. It defied words. And, the little 'thing' that was growing inside her...Was it going to be a boy or a girl? It was not yet time to determine by ultrasound. She wondered what life would be for her as Mrs. Jennifer McCarthy, if he should ask her to marry him. She had always related to him, loosely though, as a cousin until he was outed. And then their first lovemaking erased all traces of that and set the stage for a new kind of relationship, which was as yet to be defined. But judging from his excitement at the news of her pregnancy, she believed she knew what that new relationship would be. She smiled and picked up her handbag and left for work.

# GALVESTON, TEXAS

## SUNDAY, MARCH 17, 2013

CLETUS NICHOLAS MCCARTHY did ask Jennifer to marry her. Though, she had nursed the hope of one day being asked that question, she had not thought it was going to be so soon and so abruptly. Of course, he had carefully planned it and hid it from her so that the surprise would be all the sweeter. After learning from Jennifer that he was going to be a father, it took him only a couple of days to make the decision. He had immediately confided in his parents, Hannah and Stephen, who were initially alarmed at the prospect.

"Son, couldn't you let one scandal die down before you start another?" Hannah had asked, half chiding and half exasperated.

"No, Mom," Cletus replied with a note of humor in his voice. "I always enjoy the cascading effect of things. Get it all out up front in one package, let the public feast on it to their hearts' content, and then have peace. By the way, I don't consider asking the mother of my child to marry me a scandal. Not marrying her would be the scandal." Put in that light, Hannah McCarthy was robbed of further protest, but she was still squirming visibly and seemed irked that her husband was very calm about their son's decision.

"Well, just having everything happen bang, bang, bang makes me nervous. First, you got sued and exposed for being IVF-conceived, then you went and quit the priesthood before you told your shadow about it. And now…" she broke off, agitated, and addressed her husband, somewhat querulously, "Honey, you haven't said anything."

"Calm down, honey," Stephen replied. "Yes, I haven't said anything because, for one, we saw it coming, and besides, Jennifer and Cletus are adults. If they have decided in that direction, we need to respect it."

"You saw it coming?" Hannah asked, looking incredulous and miffed at the same time.

"Yeah. Didn't you? How else would you interpret the constant teasing battles?" Stephen asked in turn, chuckling incredulously too. "It stuck out a mile, honey! They've been in love for years!"

"Alright, alright," Cletus raised his hand as though he was going to flag off a race. "Mom, Dad, calm down. Let there be peace. It's a decision that I have carefully thought out, though I haven't shared it with Jennifer yet… and don't any of you dare let her know before I do, either!"

"Lord have mercy!" Stephen said. "Son, we will not, or, let me speak for myself: I would never let the cat out of the bag. My mouth is sealed." He joined his thumb and forefinger and made a zipping sign across his mouth.

"Well, I don't know," Hannah said, fidgeting. "I know Jennifer is pregnant, but I think you are moving too fast."

"Mom!" Cletus called, a shade too loud. "She is not just pregnant. She is pregnant with *my* baby. And I am going to marry her so that my child will be legitimately born. Maybe that way we can begin a new chapter for the McCarthy family and move from being a bunch of adopters and adoptees to being regular people."

His vehemence made his mother wince and recoil. Then she quickly left the sitting room and hurried up the stairs. Cletus knew he had said something hurtful. Relenting immediately, he bolted from his chair and made to go after her to apologize. Hs father stood up promptly and blocked him before he could make it to the stairs.

"Don't. Leave it to me. Let me handle this." Then he jogged up the stairs, stopped halfway, and said, "Son, don't worry about it. She'll be alright. Just go to your room and rest."

Cletus vacillated for a few seconds and eventually decided to follow his dad's advice. He went to his room feeling slightly dejected. He had recently begun to be a bit snappy at his mother whenever they spoke and she seemed to disagree with him. His slightly raised voice of the last few minutes and his mother's reaction made him suspect that she might think he hadn't forgiven her, and the thought of her possibly harboring that feeling crushed him. Knowing Hannah very well, he believed she was, probably, sobbing quietly in her room. He lay tossing about and awake that evening for a long time. Eventually, he decided he would apologize to her first thing in the morning.

As his dad had assured him, Hannah was her usual self the following morning. She welcomed him downstairs with a delicious breakfast of French toast, grits and scrambled eggs, and dismissed his apology with a wave of the hand, telling him she had thought over the whole thing and concluded that he was right. She was just being a fretting mother too attached to her son.

"I need to get me a big pair of scissors," she said, suddenly feigning seriousness.

"For what?" Cletus asked, innocently curious.

"To cut you off from my apron strings and let you be a man," she replied, looking at him as though he should have known that himself without being told. Her sudden humor cracked both men, son and dad, up. "Well, am only being a mother," she added and joined in the laughter.

Breakfast was good and the McCarthy family of three huddled around the table had a good time. Cletus seized the chance and the good atmosphere to inform his parents of his plans to visit Dr. Horacek for two weeks. He would be back in Houston after Easter week. Both parents had no objection. They even approved, thinking that a change of environment for a little while would be good for him.

All of that had happened a week previously. And now, here he was sitting in the pews of Sacred Heart Church, incognito, with Jennifer at his side, waiting for Mass to begin. He didn't feel particularly awkward now as he had the first day he attended Mass as a layman at the Sacred Heart Church in Conroe. He was beginning to get comfortable with his newfound status after having been at Mass in different churches every weekend since he became a layman. He had decided not to visit the same church more than once in case he should be recognized, although he had changed his hairstyle to disguise his appearance. And since he was always in civilian clothes now, his ruse worked. It almost amused him how easy it was for him to be hiding in plain sight. He stole a secretive side glance at Jennifer, who was also slyly feasting her eyes on the rich Victorian architecture of the church. Painted snow white and accentuated with gold linings, the walls and ornately sculpted pillars were a sight to behold. The stained-glass windows were artfully done with a million tiny pieces, all fitting into one another to produce a master piece of delightful impression. The entire edifice commanded an aura of simplicity and elegance, of innocence and complexity. And Cletus McCarthy got lured into a philosophical dream world. He mused on how the crafts, artworks, and structures produced by man had always tended to be an extrapolation of himself. Humans can be complex and yet look innocent in appearance, stately in bearing, and still be quite moronic. This combination of opposites had dogged man's nature since his creation and, perhaps, would continue....

The bell rang to signify the entrance of the Mass retinue. Cletus McCarthy's thoughts were interrupted as the Choir Director announced the processional hymn of the day.

"Good morning, brothers and sisters in Christ. Our entrance hymn is: *There's a wideness in God's mercy.* Please stand to welcome our celebrant and ministers of the Mass." The title of the song had a very assuring and peaceful effect on Cletus McCarthy. He opened his hymn book and sang along with the congregation in full throated baritone, harmonized beautifully by Jennifer's soprano.

It seemed like every aspect of the liturgy of the day was chosen or choreographed to suit his life situation. "A reading from the Book of the Prophet Isaiah," the lector stated. "Thus says the Lord…"

Cletus McCarthy scrambled for half a minute to get the correct page of the reading in the missal before remembering to abide by his own teaching to his congregation when he was a priest. "Always look up with attention at the reader and get the proclamation direct," he used to exhort them. He smiled ruefully at himself for so quickly forgetting.

"…Remember not the events of the past, things of long ago consider not. See, I am doing something new."

'Of course, God was doing something new in his life,' he thought. 'I am beginning life again as a regular and common lay man. Besides, I am expecting a baby, a child of my own who after he is born, nobody will shame because of his manner of conception.'

"In the desert, I make a way," the reader continued in the same flat and somber tone that is characteristic of readers at worship services. "In the waste land rivers…."

The Responsorial Psalm celebrated the theme of deliverance, and Cletus McCarthy believed he was being delivered from a paradoxical life that would have been very stifling for him. And when he listened to Paul in the second reading saying he forgets what lay behind and strains for what lies ahead, that did it for Cletus McCarthy. He now understood fully what members of his congregation always meant when they would say it was important for them to feel fed at a Mass they attended. He felt fully fed and ready to take on the world. He did not take Holy Communion, even though he had confessed the previous day. He denied himself the opportunity in order to be in solidarity with Jennifer, who had indicated earlier that she would not receive Holy Communion.

Post-Mass lunch at *Famous Crabs 'N Shrimps* was unusually delicious.

Cletus and Jennifer ate and laughed zestfully. They occupied themselves with small talk about seafood, about fishing, and about spring time. He carefully directed the conversation away from themselves and made what happened next a sweet surprise to Jennifer. A troop of three waiters and two waitresses walked in line toward their table bearing aloft a well-decorated platter of white cheesecake with three small lighted candles stuck into it. They stopped at the table and began immediately serenading Jennifer with *Happy Birthday to You*. She was so overjoyed that in her effort to get up and hug Cletus, she accidentally knocked over his iced tea glass and spilled it all down the front of his shirt and pants. He looked like he's had an accident that he hadn't had since he was a small child. Cletus was so amused that he started laughing so hard that the waiters and waitresses joined in. Members of neighboring tables couldn't help but join the free laughter, especially as Cletus looked up and quipped, "Reminds me when I used to wet my bed, many years ago."

"We've all been there, buddy," a gentleman at the next table concurred, and the laughter went one more round.

Jennifer was all apologies, "I am so sorry. Oh dear, I am. I just wanted to give you a hug…"

"Oh, it's nothing," Cletus replied, trying to calm her. "So, quit flogging yourself so much."

"Oh, thank you," Jennifer said.

"I'm going to do a good job of that on you later," Cletus added, drawing another round of boisterous laughter. Jennifer playfully whipped him with her cloth napkin, stifling her own laughter with a pretty pout.

After lunch, they drove slowly along Seawall Boulevard, sightseeing. The sea itself was a beautiful opal color simmering under the bright spring sun. It was pleasantly breezy. Jackdaws and seagulls hovered lazily, floating on the breeze over the waters, or flapped about contending with one another over some piece of food or another. Eventually Cletus parallel-parked his car, sandwiching it in line with others parked along one lane of the boulevard. They got out and sauntered languidly along one of the piers.

"Let's take some pictures," Jennifer suggested, eagerly. "I haven't had a picture of me on a sea background. The atmosphere is good, the sun bright and the color of the water is exquisite."

"You want to take pictures because you see me with a camera, or you knew I was coming out here for that?"

"I saw you pack the camera when we left Houston," Jennifer replied.

They started to snap each other's portraits and full pictures. Then they enlisted the service of another young couple who was passing by. After a few snaps, Cletus went and whispered to the couple, out of Jennifer's earshot. Then he ran back and stood beside her for one more shot. What happened next took Jennifer by surprise yet again. Cletus quickly got in front of her, got on one knee, popped open a tiny box with a twelve-carat diamond stuck inside the slit of a blue velvet bed, and asked, "Jennifer Ellen Trudeau, will you do me the honor of being my wife?"

"What?!" Jennifer shouted, brows raised, eyes popping, mouth ajar. She breathed heavily for a second before finding her voice. "You are crazy!"

"Yeah, since we became conscious of each other as we grew up, I have been. And I think it's time to cure me of the craziness," Cletus prattled graciously, looking up at Jennifer with a smiling face like a toddler eager for maternal ministrations. Jennifer was still wordless and breathing heavily. She looked at the couple filming the little drama, looked at Cletus kneeling in front of her and looked at the couple again. Other strollers had stopped briefly to watch the well-known event going on. "Well, we aren't going to be here all day. And besides the pier board is *good* wood, you know, hard and unyielding."

Jennifer looked around at the many eyes now trained on her from smiling faces, all waiting to begin applauding. She breathed faster and, almost panting, shouted, "Yes! Yes! Yes!" three times, as Cletus slipped the ring onto her finger. Then he got up, swept her off her feet, and kissed her hard on the mouth. The dam of applause broke. Laughter and claps intermingled with the cooing of oohs and ahs greeted the newly engaged couple. After what seemed like the longest kiss that a couple ever took on a pier, Cletus and Jennifer tore themselves away from each other's mouths and posed for one more picture. Then, hand in hand, they walked back to their car amidst the waving and congratulations from the small crowd that witnessed the little ceremony. Later that afternoon, driving back to Houston, they chatted all the way about their future together. Jennifer was almost like a tipsy teenager in love. She gave her man more than his fair share of smiles for a day, and wouldn't finish a sentence without patting him on the hand or rubbing him gently on the shoulder.

———

Barbara and Crystal drove over to the McCarthys' that evening, to share in the engagement party which Cletus insisted was a family affair.

It was not really a party, but a gathering of family to wish the engaged couple well. Not all in the family were there. Emma and Trevor Henson were out of town on a two-day visit to Corpus Christi with their daughter and son-in-law. John McCarthy had taken Stacy Donovan to Beaumont for the weekend and they were not getting into Houston until near midnight. But they all got the news by phone and, John and Stacy were so happy to announce that they, too, got engaged while in Beaumont. Thereafter, and for the next few days, the two newly engaged couples had to spend a lot of time arguing to convince family members that they did not conspire to get engaged the same day. Dr. Josef Horacek got the news by phone, too, and expressed his happiness for the couples. The party went on well into the evening. Barbara helped Hannah run the kitchen. Crystal forgot to hang out with her brother and, instead, did more of that with Jennifer. Cletus, Josh, and Stephen hung around the barbecue pit, beer cans in hand, flipping T-bones and discussing sports, including the latest homeruns and touchdowns. Eventually, Cletus couldn't keep it all in the family. Their neighbors, the Roberts and the Tates, got to hear about it and breezed in to wish the newly engaged a happy life together. By ten o'clock that night, everybody was heading home, the following day being a work day. Hannah and Stephen stayed on in the sitting room watching the news while Cletus and Jennifer went upstairs to his room. They slept together in his room that night, the first time to do so, with the full knowledge of Hannah and Stephen McCarthy.

For Cletus McCarthy, life was good. He was well on the way to new beginnings, a new life, and, in fact, a new chapter in the history of the McCarthy family. He was traveling in three days to Norfolk to spend time with Dr. Joseph Horacek. He made plans to scout out the possibility of moving there with Jennifer after their wedding. If he found Norfolk not very beckoning, New York was going to be the next option. Dr. Horacek had promised him he might be able to get him a good teaching job at the university Theology Department. But that was a long shot, as those he knew in that department were only casual acquaintances. But it was good to give it a shot. Then there was the baby on the way. They talked far into the night, making plans for the baby, and, possibly, other babies along the line. When it came to deciding how many they would have, it appeared they weren't ready to be on the same page, so they agreed to reserve that discussion for another time and went to sleep.

# PART VI

*If I die young, bury me in satin.*
*Lay me down on a bed of roses....*
*Lord make me a rainbow,*
*I'll shine down on my mother*
*She'll know I am safe with you*
*when she stands under my colors....*

- THE PERRY BAND

## THURSDAY, MARCH 21, 2013

TROOPER DANA AND his partner trooper Jackson had just finished their supper at the tavern on County Road 31, running perpendicular to U.S. Highway 58. The time was 9:20 p.m., and it was Thursday night. They always loved Thursday night patrol because they got to have a free treat at the *Purple Hearts*. It was not clear why the proprietors named the tavern *Purple Hearts* except, maybe, for the fact that it had an adjourning gentlemen's club where lonely bachelors would go to have the time of their life with pole and lap dancing girls. Set behind a large gas station and almost a mile from the nearest residential area, it was a popular place. And not a few love-starved husbands sneaked in there to have stolen treats, too. Dana and Jackson did visit it on very few occasions under the guise of just patrolling to keep the peace. After they had eaten their meal that evening, they debated whether to go in for a few minutes before hitting the road for their night patrol.

"Heads, we go in, tails, we continue on patrol," Dana said, bringing out a quarter from his wallet. He tossed it, caught it in midair, slapped it on the back of his left hand, and took off his right hand. They lost. As they trooped out to their vehicle, Jackson grumbled, blaming Dana for being jinxed with bad luck. Dana ignored his partner and started their police car, pushed the gear lever to D, and moved on. He nosed the car onto County Road 31, and took a left loop to merge onto US 58.

"Is the skyline red, or is it my eyes?" Jackson asked rhetorically, peering ahead.

"Please, don't tell me you're Moses, and you're seeing the burning bush," Dana teased. "I'm in no mood for religion right now."

"It's not religion, man," Jackson replied, getting serious. "The skyline ahead is red. And that's unusual this time of the year in this part of the hemisphere."

Trooper Dana peered ahead and thought his partner was right. The skyline far ahead of them was getting very red and orange bright at the base where the sky met the Earth on the horizon, as they approached. And the redness also seemed to be dancing, sparring with the rest of the dark sky dotted by the stars that had begun peeping out and twinkling.

"You know, you're right, Jack," He said, still peering with mouth slightly ajar as he drove on. "Must be a house on fire or something."

"Well, who's Moses now?" Jackson teased. "We don't know yet whether it's a fire or just some weather phenomenon. Can you step on the gas?"

As if on cue, their radio crackled to life, "Highway five eight, come in! Highway five eight, come in! This is headquarters. Over."

"This is highway five eight. Trooper Dana, Trooper Jackson checking in. Over," Jackson responded to the radio inquiry while Dana drove on.

"Inferno, reported on five eight East. Repeat, inferno on five eight East. Check out, over," the voice from headquarters was a trifle impatient, and Dana suspected it was something serious. So, he turned on the signal lights and the sirens and stepped on the pedal while Jackson confirmed the execution of the order.

"Inferno sighted. Trooper Dana, Trooper Jackson on case. Repeat: Dana and Jackson, on case. Sign off."

They sped on, passing other vehicles to check out the supposed 'inferno'. As they got closer and closer, it seemed that they were going to witness something other than a house fire. Eventually, they reached the scene and were surprised to see a long line of vehicles that had slowed down or cleared the road to park on the shoulder, extending almost a mile from the actual scene of the fire. Dana slowed down the car, but kept going to get as close as possible. What they saw was unbelievable. What looked like a gas tanker was on its side, sprawled diagonally across the road. Huge balls of fire, taller than twenty feet, were leaping into the air and disappearing in thick black smoke. It was impossible to drive past the scene because it engulfed the entire road, practically shutting it down. The heat emitted by the inferno was such that the nearest vehicle was parked almost a quarter of a mile from it. Troopers Dana and Jackson could not go beyond that point because they, too, had begun to feel the intense heat. People were milling around with their cell phones glued to their ears, some gesturing frantically as they talked. Everyone was in panic and sorrow because it was impossible to move in to help. Dana and Jackson got out and tried to find out from those standing by or moving around what happened. No one could give them any coherent piece of information. All they could gather was that an eighteen-wheeler gas tanker coming out from a side road to merge onto US 58 apparently lost control and careened into two or three other vehicles. The impact of the tanker as it hit the tarmac, sliding, produced sparks, and ignited with a big bang into a huge ball of fire.

The two troopers got on their radio and relayed to headquarters what they saw and what little information they had gathered from the bystanders. They were yelling because it was almost impossible to hear one another because of the din of excited commuters and motorists, and the series of loud cracklings and minor explosions that kept coming from the scene. There were loud hissing sounds, too, which occasionally seemed to shrink the flames. But then the flames would leap even higher once the hissing sound subsided. It soon became clear where the hissing came from. The human silhouettes darting about on the other side of the flames were firefighters who had arrived at that side of the inferno and were frantically battling the flames to put them out. Angry sirens and blinking red, blue and yellow lights rushing up from the side that Dana and Jackson came announced the arrival of another firefighting unit. They lost no time getting into battle too. The whole scenario was chaotic with the noise of the engines from the firefighting arsenal on both sides, the noisy and confused crowd, the still revving engines of the vehicles lined up along the road on both sides, as far as the eye could see because it was impossible to pass through from either way, and the yells and shouts from the firefighters as they barked out and relayed commands to one another.

Eventually, the high-leaping, angry flames were dwarfed by the steady assault of the forceful pressure from the firefighters' hoses, each shooting out gallons of water at a speed of almost sixty miles per hour. The heat waves and the acrid stench that came from the smoldering heap were hellishly suffocating, and the thick black smoke that rose from it covered the heavens above, shading out the twinkling eyes of the stars. Then the forms of the charred vehicles involved in the accident gradually became discernible. Dana and Jackson drew nearer and could count not less than one sedan-like and two van-like frames, all seemingly crashing into the long burnt-out hulk of an eighteen-wheeler tanker, sprawled diagonally across the road. Was it some human error on the part of one or all the drivers involved, or was it just the freakiest coincidence of uncontrollable variables? No easy and immediate answers were forthcoming from the doomsday scenario of that late evening. The only sure facts were that all commuters of the vehicles involved in the accident were dead, charred and consumed in the hellish flames like a burnt offering. And Cletus Nicholas McCarthy was presumably one of them.

Later that evening, Dr. Josef Horacek was in his sitting room watching the late-night news. It was way past his bed time, but he stayed up late because the estimated arrival time of Cletus McCarthy was anywhere between ten and eleven o'clock, depending on the traffic situation as he entered Norfolk. He had tried twice to get him on the phone to ascertain his progress, but had not been able to get a ring from Cletus's phone. All that met his ears were a series of beeps announcing an engaged phone line. Wondering whether he switched off his phone when he was driving or was talking all the time with the folks back in Houston, Dr. Horacek had decided to keep calling every so often. Perhaps he would catch Cletus stopping to get gas or a snack. He was just finishing his coffee as the local TV station announced the eleven o'clock news time.

He saw it before he heard it. The accident on US 58 scrolled slowly past the base of his TV screen, as the news anchor introduced the news for the evening. Given as breaking news, they could not give any meaningful details other than the fact that multiple vehicles were involved in a fatal head-on collision with a gas tanker on US 58 and busted into flames. They reported that fire fighters were able to put out the flames only after they had battled it for almost an hour, and that it was apparent that there were no survivors. They promised further information as details came in from the ongoing investigation.

Not feeling comfortable, Dr. Horacek tried Cletus's number one more time. He got the same busy signals. His gut sank, and he suspected that something ominous had happened. His next phone call was to Barbara, who also informed him that she had lost contact with Cletus.

"He called to check in and tell us his progress every three hours," Barbara said. "I haven't heard from him in about seven hours."

Dr. Horacek indicated he hadn't, either, but decided not to give in to his worst fears. He clicked off his phone, afraid that Barbara might start asking probing questions. He was debating in his mind whether to call the McCarthys or wait an hour or two, and then the phone rang in his hand. It was Stephen McCarthy's voice on the other end of the line. He inquired whether Cletus had arrived safely. Dr. Horacek hesitated for a few seconds before responding in the negative. Stephen indicated that he and Hannah had lost contact with their son who was touching base every two hours or so. Dr. Horacek, not wanting to cause any panic, assured Stephen that Cletus would probably arrive very late. He might have been caught in bad traffic. After promising to call and inform them when Cletus would arrive, he hung up. Not feeling comfortable just sitting there watching the news, but not getting any detailed information or any phone call from Cletus, he decided to drive out to the scene of the accident. From the news report, he figured that the accident scene was about sixty to sixty-five miles away. 'I could do that in under an hour', he thought to himself as he picked up his car key and headed for his garage. Inside the garage, he hesitated, wondering whether he was going on a wild goose chase. Then he figured that since he had his phone with him, if Cletus called, he would answer and turn around to drive home, and they would only laugh about his panic with relief. He drove up to the front of the clinic and got one of his two night janitors, Fu Pham, to accompany him.

"Did you watch tonight's news, Fu?" Dr. Horacek asked, wanting to start a conversation to keep his mind from wandering wild with suspicions.

"No, boss," Fu replied, shaking his head vigorously. "I no watch news when I work."

Dr. Horacek threw him a side-long glance and felt like punching him on the nose and sending him flying out of the car, and driving on. He wondered why Fu thought it was necessary to lie. His kitchen window and the window of the clinic's lounge were a mere fifteen feet apart. And he always observed Fu watching movies on the television. Though they always pulled the curtains closed, from their perspective, they had no way of knowing he could still see them through the cracks between the drapes and the window frame. He decided it was no use trying to converse with a schizophrenic janitor whose only understanding was that his boss was asking questions to catch him. He drove the rest of the way in silence. No call came from Cletus McCarthy throughout the seventy-one-mile drive. It had turned out to be further than he thought, but he still made it in fifty-four minutes, according to his GPS timer. He was glad he ran into no cops on the way. As he pulled up, he could sniff the acrid smell of burnt rubber and gas and flesh. It stank and stung the nostrils. There were only two police cars still blinking their colored lights. Other vehicles belonged to the FBI and the local TV station, the crew of which were packing in their cameras and other equipment, ready to go for the night. A caterpillar had been called in and it managed to push the rear end of the burnt-out tanker out of the way, just enough to make room for vehicles to crawl past each other on the shoulder of one side of the road, from opposite directions. Whiffs of smoke were still oozing from some parts of the burnt-out vehicles and about four policemen and three FBI agents were still foraging in the charred heaps to salvage anything that could serve as evidence to explain what happened. Some relatives of the suspected victims who had arrived before Dr. Horacek were huddled together at different spots bewailing their lost loved ones. He got out of his car and walked up to one of the policemen and introduced himself, explaining why he had driven almost one hour to the scene. The policeman introduced himself as Trooper Dana and led him to a little heap on the side of the road. Three of the FBI agents, a woman and two men, wearing gloves and holding tongs, were gingerly turning some half-burnt items and trying to piece together as much information as they could that would help in identifying the victims.

Dana introduced Dr. Horacek. "This is Dr. Horacek. He has reason to suspect that his son is among the victims."

"Do you want to take a look, Sir, at some of the retrieved items here?" The female agent asked politely. "Some of the items are burned beyond what we can read, but some were merely scorched."

The items ranged from flasks of water and coffee mugs to half-burnt shoes and wristwatches. There were a few blackened cell phones, some bent from the scorching heat or completely burned beyond recognition. One of the phones had one corner still fresh and Dr. Horacek pointed at it, "The phone. Let me see the phone. His phone was an Apple iPhone 4 with a green plastic casing." One of the agents grabbed the burnt phone with a tong and held it for Dr. Horacek's inspection. It was impossible to really tell, even under the powerful search beam of the FBI torch light, whether the color of the little part of it that was not burnt was green, deep grey, or even black. Just then, another FBI agent walked up with an object clasped with a tong and announced that it was a wallet from the vehicle they could tell was a sports utility of some type.

"The majority of the contents are still intact, especially the cards."

They started opening the wallet, the outer part of which was scorched dark. But because the wallet was made of a special material that looked like leather, but was not really leather, it had, for the most part, withstood the flames and the heat. They used tongs and started pulling out a few cards that were not burnt. The police and the FBI agents were relieved to have chanced upon one item that could give a positive identification of at least one of the victims with certainty. They pulled out credit and bank cards, and then the driver's license. All four cards bore the unmistakable name of Cletus Nicholas McCarthy. The picture on his driver's license was the one he took in his late twenties, and he looked very handsome, with a pleasant face. Dr. Horacek looked at it for a few seconds, and then suddenly belted out a loud cry, fell on his knees, and wept loud and long.

"My son! Oh, my son, Cletus! My son! What has happened to you? Why has this happened to you? Oh, my son, my son!"

Dana, Jackson, and the lady FBI agent tried to no avail to console him. Not knowing what else to do, they gradually inched their way from him and allowed him to weep out his frustration and anger. Fu Pham was so confused at everything that happened that, also not knowing what to do, he simply wept along with his boss, wringing his hands helplessly. After what seemed like ages, Dr. Horacek was able to pull himself together. He begged and was allowed to have a peek at the charred corpse of Cletus McCarthy, which had crumbled in a heap on the burnt and twisted rubber covering of the driver's seat. He was assured that the scene would remain that way until he returned in the morning, as the FBI and the police would make sure all identifications were done and relatives of all the victims were satisfied that they had identified their loved ones before they would release the ashes to any of the families.

It was not a pleasant ride back to Norfolk that evening. Dr. Horacek felt in some sense that he was partly to blame. If he had not invited Cletus McCarthy to visit him, he would have been safe and sound in Houston. IN his heart, though, he knew that what happened was just sheer bad luck that Cletus McCarthy was on that portion of the road at that particular time. All the way back to Norfolk, he agonized over how he was going to break the news to the people in Houston, and in what order. Should he start with his wife, Barbara? Or should he start with Cletus's parents? Either way, it was going to be a very difficult task. He decided to reach home first before dialing anybody with the saddest story of his life. He had felt nothing when he received news of his wife's death along El Paso highway years ago. That was because he had never bonded with her the way he bonded with Cletus, after discovering that the experiment he'd done years ago had blossomed into such a brilliant young man. Why fate should have thrown him such a wicked curve of bad luck just then was not clear. Dr. Horacek sank into deep grief.

He dropped off his janitor and gave no response to the latter's "good night, Boss. I pray for you," and drove straight home. His movements were like a zombie's as he parked the car in his garage and went and sat in the sitting room, lost in deep thought. After what seemed like ages, he picked up his cell phone to make the calls that he could not dodge. Two more calls had come in from the McCarthys and he wondered why he did not hear the phone ring. Instead of returning those calls right away, he decided to call Barbara first with the bad news, strictly warning her not to relay it to Crystal until morning. Then he dialed Stephen McCarthy.

THE FUNERAL MASS was scheduled to be held at the Co-Cathedral of the Sacred Heart, in downtown Houston. Umberto Cardinal Pacino Felice had insisted it should be so. Everyone knew why. It was the least the Church could do to show solidarity and compassion to the McCarthy family and to demonstrate that even though Cletus had applied for and obtained the lay status, the Church could not turn its back on him at such a time. Most commentators had already made angry accusations to the effect that the Church had used him as a pawn to further its moral indoctrination, but abandoned him to his fate when he fell into the post-partum depression and identity crisis following the trauma of being outed in court. A good number of the priests saw it that way, too.

"Rome should not have granted him the request for laicization," Fr. Polanski had observed, a few days earlier, at the gathering of a handful of the priests who got together at his place to discuss how to help the family plan the funeral service. "They simply let him punish himself for a wrong that wasn't his fault."

"Looks to me like they considered him an embarrassment to the Church," Fr. Gary Logan, one of the young priests known for his controversialist views of the Roman Curia said. "They had probably wished he hadn't been ordained. Cletus just handed them the chance of their lives on a golden platter and they jumped at it."

"Hopefully, someone doesn't snitch to Rome before the funeral date that he's going to have a priestly burial with full honors," another priest interjected with a hint of disapproval for anybody who would do that.

"Well, he is still a priest," yet another replied. "He only chose to live in the lay state."

"Yeah. Once ordained, you are a priest forever, according to the order of Melchizedek," Fr. Logan concurred. "I would be greatly surprised if the Cardinal had decided otherwise. He deserves to be buried a priest."

The pre-meeting conversation went on for a few more minutes, moving from supporting the decision to bury Cletus McCarthy as a priest to the momentary policy about the ordination of IVF-born candidates. Some of the priests figured that since there might be the possibility of other IVF-conceived or surrogate-born seminarians in the pipeline, there was need for the Church to get out a canon legitimizing the ordination of such candidates once they have fulfilled all requirements. They agreed to prod Fr. Brady Callahan to petition Rome to expedite action in promulgating such a canon. Eventually, Fr. Polanski called the meeting to order and they began discussing the business of the day.

That was five days previously. Now the Co-Cathedral Church was packed full on Saturday, April 6, the day of the funeral. The usual wake and Vespers with Office of the Dead that would have taken place the prior evening were shifted to that day. Everything was to be done the same day. At 9 a.m. on the dot, Cardinal Felice, wearing a violet Cope and Mitre, walked up to the door to receive the casket of Cletus Nicholas McCarthy. He was flanked by altar servers and his personal Master of Ceremonies. The crowd on the front steps and landing was thick. The McCarthy and the Horacek families, all swathed in black, formed a semi-circle behind the casket. There was scarcely a dry eye among them. The ladies—Hannah, Barbara, Crystal, and Jennifer—had swollen eyes from copious weeping. They kept sniffling with effortful restraint and continually dabbed their eyes, which couldn't stop flowing with tears. The men—Stephen, Josef, John, Trevor, and Josh—had red, watery eyes, and tautly clenched lips. They were visibly battling anger lumps in their throats as they kept straining to swallow gulps of saliva, but gallantly stayed choked on their ties. The crowd kept squirming as is characteristic of such gatherings, with people shuffling and juggling for a better spot to catch a better view of the action up front. Some strained to see the casket, others tried to catch a glimpse of the McCarthy and Horacek families. Cardinal Felice moved closer to speak the rite of reception.

"In the name of the Father, and of the Son, and of the Holy Spirit," he chanted. The people responded with a resounding 'Amen.'

He continued to read the brief opening prayer, and when he concluded, the organist played the *Dies Irae, Dies Illa*. A choir of priests in black cassocks and white surplices picked up the doleful timbre of the music and chanted the holy dirge in the most somber, Gregorian tone they could muster.

> *Dies irae, dies illa,*
> *Solvet saeculum in favilla,*
> *Teste David cum Sybilla.*

The procession slowly began to move into the church with the Cardinal leading the way. The choir of priests stationed itself in the section right of the altar and continued its chant. The casket, draped with a white pall marked with a large purple cross band running the whole length and width of it, was stationed centrally by the three steps leading up the sanctuary, and perpendicular to the altar. The Book of the Gospels was placed on top of it with a purple stole on top of the book. The Cardinal and his train of ministers remained standing in the sanctuary, as well as the people who had filled up the pews. Then the choir belted out in a crescendo:

> *Ingemisco, tamquam reus:*
> *Culpa rubet vultus meus:*
> *Suplicanti parce Deus.*

As if on cue, Hannah McCarthy lost it. The loud shriek caught everybody off guard. The other three ladies—Barbara, Jennifer, and Crystal—let go in unison, joining Hannah in her bitter wailing. The somber chant fell apart for a second or two, but quickly regained tempo and coherence. Church wardens and ushers rushed in to help the men of the McCarthy and Horacek families calm down their grief-stricken women. It was a daunting task, as the women wept with abandon and refused to be consoled. As if to really make a point before God, on behalf of Cletus Nicholas McCarthy, the choir, for its part, waxed stronger with the chant in its bid to, perhaps, overshadow the wailing. The loud, but dolefully plain, chant blended with the wailing to produce such a fearsome aura that everybody trembled. Children were so scared that they joined in the wailing, too. Greg Sullivan later observed that it was like judgment day.

Eventually, the choir of priests finished their chant and sat down. The sorrows of the ladies were also finally assuaged and reduced to heaving and sniffling, and Church wardens went around dutifully serving boxes of Kleenex wipes. A couple of cantors went to the microphone and spoke the

Office for the Dead. For almost an hour, the clergy recited the Office. Then the Cardinal read the closing prayer and left the sanctuary with his train. There was no viewing because the casket could not be opened for obvious reasons. What was put inside the casket at the accident scene in Norfolk on US 58 and driven back to Texas were the ashes of Cletus McCarty, swept from the driver's seat of his burnt-out vehicle. After a fifteen-minute hiatus, the Cardinal and his Mass train came in again for the funeral Mass.

The funeral Mass itself took just an hour. The readings were carefully chosen to reflect the mood and the occasion. The first reading from the Book of Wisdom iterated that the just man, though he die early, shall be at rest, and the second reading gave the assurance that hope cannot fail believers because the love of God has been poured into their hearts. The Cardinal gave a very profound homily. At one point, he dwelt on how Cletus McCarthy was the perfect offering that enriched the lives of many apart from his parents. He was offered to them at birth to fulfill their parental vocation, he offered his life to serve the people of God as a priest, and, finally, became the lamb of sacrifice offered as a holocaust to God to open the door of mercy for others after him. He regretted that line immediately, as it set off the storm of wailing again, a storm that took more than three minutes to calm down. After that, he studiously avoided any overly sentimental utterances, and the rest of the Mass continued tamely to the end. Bishop Montana did the Prayer of Final Commendation and the funeral procession left for the cemetery.

Stephen and Hannah McCarthy had insisted that Cletus be buried in the family plot they had bought at Rest Haven Cemetery along North Freeway, instead of the Archdiocesan Cemetery in Dickenson. The funeral procession left the Co-Cathedral of the Sacred Heart and snaked its way along Jefferson, connected with Dallas Street, and headed to the cemetery along Interstate 45 North. The crowd was uncommonly large and it formed a procession of almost two miles, slowing traffic on I-45 and holding up other traffic streams from tributary roads pouring into it. It was an amazing sight to see. A great number of motorists voluntarily pulled off on the shoulder at the sound of the sirens and the numerous colorful lights from the police escorts' motorcycles. Faces that peered through car windows seemed sad and inquisitive at the same time. The air seemed to stand still. Though it gave no indication of imminent rain, the sky spotted huge swaths of clouds that made it impossible to tell the position of the sun. The very atmosphere itself seemed to be in mourning for Cletus Nicholas McCarthy as he went to his eternal rest.

"Man!" Fr. Brady Callahan exclaimed. "Feels like the funeral of a god. Never seen this type of crowd at a funeral for a long time. Not since that of Bishop Nold."

"Nold's funeral pulled only half this crowd," Bishop Montana said from the back of the car, in his characteristically husky, but strong, voice. "I think it must have something to do with the publicity his case got. I'll tell ya, that case garnered a lot of well-deserved sympathy for him."

"It *is* the funeral of a god, indeed," Fr. Polanski replied, waxing prophetic. "When his vehicle burst into flames on Norfolk Highway 58 that fateful evening, and the spirit of Cletus McCarthy rose in the fumy smoke toward Heaven, a god had died. I believe the Cardinal hit the nail on the head in his homily."

"We're gonna miss him for a long time," Fr. Brady said, dolefully.

"Yes, we are certainly gonna miss him," Bishop Montana concurred.

Fr. Brady, Fr. Polanski, and Bishop Montana had decided to carpool to the cemetery, with Fr. Brady driving. They fell back into silence as the hearse exited the freeway onto the feeder road leading up to Rest Haven. A single white truck that stood by the gates took over the lead while the police escorts fell off. It took more than twenty minutes to get all the traffic parallel parked. When they got out of their vehicles, Bishop Montana couldn't help but nod acknowledgement of the ingenuity of the truck driver who, on noticing the long line of vehicles, had decided to wrap them around two adjacent sections of the cemetery, forming a big letter **S**, to accommodate everyone. "He got it right," he muttered to himself.

Fr. Polanski was given the honor of officiating at the graveside for his friend. He positioned himself at the head of the casket and choked on his first attempt to speak the prayers. Bishop Montana and Fr. Brady moved in on either side of him and placed their hands on his shoulders, rubbing and rocking him gently to calm him. The McCarthys and Horaceks, noticing his reaction, broke down again in bitter wailing and sobbing. Everyone was heart-broken watching Cletus McCarthy's families on both sides, and there was scarcely a dry eye at the grave side that afternoon. Hannah McCarthy had launched forward in an attempt to throw herself on the casket, but was immediately restrained by other mourners who stood beside her and were quick enough to notice her move. It took almost three minutes before they could reasonably be calmed down. Fr. Polanski made great effort to compose himself. Eventually, he drew a deep breath, exhaled, and gallantly recited aloud the blessing of the grave.

"Eternal rest grant unto him, O Lord," he said.

"And let perpetual light shine upon him," the crowd responded.

"May he rest in peace," he added.

"Amen," responded the crow, as before.

"Since Almighty God has called our brother, his priest, Cletus McCarthy, to his eternal rest…" Fr. Polanski continued, purposefully raising his tone to emphasize the words, *his priest*. "We now commit his body to the Earth, from which he was made."

At Fr. Polanski's pronouncement of "his priest," Jennifer, who had rested her head on Barbara's shoulder, started slightly. Barbara, noticing her quick, reflexive move, threw her arm around Jennifer and gently pulled and coaxed her to lay her head back on her chest. Ever since the bitter news of Cletus McCarthy's accident and death filtered back to them in Houston, the four women—Hannah, Barbara, Crystal, and Jennifer—had forged such a close bond that they couldn't let go of their hands whenever they were together. Their pictures even appeared in the Houston Chronicle and other papers. In every case, they were always depicted locking themselves together by the crook of their arms. It was as though they were always telling the world, 'he belonged to us four, and we belonged to him'. It was always a very moving sight, all the women in Fr. Cletus McCarthy's life. Jennifer cooperatively lay her head back on Barbara's chest, reaching out at the same time to rub Hannah's forearm. Jennifer's thoughts were inundated with Barbara's words of admonition. She was not to grieve enough to the point of distressing the child in her womb. She understood her perfectly well, also being a nurse, and knew the implications of fetal distress and possible miscarriage. Jennifer wanted to avoid a miscarriage at all costs.

"That's him living inside you," Barbara kept reminding her in the days leading up to the funeral. "That child is the only handle you've got on him. Lose that, and you lose everything of the person you loved so dearly." Jennifer thought that was the most profound way to perpetuate the memory of Cletus McCarthy. And it was a very real one. She was carrying his child and, metaphorically speaking, she was carrying Cletus McCarthy in her womb. Though she had lost Cletus McCarthy, a Cletus McCarthy was growing inside her. The first Cletus McCarthy came from a test tube, produced, not begotten, according to Catholic doctrine. However, the second Cletus McCarthy would come from her womb, begotten not produced, according to Catholic doctrine. He would be the new beginning for the McCarthy family; he would start the lineage of the begotten, not the produced or adopted. She would name him Cletus. As she used to call the first Cletus, 'Cousin', she would call the second Cletus, 'Cletus Cousin McCarthy'. She smiled at the awkwardness of the name and was again startled by the abruptness of the loud chant from the choir of priests who erupted in one great *Salve Regina* to conclude the graveside service for Cletus McCarthy

*Salve Regina, Mater misericordiae,*
*vita dulcedo, et spes nostra salve.*
*Ad te clamamus, exsules filii Hevae.*
*ad te suspiramus, gementes et flentes.*
*in hac lacrimarum valle.*
*Eia ergo, ad vocata nostra, illos tuos*
*misericordes oculos ad nos converte;*
*et Jesum,benedictum fructum ventris tui,*
*nobis post hoc exilium ostende.*
*O clemens. O pia, O dulcis, Virgo Maria.*

JENNIFER LAY HER bouquet of flowers at the base of the marble tomb marker for Cletus Nicholas McCarthy, in Rest Haven Cemetery, and stood beside the baby stroller, looking pensively for a few seconds at her seven-month old son, sleeping peacefully in it. Then she sat down, cross-legged, facing the tombstone. The baby had come in October, 2013, exactly nine months and three weeks from when he was conceived. She had named him Cletus McCarthy, Jr., a name that pleased Stephen and Hannah McCarthy, since it perpetuated the memory of their son. She had not inserted "Cousin" as his middle name, though she originally intended to do so. It sounded awkward. And so, she decided to leave it out and only use it as a nickname. And besides, born on the memorial of St. Ignatius of Antioch, there was little debate that his middle name should be Ignatius. In the end, everybody opted to stay with just Cletus McCarthy, Jr.

She was not working on Memorial Day and, so, decided to pay a visit to the tomb of the man she loved, the father of her baby. It was a few minutes before 4:00 in the afternoon and there were a handful of other families milling around the cemetery honoring their dead loved ones by placing flowers on their graves. Stephen and Hannah McCarthy were going to join her at 4:30. It was a little family ritual they had begun on Memorial Day in 2013. On that occasion, after joining hands and standing around the grave and praying, Stephen had pronounced that the family would be doing that as an annual remembrance of Cletus.

Rest Haven Cemetery was breezy that day. It was cozily cool, also, because of the numerous oak, piquant, and acacia trees which provided large portions of shaded areas from the sun. The sun itself was bright, but not really hot. It was late spring. The shrubs lining the edge of the cemetery grounds and the lawns around the Funeral Chapel were in full bloom. Their flowers blended with the ones brought by families to lay on the grave of their loved ones to produce a pleasantly idyllic ambient so delightful to the eyes. Jennifer thought the name of the cemetery was very apt because it was seductively restful and peaceful. Was that how Heaven would feel? If it was this peaceful and restful on Earth, maybe it was one hundred times so in Heaven. If so, Cousin Cletus was having a swell time over there. She stared at the tombstone and smiled absent-mindedly. She felt peaceful, healed and contented. Maybe Cousin Cletus was fanning her from above, fanning his sleeping baby. Maybe he was looking down at them, very happy that they had come to visit him.

Jennifer had never thought she would get over the loss of Cletus McCarthy. It devastated her. The only thing that kept her going was the knowledge that she was carrying his baby inside her. She was determined to make sure nothing distressed the baby which might possibly lead to a miscarriage. Barbara Horacek had been her guardian angel in the meantime, prodding her, admonishing her, gently coaxing her and goading her on. Hannah McCarthy did the same to a lesser degree because she herself was almost a wreck from grief. Then all of them had taken turns counselling Crystal, never letting her out of their sight, in case she tried to harm herself out of anger for losing her newfound brother. The men had reacted in different ways, but generally did better than the women. Stephen McCarthy consoled himself with large gulps of Kentucky Bourbon. John McCarthy wreaked of Havana cigars, which he chain smoked to calm his nerves.

Josh played violent video games on his android tablet and cursed when he missed a villain, causing Hannah to take a break from sobbing and sniffling to chide, "Josh, mind your language," and then go back to sobbing again. Trevor and Emma Henson visited every other day to spend time with them. Greg Sullivan and Fr. Polanski swung over at least twice a week. Members of Our Lady Queen of Peace and St. Monica Churches visited in groups and on various days to show solidarity. It was almost three months before the constant stream of visitors to the McCarthy house slacked off. Stacy visited quite often in John's company, and on one occasion, visited with her parents, Patricia and Geoffrey Donovan, Sr. All in all, the McCarthys were not short-changed in condolences and sympathies. At one point, they even began to wish the rest of the world would let them have some private time to themselves, to heal faster. They were particularly concerned about Jennifer and the baby, and, of course, shielded her from most of the visitors.

The Horaceks had their fair share of sympathizers. Barbara's house was a revolving door to her nurse colleagues at Baylor Methodist Hospital, and elsewhere. Ima and Edidiong Eshiet visited and, together, they had all visited the McCarthys to express their profound sympathy. Edidiong assured the McCarthys that although he disagreed with Fr. McCarthy's treatment of them, and sought redress in court, he would never dream of wishing any of the McCarthys dead. He took refuge in an African proverb: "As our people say, 'It is better to have a sibling to fight with, than to have none'." The McCarthys were touched by the visit from the Eshiets and assured them that they harbored no more hard feelings. It seemed like an aeon before the stream of visitors finally stopped for the McCarthys to move on with their lives.

Late July of that year, Barbara Horacek was able, finally, to resign from Baylor Methodist Hospital and her teaching job at the college. She and Crystal moved back to Norfolk, where Crystal enrolled in the prelims in the School of Medicine and Health Sciences. She later learned from Edo-Mma that Kelechi had returned back from Nigeria and he and Josh had joined the Air Force. Edo-Mm herself had been admitted to study neuroscience at Rice University. They had sworn over phone calls and texts to remain friends forever, despite what had happened.

The weeks and months following the death of Cletus McCarthy were very interesting. It brought out the best in people, even those who initially were upset with them for flouting the Church moral teaching against IVF. Jennifer experienced an uncommon show of solidarity and understanding from her colleagues at St. Luke's Hospital in the Woodlands, where she worked. She made more friends among her co-workers than she had made when Cletus was alive. In fact, all that came to a head, when at 4 a.m., on the morning of Friday, October 17, 2013, her water broke as she was taking the vital signs of one of her patients to prepare her for a procedure. Jennifer was rushed to the maternity unit of the hospital, where she gave birth to a six-pound-eleven-ounce baby boy. Dr. Nguyen kept her at the hospital for a full week before releasing her and the baby to go home. By then, Cletus, Jr. had grown to weigh almost twelve pounds.

As if on cue, little Cletus woke and tried to turn over in his stroller. He gasped and stuttered, then yelled a cry of protest. Jennifer woke from her revelry, jumped up, and rushed to attend to the needs of her little boss.

"There, Cousin. There, there!" she coaxed. "What you need? You need Momma? I'm here, my love. My little king. We came to see your dada. Come here," she said as she picked him up and sat him in the crook of her arm, rocking him gently. "We came to see Dada. You wanna talk to Dada. Here, talk to Dada." She sat down again, cross-legged, and sat the baby down within her crossed legs and leaned him on her belly and chest. "Talk to Dad. Call him. Dada! You see, Dada was a very intelligent man, strong and friendly. Well… a little self-willed sometimes," she said, bobbing her head from side to side to indicate she could tolerate that trait in him. "He was a priest for a while, almost eight years, but then something happened, and he resigned." Little Cletus gave a grunt and a feeble squeal. "No. You won't understand," Jennifer continued, as though she was having a conversation with her little baby. "But you will understand when you grow up. I'll tell you his story again. I'll fill you in on the details. For now, though, you won't understand. I can tell you that he left before you were born. He was called to Heaven by God. This is where we buried his remains. So, that is why we're sitting here." Little Cletus gave a joyful shriek, splashing the air with his little hands. "No, you cannot see him, but he sees us. You can talk to him, though. I know you're not talking yet. You can call him Dada. You wanna call him Dada? Say Dada. Dada. Say Dada." Little Cletus pointed a tiny pinkie at the tombstone. "Yes, that is Dada. Call him Dada." Little Cletus shrieked again joyfully and energetically splashed the air again with his little hands. Then he shrieked and uttered, "Ta-ta, ta-ta, ta-ta," and pointed again at the tombstone. "Yes, call him Dada. That's Dada."

"No. That's not me, son," a man's voice said, firmly, from behind Jennifer. "I'm this way, son. That's only a tombstone. I'm here. Dada is here."

"What?!" Jennifer swirled around at the voice and saw a thirtyish-looking, handsome man in a bowler hat, suit, and tie. "Who are you? What do you want?"

"It's me, Jenny," the man said, calling her by the endearing name that only one person used to call her. He moved closer and squatted. Jennifer recoiled violently and began shouting, hugging little Cletus very tight to her chest, struggling to get up at the same time.

"Who are you? What do you want? Stay away from me and my son, or I am going to shout!"

"Jenny, take a hold of yourself," the man said harshly, almost whispering. "Don't shout. It's me, Cletus Nicholas McCarthy."

"What?!" Jennifer exclaimed loudly, in spite of herself. "You…?"

"Yeah, me. I thought you would recognize me right away," Cletus replied, smiling inanely at her discomfiture. "It's not a ghost. It's me. It wasn't me. It's me," he felt stupid babbling and decided to rush out his explanation before Jennifer caused a row at the cemetery.

"No! No! This isn't real! No! I'm dreaming!" Jennifer yelled, struggling to her feet and slowly backing away.

"Will you stop and listen? Pull yourself together!" Cletus almost snarled at her in frustration. "It wasn't me in the accident. I survived. I mean, I was involved, but I survived. I did not die in the accident."

"How do I know you're not a ghost?" Jennifer asked, looking wildly incredulous and suspicious. "How do I know you're real, and it is you?"

"You can touch me," Cletus said, removing his hat. "I am not a ghost." Then he swore, "Jesus Christ, Jenny! You're now making me play Jesus before the frightened apostles at His first appearance. Look, before you touch me, look at your far right."

Stephen and Hannah McCarthy were walking toward them. Hannah was waving and seemed to be laughing at the same time. Then Hannah broke into a strut to get to the scene before the little drama got out of hand.

"Jennifer. It's Cletus. 'Cousin' Cletus, not a ghost," Hannah said, excitedly, trying unsuccessfully to hold back her laughter at Jennifer's still clutching little Cletus protectively and half turning away from Cletus, Sr. "I had the same reaction when I opened the door and saw him."

"Won't you tell her how you ran away shrieking?" Stephen McCarthy teased his wife.

Little Cletus shrieked at seeing his grandmother.

"Yes, my little angel. It's Nana. Come here," she said, taking him from Jennifer, who let go of the baby grudgingly, still looking confused. "Let's go home before people notice us, please."

"Come on, Jennifer. Let's go," Stephen McCarthy said, beginning to wheel the stroller toward where he parked their car.

"Jenny, relax and pull yourself together. I am real. I am not a ghost. It's a long story. Let's get home and I'll tell you everything. I witnessed the accident. In fact, I almost got involved in it, but I escaped it by a fraction of a second. I like the fact that everybody believes I died. It gives me the room to begin life again without the old baggage and without people always staring at me with unwanted curiosity."

"But…?" Jennifer turned and looked at the tombstone where she had laid her bouquet.

"Yeah. Someone else's ashes are down there, not mine. It wasn't my time yet and God did not want me to die. I know the flowers were for me, but leave them there. The poor guy down there probably needs 'em more than I do. Let's go," Cletus McCarthy said and started walking in the direction where he parked his car. Then he turned to his mother and asked, "Mom, can I please hold my son for the first time?"

"Oh, sure, son. Hold," Hannah said, handing him the baby, who looked at the face of the stranger with quiet curiosity.

"Auntie, Hannah?" Jennifer found her voice.

"Yes, dear. Are you okay?" Hannah asked.

"Pinch me," Jennifer said. "Pinch me so I can wake up. I think this might still be a dream."

"Okay. There," Cletus McCarthy said, pinching her hard on her forearm.

"Ouch! That hurts!" Jennifer protested.

"Well, at least you're awake," Cletus said. "And you asked for it." Hannah and Stephen laughed.

"I asked Auntie Hannah to pinch me, not you," Jennifer said, and beat Cletus on the shoulder with her purse. Then she added in a loud whisper, "Ghost!"

Stephen, Hannah, and Cletus McCarthy broke out again, laughing. Cletus Junior, not wanting to be left out, shrieked loudly with joy as the little group walked to their vehicles to drive home.

---

The thirty-minute drive from Rest Haven Cemetery to Hollow Wood Circuit took ages because of the traffic. Cletus McCarthy thought too many folks spent their Memorial Day holiday behind wheels on the roads than they did beside their barbeque pits and beer coolers. Eventually, they made the exit to Saw Tooth Canyon Drive and then wheeled onto Hollow Wood Circuit. He put on his long coat and bowler hat and looked like Sherlock Holmes incarnate, stoutly walking in to investigate a crime scene. His disguise hugely paid off. It would have taken a close acquaintance quite a while to recognize him as Cletus McCarthy. If the neighbors noticed him, they probably thought a gentleman from the FBI was visiting the McCarthy's for some more information on Cletus McCarthy's death a year and three months earlier. Or, that a wealthy gentleman courting the single mother, Jennifer, was just visiting with her for the holiday. He moved briskly inside the house. Jennifer followed with little Cletus. Then Hannah and Stephen brought up the rear, with Stephen dragging the stroller after him.

Once inside, he relaxed and started shedding his disguise. He hung his great coat and suit on the back rest of a chair, and dropped his hat on top of the television set. Then he took little Cletus from Jennifer and sat down, looking at the child's face with a smile.

"He's a chip off the old block, son," Stephen McCarthy said, putting the stroller by the corner near the big couch. "In a few months, he'll be quite a handful."

"Yep. I can see every bit of me in him," Cletus concurred with his father. "Let's just pray he doesn't grow up stringing bad luck like his dad." Jennifer moved closer and gingerly laid a hand on his shoulder, rubbing it gently and looking him over slowly, like a prospective buyer appreciating a horse before making a final offer.

Hannah noticed her behavior and, struggling to stifle her laughter, said, "Jennifer, it's him. It's Cletus. You'll be convinced once he tells you his story."

"I know," Jennifer replied. "I'm just rubbing him so he can feel that he's still a human being. You never know with Cousin. He might begin to think he's Jesus risen from the dead."

"Okay! That's what was going on in your mind at the cemetery. I knew it! You thought you were Mary Magdalene seeing the risen Lord in the Garden of the Resurrection!" Cletus McCarthy said, looking excited, like a detective who had caught a culprit in a ruse. He turned and addressed his parents, "You should have seen her. She was swooning, and was about to genuflect and say 'Rabouni' when I stopped her."

"I was not about to genuflect and say, 'Rabouni'," Jennifer interjected, protesting and stifling a laugh at the same time. "I thought you were some bad guy trying to kidnap me and my son."

"I am going to tell you how I survived the accident so you can believe it's me," Cletus said. "Actually, I did not survive it. I escaped it."

"Quit bragging and tell me how you faked your own death. You used to be a pretty straightforward person, and now you're becoming a counterfeiter," Jennifer teased, drawing a seat to sit down.

Hannah rolled her eyes and looked at her husband and said, "Honey, do you want supper, or are you going to stand there all evening watching those two? They were born to fight. So, if you're hungry, tell me what you want for supper."

"Yes, honey. I'm hungry," Stephen McCarthy said, nodding his head for emphasis. "No, I'm not standing and watching them all evening. I'm just wondering whether history is not witnessing another 100-years war in the making. I can't believe they're picking up right where they left off." He chuckled incredulously.

"I think the little man is asleep," Cletus said. He got up slowly and placed the baby in the stroller, then came back to his seat. "He doesn't want to listen to his dad's boring story." He turned, slightly facing Jennifer and said, "Since you weren't here this afternoon when Mom opened the door and I walked in, let's begin our story there."

"Oh, my goodness! He's going to tease me about it forever," Hannah said. "Can we just skip that part, please?"

"Okay, Mom. I'll just give a summary of that and go on. She shrieked in horror and ran upstairs."

"I shrieked and ran because I thought I was seeing a ghost," Hannah confirmed. Then she added, for Jennifer's benefit, "He just walked past me at the door: bowler hat, great coat, and all, and came in straight into the sitting room. I rushed after him to challenge what kind of audacity he thought he had to barge into my home like that, thinking he was some kind of investigator. Then he removed his hat, coat, and suit, and said, 'Mom'. I immediately recognized him and nearly fainted. That's when I shouted, calling Steve, who was upstairs."

"The drama was much bigger than what you and I had at the cemetery," Cletus took over the story. "It took me a whole lot of effort to calm them down and make them understand I didn't want the neighbors to hear what was going on. It would have destroyed my chance of beginning a new life somewhere where I'm not known. Can you now understand, Jenny? To the rest of the world, Cletus Nicholas McCarthy, the IVF-conceived priest outed in court, who resigned his priesthood shortly thereafter, is dead, buried, and long gone. That chapter is closed. It was an idea that came to me in a split second. And I said to myself, 'if you are going to invent a new identity for yourself, and put the past to rest, this is your chance to do it. Otherwise, it is going to dog you throughout life. The accident provided a perfect cover."

"I'm beginning to understand," Jennifer said, nodding affirmatively.

"Good," Cletus continued. "When I kissed you and left, embarking on the two-day odyssey to Norfolk, it didn't cross my mind that events would take this turn. Remember, I kept in touch with you throughout the first day till I took a break for the night? And I did the same the following day until about five in the evening? I also kept in touch that way with every other person till I was less than 150 miles from Norfolk, when I had to stop at a rest area to pee. And that's where things began to get weird."

Cletus didn't really need to pee. He'd informed Dr. Horacek earlier about the exact time he would arrive at his house, according to his GPS calculation, but later realized that, having cruised much of the way at well over the speed limit, he was going to arrive almost one hour early. So, he thought making a few stops would bring him closer to his target time.

"The rest area I stopped at was smelly and unclean. So, I got out again and, looking up, I saw a gas station about half a mile away. I thought to myself, 'I can whittle away a bit of time there, and, maybe have some snack'. I drove to the gas station and stopped at the outermost pump to top off my tank. So, that way, I wouldn't have to stop for gas till I arrived at Dr. Horacek's. When I went in to get a snack, I saw three young guys loafing around by the outside corner of the building. I remember faintly thinking they looked suspicious. They were smoking some kind of awful-smelling wrap and passing it among themselves. I went inside, picked a muffin from the shelf and a can of Sprite from the refrigerator, and went to the counter to pay. Suddenly, there appeared this dude from nowhere, coming to stand beside me. He was strongly built and pleasant-looking, though.

"'Good combination, buddy', he said, indicating my sprite and muffin.

"'Thank you', I said and, sensing that he was spoiling for a conversation, began wracking my brain for something gracious to say and take my exit. 'Keeps the guts from rumbling till one gets to the major meal'.

"On that, I agree with you, buddy', he said. 'I'm gonna grab me one of them muffins for the road before I leave'.

"'Good idea. See you around', I said and picked up my bag of snacks to leave.

'Hey! Wait a minute', he said, placing his hand on my arm. 'Don't I know you from somewhere'?

"My first impulse was to hand him the change I was still holding, but he didn't look like a homeless beggar. In fact, he was better dressed than I was, and trying to give him alms would have been an insult. Besides, he exuded such friendliness and confidence that I felt no threat from him. So, I said politely, 'I'm afraid, Sir, that you must be confusing me with someone else'.

"'You're out of town, aren't you'? he asked.

"'Yes, I'm afraid I am', I said, unwittingly taking the bait, thinking that would make him admit he was confusing me with someone else.

"'Let me guess. Texas', he said. 'I can tell by the accent'. I nodded, thinking again, that was it. He was going to apologize and shake hands so we could part ways. I was wrong.

"'Then, you are the guy. I can't mistake the face. I have the stack of papers', he continued as I started getting irked. I was about to tell him off and tell him to stop bothering me when he pulled me further aside and said, 'Listen. My name is Michael Parker', and then stretched out a hand for a shake. 'I am Roman Catholic. In fact, you may not believe this, but I am also an ex-seminarian. Two weeks to the diaconate at Mundelein, Chicago. I got pulled out by the bishop and asked to find me another calling. It was painful, man. But I eventually joined the police force'.

"'So, you're a cop, then'? I asked, sighing with relief as I shook his hand and we started to walk out.

"'Yeah, but not exactly', he said and, before I could ask what he meant, he added, 'My two cents about your case, and I'll let you go. It don't matter how you were born. What matters is how you will die. The former, you can't control. The latter, you can shape and reshape it. Choice is yours. Good night, buddy'.

"While he pulled me aside, I had heard a plop sound behind me, which I didn't immediately pay attention to. But I did turn around a few seconds later to see what dropped and I saw nothing. All I saw was one of the wrap-smoking guys I had spotted outside earlier, pretending to be reading the menu board above the counter as people tend to do before placing orders for what they need. Then he pushed past us at the door in one great rush. As my magical acquaintance started to go, I called 'good night' in response and touched my back pocket for my car keys. It was empty. Then it dawned on me what the plop sound was. Simultaneously, a car engine revved from the direction where I had mine and I looked up. I could not believe what I saw. The headlights of my car had come on and the car was moving without me.

"Hey! Hey! That's my car! Stop! What are you doing? That's my car!" I shouted and ran after it, but it sped off in one furious rush of mad screeches of tires on the tarmac. Just at the same time, my magical acquaintance, Michael Parker, pulled up in a police towing van.

"'Hey, buddy. What happened? You've been carjacked'?

"'That's my car those guys have pinched', I yelled back.

"'Sons of bitches'! he swore and pulled up by me nearly running over my foot. 'Hop in! Fast! Hop in! We gotta get back your car'!

"I barely had my rump on the seat when he revved off in the direction that those guys took. Seminarian-turned-policeman Parker stepped on the gas pedal like nobody's business and we gave the mad chase of our lives. I hung on to my clicked-in seatbelt for dear life. Within three miles of the hot chase, he indicated to me that he had spotted my car.

"'That's your car right there. That's it', he said.

"'Where? Where do you see it'? I asked, perplexed, because there were other cars and trucks on the road. And it was dark. So, I wondered how he could see my car when he did not even know what kind it was. That's when I got to learn some minor police detective work.

"'Watch the tail lights of that vehicle weaving in and out of traffic without signaling. And it's going faster than other vehicles. They appear to be in a great hurry. So, who can do all those things except the guys hurrying to get away with your baby'? Then he doubled his efforts on the gas pedal and started weaving in and out of traffic himself. The speed was so giddying that I nearly begged him to stop and call off his chase, and let the thieves go, if only I could still have my life in one piece. But he seemed quite calm, and even looked like he was enjoying the chase. I thought I was going to die chasing my stolen truck. Eventually, he switched on the blue and red flashing lights and the siren, still deftly manipulating the steering wheel, switching lanes with short or no notice at all. The lights and the siren were a tremendous help, as other traffic easily gave way and we started gaining on the thieves. It was the nightmare of my life. Eventually traffic became scant and the thieves increased their speed and were going insanely fast. My companion took that as a dare and got furiously hot on their tails till we were less than a quarter of a mile from their rear. And that's when Murphy's Law set in. It happened so quickly that, to this day, as I am sitting here, and I still believe it was a miracle that Michael and I survived."

"What is Murphy's Law?" Hannah interjected.

"Whatever can go wrong…" Stephen McCarthy started, paraphrasing.

",,will eventually go wrong'," Cletus McCarthy completed the statement for him.

"I did not see it myself. It was Michael's dread-filled exclamations that alerted me to what was about to happen with no remedy at that point. First thing I noticed was a sudden jerking movement as he abruptly removed his feet from the gas pedal and started slamming on the brake.

"'O Jesus Christ of Nazareth! Don't let it happen! No! This is not happening! Lord, don't let it hap…' Michael shouted and, at the same time, almost standing on the brake pedal of his truck.

"Out of the dark shoulder of Highway 58, to the right of us, sped out an eighteen-wheeler tanker, off a slight incline, joined the main road at a sharper angle than usual. It went diagonally straight across the highway, cutting in front of the speeding thieves. The tanker driver had apparently lost control and was, perhaps, trying in vain to correct his bearing. As he was about to hit the left shoulder of the road, he wheeled sharply to swerve back to the right lane where he should have been in the first place, but his efforts made things even worse. The long tanker part of the truck could not withstand the force of such a sharp curve. It careened and tilted and, with the force and speed with which it was thrown, crashed on its side with the loudest smacking sound that I had ever heard in my life. It slid on for almost a quarter of a mile with the noise of a very loud rumbling of thunder, with sparks flying from the crushing friction.

"All I saw at that moment was the vehicle we were chasing swerve to the left. It suddenly shot up in the air and began to tumble into the blinding sparks of the overturned tanker. Then everything went black as my companion and I kept shouting, 'O my God! O my God'! I felt the jolting and bumping movements for a second or two before everything calmed down and I opened my eyes and saw Michael unbuckling his seatbelt.

"'Come on! Let's get out and sit down on the ground', he said. I followed his voice and obeyed sheepishly. I unbuckled my seatbelt and pushed open the door and stepped into weeds and grass. I had no idea where we were for a second. Then it gradually became clear that we were inside the grassy portion of the right shoulder of the road, almost emerging onto the side road where the doomed tanker had come from. 'Are you okay'? Michael asked as he came over to my side.

"'Yeah', I replied, taking a step away from the truck and checking out myself for any injuries. Satisfied I had none, I looked up to get a good handle on our bearings as Michael was still peering at me in the semi-darkness and again asking, 'Are you okay'?

"What Michael told me later was that we had rolled over, too, as he slammed the brake as hard as he could, trying to swerve to the right to avoid running into the pile ahead. Fortunately, we rolled over into the grassy knoll only once and then our vehicle stopped, landing standing upright, on its tires. I had lost that part when I blacked out in fear. Other vehicles that came after us had stopped with their headlights and hazard lights fully on. A few were honking, probably to warn others, and a handful of commuters far behind us had started coming out of their vehicles. Michael started running toward the pile-up which was just, probably, about forty feet away. I followed, again, pulled by some invisible force. Smoke was building over the pile-up and loud hissing sounds could be heard, as when you pour water on a red-hot iron.

"I don't know who saw it first, but Michael insisted he had seen it. Someone started shouting for those who were approaching to fall back.

"'Go back! Run back! For Chrisake, run back! It's gonna explode'!

"As if on cue, there was a very loud explosion with a blinding flash. Michael grabbed me by the shoulder and threw me on the ground with him. Then he pulled me, yelling, 'Get up! Run, run with me'! I struggled to get to my feet and ran to safety with Michael. From our safe vantage point on the access road, we could see the vehicles that had gotten too close to the pile-up scramble to back up or turn around to head for safety. It was the largest inferno I had ever witnessed. The fallen tanker and the two unfortunate vehicles that had run into it blazed furiously, with flames jumping as high as thirty feet into the air with a series of loud explosions. We watched in disbelief. The hope of ever saving anybody from the wreckage, or ever retrieving their bodies, was gone in the flames. Nobody could get within thirty feet of the blazing heat. Even Michael was so stunned that he stood speechless for almost two minutes before he suddenly remembered to be a cop. He yanked open the door of his truck and pulled out the speaker. Fortunately, his radio crackled to life.

"'Mayhem! Mayhem on five-eight East! Tanker and trucks ablaze, mayhem! Head Office, come in'!

"'Head Office, alert. This is Corporal Dwayne. Come in'. Just then a voice came on the other end of the radio.

"'Mayhem in traffic, five eight East. Tanker and vehicles in infernal blaze, come in', Michael called in again.

"'Head Office, alert. Will send in help. Over'.

"Michael hung up and switched off the radio before Head Office could say more.

"From a distance, we could hear the horns and sirens. Someone had called the fire department. We stood and watched for a few more minutes. Then, Michael pulled me by the hand.

"'C'mon, buddy. Let's get out of here. Let's get to where you can pull yourself together. Cops will arrive in a few minutes to take care of the situation'.

"'But...my car'! I protested.

"'C'mon. We'll take care of that in the morning. Whatever's left of it', he replied, pulling my hand. I climbed into his truck and he brought the engine to life and eased back out of the grassy knoll onto to the access road.

"I protested again, ineffectually, and pointed out that the police might want to take a statement about my stolen vehicle. Besides, when I pumped gas at the station and later dashed into the convenience store, it was only to pay for my gas and a snack. And so, I had not taken my phone out of the car charger. My second wallet containing my driver's license and other cards was in the glove compartment of the car. What that meant was that I was without anything to identify me as Cletus McCarthy at that moment. I couldn't even call anybody in Houston, or call Dr. Horacek in Norfolk. Michael offered to lend me his phone, but I had nobody's number in my head. He kept driving and I couldn't ask him to let me out. I had no clue where I was, or, if he let me out, where I would go. He kept talking about getting everything straightened out in the morning. I had no choice, but to grudgingly follow him to where he was going, so long as he had promised me things would make sense the next morning, which he did.

"Things did begin to make sense the next morning. I woke up with the sun's rays coming in through the window, and it took me almost fifteen seconds to figure out where I was. The bedroom seemed strange, though well furnished. Slowly, the events of the previous evening came fully into my consciousness. I sat up with a start and began to recall what it was I was going to do. There was a knock on the door and it opened a crack first, and Michael spoke through it.

"'Hey, buddy. Are you awake'? He pushed the door wide open at my grunting response to the fact that I was awake. 'I figured coming such a long ways from Texas, you needed the sleep. So, I allowed you to sleep while I rushed to the station to return the truck before anybody noticed it was missing'.

"'The truck'? I asked, barely understanding what he meant.

"'Yeah. The one we used in the chase? I borrowed it from the local station because I still had the spare key from manning it last year before it changed hands'. It was then that he told me he was on probation for manhandling a suspect in a case he was investigating. He was put on leave with pay, and was not supposed to use any of the police cars. He borrowed the truck anyway, according to him, because he needed to get to the convenience store that evening. His personal car was low on gas and he figured he could use the police tow van, which people rarely used. That way, he would save the gas in his car. Unfortunately, he ran into me and the car thieves and got involved in the chase before he could ask himself what he was doing.

"'If they knew I took out the police truck without permission, I could be canned, man, for violating my probation'.

"That explained why Michael was so shy of the accident scene. But there I was in his guest room, with no clue of what I was going to do without my driver's license and without anybody's phone number in my head to call. I had stored all my contacts in my phone, and always dialed them by name, not number. So, all your numbers were lost to me. Not knowing what to do next, I got up and stretched.

"'Okay, I guess you're going to do your morning routines first. After that, we'll have breakfast and then try and figure out how to contact your folks. By the way, my name, again, is Michael Parker'.

"'I'm Cletus McCarthy', I said, and we shook hands again.

"'Come out for breakfast when you're ready'. With that, he closed the door again.

"I rushed through my toilet routines because I was eager to get Michael to help me establish contact, either with you here in Houston, or with Dr. Horacek in Norfolk. As I entered the dining area, which was a small kitchenette instead of a full-fledged kitchen, I saw breakfast things were already laid out. A pretty young woman, looking late twentyish, was scrambling eggs in a saucepan on the stove. She slung a baby in a pouch-like backpack on her back with its head, legs, and hands sticking out, making it look like a turtle with its appendages sticking out of its shell. Michael was playing with a little girl who looked no more than five.

"'There you are, Cletus, looking quite fresh and lively for a dead person', he said, smiling impishly.

"'What do you mean, "a dead person'?" I inquired.

"'This is my wife, Terese. She prefers it spelt T-E-R-E-S-E, and pronounced that way, too. And this is Eileen, our daughter, and Michael, Junior, on his mom's back. Honey, this is our guest I brought home last night. Eileen, honey, say, "Good morning" to Uncle Cletus," he rattled through his intros as though he was afraid I was going to interrupt, which I did.

"Why did you say I'm quite lively for a dead man?"

"'Good morning, Sir', Terese greeted me very sweetly. 'Pardon me. I was already in bed when you came in last night, so I couldn't see you. Welcome to our place. Thank God you were not really involved in the accident/.

"Michael pushed a stack of papers in front of me and urged me to read. The front-page caption jolted me: **FIRST IVF-CONCEIVED PRIEST MEETS DEATH IN INFERNAL ACCIDENT.**

"A picture of the previous night's blaze followed. I looked at it for several seconds before I started reading. The story was told to the effect that I had set out from Houston to visit the man who admitted to fathering me, Dr. Josef Horacek, in Norfolk. Unfortunately, I met my death when I ran into a natural gas tanker that fell on Highway 58. My vehicle burst into flames and I was charred beyond recognition, except for the remnants of my driver's license, a piece of my wallet, and fragments of other documents which were pieced together. Dr. Horacek was able to make a positive identification of me from those fragments, indicating that one of the vehicles that ran into the fallen tanker and burst into flames was my car and I was inside at the moment of the accident. It went on to lament what a loss I was to the Catholic Church, even though I had gone into the lay state of life. The paper almost deified me, calling me a hero of the ethical soundness of human reproductive technology. One of the Norfolk tabloids that Michael had also bought that morning carried the same story with my picture in it.

"I read through the stories a second time and I did not like the tones of them. I resented their making me into a banner for the justification of the IVF procedure, though at that time, I had nothing against it. When I put down the paper and my host urged me to eat my breakfast before it went cold, it dawned on me that, as far as the world was concerned, I was dead and gone. Cletus Nicholas McCarthy, the first IVF-conceived Roman Catholic Priest of Houston, Texas, was dead and gone. What remained of him in the minds and hearts of people was the story.

"It might have been then that the idea to remain dead to the world started forming in my mind. I cannot really tell now. All I can remember is that I figured that if I resurrected myself, falsifying the story in the papers, I would begin another storm of publicity that would add to my stress and continue dogging me through life. If I were to start anew, living my life with the public glare off me, I would fare much better. Yet, the question remained how. First, I had to battle with what it would feel like refusing to call and indicate that I was alive and nobody should worry about me. Then I would figure how to get a new set of documents and, maybe, change my name. The latter was going to be somewhat easy, but the former was going to be a tough act to pull off because I would have to contend with the thought that I was being insensitive to the feelings of my loved ones.

"After breakfast, when my host asked me where I wanted to start, and suggested that I start from Dr. Horacek's end, I pulled him aside and confided in him my thoughts. Maybe I should not have sought his opinion on it because he jumped at the idea with the excitement of a toddler with a new toy. And so, what was just an idea in my mind to toy with as a possibility, started becoming a reality as Michael practically and alternately cajoled, coaxed, and blackmailed me into bringing it to fulfilment. All my identification cards had gone up in the flames of that accident. I couldn't use the only credit card I still had on me without blowing my cover. Michael knew all the places and the persons who would supply me with my new identity. My driver's license came from the Norfolk Department of Public Safety. My health and dental insurance cards came from the Norfolk Aetna Insurance Company. He insisted I have two credit cards: an Amex and a Visa. All these items took a period of three weeks to gather, and they came with my new name." Cletus paused for effect, took a deep breath and exhaled.

"And what's your new name, if I may ask?" Jennifer inquired, curiously.

"Not very different from my real name, especially in sound," Cletus replied. "Clarence Victor McCarty. That's my new name."

"Clarence Victor?" Jennifer asked, looking incredulous and amused at the same time.

"McCarty," he replied. "You don't seem to like it. Do you?"

"I don't know," Jennifer said, still looking amused and confused.

"That's what he told us to call him from now on," Hannah chipped in. "And I said, 'To me, you'll always be Cletus Nicholas McCarthy. Since we were about to get into a fight, we settled for a compromise: C. McCarthy."

"C. McCarthy?" Jennifer asked again.

"Yes. For him, C. will be Clarence, and for me, C. will be Cletus."

Jennifer broke out laughing and everyone else joined in.

Thus, Cletus/Clarence was adamant on breaking with his past in some way, even if he was not sure he was doing the right thing. Within one week, he had depleted whatever money he had on him and needed a job. Michael wasted no time finding him a job in the local grocery store. He stayed on it, marking time until he should have his new identity in place. After the third week, when all his particulars were in, he applied for and got a teaching job with the local community college, teaching Literary Studies and Contemporary History of the United States. He also got a one-bedroom apartment for himself and started his new life in full swing. The

Parkers remained his closest friends and allies. He made acquaintances among the locals, but stayed very guarded, not allowing them to get too close to pry into his real identity.

"My one aim was to make enough money to be able to come and get you to live with me in Norfolk. So, that's why, after I had established my new identity, I did not immediately try to contact you. Besides, I figured it was good to let you get over mourning me and heal completely before I made my appearance. I was planning for the time when I would come in person. I cannot tell you how many times I googled your names on the Internet to get your phone numbers, and just at the moment when I should have call any of you, I would lose the nerve, for fear you might get so excited and blow my cover before I could control it. As I sit here telling this story, I cannot belief how I made it through for a year and two months without going nuts. I had to pray a lot. I prayed as I had never prayed, even when I was a priest. I am still teaching at the community college and the salary is good. So, I figure if you get a job with any of the health systems there, we won't do badly with our new life.

"So, what about the Horaceks? I hope you know Barbara and Crystal moved to Norfolk?" Jennifer asked.

"We told him about the Horaceks," Hannah said. "But my question is: Are you going to hide your new self from them? What are you going to do?"

"No, Mom," Cletus replied. "I can't do that to them. That would be too callous, though it is not like they have the right to know."

"We became family with them," Hannah said. "I want us to continue that family tie."

"I think your mom is right, son," Stephen McCarthy chipped in for the first time. "Better more friends than privacy."

"That's what I'm saying. We will figure out how to reveal myself to them …"

"…'how to reveal myself to them…' Gosh! He's still thinking he is Jesus Christ risen from the dead," Jennifer mimicked, looking at Stephen and Hannah.

"There you go," Stephen said, chuckling.

"I should have let you cry out that *Rabouni* at the cemetery," Cletus rebutted.

"Now! Now, before you guys continue your war, how long are you with us for?"

"Only tomorrow. I am flying back early the next day because I have lectures in the afternoon. Jennifer will resign from her work here and join me," Cletus said, standing up to stretch.

"I won't do any such thing unless you come back for us."

"Why?'

"That's the only way I will be sure you are real," she said, pouting defiantly.

"Real? What are you talking about?" Cletus asked, confused.

Jennifer stood up and appraised him up and down and said, "Everything about you now is fake: You have fake driver's license, fake health cards, fake credit cards, fake clothes, fake names… Now tell me what else is fake about you. And give me one good reason why I should trust you. One concrete evidence why I should believe that you, Cousin, standing here, are *you*."

Hannah and Stephen McCarthy started laughing, knowing that Jennifer was warming for her mock fight.

"You already have the concrete evidence with you," Cletus replied, casually.

"With me?"

As if on cue, the baby in the stroller stirred and went back to sleep.

"Yeah," Cletus said, nodding toward the stroller. "Him. I didn't fake that."

"Good talk, son," Stephen McCarthy shouted gleefully and earned a slap on the shoulder by Hannah.

Jennifer also started slapping Cletus on the chest several times, alternating with both hands.

"Jesus Christ of Nazareth! Pop, the ladies have declared war on us poor menfolk!" Cletus said and grabbed Jennifer by her two arms, pulled her into a bosom embrace, and kissed her. Jennifer went limp and molded herself pliantly in his arms.

"Hey! Get out of here, you two. Get a room!" Hannah McCarthy said.

Jennifer slapped Cletus one more time and took off, running up the stairs with him in hot pursuit. The bedroom door banged and Jennifer giggled. Hannah rolled her eyes and sighed in longsuffering resignation.

"Oh, God! I shouldn't have done that."

"What?" Stephen asked.

"Send them to his room," Hannah replied, giving her husband a concerned look. "I literally sent them to his room for baby number two!"

Stephen looked at his wife for a fraction of a second, broke out laughing, drew Hannah toward him, and kissed her.

"Honey, relax. Let them do what we couldn't do. Let them make as many babies as possible. We have switched from being adopters to being begetters," Stephen McCarthy said and kissed his wife again.

Hannah looked at her husband and then at the stroller with baby Cletus, Jr, sleeping soundly. She started laughing and he joined her and they fell onto the couch hugging each other and still laughing. Then, Stephen suddenly stopped laughing and wondered aloud, "Who, in Heaven's name, did the entire Archdiocese of Galveston-Houston bury on April 6th, 2013, with full priestly honors?"

"I don't know," Hannah replied, then added, "Probably the thief who stole our son's car."

"Very uncanny how thieves always get lucky enough to secure their salvation at the moment of their death," Stephen McCarthy said, looking at his wife. Hannah looked back at him, and both started laughing again, falling back on the couch.

# GLOSSARY

*Meetingitis* – illness condition contracted as a result of attending too many meetings.

*Donum Vitae* – "The Gift of Life": Vatican document on the sanctity of life.

*Humanae Vitae* – Of Human Life:" Paul VI's Encyclical on human reproduction.

*In nomine Patris, et Filii, et Spiritus Sancti* – In the name of the Father, and of the Son, and of the Holy Spirit.

*Gratia Domini nostril Jesu Christi, et caritas Dei, et communicatio Sancti Spiritus sit cum omnibus vobis* – The grace of Our Lord Jesus Christ, the love of God, and the communion of the Holy Spirit be with you.

*Et cum spiritu tuo* – And also with you.

*Fratres, agnoscamus peccata nostra….* – Brethren, let us acknowledge our sins….

*Hoc est enim Corpus meum* – This is indeed my body.

*Lava me, Domine, ab iniquitate mea* – Wash me, Lord, from my iniquity.

*Novus Ordo* – The New Order.

*Ferende sententiae* – Punishment that is effective only when imposed.

*Latae sententiae* – Automatic penalty or punishment.

*Porque…. –* Because….

*Hablas Espanol, Padre? –* Do you speak Spanish, Father?

*Un poquito –* A little.

*Lo siento mucho –* I am very sorry.

*Ave, Maria, ora pro nobis –* Hail, Mary, pray for us.

*Ecce in peccatis meis. Peccator homo sum –* I (was born) in sin. I am a sinner.

*Sanatio in radice –* Radical sanation or cleansing.

*Va bene, che peccato –* It's ok (alright), it's a shame.

*Grazie, signore –* Thank you, Sir.

*Haba! –* (An exclamatory expression of protest).

*Buongiorno, Padre –* Good morning, Father.

*In loco patris –* In place of the father (a stand-in as father figure).

*Ex opere operantis –* Efficacy dependent on the holiness of the Church, not by merit of the act.

*Mio fratello…benvenuto. Mi aspettavo –* My brother…welcome. I was expecting you.

*Grazie, Santita. Sono lieto di essere in vostra presenza –* Thank you, Holiness. I am delighted to be in your presence.

*Certamente, Santo Padre –* Certainly, Holy Father.

*Bravo, Santito! –* Bravo, Your Holiness!

*Ex Cathedra* – From the Chair (Catholic Doctrine pronounced from the Chair of St. Peter).

*De fide* – As an article of faith (to be believed mandatorily).

*Movimiento Familia Catolica* – Catholic Family Movement.

*Dies irae, dies illa, Solvet saeculum in favilla, Teste David cum in Sybilla* – Day of wrath, that day of doom. When eternity merges with Earth, David's testament with Sibyl's.

*Ingemisco, tamquam reus. Culpa rubet vultus meus. Suplicantis Parce Deus* – In moaning, I pour out my guilt, my blame in anguish I accept. Spare thy supplicant, O God.

*Salve, Regina, mater misericordiae; vita, dulcedo et spes nostra, salve. Ad te clamamus exules filii Hevae. Ad te suspiramus gementes et flentes in hac lacrimarum vale. Eia ergo, advocate nostra, illos tuos misericordes oculos ad nos converte. Et Iesum, benedictum fructum ventris tui, nobis post hoc exiilium ostende. O Clemens, o pia, o dulcis Virgo Maria.*
Hail, Holy Queen, Mother of mercy, our life our sweetness and our hope. To thee do we cry, poor banished children of Eve. To thee do we send up our sighs, mourning and weeping, in this valley of tears. Turn, then, most gracious advocate, thine eyes of mercy toward us, and after this, our exile, show unto us the blessed fruit of thy womb, Jesus. O clement, O loving, O sweet Virgin Mary.

John Ayang hails from Ukana Iba, in the southeastern part of Nigeria, and he studied philosophy and theology at Bigard Memorial Seminary in Eastern Nigeria. After moving to the United States and being ordained as a Catholic priest for the Society of Our Lady of the Most Holy Trinity (1998), he studied theology and Christian ministry at the Franciscan University of Steubenville, Ohio, and bioethics and health policy at the Neiswanger Institute for Bioethics at Loyola University, Chicago.

Printed in the United States
By Bookmasters